Black
Valentin

Black Valentine

Patricia Sargent

PIATKUS

With the exception of the description of the Russian invasion of Czechoslovakia in the summer of 1968, which is based on historical facts, this is a work of fiction. The characters, incidents, and dialogues are products of the author's imagination and are not to be construed as real. Any resemblance to actual events or persons, living or dead, is entirely coincidental.

Copyright © 1988 by Patricia Sargent Zegart

This edition first published in Great Britain in 1989 by
Judy Piatkus (Publishers) Ltd of
5 Windmill Street, London W1

British Library Cataloguing in Publication Data
Sargent, Patricia
  Black Valentine.
  I. Title
  813' .54 [F]

ISBN 0-86188-858-8

Printed and bound in Great Britain by
Courier International Ltd, Tiptree, Essex

For Dan and Caroline, as always, with love, and in memory of my father, who would have enjoyed this.

Black Valentine

How it began...

Prague: 11:00 P.M., August 20, 1968

The man worked with quick, deft movements. Hunching over the long, scarred mahogany table, he drew a sheet of paper from the file folder with his left hand, adjusted it under the circle of light thrown by the gooseneck lamp, and with his right hand focused the small camera to his eye. A soft click. He picked up the sheet, set it aside facedown, and slid the next one under the light. He focused, clicked, placed that sheet neatly on top of the preceding one, and drew another under the light. Click. Another... Click. And another...

Outside, through the narrow, medieval streets of the city, sirens wailed like mourners lamenting the dead; blaring horns echoed warnings into the night; footsteps beat rapid tattoos on the sidewalk just above him as their owners hurried toward home and safety. These frantic sounds reached the man's ears dimly, muffled by the thick stone walls of the basement room, and he paid little heed to them. Except for raising his head from time to time to listen for a thoughtful second, he didn't interrupt the rhythm of his movements. Nor was he disturbed by the scrape of chairs, the tread of feet, the jangle of telephones in the room overhead. None of these were the sounds he must listen for. Before they came, he had a job to finish.

He was a tall, slender, handsome man, about thirty-eight years old, with thick, light brown hair that waved back from a broad forehead, keen brown eyes, a finely molded nose, and

1

the strong high cheekbones of the Slav. His mouth, ordinarily wide and generous and quick to smile, was a thin line now as the lips pressed together in tense concentration. Outwardly he appeared calm, his hands steady, his movements precise. But the signs of inner strain were apparent in the red spots of color that glowed on his cheeks, and though the room was cool, beads of sweat dotted his brow and upper lip.

The basement room where he worked was large and rectangular. It lay in darkness except for the lamp on the table and the pale beam of light that filtered through one of the slit windows set high and deep into the stone wall. Motes of dust moved lazily through it. Ancient dust in an ancient room, the air stale and musty as though held captive for hundreds of years. With its minimal furnishings of the table and four straight-backed chairs, it was obvious that the room was not designed for comfort. It was a storage place only, a storage place for secrets, thousands of secrets, all neatly tagged and categorized in their separate folders and in their proper filing cabinets. The cabinets themselves, short and squat or tall and thin, dulled with age or new and shiny, ranged in rows along the walls, mute guardians of small indiscretions and major betrayals. A drawer of one of the newer cabinets stood open and empty. Those files that had filled it lay on the table under the light, their pages being exposed one by one to the eye of the camera.

It was midnight when the man finished. The hour of concentrated effort had left his face pale and drawn with fatigue and had etched tiny lines around his eyes. His hands trembled a little as they tucked the camera carefully into the inside pocket of his jacket along with the second exposed roll of film. The time it had taken to change rolls had slowed him slightly, but he was satisfied with the job. As for the fatigue... He accepted that with a shrug. The long night wasn't over yet. He would simply have to live with it for a few more hours.

After a quick stretch of his aching body, arms thrust high, back arched, he bent again over the table. Reaching into a drawer, he found a rubber band and snapped it around the file folders. He was tucking the bundle into his worn briefcase when from overhead came a steady *thump-thump-thump*. The man glanced swiftly up at the ceiling, nodded, and muttered something under his breath. His movements quickened. He snapped the briefcase closed, shoved it under his arm, switched off the lamp, and hurried for the door, shutting the empty file drawer closed as he passed it.

From his pocket he drew out a large brass key and unlocked the heavy oak door. As he put his hand to the knob, the door was thrust open from the other side with such force it sent him stumbling back. A man stepped across the threshold. He was short and powerfully built, with thick black hair, a curly black beard and very pale gray-blue eyes like chips of ice.

For one frozen moment out of time the two men stood motionless, staring at each other. The newcomer recovered first. The cold eyes swept from the man's face to the briefcase under his arm and back to his face. A small, savage smile gleamed briefly in the depths of the beard, but as his hand went to his pocket, the taller man moved. He sprang forward, arm raised, the brass key protruding between the fingers of his clenched fist. He swung his arm in a sideways arc. Fear lent power to the blow. The fist caught the other man on the temple and sent him reeling. Another blow followed. The heavyset man crashed against the corner of a metal filing cabinet and slumped to the floor.

Ashen-faced, his breath rasping in his throat, the man stood over the still form, watching the slow trickle of blood flow down the cheek from the wound in the temple, watched it without really seeing it. His violence had been pure defensive reflex. Its aftermath of shock held him rooted to the spot.

He might have stood there indefinitely if the urgent *thump-thump-thump* hadn't sounded overhead again and roused him to action. He shook off the lethargy and sent a quick, searching glance around the room. Then he stooped, picked up his briefcase, relocked the door, and hurried back to the table. Without bothering to turn on the light, he brought out the metal wastebasket from beneath the table and set it in the middle of the room. Jerking open the briefcase, he spilled the files into the basket, separated them with shaking fingers, then fumbled in his pocket for matches. It took almost the whole precious box before the papers were well alight. He watched them burn, jiggling the basket frequently to give the hungry flames a chance to lick and curl around each incriminating page. From time to time he flicked a watchful glance at the unconscious man. When at last he left the room, the flames had died, leaving just a pink glow of ashes at the bottom of the basket. And as he locked the door behind him, he heard groans and the scrabble of feet on the stone floor. It wouldn't be long before the alarm was sounded and the hunt was on. Pocketing the key, he hurried down the hall to the basement exit.

In the open doorway he paused for a second. The air was unusually cool for an August night, and he buttoned the worn jacket, clumsily because his fingers were cold and trembling. He heard the sound then and, tipping his head back, looked up, listening intently to the steady distant drone while his eyes searched the black, starless sky. The sound neared, the volume intensified.

Like locusts, he thought with hatred, like a plague of locusts must sound as they descended in a destructive cloud on the defenseless fields.

The droning turned to a roar. He could make out the shapes of the planes as they swept across the sky, the screaming of their jet engines shattering the night.

The man shivered and pulled up the collar of his coat. Drawing in a deep breath, he stepped out into the dangerous night.

Throughout the early morning hours, five hundred Russian tanks and armored cars rumbled into Prague. Their smoking treads shredded the pavements and tore up the cobblestones. What stood in their way, they smashed. Street posts, telephone poles, trees, trolley cars on their tracks, automobiles parked on roadsides—all gave way before the ruthless efficiency of the invader.

By dawn Prague was an occupied city. When its citizens awoke to the new day, they found it ringed in steel and helpless. Tanks blockaded main roads and bridges and encircled key buildings. Cordons of soldiers surrounded the embassies of the Western democracies. (No sanctuary there for fleeing Czechs.) A white blanket of leaflets, like a heavy snowfall, littered the streets and parks, explaining in crude, childish phrases that their Russian "brothers" (a half million well-armed soldiers) had arrived to "liberate their Czech comrades" from those dreaded enemies of socialism, the counterrevolutionaries and imperialists.

A few "counterrevolutionaries" managed to escape. Many were caught in the net.

I

New York: February 1988

The Colonel tipped his head back and smiled up at the young man who stood beside the door. The young man returned the smile with a tentative one of his own and at the same time bent his knees a little and allowed his broad shoulders to droop in an effort to minimize the difference in their height. It seemed subversive somehow on his part to tower over the Colonel.

If the Colonel noticed the sudden loss of a couple of inches in the young man's height, he gave no sign of it but went on smoothing his thick black hair that was only lightly touched with gray at the temples. He then pulled on an astrakhan fur hat and adjusted it rakishly over the right temple, effectively concealing the small jagged scar.

"Well, Dmitri Alexandrovitch, my young comrade-in-arms," the Colonel said jovially, giving a final pat to the headgear, "they've promised us some snow for a change, I hear. It might make us feel a little homesick, but we should enjoy it all the same, shouldn't we?" With a sudden, brief, malicious smile, he added, "Though it will probably send all these soft-living New Yorkers scurrying for cover, hmm?"

The young man nodded solemnly and agreed that it probably would.

The Colonel went on, wagging an admonitory finger in a heavy-handed joking manner, "But just let them spend one winter in Moscow, Dmitri Alexandrovitch. That would teach them what snow really is. Isn't that so, my friend?"

Again the young man agreed that that was so and forced a smile because the Colonel seemed to expect it. Then, abruptly,

7

joking time was over, and the Colonel turned his attention to his dress, buttoning his coat, a fine black wool that was lined with the same fur as the hat. He adjusted the cashmere scarf around his throat and flipped the black beard out over it, smoothing it down carefully. All his movements were unhurried, precise, almost finicky. Dmitri Alexandrovitch, watching the man covertly and noting the white carnation in the buttonhole of the coat, thought not for the first time that the Colonel was a very fancy dresser with more than his share of vanity. But always, when this thought came to him, he pushed it away quickly for fear the Colonel might read his mind and find treason there.

"You admire my flower, comrade?"

The sly, malicious smile gleamed at the young man through the black beard. The Colonel *had* read his mind! But the man only said amiably, "Just something to cheer up a drab day. And your mother, Dmitri Alexandrovitch, how is she?"

The swift change of subject left the young man dumb and gaping.

"The last time we spoke you told me she was unwell."

"Ah... It was the flu, Comrade Colonel. Yes, the flu. She has recovered, so my sister writes me. Still a little weak, but that is to be expected. It's very kind of you to be concerned."

"Not at all. I'm concerned about all my comrades here at the mission," the Colonel said blandly, pulling his fur-lined gloves from his pocket. "We are in a strange land, far from home. We must look out for one another. I'm glad to hear she's better, but tell her she mustn't rush things. Influenza is very treacherous." The pale gray-blue eyes flashed up to the young man's face and down again. "Like so much in this world, Dmitri Alexandrovitch," he added in a soft voice. "Though perhaps you are too young to know about such things as treachery, hmm?"

Dmitri flushed. "No, Comrade Colonel—I mean, yes—I do understand about such things."

The Colonel nodded, sighed, and arranged his coat cuffs over the tops of his gloves. Then he raised his head and, fixing his pale eyes on Dmitri Alexandrovitch, studied the young man's face for what seemed like a long time.

It's as though he has never seen it before, Dmitri Alexandrovitch thought, or as though he wants to memorize it in every detail. Under the man's direct, uncompromising gaze, he grew uneasy. You never knew what was going on in the Colonel's mind, he thought. He wore his outward joviality like a cloak, concealing the real man underneath, but Dmitri had no doubts about that hidden man. He had heard a great deal about him here in this rumor-ridden building, and he had seen him once. Only once, but that was quite enough. A few weeks ago Dmitri had made the mistake of finishing his cup of tea before bringing the Colonel the day's mail. A matter of five minutes only! But for a few seconds then the real Colonel, a cold-blooded, merciless man, had looked out at him from behind those pale eyes, and Dmitri Alexandrovitch had seen Siberia reflected there.

"Well . . ." A gloved hand clapping him on the shoulder startled the young man out of his reverie. "You're a good boy, Dmitri, a good boy." The Colonel smiled at him, his teeth like a flash of lightning in the dark cloud of the beard. "Please pass on my respects to your mother when you write her again."

What did he mean by that? Dmitri asked himself fearfully. Why this sudden interest in his mother? But before he could speculate further, the Colonel had picked up his umbrella from where it leaned against the wall, hooked its curved walnut handle over his wrist, and turned toward the heavy glass door. Breathing a long but inaudible sigh of relief, the young man leaped to open it for him. He watched the broad, sturdy figure climb the steps to the sidewalk, saw him greet the two New York City policemen who stood guard at the mission's entrance, saw them laugh at something the Colonel said. Unfailingly the Colonel made some remark to them whenever he left the building, and unfailingly they laughed. How could the Colonel find a new joke every time? Or did he always make the same joke and the policemen laughed out of simple politeness?

The first flakes of snow were drifting down from the leaden sky as Dmitri Alexandrovitch closed the door. Turning his eyes to the television screen of the security camera that monitored the street, he watched the Colonel walk briskly down the block

9

toward Lexington Avenue. Midway, the Colonel halted, turned, and raised his head to stare up at the roof of the Soviet mission building, where out of a garden of shrubs and tall-growing plants sprouted the complicated maze of wires and tubes that formed a sophisticated antenna. Dmitri Alexandrovitch only knew that it was there, plucking signals from the ether, sending signals out into it. He had no desire to know more. It was the business of others, a small elite group of men and women who worked behind locked doors in that room at the top of the building.

Now the Colonel had turned back to continue on his way. There seemed to be a jauntiness in the man's walk, a kind of light-stepping quality that Dmitri hadn't noticed before. And as he watched the monitor screen, he saw the man pause briefly at the corner and look back the way he had come. Then to his astonishment Dmitri saw the Colonel twirl his umbrella a couple of times with a debonair kind of abandon, executing at the same time a quick little dance step that carried him around the corner and out of sight.

The young man was still staring dazed at the screen when someone pushed him rudely aside, rushed out through the door, and headed after the Colonel. The man bore a remarkable resemblance to the Colonel, having a black beard as well, though he was a little shorter and heavier and not as elegantly dressed.

Dmitri Alexandrovitch watched this second man disappear around the corner in his turn, wondering in surprise if Krassotkin was following the Colonel. That seemed very odd. But it was a day for oddities, and anyway, Dmitri Alexandrovitch thought gloomily, everyone was followed at one time or another, so why not the Colonel? He drew his gaze away from the monitor with a sigh. Who followed the followers? he brooded. And those followers? And so on and so on. Was there no end to that sort of thing? He felt glad all of a sudden that he was of no importance at all in the hierarchy of the USSR Mission to the United Nations and glad, too, that it was almost time for his tea break.

As for Colonel Sergei Sergeivitch Makarov and his follower,

Nikolai Pavlovitch Krassotkin...Dmitri Alexandrovitch never saw either of them again, and about that he had no regrets.

In a third-floor apartment of a building on the northeast corner of Lexington Avenue and Sixty-seventh Street, a tall thin man with cropped hair and neat features stood in front of a large picture window peering through the viewfinder of a sixteen-millimeter camera mounted on a tripod. The window was covered by a venetian blind slatted to restrict observation from the outside. It looked south, and within its broad field of vision lay the USSR mission and its environs.

"Here we go," said the man at the window. "There's our fancy Dan right on time." He pressed the camera button, and the soft whirr of its motor competed with the street noises that filtered through the sealed window. Over the sounds the man's voice went on reporting in staccato phrases as he spoke into a tape recorder. "Prancing up the steps. Having usual amusing conversation with New York's finest. They dutifully laughing. What the hell do they always find to laugh about? Now proceeding down street. Stepping along very jauntily, I must say. Good news from Moscow? Promoted to general? Jesus Christ!"

"Don't stop there. Your audience is spellbound." This remark came from the second man in the room. He was sprawled in a leather armchair nearby, smoking a cigarette and gazing at the ceiling through half-closed eyes.

"Man, it gets funnier and funnier. He *danced* around the corner. Now have you ever seen that before? I mean he literally did a funny little dance step right there at the corner, twirling that damn umbrella of his! And—oops, wait for it! What are those sneaky Russian bastards up to now? Here comes Krassotkin barreling hell-for-leather after the Colonel. How about them apples? All according to schedule, Makarov leaves at his usual time to make his usual rounds—"

"We *assume*." The man in the armchair had joined the other man at the window. From the ledge he picked up a pair of binoculars and focused them on the street below. After a moment he said thoughtfully, "A break in the pattern. Our

11

Colonel has a tail. Now that's an odd and interesting development. Something's up. Something is definitely up."

The man propped the binoculars on the window ledge, grabbed his coat from where it lay draped over the back of his chair, and headed for the door. "I'd better start earning my salary. Keep the home fires burning, sweetheart."

"I'll call the old man, and don't for chrissake leave me stranded here. Keep in touch."

"You know me, old friend."

"Damn right I do, and I repeat—"

But the door had already closed with a firm click, and Adam Breen was alone. He shook his head, switched off the camera, and went on murmuring into the tape recorder.

The snow was falling more thickly now, sparkling damply on the bent heads and shoulders of the pedestrians, turning to slush underfoot, and what was left of daylight on this late February afternoon filtered with sullen reluctance through the heavily overcast sky.

The weather had no adverse affect on the Colonel. He moved along at a brisk pace, swinging his umbrella like a cane in rhythm with his steps. A forward swing of the umbrella coordinated with the forward swing of the left foot, umbrella and right foot touching the ground simultaneously. The almost military precision of his movements amused the Colonel, and he smiled faintly under his beard.

It would be pleasant, he decided, to walk to his rendezvous in Greenwich Village. He had plenty of time, and he had always enjoyed walking in the snow. Who knows when he would again have the opportunity? More important, it would give him time to review the complicated and tricky game he was playing. Not that he hadn't played similar games in the past, but his life could very well hang on the outcome of this one, and nothing must go wrong.

He broke stride briefly to pause in front of a shop window, where he appeared to examine with a critical eye a display of women's underwear that was decorated in key places with red-and-black hearts. His judgment that it was vulgar but interesting and typically American (for where would you see such a decadent display in Moscow!) was an irrelevancy. In fact his gaze was fixed on his tail's reflection in the window, that distant shadow walking parallel with him on the opposite side of the street, keeping pedestrians between himself and Makarov, pausing when he did and gazing in his turn at window displays with every sign of keen interest.

No need to ask why Krassotkin was dogging his footsteps. Moscow Center would have taken the appropriate action, and if the man became a nuisance, he could be easily neutralized. It's what he stood for that was important—a visible confirmation of the forces now arrayed against himself. From the moment he had departed from his daily routine, from the moment he had walked on past Sixty-sixth Street without turning west to pay his customary visit to the Polish UN mission, he had tipped his hand. And all they needed was that one sign. Andropov's death had left the field wide open to his enemies. One slip and they'd be on him like a pack of jackals. The risks were great, yes, but he accepted them because the rewards of winning were greater. However, from now on nothing must be left to chance. All moves must be carefully calculated to bring the game to checkmate in the end. Or should he say *Czech-mate?* A savage smile twisted the lips under the heavy beard as memory picked him up and swept him back twenty years in time, swept him away from the crowded avenue in the center of Manhattan to the dead quiet of that dark basement room. He was face to face again with a frightened, determined man whose blow had left its mark on him.

But I left my mark on you, my friend, isn't that so? More than one!

Yet for all that, what had he been left with? For all those remorseless hours of interrogation in that other basement room, that tiny, windowless place for the damned where screams of pain were commonplace sounds, he had been left with a few whispered words forced through bloody lips: *I burned them! I burned them! Now let me die.*

The memory rekindled the old rage; his eyes glittered and his body burned with it. No, no, he whispered fiercely to himself.

We'll meet again, my friend. Our business isn't finished yet. Death can come after, but if I have anything to say about it, we'll meet again. Make no mistake about that.

Suddenly in midstride he halted. While a part of his mind had been occupied with the past, another had been concerned with the problems of the present. Oblivious to the bumps and jostles of impatient pedestrians around him, he stood motionless, concentrating with drawn brows and narrowed eyes. Long-range plans were tricky, no matter how carefully made. Some unforeseeable factor, some chance event, could interfere and send everything out of control. Like predicting the weather beyond a couple of days—a slight change in the wind's direction could throw the whole forecast off.

He smiled slyly all of a sudden, and as abruptly as he had halted, he moved again. Shouldering people rudely aside, he reached the phone booth at the corner, stepped inside, and made a brief phone call. Then he proceeded on his way through the falling snow, swinging his umbrella and whistling a lilting Russian folk song under his breath, embellishing the melody with delicate trills and tremolos. From time to time he checked to make sure that Krassotkin was keeping pace with him.

2

Karel Novotny came awake with a start, gasping for air, his heart pounding like a triphammer in his chest, his body drenched in sweat. He jerked his head up from the pillow and swept a terrified gaze around the room, noting with a kind of avidity each shoddy detail—the soiled wallpaper, the ancient armoire with the spotted mirror, the washbasin in the corner with the rust stain where a leaking faucet had gone unrepaired, the rickety chair and table. Finally, as his eye came to rest on his own cheap fiber suitcase where it lay on the floor, his breathing grew easier, and with a long trembling sigh he let his head fall back on the pillow.

Yes. All right. He was safe. Here in this dreary room in this nameless hotel on the Left Bank of Paris, he was safe. It had been the dream again. Always the dream. Someday, he thought with the resignation of long despair, the nightmare will win over reality. Someday I won't wake from its torment. It will succeed finally and forever in locking me in that tiny, dark, windowless room with the shadowed figures of the pain givers moving inexorably toward me where I sit helplessly in the chair, their clothes making those soft rustling sounds in the darkness.

Soft rustling sounds? No! He pulled himself to an upright position, frowning. It hadn't been the dream that had wakened him. Something else... Some other sound had reached the fringes of his consciousness. What?

He cocked his head and listened intently to the street noises

15

coming up through the window. They had a different quality from earlier. When he had dozed off, it had been broad daylight. Now dusk had fallen and the room was dark except for the faint glow from the street lamp. What he heard was the cheerful racket signifying the end of the workday—people hurrying home or to a nearby cafe for an aperitif, laughter, quick footsteps, the slamming of doors, the rattle of grates as shopkeepers locked up for the night. Nothing threatening there. And from the room next to his through the thin wall came the same soft sighs and moans and creaking of bedsprings that he had heard as he'd fallen asleep. This was less of a hotel for transients like himself, he had discovered, than a place for the whores of the neighborhood to bring their clients for a half hour of commercial love.

He was about to lie down when the sound came again. At his door. A soft scratching, a faint whisper. That was what had brought him awake. Silently he swung his legs around and down to the floor. It was cold against his bare feet and sent a shiver up his spine.

The scratching again, the whispering voice, an urgency in it. Better to know, he thought as he rose painfully and limped over to the door. He put his ear against it.

"Oh, please help me! Please open the door!" A woman's voice, low, tense with fright.

He unlocked the door, opened it a crack, and peered out. A young woman stood in the hallway. She was white-faced and breathing hard as though she had been running. She wore a thin robe, which she was clutching closed with both hands. Under her disheveled hair, large dark eyes wide with fear appealed to him. In the dim light he thought he detected a bruise on one cheek.

"Oh, please," she whispered. "Help me!"

His French had grown rusty. He strained to understand.

"It's him." She twisted her head and cast a terrified glance over her shoulder at the door across the hall. "He's drunk. He's crazy! I'm afraid—afraid he'll kill me—please..."

Uncertainly Novotny asked, "What do you want me to do?"

She moved close to the door, her face only inches from his.

16

He smelled her cheap perfume. "Just let me in for a while. Please. I won't be any trouble. I promise—no trouble at all. He'll go to sleep, I'm sure, or leave if I don't come back. Then I'll go. Oh, please, *please!*"

Novotny hesitated. He wanted to close the door. She was nothing to him. He had other concerns of far greater importance than a whore in trouble. Still, the last *please* had sounded such a desperate note, and how well he knew what it was to be desperate! After another second's hesitation, he stepped back, pulling the door wide. The girl darted past him into the room.

"Close the door quickly," she whispered. "Quickly, and lock it!"

Ignoring her for a moment, Novotny peered up and down the hallway. It was empty and silent. Too silent? A faint uneasiness stirred in him. How had she known this room was occupied? He hadn't been out of it since he'd arrived late last night. He had been quiet, resting for the most part and thinking. If she was a whore who had come to the hotel this afternoon with a client who turned ugly, how had she known he would be here to help her? And aren't these questions, he asked himself in sudden anger, coming a little late? Closing the door quickly, he swung around to face her. At the same time he flicked the wall switch, and the ceiling fixture sent light glaring through the room.

The woman was standing beside the rumpled bed, no longer clutching the robe closed. Her right arm was at her side, the other akimbo with hand on outthrust hip, the robe open wide to display the body, a thin muscular body with no softness to it at all. The crude, unsubtle pose was saying in the most mechanical way: Here it is. My stock-in-trade. Goods for sale.

He stared at her, disgust overwhelming his uneasiness for the moment. "That won't be necessary," he said coldly. "You can stay for a while—" He broke off as his gaze reached her face, struck by something that seemed completely out of character. Though there was a coy, inviting smile on her lips, the eyes had lost the wide-eyed look of appeal and were regarding him through narrowed lids with a crafty, calculating expression. There was nothing sexual there at all. She appeared to be appraising him in the way a fighter might appraise an opponent in the ring. He could see, too, how the dim light in the hall had concealed her age. She was a hard-faced woman well into her thirties. With a sharp hiss he drew in his breath, suspicion turning to certainty. This isn't a whore in trouble. This is the enemy! Oh, God, he prayed, not here, not yet!

The woman had read his thoughts in his face. Without a sound, in one quick, lithe movement, she was on him. Something flashed in her right hand. Without thinking he fell back against the door for support, instinctively dropping his left arm in front of him as a shield. The knife, wielded in a savage underthrust aiming for the belly, stabbed into the flesh of his forearm. At the same time with all his strength he swung his right fist up in a ferocious uppercut and smashed it against her jaw. The blow caught her head at an angle, snapping it back and sideways and sending her crashing to the floor. The knife flew through the air and landed with a clatter beneath the window.

For a long moment there were just the two of them suspended in limbo, the woman a silent huddle on the floor, the man a tense figure leaning against the door, watching, waiting, fist still clenched, blood dripping steadily from the wound in his arm through the shirt-sleeve and down to the floor. The man was unaware of it. All his attention was concentrated on the woman.

The sound of footsteps in the hall outside the door brought Novotny out of his trancelike state. He waited for them to move past, then he locked the door and stepped over to where the woman lay. Squatting down beside her, he noted first the unnatural angle of the head and then the glazed staring eyes. He felt for the pulse in her throat knowing he wouldn't find any. Her neck was probably broken. He had heard the crack the second his fist struck her jaw, though it hadn't registered at the time. In a peripheral way he noted also that the bruise on her face had been applied with makeup and that she wore a leather strap affair on her left arm to hold the knife.

Such attention to detail hardly seemed necessary to snare me, he thought bitterly. What a fool I am! If I had been fully awake and thinking clearly, would I have let her in? Still, it was better, he thought as he rose to his feet, that it had happened this way, far better than having her sneak up behind him in a dark alley and plunging that knife into his back.

A dizzying sense of déjà vu swept over him as he gazed down at the body. Twenty years slipped away, and he was staring at the bearded man where he lay on the stone floor in that basement room. One important difference. *He* had *not* been dead. "But that will be rectified soon," he muttered, his eyes blazing for a moment with the hatred that had nourished him and kept him alive during the long years. "Soon."

He tore his gaze away from the body and turned his attention to the wound in his arm. It was throbbing now that the shock had worn off, and the sleeve was soaked with blood. He eased the shirt off to expose a deep, jagged wound. It would take time to heal, but he mustn't let it slow him down.

Using his teeth, he ripped a long strip from the back of the shirt and draped it over his shoulder. He flipped open the lid of his suitcase and brought out the bottle of cheap brandy the old porter had bought for him last night. Using his teeth again, he pulled out the cork and took a long swallow, shuddering as the crude spirits burned their way down his throat. But they did the job; he felt stronger.

At the washbasin he held the arm under the cold running water for a long time, and when the bleeding had eased he poured brandy over it, gritting his teeth as it set the flesh on fire. Pain is bearable, he thought, winding the strip of cloth tightly around the wound, if you know when it's going to end. It's only when it goes on and on and on with no respite to look forward to that it can reduce you to a helpless, gibbering idiot.

Never mind! he told himself sharply. Forget that. Yesterday is finished. Concentrate on today and tomorrow.

From his suitcase he took his only other shirt and pulled it on. It would have to do until he could pick up another one. The torn, bloodied one he rolled into a ball and stuffed into a side pocket of the case. It would serve as more bandage later.

And now... He turned with reluctance to the body. What to do with her? He felt no guilt at all for having been the cause of her death. She had been going to kill him. He had killed her. It was as simple as that. He felt only a distant kind of pity for both of them and a terrible weariness. Slumping down on the bed, he put his head in his hands and closed his eyes.

It would have taken an act of faith to recognize the Karel Novotny of today as the handsome, vigorous man of twenty years ago. The long years spent in the Czech prisons, mines, and labor camps had stripped the flesh from his bones and laid the ashen pallor of death on his skin. They had reduced him to a haunted, hollow-eyed ruin of a man, old and sick at fifty-eight. The once rich brown hair was sparse and gray and cropped so short the bony skull was clearly visible, looking pale and fragile as eggshell. He slept little, then only during the day. The nights were spent awake, holding off the demons. Deprived of everything a person holds worthwhile—family, friends, freedom, health, self-respect—what had sustained him for the twenty years was hatred—a hatred that obsessed him for those whom he believed had betrayed him, a knife-edged hatred that each day in prison had honed ever sharper and sharper. Even when hope of escape had all but died, he still clung to the hatred until two events conspired to revive the hope. They had him working at the time in a coal mine near Plzeň. A man in his barracks with whom he was friendly was dying of cancer, and one night he had thrust a note into Novotny's hand. "If you ever get out, please, my wife..." And in exchange for that favor the man had whispered an address in Vienna. "He's expensive, but clever—and quick. A master forger."

Then two weeks later an epidemic of a virulent strain of influenza had struck down his entire barracks, and with all the others Novotny had been taken to the hospital in Plzeň. There, when his fever had subsided, he had watched for his chance. The hospital was overcrowded, its routine chaotic as a result. Prisoners were mixed in with regular patients, and the overworked staff weren't concerned with any differences. The few guards who were there seemed mainly interested in keeping their distance from the sick. It was now or never.

Novotny could still feel the clammy cold tile of the

bathroom floor beneath his bare feet, and with a shudder of revulsion he recalled how the orderly's plump neck had felt in his hands and how long it had taken him to die! In the bathroom cubicle he had stripped the man of his shoes, socks, pants, and white jacket, had put them on quickly, and had left him propped up on the toilet. A quick search in a utility closet provided him with a hat and an overcoat. No one had paid the slightest attention to him as he'd hurried along the dimly lit corridor and out into the cold night.

After that, everything blurred together. The fever returned, and most of the time he was too ill to care what happened. If he made it, fine. If not, what did he have to lose?

Against all odds he had made it. He traveled at night. During the day he holed up in barns or made a burrow in the woods like an animal. He stole food; he begged rides when he thought it was safe; and three days after his escape, he had staggered into the cottage by the Sázava River, where, twenty years before, though he didn't know it, his family had spent their last day in Czechoslovakia.

The cottage was derelict now, the windows broken, the doors hanging on hinges, the roof half caved in, but he didn't mourn over it. It was shelter, and if he was lucky, his cache would still be there. It would be the end for him, of course, if the enemy found him there, but so be it. He had crawled upstairs, found a torn and filthy mattress in a bedroom, and, wrapping his coat around him, he'd slept for twenty-four hours.

Novotny never knew that the enemy had come before he arrived at the cottage or that they came again after he left—and found the three bricks on the hearth and the gaping hole in the fireplace from which he had removed his cache of money. German marks, French francs, British pounds, American dollars—savings from payments made to him by his case officer, Nicholas Savini, for services rendered over the years. Some fifty thousand dollars. It was little enough compensation, Novotny thought grimly, for a man's life, but never mind, it was more than enough to accomplish his goal. And that's all he asked now.

When a man crosses "black" across a border, has plenty of money for bribes, and finds guards willing to take a chance, his crossing can be relatively safe. He has no need of a passport, either, under the circumstances, but afterward there is no place he can go without that precious document.

Karel Novotny hadn't wanted to stay in Vienna. With its large intelligence community there was always the danger that an American or Russian agent might spot him, but he had no choice. The forger was there. He remained hidden in his room in the seedy hotel in a working-class district in the city, going out only when he had to. Once to send that important cable to his old friend, good, reliable Josef, praying as he did so that his friend was still in the same location. The answer came back speedily. Josef was there. Luck was with him. And again, just before he left Vienna, he posted two letters. The one was the dying man's note to his wife. He had promised. He only hoped she would be allowed to receive it.

Footsteps passing in the corridor outside his room roused Novotny from his lethargy. He raised his head and gazed with feverish eyes at the dead woman's face without seeing it. Other faces superimposed themselves, one after the other. The four faces of betrayal. Three he would recognize no matter how time might have changed them. Every feature was etched on his memory. The shape of their noses, the set of their ears, the curve of their lips... He would know them.

As for the fourth... Code name *Golconda*. That face was a blank, but he would smoke him out somehow, set a fire under him and smoke him out of his hiding place!

Perhaps the fire was already burning somewhere. News of his escape would travel fast in some circles. By now wouldn't they all know that he was free? He could almost hear the clatter of the Teletype machines, the hum of the telephone wires, the shrill, uneasy whispers: *He's out. He's escaped. Killed a guard, they say. Where's he heading? He could be anywhere.*

Someone knew. The crumpled body there on the floor was evidence of that. Which one, and how had he known? From the time he had left Vienna he had brought into play all the tradecraft he could remember. Going forward, doubling back,

22

traveling south instead of north, losing himself in crowded city streets, and finally, at the end of the tortuous, zigzag course, he had reached this shabby, nameless hotel on the Left Bank of Paris.

The weak spot was Hans Mautner in Vienna, forger of passports, with the sly smile and furtive eyes. If my friend in the coal mines knows about the man, Novotny thought, then it's almost a certainty, isn't it, that agents on both sides of the espionage fence would not only know of Mautner but would be using him. And the forger was the kind of man who would talk if the price was right—or the threat harsh enough. In that case my enemies will be on the lookout for Johann Bieber, Austrian businessman.

I should have killed him, Novotny thought dispassionately. That would have been the safe thing to do. And what was one more death on his conscience? But it was too late to worry about that now. And wasn't he forgetting...! He leaped to his feet, fatigue vanishing as he remembered it was Mautner who had recommended this hotel. "A few extra francs," he had said with his sly smile, "and don't let them cheat you, my friend, but a few extra francs under the counter will buy you invisibility. They will not find it necessary to register your passport with the police."

Too much time had passed already, he thought as he limped over to the body. Someone could be waiting nearby, waiting for her to report back, growing impatient to hear that her mission was accomplished.

He stooped and seized hold of the woman's wrists. Taking most of the burden with his right hand, he dragged the body to the armoire. Breathing heavily with the effort it cost him, he pushed and tugged at the body until it was well inside. There it sprawled amid the dust balls and debris left by long gone tenants. It was clear the room was cleaned only haphazardly. She could lie there for a while undiscovered and give him a margin of time. He closed the flimsy doors of the armoire, turned the little key in the lock, and dropped it into his pocket.

A sense of urgency dictated his movements now. A tie quickly knotted, the ill-fitting jacket eased on with care. It wouldn't do, he thought with a grim smile, to be dripping blood through the airport. He slipped into the worn topcoat and lastly pulled on the concealing hat, adjusting the brim low over his forehead.

Suitcase in hand, he cast a quick searching glance around the room, noting with satisfaction that the bloodstains from his wound were already fading and blending into all the other stains on the old carpet. Catching sight of the knife under the window, he picked it up and wiped it on the underside of the tattered rug. Then he retracted it into its plastic handle and dropped it into his pocket.

Having unlocked the door, he started to reach for the knob but stopped abruptly and stared down at his hand. It was shaking uncontrollably, and he cursed it for betraying him. He was frightened, yes, he knew that, accepted it. Even with the goad of his hatred, he was frightened of what lay ahead for him in that alien, enemy territory where he was going. He knew, too, that fear would be his traveling companion from now on, but he had to control it, not let it control him. He had taken just that one small step toward safety, had sent that brief message from Vienna to the only person he could trust. He closed his eyes for a second and sent up a silent prayer. "Please, God, let her understand—and keep her safe!"

Then, without further hesitation, Karel Novotny opened the door, stepped out into the empty hall, and hurried away.

3

The bus crawled down Fifth Avenue through the home-going crush of traffic, starting, stopping, starting, stopping. Sometimes a sudden lurching motion caught Hana off balance and flung her against the knees of the plump, fur-clad woman sitting beneath her. As she took a firmer grip on the bar overhead, she wondered how those knees could be so hard, encased as they were in flesh and fur. And each time it happened, she breathed an automatic "Sorry," though there was little she could do to prevent it, being hemmed in on all sides and forced to sway as the crowd swayed. The woman's response to her apology was a brief, icy stare while she continued her conversation with her husband. A monologue, really, and Hana only guessed that the pleasant-faced man sitting next to the woman was her husband. He had offered Hana his seat when she had climbed aboard. Hana had refused with a surprised, grateful smile.

"I really can't take the cold, Henry," the woman was saying in a querulous voice. "I just shrivel up and die inside. You know that. I don't care how mild the winter is, it's still too cold. I don't know why we didn't go to Florida this time, but I'll tell you this—I'll never spend another winter in New York —never! You're not listening to me, Henry."

"Hmm," said Henry, who against all odds was trying to read the *New York Times*. His eyes slid around and up to Hana. He winked, and Hana gave him a small grin in return, which Henry found delightful. He tried to go back to his newspaper, but his eyes were drawn again to the girl. She was gazing out of the window with a dreamy expression on her face, and he was able to study her surreptitiously. A lovely, graceful child, he thought. Well, not a child. A young woman, really, but a child as far as he was concerned. It was a face very pleasing to the eye, oval-shaped with prominent cheekbones, cheeks slightly hollow beneath them. The eyes with their thick dark lashes were large and wide-spaced and brown, a clear brown like dark honey, their expression grave and gentle and intelligent. The eyes of a fawn, Henry thought, waxing poetical. The nose was fine and straight, the mouth wide but not too wide, and the jaw, though delicately molded, was firm. There was character there, Henry decided. Crowning the lovely face was a cap of curls, the color of cinnamon. The hair was damp, sparkling under the lights with tiny diamonds of moisture. She should be wearing a hat, Henry worried, she'll catch cold. Must be about five feet six or seven inches tall. The fact that she was slender made her appear taller, perhaps. Odd how she gave the impression of strength and fragility at the same time. She had a glowing, faultless complexion, her skin having the same honey tones as the eyes, and except for a little lipstick it was free of makeup. *She walks in beauty...* And aren't you getting mushy in your old age, Henry! The girl was wearing a three-quarter-length brown corduroy sport coat with a tweedy skirt and a pale green sweater under it. She must have walked a distance before she got on the bus, Henry deduced, because her brown moccasin-style shoes were damp from the snow. Somewhere in her mid-twenties, he guessed, and noting the absence of any ring on the fourth finger of her left hand, he sighed. Would that he were ringless and in his mid-twenties instead of long married and in his mid-fifties. He sighed again, glanced at his now glumly silent wife, and returned with resignation to his paper.

Hana, unaware of Henry's detailed scrutiny, had been gazing out of the window watching the throngs of cars and pedestrians all hurrying home through the wintry evening and listening at the same time to the odd bits of conversation around her.

"...second time out the bastard told me that if I wasn't going to go to bed with him, there was no point in his wasting his time!"

"...and the more I thought about it, the madder I got. It's the basic injustice of it all, you know? Am I the captain of my fate or not? I asked him. I mean, what's it all about, anyhow?"

Hana found herself smiling rather idiotically all of a sudden, and despite the crammed, uncomfortable bus with its pervading odor of warm, damp bodies, she felt that swift surge of love and compassion toward all her fellow beings, even the plump owner of the hard knees. It was a feeling that struck her at the oddest times and always unexpectedly, like a bolt from the blue, *pěst na oko*. Here she was in this hurly-burly city, far away from the sad, gray, medieval place of her birth, and it was good, just plain, ordinary, everyday good to be alive. She had to repress a cockeyed urge to throw her arms around perfect strangers.

Of course, she told herself as the bus jerked to a halt and she followed the flow of passengers to the exit, your mood has nothing to do with the very nice contract tucked in your purse or the pleasant evening ahead with Steve and perhaps seeing brother Paul before the weekend is over. Count your blessings.

Smiling to herself, Hana jumped lightly over to the sidewalk and turned toward Washington Square Park. The arch loomed, gaunt and gray against the somber sky, as she hurried along, heading west, taking her usual shortcut through the park. Shivering a little, she tucked her chin into the collar of her coat. She wasn't dressed for walking in this weather. The morning had been mild and sunshiny with that faint tantalizing scent of spring in the air, but the weather had played false and brought back the gloom and cold of winter, the kind of damp cold that seeps its treacherous way into the bones and settles there.

The night was windless. The flakes of snow drifted straight down, thick and steady, melting on the streets and sidewalks. Car tires hissed along the wet roads while the lights in the apartment buildings around the square glowed through the mist, beckoning New Yorkers home to warmth, a drink, dinner.

On Washington Place in front of a building in the middle of the block Hana paused a moment, tipped her head back, and glanced up at her brother's top-floor apartment. The windows were dark. No beckoning light there. No warming drink with him tonight. A week, he had said. A week, perhaps. That could mean today, tomorrow, the next day. For a second longer she stood there, staring up at the blank, shrouded windows while the snow fell damply on her face. I'll phone him tomorrow, she told herself finally, and swung around to head west again toward home.

One moment the sidewalk had been empty. The next moment, as though he had sprung from beneath the ground, a man stood there, blocking her way. The momentum of her stride sent her colliding against him. Something sharp jabbed her anklebone, and she sprang back with an exclamation of pain.

"Ah—I beg your pardon!" the man said, quickly thrusting out a supporting arm.

"It's all right," Hana said, trying to sidestep the arm.

"It's not all right at all. Certainly not. Are you hurt?" He glanced down at his umbrella. Swinging it aside in a wide arc, he added, "How stupid of me, how thoughtless. I'm sorry." He raised his eyes and peered closely into her face. "Are you sure you're all right?"

"Yes, I'm sure," Hana said, giving him a polite smile. "It's nothing, truly—" She broke off, uneasy all of a sudden. What was it? Why was he making so much of a casual accident? He had apologized—profusely. That was enough, surely.

Hana made a move to step around him with a murmured, "Excuse me," but the man moved at the same time in the same direction, barring her way. It had been deliberate. No doubt of it. Fear coiled its way up her spine. Unaccountable, violent things happened on the city's streets every day, and he was gazing at her with such an odd expression on his face. Was he smiling under that beard? His cold pale blue eyes showed no sign of it. They were fixed on her face with a look of such piercing intensity that for a moment they held

Hana captive, rooted to the spot like a small animal caught in the glare of light, while in the back of her mind a long-buried memory stirred in its hiding place and whispered a warning: *Danger... Danger...* Then a cab swung over to the curb with a hiss of tires and a squeal of brakes and discharged a passenger. The spell broke. Hana darted off the sidewalk, plunged across the street, and ran until she reached the intersection at Sixth Avenue. There she paused to catch her breath, casting a quick glance over her shoulder. The man wasn't following her. He was standing where she had left him, swinging his umbrella slowly back and forth, gazing after her—a short, solidly built man with a curly black beard. Snowflakes dotted the fur hat and decorated the shoulders of the fine black wool coat with the white carnation in its buttonhole. A study in black and white, she thought. Harmless. I'm a fool. What possessed me to panic like that? My imagination working overtime.

The encounter had lasted only a minute. The vague sense of menace and the brief stirring of the shadowed memory had been so fleeting that Hana was able to dismiss both from her mind by the time she rounded the corner of Fourth Street and turned up Perry, and when she reached her apartment building, she was humming softly under her breath.

Gray paint over red brick, winter-dead ivy clinging to the black iron fire escape—Hana loved the building, she loved her place in it, she loved the little ginkgo tree planted in its square of earth at the curb. Soon it would be sprouting its pale green leaves because spring was coming, that sweetest time of the year.

She brushed the snowflakes from her hair as she took the steps two at a time and pushed into the entryway. She unlocked the inner door and in the hall paused long enough to open her mailbox and extract several pieces of mail. The topmost one was an advertisement that told her in big bold letters with a lot of exclamation points that she had a chance to win $500,000. "Okay, I'll buy that," she murmured aloud, and thrust the letters into her pocket without glancing at the rest as she headed for the stairs.

"Hi there, Emily Johnson!"

On the bottom step, facing her, sat a small skinny girl dressed in blue jeans and a white T-shirt with the red-lettered legend across the chest *Property of the New York Yankees*. A tangled mass of blond hair fell around her shoulders and half covered her face. She was the eight-year-old daughter of the building's superintendent.

"Jasmin," the child said.

"Pardon?"

"Jasmin. I've decided to change my name."

"You have? I'm sorry about that. Emily is one of my favorite names."

"It's not one of mine. It's so boring. I mean, *really,* it's so *boring!*" She brooded in frowning silence for a second over the boredom of it all, then in a more practical tone, she added, "Besides, there's another Emily in my class and we're always getting mixed up."

"I see. That is a nuisance, isn't it?"

"I don't know, though..." The blue eyes, wide and anxious, fixed themselves on Hana's face. "I'm not *really* sure about Jasmin yet. If you were me, would you like it? If you were *me,* I mean."

"Well... That's a difficult question to answer because I'm not you. I'm me. It's a pretty name, there's no doubt about that, and it certainly isn't boring. How did you decide on it?" Hana asked, playing for time.

"I read it in a book. But I haven't decided *exactly*. I wrote out a list and Jasmin's on top, but the others are awfully pretty, too. Don't you want to know what they are?"

Hana couldn't refuse the look of appeal on the small face raised to hers. "Yes, very much," she said.

From a dog-eared piece of paper in her lap, Emily Johnson read out the names slowly. "There's Ramona and Rosalind and Melanie and Lucinda and Angeline and Veronica. I had to cross out a whole lot of other names. It's just so *hard* to pick the best one."

Hana nodded and considered the choices in grave silence for a moment. At least she asked tactfully, "What one does your father like?"

Emily-Jasmin scowled down at her dirty sneakers and shrugged a bony shoulder. "He likes Emily, of *course*. He would. He picked it out."

"Of course." Hana nodded again judiciously. "You know," she added, "the trouble is, I like them all. Tell you what, let me think about them overnight—sleep on it, you know—and in the morning I'll tell you the one I like best. Okay?"

The child gave her a bright, gap-toothed grin and said, "Okay."

Hana ruffled the blond head. "See you tomorrow, then, Emily-Jasmin," she said, and stepping around the child, she ran up the stairs. She was halfway up the second flight when Emily-Jasmin called something up to her, but Hana scarcely heard. She was humming under her breath and going over in her mind the things she had to do before Steve's arrival. She had cooked the stroganoff last night. She only had to add the sour cream and heat it. Crisp salad makings were in the refrigerator. Wash them, let them drain. Take out the cheese, open the wine, noodles could be cooking while they had a drink. Good girl, she told herself. Excellent organization! Plenty of time for a relaxing soak in a hot tub.

Not that Stephen Karr would care at all if dinner were ready or not. He was a big, easygoing man whom she had met at an otherwise unnoteworthy party six months ago. They had become friends immediately that night and lovers a week later. He was thirty-six years old, a lawyer, and in the middle of a reasonably amicable divorce. There was one child, three-year-old Sara, an adorable bundle of supercharged energy. Neither Steve nor she herself felt any need at this stage in their affair to make a further commitment, content with their uncomplicated "meaningful relationship." He was a real sweetheart, Steve. Yes, she looked forward to this evening.

Hana was smiling in anticipation as she headed down the hall toward her apartment. Third-floor front. Her home, her haven. She had a ring of keys in her hand, a bulky ring because Paul's were on it as well. She kept meaning to separate them and carry his in the bottom of her bag. It wasn't as if she used his every day, and it was time-consuming picking her own out.

So do it! she told herself, inserting the proper key in lock number one. Hell, you know, is paved with good—

A soft footstep behind her, a hard hand on her shoulder, a low voice in her ear. "Miss Novotny..."

Hana froze.

Always have your door keys ready; always check for strangers nearby; unless they have a knife at your throat or a gun to your head, make noise, run, scream, kick...

Paul's cautions ran swiftly and with a kind of hard clarity through her mind. Run? She was rooted to the floor. Scream? She could scarcely breathe, much less make a sound. Panic had risen in her throat like thick fog, stifling her.

"Miss Novotny..." The low voice in her ear again, the hand tightening on her shoulder. "Please don't scream or do anything foolish. We don't mean you any harm."

We?

The hand dropped from her shoulder, and Hana forced herself to turn. She found herself facing two men. The one who had spoken was leaning toward her, watching her warily, while the other man stood behind him, silent, half-hidden in the shadows.

After waiting a moment for her pounding heartbeat to slow, Hana said, "I won't scream. I'm not very good at screaming anyway, and I don't intend to do anything foolish, as you call it." Then, deciding that offense is the best defense, she added, "But you must admit it's unnerving to be accosted by two strange men here in my own—"

"Accosted, Miss Novotny? Now, really... we only want to talk to you for—"

"Who are you?" Hana broke in. "What are you doing here? And how do you know my name?"

"We're friends of your brother, Paul—from Washington. We want to have a talk with him."

The man hadn't really answered her question, but Hana didn't realize that until a good while later. "If you want to see Paul, I don't know why you've come here," she said.

"A few moments of his time." The man shrugged impatiently. "A bit of a sociable chat is all."

"A sociable chat," Hana repeated, and a sudden uncontrollable giggle erupted from her throat.

The man frowned. He was still standing very close, almost touching her. Hana could smell his after-shave lotion, a heavy, sweet scent. And something else...an odor of mint. The combination made her feel ill.

"I don't think I understand," Hana said. "If you'll explain—"

"There's really nothing to understand, Miss Novotny," the man broke in. "All we want is to see your brother. That's simple enough, isn't it?"

His arrogance and impatience angered Hana. "Oh, yes, that's simple enough. I think I can understand that," she said. "I'll *try*, anyway. You say you want to see Paul. All right. He isn't here, you see, and—"

Hana came to an abrupt halt as she saw the man dip his hand into his pocket. She shrank back, thinking for one wild moment that he was bringing out a gun—here—outside her own door!

The man's frown deepened to a scowl when he saw Hana's reaction. He drew his hand out. It held a roll of peppermints. The scene took on a kind of surrealistic quality with the man automatically offering the roll to Hana, Hana responding with a shake of her head and a polite "No, thank you," and the man explaining as he popped a mint into his mouth that he was trying to give up cigarettes. Then it was back to business.

"You said your brother isn't here, Miss Novotny. How do you know that if you haven't been inside your apartment?"

"He doesn't live here. Surely his *friends* would know that."

"Yes, we do know that," the man said coldly, "but he isn't at his own place, and we assumed he would be here with you."

"Your assumption is wrong. I'll be glad to tell Paul, though, that you called. I'm sure he'll be sorry he missed you gentlemen."

Hana laid stress on the word "gentlemen," and the man who

was doing the talking flushed slightly, but whether it was from embarrassment or anger, she didn't know and didn't care. She plunged boldly on. "If you'd like to leave a message, I'll give it to him when I can. What shall I tell him? What is it you want to talk to him about?"

The "talking man" (so Hana had titled him in her mind, for the other man said not a word throughout the entire interview) spoke slowly and carefully as though explaining something to a dim-witted child. "We've come from Washington, Miss Novotny. We'll be here for a few days. We must talk to Paul—about a private matter. I assure you he will be glad to see us."

The smile the man gave Hana was perfunctory, a mere exercise of facial muscles that did nothing to warm the expression in the cold eyes. Her boldness vanished, fear returned. Who were these men, really? Friends of Paul? Who were acting so *un*friendly? If their visit here was legitimate, why hadn't they rung her bell in the ordinary way instead of waiting in the dim hall to ambush her? She didn't need to ask how they got into the building. Emily-Jasmin...

"Where can we reach him, Miss Novotny?" The impatience and arrogance had returned full force to the man's voice. No nonsense, it said. Tell us what we want to know.

Without her being aware of it, both men had moved closer to her. They hemmed her in, waiting, watching. A subtle aura of threat seemed to emanate from them, to hang like a cloud in the air around them, and for the second time that day her mind breathed its warning of danger—but this time it was for Paul.

Tell us what we want to know. There was nothing she could tell them.

So they stood facing each other, the pale, slender girl and the two hard-faced men, while the silent seconds ticked away. How many, Hana didn't know. Her nerves were stretched wire taut, her knees were trembling, she was unable to move. She tried desperately to think of something to say, some lie to tell them, anything that would send them on their way, but nothing would come. Her mind was blank. She could only wonder how long they would be able to stand here like this.

Then from the floor below came welcome sounds to break the silence—quick, light footsteps and cheerful whistling. As though a puppeteer had suddenly relaxed the strings that held them, the tension snapped and all three moved at the same time. Hana let out a long, sighing breath and stepped a few inches back against the door. The men moved several paces away from her, the silent one glancing toward the stairway as he did so. The snick of a lock could be heard, a door opening and closing.

Taking advantage of the break, Hana spoke quickly. "I haven't heard from my brother for several days. I'm not even sure he's in town. If you will give me a phone number where he can reach you, I'll be glad to pass it on to him when I see him."

With an effort of will Hana forced herself to look steadily and calmly into the face of the "talking man." She saw him cast a sidelong glance at his companion, who raised one eyebrow and gave an almost imperceptible nod of his head. After this wordless communication, the "talking man" pulled a notebook from his pocket, wrote on it, and tore off the sheet. There was something almost savage in the way he ripped the paper off.

"Tell him to call this number any time, day or night, and as soon as he can." There was no longer even the semblance of courtesy in the man's manner now. He was very angry and didn't bother to hide it. Without a "please" or "thank you," he thrust the slip of paper at Hana. "It's important—it's urgent—that he get in touch with us. Tell him that. He'll understand."

Hana took the paper and said, "I'll tell him." Then she waited, expecting them to leave, but neither man made a move. "I'll tell him," she repeated.

Panic was only a breath away. It took all of Hana's courage to turn her back on the men. She had to force herself to take one slow step at a time, to insert the key into the first lock, turn it casually, then the second lock. The palms of her hands were moist. They made the keys slippery, her movements clumsy. It seemed to take forever. What must it be like to have only one lock on your door? None, for that matter! At last the door was open. She stepped into the foyer. Then panic took over. Suppose this was what they were waiting for—waiting to push their way in behind her! In a flash she had slammed the door shut, twisted the dead bolts, and slid the guard chain into its slot.

Feeling both relieved and foolish at the same time, Hana listened for the sound of retreating footsteps. She heard nothing. They were still there on the other side of the door, waiting. She imagined she could hear them breathing, or was that her own breath, fast and shallow in her throat, that she heard? What were they waiting for? The sound of other footsteps here in the apartment? A voice greeting her?

The only furnishings in the little foyer were a coat tree in one corner and a small upholstered bench along the wall. Hana sank down on the bench. She was angry again, and out of a perverse, childish need to get back at the men for frightening her, she sat very still, resting her elbows on her knees and her face in her hands. Not a sound would they hear from her! A contest of wills. Confusion to the enemy. She closed her eyes. Twenty years vanished like smoke in the wind.

"Confusion to the enemy... Hang on, Hanička, hang on. We'll be safe soon." They crouched together in the undergrowth, half-buried in the tall weeds and shrubs. Paul's arm was around her waist, trembling against her own trembling body, while he whispered encouragement in her ear. Her mother sat a few feet away beside old Jan, their guide. She managed somehow even in these nightmare circumstances to look aloof and remote. Her face with its strong bones was like a black-and-white etching against the greenery. Raindrops hissed on the leaves of the trees in the Moravian forest and made delicate patterns on the river—meaningless sights and sounds. Their ears were attuned only to the harsher sound of the enemy's footsteps. A sudden urgent wave of Jan's hand, and they flung themselves down, pressing their faces into the wet earth. She held her breath as the heavy tread moved closer. Voices above her, querulous, complaining about the weather. Closer, closer... Her lungs would burst, and, oh, God, they were going to step on her! Paul's hand squeezing her so tightly the bones must break. Footsteps...

Footsteps...? Hana's eyes flew open, her head snapped up,

and for a confused second she struggled to separate the echoes of the past with the reality of the present. The sounds she had heard... Were they real or in her mind? Silently she rose and pressed her ear to the door. The regular tread of feet moved along the hallway, down the stairs, and faded away. A long moment of unnatural quiet followed while Hana remained motionless beside the door until a sudden eruption of noise overhead broke the silence.

"Annie, will you come *on,* for chrissake! I'm starved. Why do you always—"

"I'm coming, you grouch, I'm coming!"

"Elephant and Castle hamburgers?"

"Okay, and coffee and dessert at Lanciani's."

"I don't have—"

"My treat. It's payday."

A door slammed. Feet clattered down the stairs. Hana drew in a deep, relaxing breath and smiled slightly. Her upstairs neighbors going out to dinner in their usual decorous fashion restored some sense of normalcy for her. Dropping her shoulder bag on the bench but without taking time to remove her coat, Hana hurried into the living room, slipped around the screen that divided her work area from the rest of the room, and peered through the nylon-curtained window down to the street. She watched the two men emerge onto the sidewalk, where they paused for a moment, both turning up their coat collars against the cold, both pulling on their gloves. Their movements seemed machinelike, synchronized, as though they had rehearsed them. She guessed that they spent a lot of time together. Neither wore a hat. Snowflakes settled thickly on their close-cropped hair like lacy white caps. She saw them tip their heads back and stare up at her window. They couldn't see her in the dark room, she was sure of that. Nevertheless she drew back into the protective shadows. The one man said something, the other man nodded sharply. Then they both swung around and marched off in the direction of Greenwich Avenue—two tall, thin men, dressed in anonymous clothes with lean, sharp-featured faces, resembling one another enough to be brothers.

Hana continued to gaze down into the street long after the

men had disappeared from view, the soft honey-brown eyes grown remote and bitter. The past was crowding in on her, its disturbing memories stirring restlessly in that dark hiding place in her mind where she tried to keep them shut away— shadows, vaguely outlined and frightening. Weeks, months would go by and she was untroubled by them, but today within half an hour's time they had successfully invaded the present and were clamoring for attention. Unlawful trespass, Hana thought with a wry grimace. It had started with the chance encounter on the sidewalk in front of Paul's apartment house that hadn't been chance. She had tried to convince herself that it was, but there had been something too contrived, too deliberate, about it. And she couldn't avoid the fact, too, that there had been something obscurely familiar about the bearded man, something that had alarmed her and sent her running in panic. And when she'd arrived home—two rough-mannered men demanding to see Paul . . .

And why, she asked herself, did she link these three men in her mind? Because she sensed the same timeless air about them? Hadn't she seen their like on the ancient cobbled streets of Prague, quiet, soft-walking men with those same cold, arrogant, watchful eyes? No one living in a police state was ever too young to know who they were and to feel an instinctive fear of them.

Yet wasn't her own brother akin to them? A part of their dark, closed world? She shivered in her damp clothes as she remembered her swift, involuntary reaction when Paul had told her what he planned to do after he finished college.

"Oh, no, Paul, how can you want to be like *them?*"

"They do a job I believe in—and this isn't Czechoslovakia."

"They're all the same—the secret police of this world—no matter what initials they go by. STB, KGB, CIA . . . They're all the same!"

"Come on, Hanička, be reasonable. They're not the same. There's a big difference between—"

"A degree of difference, I'll give you that, but only a slight degree. Put them all in long leather coats and boots and who could tell where they come from? You can't convince me otherwise, Paul."

Throwing up his hands in surrender, Paul had said, "All right. I won't argue with you." He'd smiled. "You're entitled to your own opinion. It's a free country." The smile had vanished and he'd added in a low, hard voice, "Besides, there are other reasons, Hanička. You should know that. It isn't so simple..." A spasm of pain had twisted his face and he'd fallen silent.

Not so simple—no. Hana had known he was thinking of their father, arrested and tried for treason all those years ago. She'd heard him whisper, "We left him."

Deserted him, he'd meant. Left him to the tender mercies of the Russian vultures. How often had she pictured him in the bleak courtroom in Pankrac prison, lost and alone—that kind, loving man, their elegantly handsome father. She closed her eyes and felt again that long-ago soft kiss on her forehead, heard the scarcely audible whisper in the dark bedroom, "I love you, my little Hana. Remember that." Then he was gone, a tall, thin shadow, merging into other shadows. Had she dreamed it, or had it really happened? She had never seen him again.

"We were children, Paul!" she'd cried, her voice harsh with pain. "It's irrational—your guilt. What could we have done?" What *could* they have done—a traitor's family—an eight-year-old girl, a fourteen-year-old boy, and their mother. Hadn't their mother made the only decision left to them—to flee, to go "black" across the border? Who knows what would have happened if they had stayed?

"No, Hanička, there was nothing we could do then," Paul had said. "But soon..."

Soon, if things went as he planned. "He's dead, Paul," she had insisted, white-faced and trembling, for how could she bear to think of him enduring a desperate kind of living death in some terrible prison camp? "Can't you accept that?"

The answer had been flat and final. "Not until I have proof."

Proof... Only by working within the intelligence community would Paul ever have a chance of finding out what had happened to their father. And if he discovered their father was still alive, what then? Hana wondered. Paul, the romantic, seizing the magic sword, rushing to the rescue on a white charger? Perhaps by now he knew the truth and hadn't told her, for by some unspoken agreement they had not referred to the painful subject again, and a few months later he had graduated magna cum laude from Dartmouth and, carrying his honors, his youth, and his idealism, had gone off to Langley, Virginia, to offer them to the CIA in the service of freedom.

Hana drew her gaze finally from the empty, snow-veiled street, pulling the drapes closed across the windows with finality as though blocking out the past, and switched on the lamp. Its warm glow lit up this small area, which she called her "studio." It was simply the one end of the living room that gave her the most light. Its furnishings were few and completely functional. Her work table was a large pine plank, six by three feet, which she had bought at a lumber yard, sanded smooth, and coated with polyurethane. It rested on two chests of drawers, one at either end, and these served to hold her art supplies as well. On the board stood an electric pencil sharpener, a stack of tablets, and a large ceramic cup filled with drawing pens and pencils. The work lamp, adjustable to a variety of angles, was clipped to the plank. The only other furnishings were a vinyl-padded stool for her to sit on and a four-drawer filing cabinet for storing copies of her old work, ideas and sketches for new, the lease to her apartment, and anything else she didn't know what to do with. Hana earned her living as a free-lance illustrator—children's books and adult book jackets, for the most part—and she was slowly but surely gaining recognition in the publishing world for her clean-lined, bold drawings.

Hana was heading for the hall to hang up her wet coat when the phone rang. She swung around and hurried over to where it sat on the table beside the sofa.

"Hello..."

"This is Novotny?"

"This is Hana Novotny, yes."

"It is to Paul Novotny I wish to speak, please."

"He's not here. Can I take a message?"

"When do you expect him?"

"He doesn't—that is, I don't know. Who's calling, please?"

"We will call back."

"Who—" There was a click, and the line went dead.

Hana cradled the receiver, frowning. *We* will call back? Odd, that *we*. The voice had been harsh and faintly accented. And how had this strange *we* known enough to call her to get in touch with Paul? His phone was unlisted, hers was listed as H. Novotny. Were they simply calling all the Novotnys in New York City? And who was calling? And why? And what good are all the questions when I have no way of finding the answers, she told herself, and impatiently turned her back on the telephone.

She couldn't, though, turn her back on the cold, heavy feeling of unease that was settling in the pit of her stomach. For Paul, not herself. Something was wrong. Something was badly wrong.

She stepped into the foyer and slipped off her wet coat, draping it carefully over the hall tree to dry. Then she removed her damp shoes and aligned them with equal care under the little upholstered bench. It was as though minor disorders must be put precisely right before she could cope with the major disorder that had appeared in her life.

As she straightened up, Hana's eye was caught by a crumpled piece of paper lying against the door. When she picked it up and smoothed it out, she saw it was the phone number the "talking man" had given her. Barefoot, she padded back into the living room, studying the paper. No area code. A New York number, then. For a split second of indecision her hand hovered over the phone. Then she lifted it and dialed the seven digits.

The ringing seemed to go on and on, and Hana thought with relief that assuming the place was an office of some kind, it would, of course, be closed by now. It was well after six. She was about to hang up when the ringing ceased abruptly and a woman's voice sang in her ear, "AIC Associates. Can I help you?"

"AIC Associates..." Hana echoed, and then went dumb, unable to think of anything to say. She had acted on a stupid impulse without thinking it through. Just hang up, she instructed herself, but the voice was singing in her ear again, "AIC Associates. Whom do you wish to speak to?" and before she could stop herself, she was stuttering, "I...uh—J-John White...? Is John White there?"

"There is no one here by that name. You must have the wrong number."

"I see. I'm sorry," Hana muttered.

Not the wrong number, she thought, cradling the receiver gently. Just the wrong questions.

It was a handsome building of weathered brick, its ground-floor exterior having something of an air of a church about it, for it had beautiful stained-glass windows and a massive oak door with gleaming brass fittings. One might almost expect upon walking through that massive door to be greeted by the faint, sweet scent of incense and a Gregorian chant or two. Instead, one simply found good-sized offices with innocuous and unelaborate furnishings. The building was twelve stories high with an antenna on its roof that rivaled in size and complexity the one on the USSR mission farther uptown.

Flanked on the one side by a sedate apartment house and on the other by a restaurant decked out to look like a British pub, the building had a kind of arrogant and indefinable air of holding itself aloof from its neighbors. A plaque fixed to its oak door informed any interested observer that it housed the AIC Associates, but it was so small and unobtrusive that it was rarely noticed.

The building fronted on the fenced-in park of the Tudor City apartment complex, while its rear windows looked down the steep escarpment to the United Nations Plaza beneath and to the East River beyond.

To the man sitting in the clean, white-walled room on the top floor surrounded by the sophisticated electronic equipment, the view of the United Nations buildings and the river was unremarkably familiar. He yawned and leaned over to press the button activating a tape recorder. As he did so, a buzzer sounded. Hand suspended in air, he swiveled his chair to check the TV monitor, then swung around and pressed another button. In a moment the door slid open, and the "talking man" and his companion entered the room. Without speaking, the occupant gave them a brusque nod, then turned back to his original position and switched on the tape recorder.

AIC Associates. Can I help you? AIC Associates. AIC Associates. Whom did you wish to speak to? I...uh—J-John White? Is John White there? There is no one here by that name. You must have the wrong number. I see. I'm sorry.

With a bored expression the man reached over and switched off the tape recorder, lifted his brows at the other men, shrugged, and picked up the phone.

4

"I apologize, gentlemen, if I'm upsetting your dinner plans," Gilbert Halliday said, "but it can't be helped. This is a matter that won't wait. So, please, make yourselves comfortable. You all have drinks? If you want seconds, just help yourselves."

A very cool customer, Herbert Redstone thought, admiring the man's easy, unhurried manner as he moved among his guests and over to the well-stocked bar built into one of the bookcases that lined the walls. He watched him busy himself with the Pinch bottle Scotch and the Waterford crystal glasses, trying to detect signs of the pressure the man must be under. There were none. Elegant in his country-squire garb—cashmere turtleneck sweater, Irish tweed jacket with leather elbow patches, and subtly tailored slacks—Halliday seemed completely relaxed, as though this were a simple social evening with a few friends over for drinks.

Redstone knew the man must be approaching sixty, but he had that craggy kind of face that looked old at thirty and young at fifty. He was a wealthy man, a millionaire at least, and Redstone, sipping the fine Scotch, wondered vaguely why someone with all that money should want to take on the ball-breaking job of running a huge intelligence agency with stations all over the world and having to cope at the same time with the additional headaches that came with it—the White House, congressional committees, the press, the intelligence community at large, and God knew what else. Did he enjoy the power? Was it out of a sense of patriotism? Pride, perhaps, because he considered himself the best man for the job? A com-

44

bination of all three, probably. At any rate he was generally acknowledged to be one of the more able directors of the agency, if an enigmatic one as well, keeping his private thoughts hidden for the most part behind his politician's smile.

Now, drink in hand, Halliday had taken his stand in front of the fireplace, facing the seated men. It was then that Redstone noticed how old and tired the man's eyes looked, how pinched and white the skin was around them. That's where the pressure was hidden, he realized, behind those shrewd blue eyes. He felt some relief to discover that the man was human after all.

"We have a problem," Halliday was saying in a level voice. "Our man has walked *out*, but he has not walked *in*." There was just a heartbeat of a pause while Halliday's cool gaze went swiftly from one face to the other. "Before I go any further," he went on, "I must stress that there will be no notes taken of this meeting, no records of any kind will be kept. What we say here is strictly between us and these four clean walls." A wintry smile creased his face for a second. "It will not be brought up at the regular staff meetings. Except for the five of us in this room, this discussion did not take place. We're the only ones privy to *Valentine,* and that's the way it will remain. If it comes off, fine. There'll be time enough then to go public with it if we think it's the thing to do. And if it doesn't come off, we're the only ones who will be the wiser—and the sadder. You understand now why I asked you to come here."

Here being this pleasant, attractively appointed room in Halliday's home in the Virginia countryside. Deep leather armchairs, a leaping fire in the huge fieldstone fireplace, fine and plentiful liquor... All the comforts of gracious living, Redstone thought wryly, but they brought no cheer into the room. On the contrary, they only seemed to emphasize the oppressive, somber atmosphere, and he felt acutely ill at ease. He wished to God he were thousands of miles away, back in the field, back on his home ground in Czechoslovakia. He was a field man, that's where his skills lay. What was he doing here with the top brass, odd man out?

"Just watch and listen," his boss had told him. "Catch the nuances. Don't analyze. Be passive, a sounding board."

"First impressions..."

"Precisely. That's what I want. When you know people well, you sometimes see what you expect to see, what you've become accustomed to seeing. It can blind you to what's really there. These people are new to you. You may sense something I miss."

I doubt that there's anything you miss, Savini, Redstone had thought. Aloud, he'd said, "Is there something special I'm supposed to be looking for?"

Savini hadn't answered immediately. He'd swung the BMW off the road onto a circular driveway and pulled to a stop in front of a sprawling white clapboard house. With his hand on the door latch he had fixed his dark-eyed gaze on Redstone's face and with a thin smile said, "I believe it was La Fontaine in the seventeenth century who observed in his wisdom, 'It is a double pleasure to deceive the deceivers.'"

Before Redstone could respond to that or ask any more questions, Savini had stepped gracefully out of the car and was ushering him up the steps, across the broad, pillared veranda, and into the house.

The smooth bastard wouldn't have said any more anyway, Redstone thought angrily. Clandestine by nature, by training, and by occupation, there's nothing he enjoyed more than the cryptic statement. He cast a furtive glance at his boss sitting beside him, a slender, silent figure, his sleek dark head bent toward the fire, his dark eyes hooded. The firelight, playing over the olive-skinned, ascetic-looking face, highlighted the thin lips, the long, thin nose, the narrow cheekbones. A twentieth-century Medici priest, Redstone thought, with that secretive mouth and the ruthless grooves down the cheeks. One long white hand held a glass of Perrier water. On its third finger glowed a ruby ring. He was dressed as always in a very dark, almost black, gray suit and a snow-white shirt. Redstone caught the gleam of gold cufflinks in the French cuffs. Nicholas Savini, his boss, deputy director for operations, dubbed the "Monk" behind his back.

"The original plan, as some of you know," Halliday was saying, "was for Makarov to rendezvous with Paul at four-thirty at Paul's apartment—"

"Paul's apartment? That's news to me. Since when is No-votny's apartment safe?" Gravel-voiced Wesley Drumm interrupted. General counsel for the agency, he was a big burly man with a square jaw, a jutting brow, and deep-set brown eyes under bushy eyebrows. A hard-drinking, chain-smoking man, he was possessed of a restless energy and seemed always in motion, even when sitting down. But behind the outward bluff and bluster, Redstone knew, a quick, shrewd mind was at work. "And since when," he went on, stabbing the air with his cigarette, "do we take a chance like that, Gil, when so much is at stake?"

Halliday held up a large, bony hand. "Hold your horses for a minute, Wes. We'll get to that. Let me finish. Paul was ready and waiting at his place when he got a phone call—that was about three-fifty. It was Makarov. He was changing the time of the rendezvous to five-thirty and changing the place..." Halliday hesitated for a moment.

"To...?" Drumm prompted.

"Tompkins Square."

"Jesus Christ! And Paul agreed to that? What the hell...!"

"He was given no opportunity to argue the matter, so he said, and he was to have phoned when the contact was made." Halliday paused for a split second before adding in a flat voice, "But up to now I haven't heard from him."

For a long uncomfortable moment no one spoke, and Redstone wondered, as he stared around at the grim faces of the four men, what after all *was* there to say when a valuable defector and an agent go missing?

"Six-thirty..." A soft voice broke the silence. "In this kind of exercise a lot can happen in an hour." The comment was offered by General Miles Thorsen, deputy director of central intelligence, second in authority to Gilbert Halliday, a small plump man in his mid-fifties whose dandified appearance belied his military title. He had a great fondness for fancy waistcoats, and this evening he wore one of paisley in muted shades of yellow, burgundy, green, and blue. It was worn over a cream-colored sport shirt. A chocolate-brown corduroy jacket topped these and dark brown flannel slacks, pale yellow socks, and expensive brown loafers completed the outfit. The General's round face habitually wore a look of amiable candor, and Redstone, studying him, thought how deceptive that look was, how completely at variance with those hard, steel-gray eyes behind their horn-rimmed glasses—eyes that had a way of darting swiftly from face to face, scrutinizing, probing, assessing. They made Redstone feel acutely uncomfortable and guilty as hell for no reason at all.

"Exercise, hell! It's a damn sight more than that!" Drumm growled. "I shouldn't have to remind all of you that we've stepped out of bounds here. An operation like this—if it isn't brought to a conclusion damn fast and damn quietly—if we don't get our man under cover before anyone gets wind of what's going on, we'll have one hell of a lot of explaining to do—"

In a soft, acid-coated voice, Thorsen interrupted. "An unfortunate choice of word, no doubt. Thoughtless of me. I appreciate your setting me straight, Wes, but I'm sure we're all aware of the seriousness of the situation."

No love lost there, that's for sure, Redstone thought, though that wasn't an impression he would have to pass on to his boss. A sidelong glance showed him that Savini had raised his head and was gazing speculatively at the two men, a long, considering look as though measuring them for a rope.

"What about the alternate safe house, Gil? Has that been checked out?" Thorsen asked.

"Naturally," said Halliday. "But there's nothing there. All quiet. The big question is—have they made contact? If they have, why haven't we heard from Paul? If they haven't, what's gone wrong?"

"Let us assume," Thorsen said in his soft, precise voice, "that they had a tail on Makarov—"

"You're stretching it there, Miles," Drumm interrupted. "How likely is that?"

Thorsen held up a plump white hand. "If you'll allow me to finish... *Assume* is the operative word, Wes. I'm trying to account for his call to Paul. If Makarov was being followed, then the moment he bypassed the Polish mission, they'd be on to him. He would need the extra hour to lose the tail. Ergo, the phone call to change the rendezvous time."

"All right," Drumm said. "Provisionally I'll buy that. But why change the location?"

"You've put your finger on the problem, Wes," Halliday said. "That's what bothers me. Makarov's safety lay in placing himself in our hands as fast as possible."

"Krassotkin or Shatov, the bully boys... Might they have got to him before he got to Paul?" Drumm asked. "And is his corpse floating somewhere in the East River—which would make this whole goddamn conversation academic as hell!"

"Anything's possible," Halliday said, "but that doesn't tell us why Paul hasn't phoned. Whether the rendezvous was kept or not, we should have heard from him by now."

"*If* he could call," Drumm growled. "*If* he could get to a phone. Perhaps he's floating in the East River as well. Tompkins Square—hell! Anything goes there. They could be drawn and quartered and their heads put on pikestaffs and who would notice?"

"Could Makarov have changed his mind for reasons of his own?" asked Thorsen.

"In that event we'd certainly have heard from Paul," Halliday said. "Almost anything could have happened, couldn't it? A simple street accident or caught in an elevator between floors. Who knows? I'm groping in the dark. Which is why I asked you to come here—to cover the contingencies, where possible."

"The contingencies, yes..." Miles Thorsen murmured. "I did say, Gil, that I thought Paul was the wrong man for the job. You'll remember that." He removed his spectacles and, pulling a handkerchief from his jacket pocket, began polishing the lenses, breathing on them from time to time. "He's too impulsive, too much the romantic," he went on. "His reactions in the event of something unforeseen happening are—uh—unpredictable." The man blinked nearsightedly up at Halliday, who made an impatient movement with his shoulders.

Thorsen hurried on. "It was highly irregular for us to let Makarov set conditions. I felt, and still feel, extremely uncomfortable about his insisting that Paul bring him in—alone—without backup. That he should have set any conditions at all, of course, is highly irregular." Thorsen held his spectacles up to the light and peered at them for a moment before replacing them on his nose. Tucking the handkerchief back into his pocket, he added, "We should have insisted on following our usual rules here. If we had, we wouldn't be faced with this problem now."

"He's having it all his own way, the bastard," Wesley Drumm growled. "He wants Paul. No backup. He wants two million bucks before—*before,* mind you—there's been any debriefing. Deposit two million in an account in Nassau under his new identity, he instructs us, the arrogant bastard, before he's even opened his mouth. And when he does open it, how do we know anything worthwhile will come out?"

A brief flicker of annoyance crossed Gilbert Halliday's face and he said in a cold, clipped voice, "I thought we had settled that last point, Wes. I've asked Parkman in Finance to come up with a plan that will assure Makarov the money is waiting for him, but it will not be available until we are satisfied with his debriefing. I'll add, just to set your minds at ease, gentlemen, that the Colonel is not going to be able to comb his beard, wash his hands, or pee in a pot without company once he's safe in the safe house."

From his post at the bar Drumm raised his glass and said, "Bravo!" Halliday smiled at him, Drumm returned the smile, and the tension in the room eased.

Friends, Redstone remembered. Drumm and Halliday had been friends for a long time. They could have their disagreements, but it didn't seem to disturb the basic respect they had for each other. And that wouldn't be news to Savini, either, he knew. For all the watching and listening he was doing, nothing much was coming of it! And feeling useless and irritable, he turned his attention back to Halliday.

"I can appreciate Wes's objections," Halliday said. "I can appreciate yours, Miles, because, believe me, I've been over the same ones and others as well countless times in my mind—ever since the Colonel contacted us a week ago."

On Valentine's Day, Redstone thought. Therefore code name *Valentine*. Seemed altogether too whimsical.

"But we mustn't muddy the waters with the money thing. That's the least of our worries. As for Paul...Makarov was adamant. Paul would bring him in, or he wouldn't play. He would take his marbles and go home to Moscow. If it came to the crunch, would he have stuck to that decision? I don't know. What I do know is that I had to decide in a short time how much we wanted this man, how badly we needed him—assuming his briefing will be as productive as it should be. I had to weigh the obvious problems in the way he wanted to play it against not playing it at all and losing him. I decided to chance it." Halliday paused for a second and took a long swallow of his drink as though fortifying himself. When he resumed speaking, Redstone was surprised to hear a strong undercurrent of passion in the man's voice. "I want this man. We need this man. You all know what a coup of his kind can mean to the agency—particularly at this time. I don't have to spell it out for you. You know the reasons. I'll go to almost any lengths to bring him in. That's why I threw the book out of the window. That's why I'm playing by his rules, not ours. That's why, though your objections, Wes, and yours, Miles, are all valid, you can forget them. It won't change my decision. It stands."

A complete silence settled over the room when Halliday finished speaking, broken only by the hiss and crackle of the logs in the fireplace. Redstone, glancing at the men's faces, knew exactly what they were thinking. A defector of Makarov's caliber would make all the difference to the agency. For such a long time now, since Watergate, they had all been stumbling through mine fields. Little explosions and big ones destroying their efficiency, the latest explosion being the Iran-contra affair. They tried to work in the full glare of publicity. The CIA had become the whipping boy for failures in foreign policy, for catastrophes anywhere in the world.

"Our surveillances are surveyed, our watchers watched, our agents exposed throughout the world. It's ridiculous. A *secret* service? We might just as well be doing business in a storefront window." So Savini had said only yesterday in a rare display of emotion. A moment later, more calmly and with that thin smile of his, he had added, "It is paradoxical, of course, isn't it? A secret service in an open society... The one will always be inimical to the other, won't it?"

Yes, no doubt that was true, Redstone thought bleakly as he gazed at the faces around him, and yet... Could there be some other less abstract and much more sinister reason for their problems? He tried to shake off his deepening depression.

I need another drink, he decided. But before he could move, Savini's voice broke the silence. Issuing from the depths of the armchair, it seemed to float disembodied through the quiet room.

"No one could possibly question the value of the information Colonel Sergei Sergeivitch might give us. His debriefing could go on for years. A mine of information. Like hitting the mother lode. Invaluable..." Savini raised his sleek head and let his dark, oblique gaze rest on each man in turn. "Invaluable," he repeated. "Such information couldn't be calculated in terms of dollars and cents—if his defection is bona fide."

And there it was, out in the open, the bugaboo of any intelligence body—the plant, the defector who wasn't a defector, the feeder of false information.

At the same time Redstone detected the thin note of venom in Savini's voice and remembered that the man had reasons of his own for hating Makarov. We have long memories, he thought, and he wasn't really surprised that Savini's hatred still smoldered beneath the surface after twenty years. His entire Czech network, the result of long and careful recruiting, of meticulous planning, had been blown, destroyed by Makarov in a matter of days. Savini's principal agent, Karel Novotny, had been the first to fall. The others followed, toppling one by one like a house of cards. Some had vanished without a trace, others had been arrested and tried with Novotny. And yet... Redstone couldn't bring himself to believe that Savini would allow his private feelings to affect the welfare of the agency. As far as anyone knew, he had no interests outside it. He was unmarried, he had no family. With the single-minded zeal of a solitary monk, he had devoted twenty-five years of his life to the arcane world of espionage.

"Is he bona fide?" Halliday's voice interrupted Redstone's thoughts. "He's a walk-in, and *every* walk-in is suspect. That's something we always have to take into consideration in these cases. It would be superfluous for me to say that we will, of course, do so in this case. But there's no way, Nick, of making a judgment of any kind until we have the man under wraps and the debriefing starts."

Drumm asked, "Do you have any evidence—anything at all —for suspecting the man?"

"I only want to be sure, Wes, that we cover all the ground. When a man decides to defect, he has his reasons. Good or bad, he has his reasons. Makarov is a wily fox. What's behind his defection?"

"I don't know what's *behind* it," Drumm said with a harsh laugh, "but I know what's in *front* of it—two million dollars!"

Savini went on as though Drumm hadn't spoken. "We know he had a bad time as a result of his misreading the Afghanistan situation. He was kept at a humble desk job for quite a while, and his promotion was not put through. What would have happened to him at that time if he hadn't been a particular protégé of Andropov we don't know, of course. Andropov's death may have placed him in jeopardy. He's arrogant and ruthless. He's made enemies, some of whom are in control now—"

"I'm not so sure your reading of the Colonel's situation is accurate, Nick," Thorsen broke in, soft-voiced as always. "He had a fall from grace, true, but would a man still so out of favor be directing the whole complex structure of East European agents in New York? How many at last count—something over three hundred?"

"That we know of," Drumm interjected.

"Therefore I find it hard to believe—"

Halliday broke in, saying firmly, "Forgive me, gentlemen, but there's no point to this discussion, no point at all. It's a waste of time, and time is valuable. You have my view on this matter and I have yours. But there's something else we must consider before we finish here—another problem—or perhaps a part of the same problem. Redstone here"—he nodded his

head at Herb Redstone—"has brought us word that Karel Novotny escaped from prison—"

"Jesus Christ," Drumm said, "I thought the bastard was
dead!"

"An exaggerated rumor," Halliday said with a faint smile.
"If you'd tell these gentlemen what you told me, Redstone."

"It's not all that much, I'm afraid," Redstone said. "He
escaped about ten days ago. As I understand it, he was ill and
they were transferring him to the infirmary in Plzeň. Security
was probably loose, but he must have had some kind of help,
too, though we don't know who or what, and it isn't something we'd ask loud questions about. My people had no idea.
Rumors are flying, of course, and within Czech official circles
it is said that this dangerous spy—you can imagine how dangerous he is after twenty years in Czech prisons!—was aided
by the Americans, meaning us, of course, but then they would
naturally say that. They probably really believe it, though there
isn't a grain of truth in it."

"And where might he have escaped to?" Thorsen asked.
"Have you any idea?"

"If he's still in Czecho, he's well hidden, but my guess is that
he's out of the country by now. It's more than a guess, really. A
contingent of border guards are under arrest, and my infor-
mant, who is usually pretty solid, says they are accused of
being lax on duty, or worse, meaning they let him slip through
as a result of carelessness or bribery."

"If we have no idea where he is," Drumm said, "I take it
then that he hasn't been in touch with any of our stations in
Europe?"

"He's had no contact with our people at all. They've all been
alerted and are on the lookout, of course."

"You'd expect, wouldn't you," Thorsen asked, "that he
would head for the Vienna station or Frankfurt?"

"He bypassed them completely. Never even stopped in to say
hello."

Thorsen frowned at the facetiousness of his remark, and
Redstone shrugged.

"Why bypass our people?" Thorsen persisted. "He realizes,
doesn't he, that we'd take care of him?"

"Well..." As Redstone hesitated, unsure of his ground, Savini stepped in.

"Perhaps," he said, "his interpretation of those words would differ from ours, Miles."

"What the hell!" growled Drumm.

"There's never been any doubt in my mind," Savini said in a flat voice, "that someone betrayed Karl Novotny in 1968, someone sent him straight into the arms of the Russians."

"An unsolved mystery." Thorsen's voice was quite bland, but the eyes behind the spectacles, fixed on Savini's face, were hard as pebbles. "And now we have another," he went on. "Novotny escapes and Makarov defects. A rather strange coincidence, wouldn't you say, Nick?"

"I hate coincidences. Don't trust them," Drumm said.

"Nor do I, Wes," Savini said. "And I'm glad you brought it up, Miles." The thin smile flashed at the deputy director, white teeth agleam for a second in the olive-skinned face. "The timing is interesting. Novotny escapes. Makarov decides to defect. I'm surprised, Miles, that you didn't include the Colonel's insistence that Karel Novotny's son bring him in. All of which gives us plenty to think about, doesn't it? Particularly when you consider the third mystery in this series—the link between Makarov and Novotny—the case of the missing files."

"The files, yes." Thorsen nodded his head slowly up and down above his folded hands while his half-closed eyes never left Savini's face.

"Yes," Savini said quietly, "the files that went missing from STB* headquarters the night of the invasion."

Redstone, having resumed his watching brief after making his contribution to the meeting, was both disturbed and fascinated now by the subtle play of emotions here, which he couldn't identify or understand. He watched Nicholas Savini lean forward in a swift graceful movement and place his glass of Perrier on the coffee table in front of him, the ruby ring on the long, slender hand winking slyly in the light. When the man raised his head, Redstone saw that all traces of the smile had vanished from his face, and the grooves down his cheeks

*Czech secret police.

seemed to be scored more deeply than ever. The black eyes remained unreadable.

"We all assumed," Savini said in a low voice, "that the outcome of Novotny's trial twenty years ago was a foregone conclusion—that he would get the death penalty. And we were all astonished when he was sentenced to life at hard labor instead. We heard rumors that Makarov had interceded. The rumors were later confirmed. He wanted the man alive. Why? There could be only one reason—the files. Makarov had to get his hands on those files for whatever information they contained. For a long time after Karel Novotny was imprisoned—and it must have seemed very long to him—Makarov visited him regularly at Pankrac prison and interrogated him about the missing files. Did Makarov get the information he was after? If he did, wouldn't Novotny be dead by now? And if he didn't, where are those files? Did Novotny burn them? He said he did, and it's probably true. The actual files would have been too bulky to carry with him on that dangerous night. Which means—I think it's logical to assume—that before he left STB headquarters, he filmed them. And later that night, somewhere, somehow, he managed to hide the film in a secure place before heading for our embassy. His intention probably was to have one of us pick the film up later when it was safe to do so."

"If he had concealed the film somewhere in Prague," Halliday said, "then dangerous though it was, he must have picked it up after he escaped. I can't see him leaving it behind—not after having withstood the tender ministrations of the Colonel to protect it."

"Either that," Savini said, "or he gave it to someone that night to hold for him."

"Chancy," said Drumm.

"The circumstances at the time," Savini said dryly, "weren't ideal. He'd have been forced to take a chance, but he would only have given it into the care of someone he trusted. A member of his family, perhaps."

"Paul?"

"He's the first one to come to mind," Savini agreed, "but if Paul had the film, he would have passed it on to us when he first started working for the agency."

Thorsen murmured something under his breath that sounded to Redstone like "I wonder," but Savini paid no attention. "As for Novotny's wife, Maria," he went on, "their relationship at that time was strained, to put it mildly, and I'm sure he wouldn't have taken her into his confidence."

"The only one left, then, is his daughter," Drumm said. "You think he would have given the film to her? Is that what you're getting at? She was only a child then."

"Think about it," Savini said. "He tells her how important it is to him. He tells her he's trusting her to keep it safe for him, that it's their secret, a pact between the two of them. This involves her father whom she loves. And don't all children enjoy conspiracies—the I've-got-a-secret syndrome? We all know what that is, don't we?" Savini cocked a cynical eyebrow at his listeners.

"A secret for twenty years..." Halliday murmured. He left his post at the fireplace and perched his lanky body on the arm of the sofa. "That's a long time, Nick. A lot of water under the bridge. Might she not have confided in Paul by now? They're very close, I understand. And if she thinks her father is dead, she would turn to her brother."

"I'll give you an alternative. A more valid one, perhaps. That she has the film and doesn't know it, that Novotny concealed it in something that was precious to her, something she wouldn't leave behind when the family fled the country."

Halliday nodded. "Both theories are valid, but if we're on the right track at all, it's the latter one I'll buy because—"

The phone on the leather-topped desk rang, interrupting him. He went to it and picked it up. "Halliday here." He listened for a brief moment to what it had to tell him, said, "Thanks," and cradled the receiver with a gentle click. Turning to face the men, he said quietly, "That was Jake. Nothing to report on the Colonel or Paul yet, but the sister called there. She asked for John White."

"Instead of John Doe or Bill Smith," said Drumm sarcastically.

Halliday nodded absently as he walked back to the sofa and resumed his perch on the arm. In a soft voice he said, "She's looking for her brother." He paused, staring thoughtfully at the floor for a long moment. When he raised his head, he directed his gaze at his deputy director for operations. "Then if we go along with your theory, Nick, she's the key. Where would Karel Novotny go if he's heading for the States? This is alien territory for him, he's alone and running scared. He doesn't trust us. That would let Paul out even if he were available. Not to his wife, you say. He would go where he could find a safe haven, to the one person we assume he trusts—whether she holds the secret or not. Yes." Halliday stood up abruptly. "The daughter is the key." His voice had hardened. The blue eyes no longer looked tired. There was a glint of steel in them. "We'll keep her under surveillance. Who knows? She might lead us to all three of the men we want, if we're lucky—and to the film as well. We want that damned film, don't we—if it still exists."

The room was silent. Firelight flickered on the still, expressionless faces around him as Redstone studied them covertly. The atmosphere had changed in a subtle way. He sensed an undercurrent of uneasiness, a faint smell of fear. Were they thinking of the secrets the film would disclose when they got their hands on it—secrets better kept secret, perhaps? Or was he being too fanciful? He was tired, still suffering from jet lag.

A few minutes later the meeting broke up. The four men left their host and went out into the winter night. Redstone paused on the veranda a moment, pulling on his gloves while he took in the scene around him. On his right he could see a small orchard at the end of a long sweep of lawn, on his left the outline of an empty swimming pool. In front of him the ground sloped gently down to meet the road several hundred yards away, where thick hedges gave privacy and concealed the chain-link fence.

Everything lay under a shroud of new-fallen snow. The storm had rolled away to the north, and the light of the half-moon already riding high in the deep blue sky cast a faint silver sheen over the landscape. Nothing moved. It was completely peaceful. Betrayals, defections, hunted men... All that could be part of life on another planet, but even as the thought occurred to him, Redstone's mind focused sharply on what had been troubling him for the past couple of hours. Of the four men at the meeting tonight, three had been in Prague during that fateful time in 1968. He had read the file material hurriedly, and he might have missed some details, but he remembered that Thorsen had then been serving on the military attaché's staff at their embassy, Savini had been head of the United States Information Service, and Drumm...He had been heading a U.S. trade commission to Czecho at the time, if he recalled correctly. As for Halliday himself, he hadn't been in Prague at the time, but he had been in Europe—at Camp King, the defector reception center near Frankfurt, Germany. A phone call, a plane ride away from Prague.

A deceiver among them? A hostile presence high up in the agency, subtly manipulating it for his own sinister purposes? Soft-voiced General Miles Thorsen, the deputy director, with his round cherub face and his hard probing eyes? Big, bluff, outspoken Wesley Drumm, general counsel? Or Gilbert Halliday, the director himself, with his lined, ageless face and smooth politician's smile?

Impossible!

Damn Savini!

Savini *himself*...The clandestine man, the keeper of the secrets...What better way of diverting suspicion from himself than by accusing another?

These men were all privy to the deepest, darkest secrets of the agency. There was no "need to know" restraint at this top echelon, and traitors come in all shapes and sizes, don't they? Look at the notorious English traitor Philby, who for over twenty years repaid his country's trust with treason. Didn't his shadow still darken the British secret service?

Beware, as long as you live, of judging people by appearances. The wise La Fontaine again. Maybe he should quote *that* to Savini.

Damn, damn Savini!

I need a drink, Redstone decided. Hell, I need several drinks.

It was only after he'd stepped out onto the snowy drive and headed for the car that Redstone gave a thought to Hana Novotny and allowed himself to feel brief compassion for the girl who was caught innocently in the middle of this mess.

Another man who had been sitting beside the fireplace in Halliday's comfortable room was also thinking of Hana.

What a fool I was to forget about the girl! Careless, and I can't afford to be careless. It was a mistake my being in the apartment that night. If she saw me there, if she becomes a threat now and starts remembering too much about what happened twenty years ago, then she'll have to be taken care of, that's all.

As for Karel... From Tinker to Evers to Chance. From Sergei's man in Vienna to Mautner to Karel. Simple to track down a man if he's fool enough to go to someone like Hans Mautner. Who of us in the Vienna area didn't know of that weak, greedy man? And if it hadn't been for that clumsy idiot of a woman in Paris, I wouldn't have to worry about Karel any longer. With the man dead I was willing to gamble that the film might never surface from its hiding place. In any event, how damning is it for me? Was I named in the file? Or just my code name—Golconda?

Those questions may never be answered, but it occurs to me that there's another person I must consider now—Maria. She represents a clear and present danger. I'll have to instruct my elegant young friend, when he phones, to settle with her.

I must face the fact that I'm on my own from now on. Any help from Sergei is out of the question. Too dangerous. Even if I knew where to reach him, I no longer dare trust him.

5

The phone rang three times while she was in the bath. Each time Hana struggled out of the tub, grabbed her terry-cloth robe, and rushed to the living room, dripping water in her wake. The first call brought a low-voiced demand to speak to Paul Novotny. Closing her eyes and pressing the receiver snugly against her ear, she concentrated on the voice.

"He's not here," she said softly.

"When will he be there?"

"Who's calling, please?"

"Paul Novotny—I wish to speak to Paul Novotny." There was a barely concealed note of anger and threat in the voice.

Hana tried to ignore it and repeated softly, "He's not here. Can I take a message for him?"

A silence followed. Hana thought she heard whispering in the background. Then the voice said abruptly, "I will call later," and the line went dead.

It had been a replay of the earlier call with the same harsh, slightly accented voice. The only difference was he hadn't said *we* this time.

Hana followed her damp trail back to the bathroom, trying to picture a face to match the voice, but what appeared before her mind's eye was the face of the bearded man, and his voice had been smooth, had had none of the rough tones of this man's. Was her subconscious making some mysterious connection?

She had just climbed back into the tub when the phone rang

again. This time when she answered, there was no response at all. Just an eerie sound of breathing came down the line. With an exclamation she dropped the phone into its cradle as though it were something nasty. Which it was—very nasty indeed! And was it connected to the previous calls, or was it someone who got his sexual kicks out of breathing at women over the telephone?

Too coincidental to be the latter, Hana thought, but what could they hope to achieve by it? She drew in a deep, shuddering breath and headed slowly back to the bathroom, admitting that what they could achieve was a very frightened Hana Novotny, that's what. They're using the tactics of a bully. The thought ignited a small flame of anger inside her that momentarily eased the fear. Yet when the phone rang the third time and because she was both expecting it and not expecting it, the shrill sound in the quiet apartment sent her heart leaping in her chest. Don't answer it, she told herself. Confusion to the enemy, as Paul would say, but the thought of Paul sent her scrambling out of the tub and rushing into the living room.

"Hana, is something wrong? I've been trying and trying to reach you and all I get is a busy signal." Steve's warm, familiar baritone greeted her.

"Ah..." she sighed. "Steve..."

"Your voice sounds funny, Hana. Are you all right? Did you leave the phone off the hook?"

"No—I mean—I'm all right, and I didn't leave the phone off the hook. I'm sorry if you've been trying to reach me. There've been—several phone calls. That's all." *That's all*. For a brief moment Hana was tempted to pour forth all the odd and frightening events of the past couple of hours into Steve's sympathetic ear, but the urge died as quickly as it was born. To do so might ease her own anxiety, but whatever was going on must have something to do with what Paul was working on, and she couldn't discuss that with anyone. As far as Steve knew, Paul was a statistician on the administrative staff of the United Nations headquarters here in New York and—

"...our date tonight." Steve's voice broke in on her thoughts.

"What was that, Steve?"

"About our date tonight..."

"Our date, yes," Hana said, realizing guiltily that she had forgotten all about it.

"I'm sorry to do this, Hana, love, but I've got a problem. Sara is here. Lynn brought her over tonight instead of tomorrow because she wants to go off early tomorrow for a ski weekend in Vermont. I said okay, but the trouble is Sara has a runny nose and a bit of a temperature—"

"I'm sorry to hear that," Hana said automatically, her mind not really on the problem of Sara.

"Of course Lynn didn't bother to tell me about that—though in fairness to her she may not have realized it—but I don't want to leave Sara with a baby-sitter if she's coming down with something."

"No, that wouldn't be a good idea," Hana agreed. She picked up a pencil and began to doodle on the pad beside the telephone, knowing what Steve was leading up to and wondering how she could get out of it without hurting his feelings.

"I just wondered—why don't you come over here, Hana? I can promise you potluck...pretty wild, but you won't go hungry. There's some good Bordeaux to dress it up, there's a roaring fire in the fireplace. Sara will go to sleep—early—after which we will be left to our own devices. How about it? Am I tempting you?"

"Oh, Steve, on a night like this it sounds ideal, but the problem is..." Hana paused for a conscience-stricken moment, remembering the stroganoff ready and waiting in the refrigerator, the good Mondavi cabernet sauvignon in the cupboard, the salad makings. She only had to tuck it all in her canvas tote bag and call a taxi. But suppose Paul should call? Suppose he should need her? The lie came glibly to her lips. "As a matter of fact, I was going to phone you. I'm afraid I'm in Sara's boat—coming down with something. I've got that achy feeling in the bones—you know—and a headache, scratchy throat. I wouldn't want to complicate Sara's problem."

"Oh, Hana, what a damned shame!" And his voice was full of concern as he went on to give her instructions about drinking plenty of fluids and getting a lot of rest, all of which she agreed to follow. "And if you need me for anything, call me," he urged. "Any time. I'll be here."

"Don't worry. I'll send up a flare if I need something," Hana said, and hung up, hating herself for lying to Steve. She had looked forward to the evening with him, but now how could she be snugly comfortable on this snowy evening with him and little Sara knowing Paul might be in trouble? It could be a kind of betrayal.

All for one and one for all! She could see him, a skinny boy with tousled hair, standing on the worn sofa in the apartment in Prague, brandishing their father's umbrella over his head, herself giggling. *"There are only two of us, Paul."* A parry, a thrust. *"Use your imagination, can't you, Hanička?"*

She felt suddenly very tired. How quickly all the brightness had vanished from her day! It seemed strange to remember that only a short time ago she had felt that strong sense of kinship with all her fellow creatures and that giddy joy at just being alive.

With a sigh she dropped the pencil on the table beside the pad and started to rise, but her eye was caught by what she had doodled while talking to Steve. For a long moment she sat still, staring at the crude sketch. The bearded man's face. Her fingers had drawn it without any conscious instructions from her mind—like automatic writing. It frightened her. Somewhere, somehow, she knew that face. It came out of the bad time twenty years ago. She turned the pad over abruptly, blocking it out, and rose. What she needed was strong coffee and some food. Tightening the cord of her robe, she padded barefoot out to the kitchen, where she fussed with the Melitta coffee maker, put in a fresh filter, set water to boil, and meticulously measured the coffee. While she waited for it to drip, she took some Blarney cheese from the refrigerator and sliced chunks of it on sesame-seed crackers, debating at the same time about whether she should have a drink. She decided against it. In case there should be more strangers visiting or nasty phone calls, she would need all her wits about her.

She sat down at the small pine table beside the window,

sipped the coffee, dark and steaming in the heavy earthenware mug, and munched on the cheese and crackers. The snow had changed to sleet. Hana watched it splash against the windowpane and remembered the last time she had seen her brother.

A week ago she had stopped by his apartment on her way home from the library, where she had been doing research for a jacket cover she was designing for a book on medieval costumes. He had greeted her with a kiss, put a glass of white wine in her hand, brought out some pâté and thin slices of dark bread, talking all the while of inconsequential things in which, she could see, he took no interest at all. He was in a fever of excitement. The room seemed to vibrate with it. Red spots of color shone on his cheekbones, and the glow in his brown eyes darkened them to black. In silence she watched him as he paced the limits of his elegant living room.

"Tell me about it," she said finally.

"About it?" He paused in midstride and raised a questioning eyebrow.

"Stop faking," she said, smiling. "You know very well what I mean. You'll set the room on fire if you don't sit down and relax. Spontaneous combustion..."

"Something's come up," he said, and resumed pacing.

"I can see that." She sat quietly, waiting, sipping her wine.

"It isn't anything I can talk about, Hanička. Not now. I wish to hell I could. It's important. My God, it's important! For a lot of reasons—" He broke off abruptly and came to a halt in front of her. "It could be a little tricky, but I'm not worried about that. It's going to answer a lot of old questions." His voice was as taut as a bowstring, Hana noted, and there was a reckless light in his eyes.

"A week, perhaps," he went on. "Afterward, when it's finished, I'll tell you what I can." He hesitated a moment, then repeated in a hard voice, "When it's finished."

Hana wanted to ask the question that was always uppermost in her mind at times like these: Was it dangerous? But she knew he couldn't tell her the truth if it was, and what was the point in setting the alarm bells jangling in her mind? Not that they wouldn't be jangling anyway. As he often did, he read the question in her mind and gave her that brilliant smile that always wrenched at her heart. "No need to worry, Hanička," he said softly. "It's all under control." Reaching down, he ran a finger across her forehead. "So stop frowning and let's eat. I'm starved." The subject was closed.

They walked up Sixth Avenue to a French restaurant on Twelfth Street where they ate entrecôte au poivre and drank a lot of red wine with it. After brandy with their coffee they were both rather tipsy, and they strolled home through the rainy February night, singing "Raindrops Keep Falling on My Head" and laughing a lot at nothing.

When they parted at the door of her apartment house, he stood looking up at her for a moment, brown eyes gleaming with that reckless light again, the brown hair a damp, curling halo under the streetlight, and with a strange smile said, "I'm off to slay the dragon." Then he turned quickly and walked away, calling over his shoulder, "I'll see you soon, Hanička."

Watching him go, she was suddenly cold sober and very frightened. "Take care, take care, Pavel!" she called after him, only slightly surprised at how easily the Czech form of his name came to her lips. It happened at rare times when she was under emotional stress. A kind of regression, she supposed, not really caring.

He gave her a broad wave of his arm without turning around or breaking stride. She heard him whistling.

Hana returned to the present to find she had finished the cheese and crackers and had drunk all the coffee. And Paul's voice seemed to be repeating in her mind, *A week, perhaps.*

She rose, picked up her plate and mug, and set them in the sink. After running water over them, she went to the living room and, picking up the phone, dialed Paul's familiar number. She expected to hear it ring uselessly in an empty apartment. Instead she heard the buzz-buzz of the busy signal like an angry bumblebee caught in the line. Her mood lightened immediately. Paul was home. All was well. She hung up, smiling at her quick, childish reaction.

She waited a moment, then dialed again. Still busy. She paced back and forth for a while, glancing indecisively from the phone to the window. Dark had descended over the city—

as much as it ever did. The rain had changed back to snow, and the pale nimbus of the streetlight directly beneath her window was filled with swirling white flakes, giving the illusion that the light itself was the source of the snow. A few people hurried along the sidewalk, collars up, heads down. Across the street SueEllen's little Collectibles-of-All-Kinds Shop was dark except for a faint light in the back. End-of-the-week bookkeeping time, Hana thought absently. Then, with a last glance at the telephone, she headed for the bedroom.

It took only a few minutes to dress. Heavy woolen slacks, the bulky Irish fisherman's sweater that Steve had given her for Christmas, a dash of lipstick, and a quick comb through the hair. In the foyer she pushed her feet into fur-lined ankle-high boots and tied the laces snugly. She pulled a green knit hat over her head and thrust her arms into the sleeves of the corduroy coat. Feeling in her pockets for gloves, she found the mail she had put there earlier. Not surprising she had forgotten it. Pulling it out, she glanced hurriedly through it. The advertising circular, the telephone bill, Visa bill, and a letter.

A letter... One does not expect the dead to come alive on the face of an envelope, and Hana's mind was already so preoccupied by all that had been happening in the past couple of hours that for a long, uncomprehending moment she stared at the Austrian stamps, the Vienna postmark, and the strange, familiar, haunting handwriting. Then her fingers began to tremble as though the message had been received tactually before the mind could grasp it. That precise, spiky handwriting ... How long had it been since she had last seen it?

He was alive.

Her stomach churned, the blood pounded in her head, she began to shake.

He was alive.

The floor seemed to buckle beneath her, her legs wouldn't support her, she sank down on the bench, wrapping her arms tightly around her chest, and closed her eyes, waiting for the shaking to ease. She saw his face in her mind's eye, the sad, tired brown eyes, the smiling mouth... *I love you, my little Hana. Remember that.*

He was alive.

67

When she finally opened her eyes, she was surprised to find that, though her whole world had shifted, tilted off balance, nothing had changed in the little foyer. The hall tree still stood in the corner, her charcoal drawing of Paul still hung on the wall beside it, the bench she sat on was firm beneath her.

Very carefully she opened the envelope and drew out the single sheet of thin paper. The message, written in the same spiky hand, was brief and without greeting. It read simply *Kde Domov Můj*. Praha.

She didn't remember much about the walk from Perry Street to Washington Place. In a kind of daze she strode along through the snowy streets, head down, shoulder bag swinging, gloved hands thrust deep into pockets, the fingers of one gripping the letter to reassure herself it was real and not something she had dreamed. She had thought him dead for so long that adjustment to the knowledge that he was alive would take a lot longer than a few minutes. As for the strange, cryptic message ... She wouldn't for the moment worry about that. Paul might understand it. All that really mattered now was the fact that their father was alive.

A sudden sense of urgency quickened Hana's footsteps, forcing her into a run, across Sixth Avenue, up Washington Place. A cold wind whistled down the street, whipping snowflakes into her face as she ran up the steps of the apartment building. Shivering, she put her hand on the knob of the outer door, then froze. A cold, prickly sensation between her shoulder blades told her that someone somewhere on the shadowed street was watching her. Half expecting to look into a pair of pale blue eyes above a curly black beard, she cast a quick glance over her shoulder. All she saw was a lone pedestrian on the sidewalk across the street, walking slowly, head down, paying no attention to her at all.

She shook her head. Get a grip on your imagination, she told herself as she unlocked the inner door.

The hallway of the apartment house was long and narrow and ill lit. It ran from front to back of the building, ending with a stairway on the left and a small temperamental elevator on the right. The superintendent lived in the basement. There was no doorman. "Wouldn't have one," Paul had said. "Nosy types—doormen."

Halls and stairwell were painted a uniform dull gray that did nothing to relieve the bleak atmosphere. And that made it all the more surprising when one entered Paul Novotny's apartment. It was on the top floor, light-filled and airy, with cream-colored walls and thick cocoa-brown carpeting throughout. The furnishings were an odd mixture of antique and modern, arranged with a kind of artful informality. The end result was one of comfort, charm, and elegance.

Not that Hana was concerned with the decor when she stepped into the foyer after ringing the bell and getting no response. He's probably in the shower, she thought as she unlocked the door.

A dim glow of light spilled over into the foyer from the living room. Otherwise everything was in darkness. In a soft voice she called, "Paul?" then waited, head tilted sideways, listening. No sound of a shower running. No sound of life at all, and there was an alien quality about the silence around her that she couldn't define.

Yet not completely silent, either.

As she still hesitated in the foyer, Hana became aware of a faint sound, a steady high ringing, coming from the direction of the living room. Increasingly uneasy, she moved slowly to the arched entranceway. There she halted, startled and alarmed by the disorder in the room. The chair beside the heavy oak desk was tipped over backward as though the person sitting there had risen with a rapid violent movement. The desk lamp lay on its side, unbroken and still lit. Papers were scattered over the carpet, and the telephone receiver had been knocked from its cradle and dangled to the floor.

One part of her mind noted quite calmly that she could have called all night and not received an answer, while another part fought down panic and tried to assess what had happened.

A burglar... It looked wrong somehow for that. More like a struggle, brief but contained, because, except that one of the upholstered chairs in front of the fireplace had been shoved out of its customary spot as though someone had bumped hard against it, the rest of the room was untouched.

She called, "Paul," again as she moved into the room. Not because she expected an answer, only to hear the normal sound of her voice. Then, without really thinking of what she was doing, she pulled off her gloves, stuffed them into her coat pocket, and began to set the room to rights. She replaced the receiver in its cradle, uprighted the lamp, and picked up the chair. Kneeling down, she swept the tumbled papers into a neat stack. As she rose and placed them on the desk, she caught the odor of something unpleasant in the air, something heavy and fetid. She sniffed and looked around. Nothing here to account for it. The kitchen...?

But when she switched on the light there, everything was as clean and orderly as always. The copper pots sparkled at her from their soldierly row on the wall, the stove gleamed coal black and snow white, the refrigerator hummed busily in the corner. The only thing amiss in the otherwise immaculate room was the open bottle of wine on the table beside the window and the glass with dregs at the bottom. Paul would have washed the glass, corked the bottle, and put it away.

She sniffed the bottle. Just the fruity odor of a light red wine. She opened the refrigerator and checked its contents. Milk, cream, romaine lettuce, endive, fresh mushrooms, broccoli, scallions, and a container of chopped liver. A thick steak, neatly wrapped in waxed paper, was in the meat compartment, and a piece of Stilton cheese reposed on the lowest shelf beside two bakery boxes, one containing crisp dinner rolls and the other an assortment of pastries. All the makings of a good dinner and, judging from the size of the steak, dinner for two. Who? His current girlfriend? They changed so fast she couldn't keep track. She had no sooner taken a liking to one than she vanished, never to be heard of again.

"What happened to Alice?"

"Who?"

"Alice in Wonderland—long blond hair and big blue eyes."

"Oh, *that* Alice. We split. Too possessive."

"And possession not being nine-tenths of the law?"

"Not with me it isn't."

The current one, if she remembered, was a tall, dark Spanish beauty who was studying the flute at the Juilliard School of Music. Very serious. Hana had never seen her smile. Lola something. Ortega? Ortiz?

No, it doesn't make sense, she thought, remembering the reckless light in his eyes, the feverish excitement. Even if the job were finished, she couldn't see Paul settling down so soon to a light-hearted meal with a girlfriend.

She closed the refrigerator door, stared at it, pulled it open again. You're not thinking clearly, she told herself. Everything in here is fresh. Paul has been here. He shopped today.

That is, *someone* shopped today.

She swung the refrigerator door closed, switched off the light, and stood still for a moment thinking. How to account for the mess in the living room? Someone came to see her brother. A dinner guest? There was a fight, a struggle. Why? Paul left. Again, why? Because he *had* to. He would never have turned his back on that disorder otherwise.

A lethargy compounded of fatigue and fear held her in the dark kitchen. Too much had happened in the past few hours. Too many shocks. She wanted to go home, crawl into bed, and pull the covers over her head like a child.

But there was Paul.

There was her father.

She gripped the letter in her coat pocket like a talisman as she walked with reluctant steps out of the kitchen, through the living room to the bedroom door. A moment's hesitation, then she forced herself to fling it open and walk in.

The drapes were drawn, the room was dark, and the foul stench hung in the air. She groped blindly along the wall for the switch, and in the sudden glare of light she saw the body through the open bathroom door. It was propped in a sitting position against the toilet, its pale eyes staring at her above the grinning mouth and the black beard.

It isn't Paul!

But even as the thought darted through her mind on a surge of blinding relief, she knew she wasn't alone. Her ear caught just the whisper of warning, the soft scuff of shoe on floor. Then there was an explosion of light and pain, and she was falling into blackness, carrying with her the image of a white carnation lying on the chest of the dead man with drops of blood like polka dots spattered on it.

"Feeling better? Feeling better?"
Feeling better. Feeling better.
"Come on. Back to the land of the living, girl. Open your eyes."

A strange dark place, a strange voice, meaningless words that bounced around in the empty chamber of her head, reverberating painfully against her skull. "Ah-h-h," she groaned. Her heart was pounding, and when she tried to open her eyes, she found that her eyelids were glued shut.

"Feeling better?" the voice said again. "One nod for *yes,* two for *no.*"

It was a pleasant voice, light and gentle, with a touch of music in it. She wanted to accommodate it. She nodded her head. The movement brought a stab of pain, and she groaned again.

A cool hand was laid on her forehead, the light voice said, "It hurts, yes. I think we'll have a doctor look you over."

"No, thank you," Hana whispered. Why should the suggestion cause panic?

"Very good," the voice went on. "Politeness under these circumstances deserves commendation. I commend you. No doctor... We'll see. Open your eyes, sleeping beauty, and tell me what you see. A prince in frog's clothing or a frog in prince's clothing. Your answer will decide the doctor question."

The cool hand was removed from her forehead. It had felt reassuring, and she wanted to tell him to put it back. She managed this time to open her eyes. Light stabbed at them like a laser beam. She closed them with a groan.

"Ah, sorry about that," the voice said. She heard movement. "All right. I've dimmed it now."

Through cautious half-open lids, she studied the shadowy

figure beside the bed as it came slowly into focus. A broad-shouldered man dressed in faded jeans and a blue turtleneck sweater. He had a bony, clever face, a crooked nose, and a wide mouth. An unruly mop of dark hair covered his head. But it was the eyes that drew and held her attention. They were an amazing blue green, like seawater, with gleaming silver highlights, heavily fringed with dark lashes. They were smiling at her.

"Frog or prince?" he asked in his light, musical voice.

"Frog," she croaked, closing her eyes against the gleaming seawater. "Let me sleep."

She heard him mutter something that sounded like "that goddamn sorcerer," and then she felt the bed jiggle as he sat down beside her.

"The banter is to keep you awake, girl." The cool hand rested gently on her forehead again, cool fingers on her wrist. "I don't want you to sleep if we have a concussion on our hands."

She muttered, *"We...? Our...?"*

"You know what I mean."

She felt his breath on her cheek. When she opened her eyes, she found herself looking directly into the seawater eyes, an inch away from her face and gazing intently at her. She tried to pull back. He shook his head, smiling.

"No need to panic. Just looking. I'm no neurosurgeon, but I've had a little experience with this sort of thing. Any double vision?"

"I don't think so."

"You'd know if there were. Any nausea?"

"No. Achy all over, but mostly in the head."

"All right. We'll take care of that." He straightened up, adding in a low, thoughtful voice, "It seems to have been an expert blow. What do you remember?"

An expert blow? She stared at him, her mind blank. "That's a good question," she said finally. "But at the moment I can't answer it."

She felt the stirrings of panic again. Carefully she turned her head to the left, where through a half-open closet door she could see a rack full of men's clothes, elegant and expensive. Suits, slacks, jackets. A shoe stand on the floor held a variety of expensive shoes. Against the wall of the room beside the closet door stood a familiar bureau with a photograph on top. Her photograph. She was in Paul's room, on Paul's bed. She felt inordinately pleased with herself for having figured that out. But why? The pleased feeling vanished, and her head began to throb as a terrifying jumble of images tumbled helter-skelter through her mind—a fallen chair, a lamp tipped over, a scattering of papers, a full refrigerator, a smell... A smell! Order out of the swirling chaos. She heard again the whispered sound, saw the body. With an indrawn hiss of breath she twisted her head around toward the bathroom. The throbbing in her head became a jackhammer, but she ignored it as she stared through the bathroom door.

So vividly had the picture of the dead man been imprinted on her mind that at first Hana wasn't aware that what she was seeing, slumped against the toilet, was only the remembered image and not the real thing at all. The bathroom was empty. She blinked several times, thinking her senses were playing tricks on her, but the bathroom remained empty. No body lay propped against the toilet, no red polka-dotted flower decorated a dead man's chest. The room was spotless. There was no longer even a smell. Or rather there was a smell—a pleasant one, the faint fragrance of cologne. She recognized it as Paul's after-shave lotion.

"Tell me about it, sleeping beauty."

She turned her head and stared at him, her eyes blank. For a moment she had forgotten about the stranger sitting beside her. "About it?" she asked hoarsely. Her voice wasn't under control, and the jackhammer was pounding full force now. She raised a hand to her head. "There'll be some aspirin in the medicine cabinet in the bathroom. Would you mind getting me a couple?"

"I'll be glad to," he said, rising. "And while I'm doing that, I hope you'll be thinking of a good answer to my question."

"I don't—" she began, but he had vanished into that remarkably clean bathroom.

When he returned, he held a small flowered paper cup from the dispenser and two aspirin. Hana sat up, swallowed the tablets, drank the water, and handed him the cup.

"Thank you," she said, and swung one leg slowly off the bed.

"What the hell do you think you're doing?"

"I'm getting up," Hana said, moving the other leg and gritting her teeth against the pain. "I have things to do."

"You should be taking it easy for a while. Don't you know what kind of trauma a knock on the head like that causes?"

"I'm getting a pretty good idea."

"If you pass out, girl, I'm warning you, I'll take you straight to the hospital. Just sit there for a bit of a while. I'll make some coffee—strong."

"Please make yourself at home," Hana said weakly, holding herself upright by clinging to the bedpost.

"Thanks. I'll do that." At the door the man turned and looked at her for a moment in silence. Then he said softly, "We can have a fine little chat over the coffee. I'd like to know why you did that double take when you looked into the bathroom. I have twenty-twenty vision, you see. You went pale as death. I suspect we have a good deal to talk about, Hana Novotny."

Before she could think to ask him how he knew her name, he had left the room, leaving the door open behind him. "Probably his sorcerer told him," Hana muttered. He's right, though, she thought grimly, there's a great deal to talk about, but not to this man, whoever he is. It's to Paul I must talk—about their father and his cryptic note, about a black-bearded man with eyes like hoarfrost, alive on the sidewalk, dead in Paul's bathroom, now vanished.

Hana closed her eyes and leaned her hot, aching head against the bedpost. Someone had gone to considerable trouble, she realized, in removing the body and cleaning up the bathroom. The same someone who had knocked her out, no doubt. The frog prince? This stranger with the extravagant seawater eyes? Somehow she didn't think so. She had felt no sense of threat in his manner. Or were those famous last words? But why should he strike her on the head, pick her up and lay her comfortably on the bed, then wait around for her to come to—in the meantime removing her hat and coat and placing them tidily on Paul's reading chair by the window? Her purse, she noted, was hanging by its strap from the arm of the chair, and the boots stood neatly aligned on the floor beneath. None of it made any sense at all.

And how had someone—whoever it was—managed to get the body out of the building? Two men supporting a drunk? And why take the risk of removing the body at all? The thought like a thief stole into her mind: To protect Paul. Immediately she reminded herself that there could be any number of reasons, and what point was there in playing guessing games? Still the thought tucked itself into the back of her mind, where it tormented her from time to time.

She opened her eyes and by clinging to the bedpost eased herself to a standing position. Her head swam in one direction, the room in another, and she waited for the dizziness to pass, listening to the sounds coming from the kitchen—the bang of a pot on the stove, the soft plop of a gas jet, whistling—homey, cheerful sounds that seemed alien under the circumstances.

She made it to the chair, and after waiting for a second bout of vertigo to pass, she slipped her feet into the boots without bending over. Then she paused, staring helplessly down at them. They seemed extraordinarily far away. She felt like Alice in Wonderland. *Good-bye, feet.* With a shrug she rose, leaving the boots untied, picked up her jacket, stuffed her hat in its pocket, and swung the strap of her handbag over her shoulder. As she made her slow and careful way to the door, she glanced into the bathroom. Something caught her eye. It was lying half-hidden under the laundry hamper, its petals withered, the polka dots faded to brown. It had been overlooked in the cleanup somehow, but it was proof, if she needed it, that the nightmare had been real.

The man was still whistling in the kitchen. Quietly she pushed the bedroom door closed and went into the bathroom. With the tip of her boot she coaxed the flower out of its hiding place, and by supporting herself with a hand on the rim of the tub, she went down on one knee without moving her head and picked up the flower. Careful not to let any of the petals fall, she plucked a tissue from the box and wrapped the flower in it. It never occurred to her to question what she was doing. She only knew she had to do it.

As she was tucking the flower into her pocket, she heard the soft scrape of a footstep behind her. Memory of the other footstep sent her spinning around on a swift surge of fear. The stranger was standing in the doorway, holding a tray. "Damn it!" she cried in a flash of unreasoning anger. "Damn it, do you have to sneak up on someone like that?"

"Easy, girl, easy," the man said in a mild voice. "I come in friendship." He held up the tray, smiling.

"I'm sorry—I thought—I'm sorry." Hana sank down on the edge of the tub, trembling, trying to regain her self-control, while the stranger waited silently in the doorway, watching her. He couldn't have seen the flower, she assured herself. The tissue, perhaps, but there's nothing suspicious about putting a tissue into your pocket.

The man said in a soft, coaxing voice, "You should be in bed, you know, Hana Novotny. You're better off there for a while, and I've got a brew here that will set you on your ear."

"I don't want to be set on my ear, thank you. I've already been there. We'll have the coffee in the kitchen," Hana said, rising, swaying. "I'm fine."

"Sure, it's always pale as a ghost you are."

"I appreciate your making the coffee, Mr. . . . ?"

"O'Reilly. Conn O'Reilly, at your service."

"I knew it would be O something," Hana said coolly, "but we'll have it in the kitchen, Mr. O'Reilly—"

"Conn."

Hana ignored that. "I'm fine," she said again firmly. Making every effort to believe it and avoiding the probing gaze of the blue-green eyes, she limped past him and headed through the living room to the kitchen, head throbbing, boot laces flapping.

The man followed behind, muttering imprecations against stubborn, irrational women who wouldn't listen to reason and who would be very sorry indeed as a result.

Still upright, though not sure how she had managed it, Hana

reached the kitchen and dropped onto a chair beside the wrought-iron glass-topped table. She was breathing heavily, perspiration beaded her forehead.

"Here. Drink up, girl." The man set the tray down, took one of the mugs, and placed it in front of her. "After a couple of these you'll feel no pain, I guarantee it. From a purist point of view this brew can't be called Irish coffee because your brother for some mysterious reason known only to himself has no Irish whiskey. Slivovitz, yes, but I've never tried that in coffee, and I wouldn't care to. Nor does he have any whipped cream in his otherwise well-stocked refrigerator."

Hana glanced up sharply at him, looking for hidden meaning behind his words, but the bony face was smiling blandly at her.

"So I made do," he went on, picking up the second mug, "with brother Paul's best cognac." He tapped a finger against the familiar-looking bottle at his elbow. "I didn't think he'd mind under the circumstances. The coffee is well fortified, it's sweet, and it's strong. Just what Dr. O'Reilly orders."

"If it were any stronger," Hana murmured, gazing down into the thick black liquid, "it would get up and walk by itself."

"What I admire about you, Hana Novotny—among other things, that is," O'Reilly said, leering wolfishly at her, "is your ability to joke under fire. The jokes leave something to be desired, it's true, but your delicate condition could account for that, and it's 'A' for effort I'm giving you all the same. Now drink up, then you can purge your soul and tell me all about it. *Slainte!*"

He saluted her with the mug, raised it to his lips, and at one gulp drank half its content, his eyes beaming at her all the while over the rim.

Hana watched him warily as she swallowed some of the hot, sweet, heady mixture. It slid easily down her throat and sent warm, soothing messages throughout her body. She took another long swallow, set the cup down, and asked, "How do you know my name?"

O'Reilly cocked an eyebrow at her in surprise at the question and gestured at her handbag where she had hung it over the chair. "That's the source of my information," he said.

78

"You looked into my purse?"

"Just to check if you had Blue Cross coverage. Now I've answered your question. Perhaps you'll answer mine."

"And what is that?"

"Don't go all coy, girl, and pretend you don't know what I'm talking about. I come in here and find you out cold on the floor, the owner of the apartment notably absent—"

"Paul? My brother? He had nothing to do with this!"

"Did I say he did? No need to leap. But this *is* his apartment and nothing to do with *what*? That's my question. One of them, that is. How did you wind up flat out on the floor in the first place? Why, when you returned to the land of the living, did you gasp and turn white like a heroine in a Gothic novel when you looked into the bathroom? And why did you round on me just now in the bathroom as though you were expecting to see the devil himself? Those are some of my questions, and we can proceed from there after you've answered them."

Hana directed a steady, brown-eyed gaze at the man sitting across the table from her. The coffee mixture was having a restorative effect, and she was feeling more in control. The pounding in her head had eased, she felt less shaky. She studied the man's clever, bony face with its extravagant seawater eyes, crooked nose, and wide mouth that quirked up at the corners. He was busy refilling his cup with coffee and brandy; the movements of his strong, square hands as he spooned in the sugar and stirred it were deft and quick. They didn't look like the hands of a murderer. The hands of a murderer... She scoffed at herself for the ridiculous thought. As though the hands of a murderer would appear different from other hands!

Nevertheless, all things considered, she found it difficult to cast him in the role of villain. But at the same time she had no intention of telling him what had happened here. Besides, who was Conn O'Reilly, anyway? What was he doing here, and what right had he to ask questions—in such a high-handed manner at that!

Hana swallowed the rest of the sweet, brandy-laced coffee and pushed the mug across the table for a refill. "You gave me your name," she said, "but for all I know you could have picked it out of the air."

O'Reilly cast his eyes heavenward and muttered something about a sainted Irish grandmother as he reached into his pocket. Drawing out his wallet, he extracted his driver's license and offered it to Hana with a flourish. "As the sovereign state of New York is my witness," he said, "Conn Brian O'Reilly himself, born on January twenty-third, 1952, thirty-six years old, in my prime, as you can very well see, height five feet eleven, eyes blue—"

"Blue green," Hana murmured as she studied the picture on the license.

"I'm pleased and flattered that you noticed," O'Reilly said, smiling. "And if you'll turn it over, you'll see there's no record of convictions. Pure as snow." He waved a hand toward the window, where white flakes were drifting thickly down.

Handing him back the license, Hana nodded gravely and said, "Thank you. That answers one of my questions, but what are you doing here and how did you get into this apartment?"

"I live on the floor below, I'm a friend of your brother, I came up to see him about something. When I found the door open, I thought it odd and came in to investigate—and there you were, sleeping beauty, stretched out on the floor, looking like death. I picked you up, put you on the bed, and the rest of the story you know." While talking, O'Reilly had been busy stirring the sugar into her drink, not looking at her except for one quick flick of a glance at her face. Now with a last vigorous swirl of the spoon, he pushed the mug across to her. "Satisfied?" he asked.

Hana didn't know if he was referring to the drink or to his explanation, so she simply nodded and sipped some of the coffee while she thought over what he had said. It was all smoothly spoken and plausible, but...

But... *Had* she left the door open? She had no memory of it one way or the other. And if she hadn't, the man who'd attacked her might have. Still, suspicion nagged her with another *but*. Why, when she was in and out of this building several times a week, had she never run into Conn O'Reilly before?

As though he had read her mind, the man was saying in his light, musical voice, "I moved in only a week ago. Your brother told me about a vacancy, and the state of housing being what it is in Manhattan, I grabbed it sight unseen—after a little something passed under the table, that is."

"I see. And what do you do for a living, Mr. O'Reilly?"

The man's face creased into a broad, clownish grin. "Sure, and very little if I can help it."

Hana stared at O'Reilly silently for a moment, then abruptly she asked, "Where were you born?"

"Brooklyn."

"Brooklyn? But—where did you spend your childhood?"

"For the most part, Brooklyn."

"You mean—in other words, this—this Irish patter of yours," Hana said indignantly, "is simply put on? A kind of comic act?"

"Ah, well, as to that..." The man teetered back on the two legs of the chair. His grin broadened, and he waved an expansive arm in the air, which sent the chair rocking dangerously. Hooking a leg around the table leg to maintain his precarious balance, he went on. "It suits me from time to time. Besides, my mother—a grand girl, you'll like her—was born in the old country up near Castlebar, you see, and she was a great one for not losing touch with our roots. So every summer she'd ship me off to her hometown, where my grandmother still lived. When I wasn't fending off the local bully boys of Ballyvary, who wanted to prove how much tougher they were than this interloper from Brooklyn, my grandmother was boxing my ears for not working hard enough at learning the Gaelic. A hard life and a sad one, so it was. And now—" O'Reilly unhooked his leg and brought the chair down with a thump. "And now that I've satisfied your insatiable curiosity, Hana Novotny, perhaps you'll do the same for me. Speaking of roots...Where is your brother, and when do you expect him back? I'd like a little chat with him."

At once Hana went silent and still as the warning bell jangled in her mind. The diversion had been brief. They were back now to the business at hand. Though the question had been asked casually, lightly, Hana was not deceived. This is what it was all about, wasn't it? Cold-eyed "friends" from Washington, harsh voices on the phone—all wanting to know where Paul was. And now this man, Conn O'Reilly, claiming friendship with her brother, appearing from nowhere. Had he been kind and helpful and amusing simply to gain her confidence and find out what he could about Paul? Is that what his game was?

"Those are two questions, Mr. O'Reilly, not one," Hana said, angry and not trying to conceal it.

"Don't be picky, sleeping beauty."

Hana raised her head quickly at the sudden hard tone in the man's voice to find the seawater eyes fixed with disconcerting intensity on her face, the light from the ceiling fixture igniting into brilliance their silver highlights. Like small searchlights they seemed to probe into her mind, and Hana had the disturbing sensation that they were reading her secret thoughts. She lowered her eyes quickly and reached for the cognac bottle.

"I don't know where Paul is," she said, pouring a recklessly large dollop of the brandy into her cup, "nor when he'll be back—from wherever he is." She took a long swallow from the mug, set it down on the glass tabletop with a thump, and, asking forgiveness in a silent prayer, added, "I'm not my brother's keeper."

"Aren't you, Hana Novotny?" The man's voice was kind and gentle again, and when Hana said nothing, he went on quietly. "Well, never mind, then. But fair's fair, isn't it? You're going to tell me what happened here, aren't you?"

Hana curled both hands tightly around the mug and, keeping her eyes down, said, "I'm afraid you'll be disappointed. It's not much of a story. I came along to see my brother. When I entered the apartment, I found it empty—or it seemed empty—and someone hit me on the head. That's all. I figure I must have surprised a burglar."

"He must have been a very tidy burglar. There was no sign of a search when I arrived."

"There was a bit of a mess in the living room," Hana said, "but I cleaned it up."

"And after you cleaned it up, you went into the bedroom..."

82

"Yes."

"And surprised the burglar there?"

"I assume so. Else why was I hit on the head?" Hana raised wide innocent eyes to O'Reilly's face. "He must have been hiding there."

"Did you see him?"

"No. I only heard a footstep behind me. That's all. That was enough—more than enough!"

"Of course. And it was the burglar you expected to see when you came to and looked into the bathroom?"

"Why—yes, I suppose so."

"Oh, sure!" O'Reilly teetered back in his chair again and flung an arm in the air. "And what might the burglar be doing in the bathroom now? Taking a shower, perhaps, or brushing his teeth! Bashing people on the head is a dirty business, right enough." The man's voice was heavy with sarcasm and rich with brogue.

Coldly Hana said, "Under the circumstances you can understand that I wasn't thinking rationally. I was only looking around, trying to—to orient myself."

O'Reilly thumped the chair back onto its four legs and asked, "You have a key to this apartment, I take it."

"Of course."

"Just my own insatiable curiosity, but why did you stay at all when you found that your brother was not home?"

"That's my affair, Mr. O'Reilly."

"Perhaps," O'Reilly said gravely. "It's just that a burglar in the building makes it my affair as well, Miss Novotny."

"He's gone now, at any rate," Hana said. And that, she thought, is that. Lifting the mug to her lips, she drained the rest of the drink, which was now more brandy than coffee. As she started to set it down, weariness suddenly washed over her in waves. Her fingers trembled so hard that the mug did a little dance on the tabletop. Not only was she exhausted, she realized, but she was dizzy as well, and the dizziness was only partly due to the blow on the head. She had had too much brandy on an empty stomach. It seemed a long time ago that she'd had the snack of cheese and crackers, and she was hungry. Immediately she felt guilty. She thought of Paul, of her father, of the dead man in the bathroom. It was frivolous, she felt, to be thinking of food at a time like this. It was frivolous to be tipsy as well, but she was tipsy and hungry all the same.

"It's time to go home," she murmured.

O'Reilly, who had been silently watching her with a bright, curious gaze, asked, "I take it you are not going to wait for your brother to come home, then?"

Hana shook her head and rose to her feet. To her dismay she found that her legs weren't steady and her head was swimming. She swayed and clutched the back of the chair for support.

"Hang on!" O'Reilly leaped up with a clatter and rushed around to her side. "Sit down," he said angrily, "before you fall down!"

Hana tried to say firmly, "I'm going home," but her voice wavered and broke on "home," and all of a sudden she was crying. Hot tears filled her eyes, blinding her, streaming down her cheeks. A strong supporting arm slipped around her waist, a soft voice spoke in her ear. "It's all right, girl. No need to carry on."

"I'm not carrying on, damn it!" Hana sobbed indignantly. "It's de-delayed reaction, that's what it is. T-too much has happened t-too fast—and t-too much damned brandy besides!"

"Sure, that's what it is right enough," the man said, and went on making soft crooning sounds in her ear as Hana gulped down the last sobs, repeating, "De-delayed reaction . . .

"I'm all right now," she said at last.

"Sure you are."

"I think I got your sw-sweater wet."

"It's a pleasure," O'Reilly said.

"Excuse me," Hana said, moving away. "I need a tissue or something."

"Here you are."

She felt a soft cloth thrust into her hand and discovered after she had wiped her eyes and blown her nose with it that it was Paul's dishrag. "Oh, God!" she cried, and burst out laughing. "Oh, God!"

"You're certainly a difficult woman to keep track of," O'Reilly said, frowning. "You're not going all hysterical on me now, are you?"

"No!" Hana gasped, still laughing. "No. It's just this—" She waved the dishrag at him. "It's such a perfect ending. From tragedy to comedy in one second. You've no idea—after everything—after everything that's happened—it's the perfect ending!"

They walked to Perry Street at Hana's insistence and over O'Reilly's objections. He wanted to call a cab. "The air and exercise will clear my head," Hana said, the laughter having long since died, leaving her face pale but her jaw obstinate.

The truth was Hana wanted to avoid the intimacy of a shared cab. If there were more questions, she was too tired to think of lies that would sound reasonable, and on the street it would be easier to walk away if the man became too importunate. But when she said she would prefer to walk alone, O'Reilly's answer was a firm "No way. I'll not hear of it, Hana Novotny. I'll not have a stranger scooping you off the sidewalk, if it comes to that. And if you'll not let me walk beside you, I'll walk behind you. Just make up your mind to that." And with a muttered "It's a free country," Hana gave in.

Outside, the snow was falling steadily from the slate-gray sky, veiling the streetlights, muffling the harsher sounds of the city. Traffic was thin—a scattering of private cars, a few taxis, all of which were occupied. Somewhere north on Fifth Avenue Hana could hear the scrape of a snow plow. There was something lonely in the sound, and in a sudden and silent about-face she was grateful for Conn O'Reilly's company. She glanced at the man. There was a rather fierce frown on his face, his head was bowed, and he seemed lost in thought as he walked silently beside her.

At Sheridan Square the snow had already drifted over the curb of Seventh Avenue, and Hana missed her footing and stumbled forward into the street. O'Reilly's outstretched hand grasped her arm and pulled her back onto the sidewalk. As he did so, a figure suddenly detached itself from a dark doorway nearby and lurched up to Hana. A small, thin rag of a man with hollow eyes and sunken cheeks, he plucked at her sleeve with a filthy hand while in a slurred, whiskey-laden voice, he whined, "Can you spare a little something, lady? I am temporarily out of funds and I haven't eaten all day. Whatever—"

That was all he had a chance to say, for O'Reilly was standing between them, having moved so fast that Hana wasn't aware that he had left her one side before he appeared on the other. O'Reilly placed one strong hand on the man's shoulder and sent him reeling back against the lamppost.

"Hey!" The drunk wound his arm around the post to keep from falling and whimpered, "Whassa matter, mister, whassa matter? Why the rough stuff? I was only—"

"Never mind," O'Reilly growled at him. "Forget it." Dipping a hand into his pocket, he brought out a bill and thrust it at the man. "Get lost," he said, and grabbing Hana by the elbow, he half dragged her across the street. The thin voice of the drunk followed them for a while, full of slurred surprise and gratitude. "Why, thank you, son, thank you. God bless you for your generosity. God bless you, son, God bless you..." His voice faded away through the snow, and as they reached the sidewalk, Hana jerked her arm free from O'Reilly's grip.

"There was no need for you to interfere so drastically, Mr. O'Reilly," Hana said in a low, furious voice. "I'd have been glad to give something to the poor man. I'm capable of handling situations like that, you know. I'm not a child. I've been living in New York for some years, and I can tell when a situation is threatening and when it is not!"

O'Reilly stared, wide-eyed, at Hana for a moment, taken aback at her onslaught. He looked slightly bewildered as he said, "Of course you can, Hana Novotny, of course you can. I'm sorry—I wasn't thinking—or rather... Well, I'm sorry. Forgive me."

Hana didn't hear any of the usual banter in the man's voice. His tone was serious and apologetic—and something else. She puzzled over it for a moment until she recognized it as surprise. With sudden insight she realized that he had surprised himself as well as her when he'd moved so swiftly between her and the drunk. His action had been pure reflex. And why? What sort of man acts with such speed and agility in a situation he thinks might be dangerous? Conn O'Reilly, frog prince, with the clear seawater eyes... Who was he? She had taken him pretty much on faith, hadn't she?

Frowning, Hana drew back from the man and without another word swung around and headed up West Fourth Street, walking fast, concerned now only with getting home, where she could sit down quietly and alone and try to make sense of everything that had happened.

Silently, O'Reilly kept pace with her. By the time they reached the apartment house on Perry Street Hana was breathless with exhaustion.

"I told you we should take a taxi," O'Reilly said, looking at her white face with concern.

"I'm fine," Hana said hoarsely.

"You keep saying that. Why is it that I don't believe you?"

"Thank you for seeing me home, Mr. O'Reilly," Hana said. And then, because that sounded too curt, too ungracious, for he had been kind and helpful after all, she added, "And I'm grateful for your—your aid to the walking wounded." She managed a faint smile as she held out her hand.

The man ignored the hand. "You're home," he said firmly, "when you're inside your apartment."

Hana shrugged, too tired to argue, and while O'Reilly held the outer door open for her, she went through and unlocked the inner door with fingers that trembled with fatigue.

The three flights of stairs seemed more like six to Hana, but she made it to the door. She was home.

"I'll not come in, sleeping beauty," O'Reilly said.

Hana stared at him. "I wasn't—"

"No, no," O'Reilly said, holding up a hand, "don't insist. Some other time, perhaps, if you play your cards right. I will be in touch, though, if you don't mind. I'd like to know..." He hesitated for a moment. "I'd just like to know that you're really all right, and perhaps you'll be giving me a more detailed report than 'I'm fine.'" He hesitated again, then added, "And when you hear from your brother, will you please tell him that

87

Conn O'Reilly would appreciate a little chat with him—as soon as he can arrange it?"

"I will," Hana said. She had already unlocked her door and was waiting for the man to leave. He made no move to do so. Instead he stood there gazing at her silently, his bony face unusually grave.

Finally he said, "There's nothing more you want to tell me —about tonight—about what happened at your brother's apartment?"

The question caught her by surprise, and Hana answered too quickly. "I've already told you all there is to tell. There's nothing more I can add."

"*Can* add or *want* to add?" The man shook his head sadly. "You're a bad liar, girl, and that's a fact. 'It's such a perfect ending. From tragedy to comedy in one second. You've no idea...after everything that's happened...' I'm sure you recognize the quote?"

Hana forced a laugh. "A touch of hysteria, that's all. It's a reaction I always have after a burglar hits me on the head."

"I see. Well... The situation will either clarify itself or grow murkier, won't it? But I'd appreciate it," O'Reilly added in a soft voice, "if you'd look out for yourself, Hana Novotny. It's taken a lot of years to find you, so it has, and I'll not be losing you now." And before Hana realized what he intended, he bent down and kissed her lightly on the cheek. When he raised his head and looked at her, the blue-green eyes were ablaze with silver highlights and he was smiling. "*A stór,*" he whispered. "Sleep well." Then, abruptly, he swung around and left.

Frowning, Hana watched him go, a broad-shouldered, easy-moving man, his unbuttoned sheepksin jacket swinging loosely out behind him as he strode down the hall, his dark hair, damp from the snow, glistening under the light. And she remembered Paul walking away from her a week ago with the same easy stride, whistling, rain-wet hair shining under the streetlights.

She had wanted O'Reilly to go. Now for an illogical moment she fought the urge to call him back as a sudden, almost unbearable feeling of loneliness swept over her in the quiet, empty hallway.

They were waiting for her in her living room, two men, so quietly that Hana had removed her boots in the foyer and hung her coat on the hall tree without hearing a sound to alert her to their presence.

She froze in the doorway, staring at them, wide-eyed and white-faced.

6

Shock, first, made her speechless. Then anger overcame the shock. "Who are you? What right do you have to be here?" she demanded heedlessly. "How did you get into my apartment?" But when Hana recognized the slim, dark-haired man standing by the window, the fear that gripped her drove all other feelings away. "It's Paul. Something's happened to Paul."

"No, it's not Paul," the man at the window said calmly. "Your brother's all right as far as we know."

"As far as you know..."

"If you'll sit down, Miss Novotny, I'll explain. We're hoping *you* might enlighten *us*. I'm Nicholas Savini. Your brother works for me. He may have mentioned my name."

Hana nodded as she stared at the narrow, ascetic face with its thin lips and hooded eyes. The "Monk," Paul had called him. She took an instant dislike to the man.

He was saying in his smooth voice, "I apologize for startling you. That was thoughtless of us. This is Herbert Redstone—"

A hand had gripped her elbow and was guiding her to the couch. A voice was saying, "Can I get you something, Miss Novotny? A drink? A cup of coffee?"

Hana sat down, then frowned up at the man standing over her. Hazel eyes gazed down on her anxiously. Nothing threatening there, a pleasant enough looking man, younger than Savini.

"I think she could use a cup of coffee, Herb. I know I could. Suppose you make enough for all of us." Savini had moved from the window and was now sitting on the chair opposite the couch.

"Right," Herbert Redstone said. "Don't bother to get up, Miss Novotny. I'll manage just fine."

How high-handed of them—as though they were the hosts, she the guest! Hana was angry again, but she was also exhausted, and her head was throbbing painfully. She rose, saying to the room at large, "I need some aspirin, but don't bother to show me where they are. I think I'll be able to find them."

As she turned and headed for the bathroom, she thought she saw the flicker of a smile touch Savini's lips. It didn't make her feel charitable toward him, however. Neither man had explained or apologized for their unwarrantable presence in her apartment, nor would they, she knew, and it would be useless to make an issue of it. They were here, and she would have to deal with them until they left. On the credit side, whatever had brought them here might give her a clue about what was going on in relation to Paul. But no matter what, she thought grimly, if things continue like this, I'll soon be accepting these abnormal events in my life as normal, rather than the other way around!

In the bathroom she swallowed two aspirins, hesitated, then with a muttered, "Kill or cure," swallowed a third and drank two glasses of water. She ran a comb through her hair and tried not to look too closely at the white face and feverish-looking, dark-ringed eyes that stared at her from the mirror. She was prepared for questions about Paul. She had some of her own to ask. But what about her father? They must know of his escape. She remembered his letter then, still tucked in the pocket of her coat hanging on the hall tree, and felt a moment of panic. But how could they know it was there? she asked herself angrily. And besides, these men were not her father's enemies, were they?

She pressed her fingers against her aching temples and felt again the overwhelming urge she had felt in Paul's kitchen—to crawl into bed, pull the covers up, and sleep and sleep and sleep. Instead, after putting on her slippers in the bedroom, she headed resolutely if a little unsteadily back to the living room.

"I'm sorry if our unexpected appearance here at this hour startled you, Hana," Savini said blandly when the three of them were settled in chairs with cups of coffee in hand. "You don't mind if I call you Hana, do you?"

Hana did mind. It's a trick, she thought, a way of putting me down, placing me at a disadvantage. *Do you mind if I call you Nicholas?* She almost asked the question but decided she was too tired to play games and said instead, "Please do."

Savini nodded his sleek hand. "Good. Then it would be best if I came straight to the point. We've come to you, you see, because we are more or less at our wit's end." A shrug of one elegantly clad shoulder and a small deprecating smile accompanied this statement. "About Paul—I told you he's all right as far as we know, but we are concerned about him. There is a possibility that he might be in trouble, serious trouble, and we've come to you for help."

Hana nodded but didn't speak. Two thoughts preoccupied her. One, that Paul might be in trouble, as Savini suggested, only confirmed her own fears; the other, that an organization as large and as powerful as the CIA should be asking for her help was ridiculous and frightening. Both thoughts only increased the feeling of uneasiness that seemed to have settled permanently and coldly in the pit of her stomach.

"I don't understand," Hana said slowly, "how you think I could help you. I've no idea where Paul is. I haven't seen him for several days."

"When precisely?"

"We had dinner together a week ago."

Savini sipped his coffee, watching her with hooded dark eyes as though waiting for her to continue.

"Nothing out of the ordinary," Hana said wryly. "We see each other quite regularly."

"Yes, so I understand. And he said nothing to you about—about where he might be going, what he might be doing, this past week?"

I'm off to slay the dragon.

"Nothing," Hana said quickly and firmly. "Paul doesn't talk to me about his work. He never has."

"I'm sure not," Savini said smoothly. "That isn't the problem, Hana. The problem is . . ." The man hesitated a moment as though debating what to tell her. Then, with an ingenuous kind of smile that sat oddly on his narrow, secretive face, he went on, "To be quite frank, our problem is we know where Paul is supposed to be at this time, but he isn't there. He should have been in touch with us, at least by phone, but he hasn't been. We are concerned, naturally. I can only tell you this much, Hana—your brother is on a very important and very secret job which involves—could involve—some danger. It's urgent that we contact him, very urgent. Now, would you know where he might go if he wanted—solitude and safety?"

Solitude and safety . . . There was something ominous in the way the man had spoken these words. And didn't he really mean where would Paul go to hide out? Why? Why, for God's sake, should Paul do that?

"I don't know," she said. "I just don't know. There's nothing—"

"Think, Hana." The man's voice was low and hard. "Think. It's a question of Paul's safety. I don't use the word lightly." He paused for a moment as though to let the words sink in. "Now," he went on, "isn't there anything you can tell me? Anything you want to tell me?"

"No." Hana shook her head. "There's nothing."

There was something, of course. There was the dead man in Paul's bathroom. She would probably tell them about that, but not yet, not yet. Who knows? That might be enough to send them away, and she'd be left still groping in the dark. As much as she wanted them to go, she wanted them to stay.

"I'd do anything for Paul," Hana said. "Any time, any place, anyhow. You must know that. But I don't know what I can do. I don't know what's going on—only that something is. Most definitely something is. There's no doubt about that!" Her voice rose in sudden anger. "And whatever it is, a lot of people seem to think that I have some information—that I know—"

"A lot of people?" Savini asked sharply.

"Phone calls. Men wanting to speak to Paul. Two men waylaying me at my door this evening, asking for Paul. Correct me if I'm wrong—they were your men, weren't they?"

"The men at your door?" Savini nodded and without apology said, "Yes, but you didn't tell them anything."

"I didn't like their manners. I wouldn't have told them anything even if I could have."

A sound that was a cross between a hiccup and a sneeze came from Redstone's chair. Savini ignored it.

"I see," he said. "Well...I wonder if you would be good enough to describe the phone calls, Hana."

Hana gave him the gist of the brief conversations, adding, "The voice—I think it was the same one each time—was harsh and slightly accented. Slav, I would say. And I think there were other people with him because I heard background noises and once he referred to *we.*"

Savini nodded his sleek dark head in the approving fashion of a teacher complimenting a bright student. Then he turned to Redstone.

"Not surprising," he said. "We knew they would pick up the trail, of course, and it's logical that they would try to do it through Hana."

Redstone nodded solemnly, and Hana, studying both men's faces, had the distinct feeling that Savini's statement had been made solely for her benefit. She didn't quite know why. To keep her off balance?

"Who are they?" she asked bluntly.

"Whoever they are, Hana, they are not friends of Paul, but they want to get hold of him as much as we do. More, perhaps. They have more to lose."

"I don't understand," Hana said.

Savini went on as though she hadn't spoken. "And they will probably take an interest in you, Hana, if they think Paul confided in you."

"You're trying to frighten me."

"I'm simply giving you the facts. How you react to them is your problem."

Hana's cheeks flamed with anger at the crude brutality of the man's remark, though again she had the feeling that it had been said for its effect on her.

"There's a great deal at stake here, Hana," Savini went on, his voice very cold. "I want you to keep that in mind. That's why, for your brother's sake, for your sake, for all our sakes, it's urgent that we find Paul. You tell me you know nothing of what's going on. I'm telling you I find that very hard to believe."

"You're saying that I'm lying?" Hana's voice trembled with anger.

"What else can I think, Hana? If you're not lying, how do you account for this?" Savini rose and stepped over to the table that held the telephone. He picked up the pad that lay facedown beside it and, turning it over, held it out toward Hana. She found herself staring at the sketch of the bearded man.

"I see," she murmured. "I'd forgotten all about it."

"How do you know this man?"

"I don't know him."

"You drew his face. How can you say you don't know him? Where did you meet him?"

"On the sidewalk," Hana said. "I bumped into him—literally—on the sidewalk when I was coming home earlier this evening." Though it seemed, she thought, more like a year ago this evening!

"Where?"

"Where?"

"On what sidewalk, what street?"

"On Washington Place. In front of Paul's apartment building."

A stillness descended on the room with the swiftness of a lightning stroke. And as Hana stared from one impassive face to the other, she had the odd sensation that both men were even holding their breath. She had *her* secret about the bearded man, but what was theirs?

"Hana..." Savini's voice, soft and silky smooth, broke the silence. "Are you telling me that this was an accidental meeting with a stranger—a man you never saw before?"

"Yes—no—I mean—" Hana broke off. How could she explain? *What* could she explain about a shadowed memory that had stirred briefly in a dark recess of her mind and had brought with it an ill-defined feeling of menace and panic?

95

Soft, insistent, the voice went on demanding answers. "I don't understand why you drew this man's picture, Hana, if you didn't know him. There must have been more to it than an accidental meeting in the street."

"I'm an artist. Faces interest me," Hana said. Yours, for example, she thought. I would like to draw your face, Mr. Savini. Not as a monk but as a cardinal, dressed in rich, red, fur-trimmed robes in contrast with that thin, ascetic face and cold black eyes. A cardinal of the Inquisition, perhaps.

"You draw all the faces you see?"

"What?"

"I said, do you draw all the faces you see?"

"No, of course not."

"You are selective?"

"Pretty much so."

"That's not good enough, Hana. You're an artist. Faces interest you. I understand that. But why *this* face? I asked you if you had ever seen this man before and you said *yes* first, then *no*. What did you mean?"

Hana didn't answer. She drank some coffee, noted it was cold, and set the cup down on the table.

"Obviously the face meant something to you, Hana. What?"

Hana closed her eyes for a moment, drew in a deep, shuddering breath, let it out in a long sigh, and said, "I'll try to explain. I drew his face because—because it bothered me for some reason."

"How did it bother you?"

"The eyes... He had very pale blue eyes above that black beard. I felt that I..."

"You felt you had seen the man before. Is that it?"

Hana nodded.

"And the man? Did he make any sign that he knew you? Did he say anything?"

"Nothing out of the ordinary. He made a fuss about bumping into me—a bigger fuss than is normal on the streets of New York. And he did stare at me hard, but—"

"But people stare at you a lot because you are beautiful," Savini said in a matter-of-fact voice.

With an impatient shake of her head, Hana said, "No, that isn't what I meant. It wasn't that kind of look. It was different. That's all. I can't explain it any better."

"All right. But you think you saw him before. Where? When?"

Hana shook her head. "You don't understand."

"Then make me understand."

"There are no facts to pin it down. There's only a feeling, a vague feeling, that somewhere, sometime long ago, I've seen him."

There was a slight pause, then in a deceptively gentle voice, Savini said, "When you were a child—in Prague. Is that it, Hana?"

Hana shrugged and looked away. "I suppose so," she whispered.

Still very gently, Savini said, "Then let's go back to that time. Let's talk about it. You might remember—"

"No!" The swift shout of denial came out of its own accord, loud and clear. It was followed by a heavy silence, during which Hana avoided looking at the two men. She kept her eyes down. Her face had flushed with anger and embarrassment for having exposed with that one sharp word a secret and painful part of herself to strangers. She had never talked about it—not to Stephen, not to friends, certainly never to her mother. Only to Paul. It was a part of him, too.

If she weren't so tired, she thought, if the dull throbbing in her head wasn't warning her of more headache to come, she would not have been caught unaware, she would have said no, quietly, with dignity. She picked up her coffee cup for something to do, saw it was empty, set it down again.

"Can I get you some more coffee, Miss Novotny?"

It was Redstone, the silent one, who spoke. (Did they always travel in pairs like this, one silent, one talkative?) He stood beside the couch, looking down at her, his eyes kind and concerned.

"If you don't mind my taking over in your kitchen again, that is." Redstone smiled.

Hana suspected that the slight touch of gaucherie was put on for her benefit, but it didn't matter. "Yes, I'd appreciate it. Thank you."

Redstone vanished into the kitchen, and Savini moved silently and gracefully around the small living room, nodding approval of the Hogarth drawing and the good Dürer reproduction that hung on the walls, ignoring Hana completely until Redstone came back with the coffee. The three cups were replenished, Redstone returned to his chair, and Savini to his.

It all seemed very precise, Hana thought, as though someone had directed the action. The stage is set, the play will begin.

Savini spoke, his voice soft and smooth as oil. "I don't enjoy asking you to do something that is painful for you, Hana, and certainly that night when the Russians invaded Czechoslovakia must have been very frightening for a child. But I'm asking you for Paul's sake to tell me what you can remember. Trust me. It's for your brother's sake."

"That sounds like blackmail," Hana said with a twisted smile. "And I don't see how it can help Paul now. It was a long time ago."

"Because something that happened then could affect what's happening now. Trust me, Hana."

"What you're asking is not only painful but difficult as well. I was only eight then, and it's hard to remember. There are gaps. It was all very confusing. I had no idea what was happening. I only knew my world was turning upside down."

"Just one step at a time. That's all. We'll take just one step at a time."

Hana was silent for a moment, sipping the hot coffee and staring into the dark hooded eyes of the man sitting opposite her. He looked so relaxed and assured, so different from the way she felt, tense and unhappy. His one long, slender hand rested unmoving on the arm of the chair. The ruby ring gleamed at her under the light. If he's telling the truth, Hana thought, that it's really for Paul's sake he wants me to dredge up buried memories, I can't refuse no matter how much I want to. Unable to sit still all of a sudden, Hana rose and carried her coffee over to the window, where she perched on the ledge, her back to the men. Behind her she heard some rustling sounds and the creak of a chair, as though they were adjusting to this move of hers.

Savini broke the silence. "Are you with me, Hana?"

"Yes." She sighed.

"The night the Russians invaded Prague... where were you?"

"I was home, of course, in our apartment on Celetná." She closed her eyes and saw a darkened room filled with heavy baroque furniture. Figures like puppets moved behind the shadows.

"With your family? Your mother, your father, Paul?"

The room emptied and vanished. She opened her eyes.

"Paul? No, I've been trying to remember where Paul was that night. I don't think he was home, else I wouldn't have felt so alone. He probably spent the night with a friend of his on Na Kampě. I think so, anyway. He did that often."

"All right. It doesn't matter. Your mother was there?"

"Yes." A hard, flat *yes*. Nothing more. There was finality there, and Savini didn't press it.

"And your father? Was he there that night?"

It was the first direct reference Savini had made to her father, and though his voice had remained as soft and unthreatening as ever, the atmosphere in the room changed subtly. Hana had that same odd feeling that the two men behind her were holding their breath again.

"He wasn't there when I went to bed," Hana said slowly. "He came into my room, though, later—much later—to kiss me good night." She closed her eyes again. The tall, thin shadow of her father stood beside her bed in the dark room.

"Very late? Would you know what time it was?"

"I'm not sure. I'd been asleep. It *felt* late, but it's hard to judge."

"Yes. He kissed you. He spoke to you?"

I love you, my little Hana. "He just said good night." The intimacy of that brief, dreamlike moment was not something she was prepared to discuss, and how could it possibly have any relevance to what they were talking about?

"He didn't say anything else?"

"No."

"This was a habit of his? Coming to your room to kiss you good night when he had been working late?"

Hana fell silent, turning the question over in her mind. It surprised her now that she had never before considered her father's strange night visit as anything other than one part of the whole pattern of strange events of that night. A nice part. The only nice part.

"No," she murmured. "Now that I think of it, it was not his habit." She turned her head and looked at Savini. "If he worked late at night, which he did often, I would see him in the morning. We would talk at breakfast before I went to school."

"So there was something special about that night—something special that brought him to your room."

"I suppose—" Hana turned her face back to the window so Savini couldn't see the tears in her eyes. "I suppose," she whispered, "that he came to say good-bye. He must have known or suspected..." Her throat closed, and the tears rolled silently down her cheeks.

"Yes," Savini said, his voice sounding distant and harsh. "Yes, perhaps he did."

A brief silence followed. Hana brushed the tears away and drank some coffee. Then Savini resumed his questioning, his voice soft again.

"I want you to think hard before you answer me now, Hana. You were eight when all of this happened, and of course there are gaps in your memory, as you said. But concentrate on this: Did you see or hear anyone come to your apartment that night? Was anyone there at any time besides your father and mother? It doesn't matter if it was someone you knew or a stranger. Can you remember? Anyone. Take your time and think about it."

Anyone?

Anyone... Something brushed at her consciousness, feather-light, like the wings of a bird. She waited, holding her breath. But there was nothing more. No shapes or shadows moved among the baroque furniture. "It's hopeless," she whispered wearily. "Nothing. Just a blank screen. So much happened in such a short length of time, and I've kept it all buried for so long..."

After a brief pause Savini nodded his head and said, "Of course." Whether he was disappointed or not, Hana couldn't tell. He showed no emotion at all. "Perhaps something will come to you later," he added. "It often happens that way, doesn't it, after the seed has been planted, so to speak, and you are no longer worrying over it. We've all had that experience, haven't we?"

Then he went on, his voice cool and matter-of-fact, to ask her to tell him about their escape across the border. The next day, hadn't it been? Right after the invasion? She must be able to remember *something* about that. Would she tell him, please, what she could remember? Anything at all that came to her mind.

Hana stared at him for a moment in disbelief, then burst into a loud tirade, almost sputtering in her anger. It was too much, she cried. How dare he? It was too much to ask! They had barged in here, uninvited, illegally! Didn't he know how exhausted she was, how her head ached?

"And what does it have to do with Paul—except that he was there? He was only fourteen. What does it have to do with now!"

"We've been over that ground before, Hana. I'm trying to put together some things that happened in the past to help me understand what's going on now. And it does have to do with Paul." Savini paused a moment, then added, "If you refuse and somehow that harms Paul, could you ever forgive yourself?"

"Oh! That's hitting below the belt!"

Savini shrugged. "How I convince you isn't important, Hana, just so I do convince you. I know I'm asking a great deal. You're afraid of it, of course. I understand that. But, come on, sit here on the sofa in comfort and tell me about it. I won't interrupt you any more than I have to. Then we'll go and leave you in peace. Please, Hana."

In pieces, more likely, Hana thought, and was able to smile a little at the crude joke, hearing Conn O'Reilly's light, musical voice telling her he admired her ability to joke under fire. But she had caught the implication behind Savini's words. Despite the rather humble-sounding "please," she knew he had no intention of going until she complied with his request. Suppose I just said, No, I won't, and clammed up? she wondered. Would the man and his silent partner simply sit there for the rest of the night, waiting for her to change her mind? But even while she was asking herself this, she found that she had picked up her coffee cup and was moving toward the sofa, half-angry, half-resigned, but knowing she couldn't take the chance of hurting Paul.

Hana sat with her head resting against the cushioned back of the sofa and stared at the ceiling as she recounted the hurried departure from the apartment in Prague that had been her home since birth. Her voice was weary, subdued, and at first she spoke haltingly as she tried to recall long-forgotten details, but as one memory sparked another, the words came faster.

"It's always hard to tell someone about a nightmare," she said, "unless it's filled with gruesome scenes, but a lot aren't like that. The nightmare quality often comes from just—just an aura. That's what it was like that night. If I'd been older, it might not have been so frightening, or if someone had explained. The whole atmosphere was doom-laden. I can't describe it any better than that.

"It was very early—just before dawn, it must have been—when my mother woke me and told me to get up and pack. We had to go away, she said. Paul was there by then. I don't know when he had come in. He looked very white and tired. We were allowed one small bag, a few clothes, enough for a couple of days, my mother said."

Savini's soft voice broke in. "Nothing else? None of the treasures an eight-year-old accumulates? Difficult to decide what to take, what to leave behind. You must have had to make some painful choices."

Hana lowered her eyes and stared at the man for a moment, wondering what he was getting at, but all she said was, "Yes, but I managed to sneak in a few extras that didn't weigh much when my mother wasn't looking. She was very distracted herself—and frightened, too, I thought, though she tried to hide it. And that was scary for me because she was always very calm, very cool, no matter what happened.

"I kept asking about my father. I couldn't understand why he wasn't there. Wasn't he coming with us? My mother told me he would join us later."

The voice harsh, suddenly, and shrill: "That's enough! Do you understand me? Your father has other things to do. No more questions. Just be quiet and do as you're told!"

"But of course he didn't join us later. He couldn't." Hana paused a moment to draw in a deep, shuddering breath. Then she turned her gaze up to the neutral ceiling and went on.

"We had to sneak downstairs so as not to wake anyone."

Avoiding the steps they knew from long usage would creak, Paul and Hana moved quickly down the three flights, holding hands, gripping suitcases, bewildered at leaving behind the untidiness of unmade beds and open bureau drawers with contents strewn on floors and chairs. Paul's whispered "Quiet now, Hanička, we don't want to wake them." Them... The gimlet-eyed superintendent and his sly-faced wife. Then outside into the cool dawn, where an unnatural brightness in the distance lit the sky and harsh, rumbling sounds filled the air with menace. No time to wonder, to ask why. Without making a sound, Paul put their suitcases in the trunk of the car, then took her arm.

"There was a car waiting for us at the curb, its engine running. The trunk was open. My mother must have told Paul what to do because after she got into the front seat he grabbed me by the arm and pushed me into the trunk, then climbed in after. When he pulled the lid down I started to scream, but Paul put his hand over my mouth."

"It's all right, Hanička, it's all right." How many times in the coming long day and night would her brother ease her fears with those few ordinary words?

"All I remember of that long, bumpy ride was Paul whispering in my ear about the invasion, about the Russian soldiers and tanks he had seen swarming through the city's streets while he was sneaking home through the dark side streets. I didn't really understand what was going on, only that it sounded bad and made the nightmare feeling worse.

"After a while I must have dozed because the next thing I knew was we had stopped and it was very quiet. My mother lifted the trunk lid and said we could get out. As soon as we did, the car sped away—very fast."

"Hana," Savini's voice interposed softly, "at either time, when you got into the trunk or out of it, could you see who was driving the car?"

Hana shook her head. "A man, I think, but that was just an impression because I wasn't paying any attention to that, particularly when we arrived and I got out of the trunk and saw where we were. I was so happy and relieved, I started to cry. We were at our summer cottage in Ledeč on the Sázava River. I thought we would stay there then like we did every summer and my father would come and we would swim in the river..."

For a second the scent of the pine trees in the rain filled her nostrils, and Hana could hear the chuckling sounds the river made that used to send her to sleep at night. Her voice stumbled, she bit her lip and blinked a few times.

Savini asked, "You weren't too far from the Austrian border there, were you?"

"That's right," Hana said, her voice husky. "And that's where we were going, though I didn't know it at the time. Mother rushed us into the cottage. I wanted to walk around outside, but she wouldn't let me. There was an old man waiting for us in the kitchen. His name was Jan. I never knew his last name. I asked Paul who he was, and he told me Jan was our guide—which meant nothing to me then.

"Jan had food waiting for us—a big loaf of dark bread and thick sausages, coffee and fruit—a feast. We had to stay inside all day, but Jan sang songs for Paul and me and played cards with us and told us funny stories, so the time went fast. Then just before dark Jan went away. When he came back, he was driving an old truck. It rattled a lot—I'd forgotten that—it rattled so much I thought it would fall apart and I didn't want to get in. But my mother made me, of course. In the back there was a lot of hay, and Paul and I had to crawl in and hide under it. I kept sneezing until Paul worked the hay away from our faces and we could breathe fresh air.

"My mother sat in front with Jan. She had tied a scarf around her head and had changed into old slacks she kept in the cottage so she looked like a farmer's wife—at least that was the idea.

"After a long while Jan stopped and we got out of the truck and walked through the forest. It had begun to rain. I remember that."

The gentle hiss of the raindrops on the leaves, the damp-earth smell of the forest filtered through the dazed exhaustion of fear...

"There were voices, footsteps. We had to hide in the underbrush while some men stood near us, talking, laughing. Maybe they were border guards. I don't know." Hana's breathing quickened, and the words poured out in a rush. "When they went away, Jan said something or made a signal and we got up and ran—like rabbits—out of the forest into a clearing. Mother was ahead of us, and Paul and I followed her."

"And when I tell you to run, run as fast as you can after your mother." Jan's voice, kind, anxious. "Exactly behind your mother. Do you understand, Paul? Hold Hana's hand. Don't let go. Keep her close to you."

"I didn't see or hear Jan, and I turned around to look. He was standing just at the edge of the clearing. He waved at me, or that's what I thought he was doing. It was quite dark, I couldn't see too well. Then all of a sudden there was a cracking sound, and he threw both arms in the air and fell forward on his knees. He began to crawl—in a circle—like a wounded animal—on all fours. Then he sprawled out and lay still. I started to go back to him, but Paul held tight to my hand and made me run the other way. My suitcase kept banging against my legs. I wanted to stop and rest, but Paul wouldn't let me, and finally when I thought I couldn't run any more, we were there. Paul let go of my hand and I fell to the ground beside the Austrian guard. I lay there, trying to catch my breath and looking at his boots. I'd forgotten that—those boots. They were creased and worn and not very clean. They looked—they looked comfortable and safe, somehow.

"When we went away with the guard, Jan's body was still lying in the clearing."

The pewter-gray eyes, stone cold, the smile without warmth: You could say that he stepped on a land mine and that's what killed him. More truth than fiction in that. But it's no business of yours. Forget it, Hana.

"My mother told me later that Jan stepped on a land mine and that's what killed him." Hana paused a moment, then added in a barely audible whisper, "He was a kind, gentle man. He shouldn't have died like that."

A silence followed that seemed to go on and on. As far as Hana was concerned it could have lasted forever. She felt empty. Nothing more. Just empty. Even the headache seemed to have receded to only a vague threat somewhere at the back of her head. They would leave now and she could sleep.

Savini's voice, soft, persistent, broke into the silence. "There are two things I don't understand, Hana. At the place where you crossed the border, didn't you see any guard towers? Wasn't there any barbed wire?"

Hana didn't bother to raise her head. She simply rolled it back and forth once against the sofa and said wearily, "I don't know. I don't remember anything like that. I only remember running."

"And this man whose face you drew, whom you thought you had seen sometime in the past... He doesn't come into your narrative at all, does he?"

For the first time Hana detected some strong emotion under the smooth voice, but whether it was anger or disbelief or disappointment, she was too tired to worry about it. "I've told you all I can," she said.

"Perhaps you think you have, Hana, but memories are tricky, and now that you've started digging into the past, you'll find, I think, that later—"

"Later!" This time Hana raised her head to stare angrily at Savini. "You said you'd go!"

"Yes, of course we will—in a little while. But I want to tell you something first, Hana. I want to tell you who this man

106

is"—Savini leaned forward and tapped the drawing with his finger—"and why it's important for you to remember if you saw him at any time in Czechoslovakia and where you saw him. This man—" the finger went on tapping—"was responsible for your father's arrest, for his imprisonment, his torture..."

Hana made a small sound in her throat and raised a hand. Savini ignored her. In short, brutal sentences that fell on Hana like blows, he described what happened that night in August 1968, after her father had come to her room to say good night. With what seemed deliberate cruelty he told her in detail of her father's coming to the American embassy for sanctuary, how someone must have betrayed him, someone he trusted must have told him he would find safety there, perhaps told him that the patrol of Russian guards surrounding the embassy had been bribed to look the other way. "I myself," Savini said, "had alerted the marines to be on the watch for him.

"But no sanctuary, Hana. Instead your father was seized by the Russian guards. No hesitation on their part to check to see if they had the right man. They grabbed him, first sight. They clubbed him to the ground with their rifles, dragged him off, half-conscious, to Pankrac prison."

"This isn't something I got secondhand, Hana. I watched it all from a window in the embassy. He worked for me, Hana. He was also my friend. It was me, I'm sure, he was trying to reach. If I could have helped him, I would have, but I was helpless, you understand. And his arrest was only the beginning of his ordeal."

Savini paused for a moment, but Hana said nothing. She'd raised her head when Savini had begun to speak and fixed her gaze on him. The gaze never wavered, but as he went on the blood slowly drained from her face, leaving it ashen. Only the honey-brown eyes had color. They were blazing.

Savini's voice continued remorselessly. "Others at your father's trial were given the death sentence. Not your father. He was deliberately kept alive by this man, who paid him regular visits in the months following his imprisonment, methodically torturing him in order—"

"Stop it! Stop it!" There was the clatter of a coffee cup overturning, and Hana was standing over Savini, shouting down at him. Her fists were raised as though she were going to strike him. "Sadist—you're a sadist! It doesn't matter anymore. Do you hear? That's past. The man is dead. Do you understand? He's dead! Somebody killed him. I saw him—his body—to-night—in Paul's bathroom!"

7

They had left at last. Be grateful for small favors, Hana told herself, as with what seemed like her last ounce of energy she bolted the door, slotted the chain into place, and headed for the bedroom, turning out lights as she went.

Her outburst had brought Nicholas Savini out of his chair like a snake uncoiling, hissing questions at her. What did the dead man look like? Had he a scar on his right temple? How was he killed? When were you there? Why were you there?

She had held her ground, answering in brief monosyllables, saying nothing about the blow on her head or Conn O'Reilly. At the end he had pulled a card out of his pocket and handed it to her, saying coldly, "You hold the key, Hana Novotny, make no mistake about it, and when you choose to remember anything more—"

"Choose!"

"—about this man, about what happened in Prague, no matter how trivial you may think it is, call me at this number. They will know how to get in touch with me."

A swift glance at the card told Hana it was the same one the "talking man" had given her earlier.

"In case," Savini said, his voice icy, "you've forgotten it. And at the risk of sounding melodramatic," he added, "I must tell you that your well-being as well as Paul's depends on your doing as I say." Without another word the man turned and left the apartment.

Redstone, following him, paused at the door. With a smile that held a touch of apology, he said, "He's upset, you see, by what you told him."

"I'm upset by what he told me," Hana said coldly.

"Of course. But, please, Miss Novotny, don't make the mistake of underestimating the importance of what we've been talking about. That could lead to very serious consequences. And if you remember anything and would prefer to talk to me instead of Mr. Savini, you can reach me at that same number." He smiled again.

Hana didn't smile back. She stared at him for a long moment, and asked in a low voice, "Is it true that you really don't know where my brother is?"

Grave and unsmiling now, Redstone answered, "It is true, Miss Novotny, it is too true." He left, pulling the door gently closed behind him.

Tomorrow, Hana thought. I'll sort it all out tomorrow. Bone weary, she dropped on the bed, fully clothed, drew a blanket up around her shoulders, and closed her eyes.

As though that had been a signal or as though a button had been pushed, images started whirling dizzily across the screen of her mind. She saw Paul's face, his eyes hot with excitement, she heard his tense voice: *"It's going to answer a lot of old questions."*

O'Reilly's seawater eyes glowed at her, the light, musical voice whispered: *"Look out for yourself, Hana Novotny."*

The narrow, ascetic face of a monk gazed at her without compassion while the thin lips described in relentless detail one man's brutality to another.

And finally, crowding out the other images, came the bearded man's face as she had last seen it, staring at her through the bathroom door with those dead eyes above the gaping mouth, the stained carnation lying on the rumpled suit jacket. Other figures appeared, faceless and silent, moving with urgent stealth around her unconscious body, carrying the dead man away, scrubbing the blood from the bathroom floor, spraying Paul's expensive after-shave lotion, collecting the dead man's elegant coat, fur hat, umbrella . . .

Coat . . . Hat . . . Umbrella . . . Where—

Abruptly, without warning, Hana slipped over the edge into sleep.

8

A slim, youthful-looking man with a pleasant, rather nondescript face stepped into the phone booth on the corner of Perry and Bleecker streets, dialed a number, and after identifying himself listened to the cool, precise voice on the other end of the line.

"The woman on University Place...I want you to direct your attention to her in the morning. It is possible she could become a threat, in which case... But I will give you further instructions tomorrow. You will take extra care not to be seen—" The man started to speak, but the cool voice rode on through his words. "There is no need for you to tell me you are always careful. I know that. It goes with the territory, so to speak. Nevertheless, I do stress it. Understood?" The man said yes, he understood. "Very well," the voice went on. "You are to make careful note of anyone making contact with her. Anyone, even if they appear to be legitimate customers. Next, be on the lookout for others who, like yourself, seem to take a special interest in her. There could be two, perhaps three, groups who might have watchers there. I want to know what they look like, what they do. Do they go into her shop? Do they speak to her? Do they make phone calls? Note everything to the smallest detail and phone me every hour on the hour at this number in case I have further instructions for you." There was a brief pause, then the voice said, "Very well. I think that takes care of everything. Now what about the girl? Did she leave her apartment again?"

The man told him she had not, that her windows were now dark and he assumed she must have gone to sleep.

"Good," said the precise voice. "You need no longer concern yourself with her. There will be someone else on her in the morning. Your money will reach you through the regular channel. Do you have any questions?"

The man said no, and the line went dead. He hung up and stepped out of the booth. After adjusting the beige cashmere scarf snugly around his throat, he headed west along Bleecker Street, his fine leather boots moving with quick, crisp steps along the snowy sidewalk. A smile played around his lips, and his blue eyes gleamed behind the wire-rimmed spectacles.

9

Hana dreamed...

She was peering out of some dark hiding place, watching three people who were sitting a short distance away at a small round table. Light coming from an unseen source outlined the three heads and cast an eerie glow over the three faces. The bearded man's was one of them. He glanced up sharply all of a sudden and looked straight at Hana in her hiding place. He jerked upright and rose swiftly from the table, frowning, mouthing words at her, and shaking his umbrella. Then, in one of those sudden changes of dream scenes, the bearded man was chasing her, gesticulating wildly, threatening with upraised umbrella, and she was running from him in terror through a dark, densely wooded forest toward a sunlit clearing where she knew safety lay. Running in that slow motion of dreams, her legs moving as though underwater. She knew he was gaining on her, and she tried desperately to pump her legs harder, harder. Then the edge of the clearing was there, just ahead of her. She cast a quick glance back at her pursuer. She saw him raise the umbrella to his shoulder—no, it was a rifle he raised, and from its barrel a bright blossom of fire erupted. She stumbled and fell. A scream, someone screamed...

"Paul!"

Hana woke, sitting bolt upright, gasping for breath and staring around the dark bedroom in terror, the echo of her cry ringing in her ears. So disoriented was she by the dream that for a long moment she remained rigid and very still with her eyes fixed on the door, waiting for Paul's pajama-clad figure to appear, eyes sleepy, hair tousled, but smiling and saying softly, "It's all right, Hanička, a bad dream, that's all. It's all right." When reality finally penetrated her dream-dazed state and she knew Paul was not there to hold her hand, she felt a moment of blank despair followed immediately by anger.

"You're not a child anymore," she muttered. "You'll have to fight it on your own."

It... The past... The bad time...

She reached out and switched on the bedside lamp. The warm glow of light was comforting. She pulled herself to a sitting position, drew her legs up, and, wrapping her arms around them, rested her chin on her knees.

She hadn't been troubled by the dream for a long time, though it used to haunt her for months after their escape across the border. In her imagination she smelled again the rancid odor that lingered in the old tobacco warehouse where she and Paul and her mother, along with hundreds of other refugees, had been given shelter in Vienna by the Austrian government. She could see those rows upon rows of people, tossing uneasily on the rubber mattresses. Some, like herself, waking from nightmares, crying out in the dark...

The dream, though distorted like most dreams, had truth in it. And tonight, prompted probably by Savini's persistent questioning and the intrusion of the bearded man into her life, her subconscious had recalled the hidden memory, had added the new scene to the old ones.

Hana closed her eyes and began to pick her way slowly through the mine field of the past. She saw herself on that long-ago night, a sleepy eight-year-old, getting up to go to the bathroom. Had it been late at night? Early morning? Before or after her father had come to her room? She had no way of knowing.

She watched her child-self move soundlessly on bare feet down the dark hall on her way back from the bathroom. There was the living room door, slightly ajar, the sound of

114

voices, a sleepy child's curiosity. Pushing the door open a little more, she had peered in. Light. Rosy light coming through the window. That was what caught her eye first. She had thought it was the dawn. Later Paul had told her that the pretty red glow was caused by fires burning on Wenceslaus Square. Then she saw the three people sitting at the table beside the window—the round table where she always did her homework. Two men and a woman, heads close together, the glow from the window lighting their faces. No, lighting two faces. She had only a dim recollection of the third person—of hunched shoulders in a light-colored jacket. But the other man, heavyset, strong looking, with a curly black beard...

She had recognized him in front of Paul's apartment building, hadn't she, but she had been afraid to acknowledge it. That's why she had panicked and run from him. And she had been even more afraid of making another connection with the past, but it was there now, staring at her out of the dream, and she couldn't evade it. She shivered and clenched her hands into fists. The nails bit into her palms, but she didn't feel it. The woman at the table had been her mother, of course. The fiery glow from the window that outlined those severely molded cheekbones and jawline made it perfectly clear.

If she had wanted to, Hana had no way of stopping it now. The present fell into shadow, the past sprang into light as the scene rushed back at her, playing itself out.

She was frightened again as the eight-year-old child had been frightened, staring through that partly open door at those three heads so close together, hearing the low, urgent whispering, sensing something secretive, conspiratorial, and knowing instinctively that they wouldn't like her to be watching them.

Had she made a noise as she moved away? Something had attracted the bearded man's attention, for he had suddenly jerked his head up and swung around to face the door. Seeing her there, he had fixed those pale blue eyes on her face with the same intensity that had held her rooted to the sidewalk last evening. Then he had said something to her mother in a sharp undertone, but here the reality differed from the dream, for it was her mother who had risen, not the bearded man. It was her mother who had come swiftly to where she stood, the gray eyes stone-hard with anger, arm raised, hissing, "How dare you pry? Get to bed and stay there!" The blow had caught her on the side of the head, the force of it had sent her reeling back. Then the door had slammed shut, and Hana, in pain but too shocked to cry, had stumbled blindly to her room.

It occurred to her now that she had never told Paul about that blow or about those three people at the table. In the race of events that followed, there had been no opportunity, and ultimately she had buried it in the darkest part of her mind. But that's what had brushed her consciousness briefly when Savini had been questioning her. That's what he had been wanting to hear.

"You hold the key." "If I do, Mr. Savini," Hana murmured grimly, "I don't know what door it fits. And oh, God, how I need to talk to Paul!"

Knowing any more sleep was out of the question, Hana threw the blanket back and climbed out of bed. After pulling off the sweater and slacks she had slept in, she put on her robe and slippers and then roamed the room, restless and unhappy.

Gray winter light filtered through the curtains. A cold wind was rising, rattling the windowpane. It was that bleak hour before dawn when nothing seems possible, when hope and energy are at their lowest ebb. When Hana's gaze fell on the scattering of objects at her dresser, in her present alienated state they looked strange, as though she had never seen them before—the lacquered tray that held her makeup, hairbrush, comb, hand mirror, and a framed three-by-five photograph. She paused in her roaming and stared down at it. Four people frozen in time by the lens of a camera. Four people squinting into the bright June sunlight. Behind them the Vltava River flowed serenely along beneath the ancient Charles Bridge, where the stone saints on its parapets bowed their heads under golden halos in eternal prayer. Across the river the jumbled red-tiled roofs climbed up the steep hill to meet the massive Hrad that crowned the summit, the ninth-century fortress-castle, seat of old Bohemian kings and new communist dictators.

Her eighth birthday, June 21, 1968.

We'll change, Hana thought, these people never will. Her mother would always gaze into the lens with those cold gray eyes, standing apart from them, a stranger, distant and aloof. Paul would always be that skinny, gawky fourteen-year-old, smiling forever that wide, self-conscious grin. And herself, awkward and bashful in a too frilly dress. How beautiful she had thought it was! She was gripping her brother's arm with one hand, with the other clutching to her breast the music box, that magical gift from her father. She had let it out of her hands only once that day when she had allowed Paul to examine it, raise the lid, set the music playing and the tiny ballerina dancing.

"I'm glad you like it, my darling. It was made especially for you."

With an ache of sorrow she turned her eyes to the fourth person in the picture, the tall, slender, handsome man, his hair ruffled by the breeze, his eyes crinkling around the edges as he smiled down at her. What a lovely day that had been, one of their last carefree days in Prague. Tensions were already building, and two months later guns sounded in the city, fires burned on Wenceslaus Square, and her father had vanished. The brutal Russian tanks put an end to the Prague Spring of Dubček, bringing the darkness of destruction and death.

Without thinking, Hana reached behind the picture where the music box stood, had stood in silence for a long time. She wound it and raised the lid. The little ballerina in her lacy tutu, all pink and white and gold, turned and twirled, twirled and turned, on one tiny pointed foot to the sweet, melancholy tune of the Czech national anthem, "Kde Domov Můj."

Where is my home, where is my home?
Brooks are running through the meadows,

117

Pines are whispering on the hills,
Orchards dressed in spring's array
An earthly paradise portray,
And this land of wondrous beauty,
Is the Czech land, home of mine.

She hadn't thought she would remember the plaintive lyric. She hadn't thought she would be moved by it, either, but she found that her eyes were wet and there was a lump in her throat.

The melody slowed, tinkling out its last notes, the ballerina stopped and stood gracefully poised, waiting to dance again. Reaching out to close the lid, Hana's hand paused in midair as her eye was caught by something. Frowning, she leaned down and peered closely at the china figurine, at an irregular hairline crack around its neck. She stared at it for a long time, puzzled. It was strange that she couldn't remember.

"...what to take, what to leave behind. You must have had to make some painful choices." Savini's black eyes intent on her face.

No painful choice with this. She wouldn't have dreamed of leaving it behind.

Hana never tried to account rationally for what she did. With a quick intake of breath, she took the ballerina's head between thumb and forefinger and pressed hard sideways. With a snap the head came off clean in her hand and she was staring at something round and black that was tucked into the hollow body. She tipped the music box upside down. Two tiny rolls of film fell into her palm.

Hana sipped strong hot coffee from an earthenware mug in her warm, brightly lit kitchen and stared at what lay in front of her on the table. She gave only a brief glance to the stained carnation, foul smelling now, reeking of death. She would get rid of it.

The second item claimed more of her attention—a soiled, crumpled sheet of paper torn from a spiral notebook. She had discovered it in her coat pocket when she was removing the

118

flower and her father's letter. It was a hastily scrawled message in pencil in her brother's handwriting. *At nine A.M. tomorrow, Saturday, be in the public phone booth on the corner of Perry and Bleecker. I will call you there. P.*

Her first reaction on reading it had been just overwhelming relief that her brother was alive and well. Her second reaction had been admiration for the man who had put it in her pocket. How swift and skillful he had been! While he was plucking at her sleeve with one hand, he was slipping the note into her pocket with the other. She hadn't felt it at all, and he'd had only that split second before O'Reilly had jumped between them. A good actor, yes. She couldn't believe he had been drunk.

"Nine o'clock, then," she murmured. "Question-and-answer time. My questions, your answers, my dear Paul."

Her gaze rested finally on the two tiny rolls of film. She realized now what her father had been doing in her room that night. He'd known that no matter what happened, she would never allow herself to be separated from the treasured music box. But beyond that fact she was not yet prepared to think, nor would she conjecture about what secrets the films might hold. And for the time being she would tell no one about them. Not Savini. Not even Paul. They were her father's property, and if what Savini had told her was true, he had paid a very high price for them.

She rose and took from the shelf over the stove a roll of aluminum foil. Tearing a strip from it, she wrapped the film in it, crimping the edges in a tight seal. What I need now, she thought, is a good hiding place.

Leaving the film on the table beside her father's letter, she picked up the flower and Paul's note and carried them to the bathroom. There she methodically tore both into small pieces and flushed them down the toilet, thinking that if Paul had chosen such a secretive way of delivering his message, it was the safe and sensible thing to destroy it.

Back in the kitchen Hana felt suddenly weak and trembling with hunger. When had she last eaten a proper meal? She could only remember drinking cup after cup of coffee.

"That won't do," she told herself. "Nourishment for mind and body. That's what I need. Then I can cope." So she measured oatmeal and water into a pan, and while the cereal cooked she ate a banana and drank orange juice. In a few minutes she was sitting at the table, eating the oatmeal and studying her father's brief letter yet again.

She had gleaned one bit of information from its envelope. Or rather she had recognized the significance of the Vienna postmark. Not surprising that the shock of learning that he was alive had caused her to overlook it. He was free and out of Czechoslovakia.

Free? Yes. Safe? No. His enemies would be hunting him down now with every resource at their command. And they were everywhere, those enemies. Here in New York alone...

She remembered Paul's description of the United Nations, where he was stationed as a statistician on the staff of the secretariat. "It's the biggest nest of spies in the world," he had told her. "A watching and listening post for every member country's intelligence service. Not a move is made, not a word uttered in that delegates' lounge, that isn't avidly recorded in someone's little notebook. You only have to greet a man with the remark that it's a nice day and you can hear the wheels start whizzing around in his head as he asks himself: Now what did he *really* mean by that!"

Restless suddenly, Hana pushed the bowl away, rose, and began pacing with short quick steps that rapidly covered the small area of the kitchen. Back and forth, back and forth, her thoughts keeping rhythm with her steps.

Why hadn't Savini told her of her father's escape? She had no doubt at all that he knew. Why, after telling her the brutal story of her father's capture and the torture that followed, hadn't he told her that her father was alive and free? It would have been the kind thing to do. But then she had sensed that Nicholas Savini would be kind only if it served some ruthless purpose of his own.

All right, I'll discount the kindness, but my father worked for Savini. That's why he was arrested in the first place, and Savini claimed to be his friend. That being the case, why hadn't her *father* contacted *Savini?* There are CIA stations all over Europe. Any one of them would have provided quick sanctuary for the fugitive. But her father had chosen not to go to one. By the same token he had chosen not to contact his own son, who worked for the CIA.

No, her father had gone his own lonely and dangerous way —and for that he must have had very compelling reasons.

She shivered, afraid for him, afraid with him, as she thought of what it must be like to be watching over one's shoulder always, to have to be on guard constantly against the casual stranger who might prove to be the deadly enemy.

Why had he gone to Vienna? Was that important somehow? Someone there, perhaps, who could help him? A friend? After twenty years? Or was it just a stopover on the way to his final destination?

You know the answer to that, Hana, she told herself. And her heart started to pound so hard all of a sudden that she had to lean against the table for support. He's coming here, of course. To New York. To Perry Street. To you, to be precise, because he trusts you. Face it. Where else could he go? That's why he sent the letter—to tell you he was coming. It's all of a piece—the music box, the film, the message.

She sat down and stared at the sheet of paper, rather worn now with much handling. Her father must have thought these words would mean something to her. He *must* have, else why had he written them at all?

The phone rang, a sudden jangle of harsh sound in the early morning stillness, making Hana jump. Her eyes were still fixed on the note as she rose to answer it, and it was then that she saw what she had been overlooking all along. The recognition of the importance of that simple notation in the upper right-hand corner of the paper turned her legs to water. She sank back down on the chair. The phone rang and rang, but Hana no longer heard.

How easy, she was thinking, to have missed it! How obvious now that she understood it! But the understanding brought with it a jolt of fear, profound and ice cold; it seized her and shook her. She clenched her fists and closed her eyes. "Oh,

God," she prayed, "don't let me make a mistake. Please, God, let me do it right!"

The phone started to ring again. She hurried into the living room to answer it. In response to her "Hello," she was startled to hear her mother's cool voice say, "Would you be able to come over here, Hana? I want to talk to you."

10

The snow had stopped in the early morning hours, a cold wind had risen, and the sun, struggling to emerge from its cloud cover, managed to send a bright beam down from time to time to set the eyes blinking against the sudden white glare.

Not white for long; dirty slush underfoot soon, Conn O'Reilly thought with a kind of perverse pleasure. He was bleary-eyed from lack of sleep, stiff with cold, and bored out of his mind. After a lengthy, headache-producing foray into the computer for what information he could find on the Novotnys and after a quick talk with the head of his department, he had grabbed a few hours' sleep. Now since seven o'clock this morning he had been sitting in a green Chevy Nova with a defective heater parked in front of a fire hydrant on the corner of Bleecker and Perry streets watching the entrance of Hana Novotny's apartment house. He had chosen the Nova because it was a common, garden-variety car that no one would glance at twice, and with his cap pulled down and his coat collar turned up, he didn't think the girl would recognize him if she happened to look down into the street.

Though if she has any sense, he thought, she's still tucked up in bed like other sensible people on this cold, blustery Saturday morning. Studying the facade of the building, he picked out the windows he figured would be hers and allowed himself the pleasure of picturing that lovely face as it would look in sleep —relaxed and vulnerable, honey-colored eyes hidden beneath long-lashed lids, toast-brown curls pressed into the pillow.

"Honey...Toast..." O'Reilly growled. "It's your stomach that's talking, Conn O'Reilly, not your heart!"

He ate several oatmeal cookies from a package in his pocket and longed for a cup of strong, hot, black coffee.

To divert his mind from the thoroughly unsatisfying breakfast, he lit a cigarette and concentrated on the jigsaw-puzzle picture he had put together based on what he had gleaned from the computer and other more immediate sources of information. One of the latter had been the letter he had discovered in Hana Novotny's coat pocket while she'd lain stretched out unconscious on brother Paul's bed. Its brief and mystifying message had been translated by a Czech-speaking friend.

Kde Domov Můj. "Where Is My Home." Title of Czech national anthem.

Praha. Prague, of course.

And Prague had been home to the Novotnys until 1968.

Okay. So what? Where did that get him?

No signature on the letter, but envelope postmarked Vienna.

Karl Novotny had escaped from a Czech prison over a week ago and had managed somehow to get the hell out of Czechoslovakia.

Right.

And he sends a note to his daughter in some kind of code that she would understand.

Right.

Or wrong?

When would he have arranged a code with an eight-year-old kid? Karel N. had been carted off to prison the night of the invasion, and it's unlikely that he would have been able to communicate with his daughter from Pankrac or wherever. Unless he was able to bribe a guard. Possible.

Or... It could have been a fun thing, some sort of game father and daughter used to play when she was little. The kind of thing she wouldn't forget.

Right. I'll buy that for the time being, O'Reilly decided as he rolled down the window and tossed his cigarette out. Then, turning slightly sideways so as to keep Hana's door in view, he rested his head on the seat and went on fitting pieces into the picture.

Karel N. had contacted his daughter with a hush-hush message. Does that mean he did *not* communicate with his old case officer, Nicholas Savini? Or with son, Paul? Chances are father would not have involved daughter in a situation that could be tricky, if not downright dangerous, if it hadn't been necessary. So that lets Savini and Paul out. Why? Novotny didn't trust the CIA? Had he grown paranoid in prison? Blamed them for his arrest? An easy sickness to contract—paranoia. One of the hazards of the profession. Or perhaps he had a sound and sane reason for his distrust.

Never mind, O'Reilly, he instructed himself. Don't ambush yourself with a lot of questions you've no way of finding answers for yet. Go with what you know.

Right.

It was a matter of history that at the time of the communist coup in Czechoslovakia in February 1948, the STB, the Czech secret police, had welcomed their KGB brothers with wide-open arms. Couldn't do enough for them. Whatever the Russians wanted was theirs for the asking. Unlimited access to the STB headquarters and their most secret files.

But twenty years later it was a different story altogether. Not only were the ordinary Czech citizens shocked and appalled by the invasion of the tanks and armed soldiers, at the sheer ruthless brutality of it, so was the STB. Perhaps that sweet, brief smell of freedom from the Prague Spring of Dubček had been as intoxicating for them as it was for everyone else. Who knows? At any rate, the STB dug their heels in and presented a united front of opposition to their Russian counterparts. And on that fateful night of the invasion fifteen STB officials disappeared from their headquarters along with top secret files listing Czech agents—their locations, their code names, the operations they were running—as well as suspected foreign agents operating within the country. Most of these fifteen officials were never heard of again, and it was generally accepted that the KGB had caught up with them and killed them. One, indeed, had been found a few days later hanging from a tree on the outskirts of Prague. Moral: Here but for the grace of the KGB...

Karel Novotny, however, was put on trial a few weeks after

being captured. A big show trial with all the stops pulled out.... *This wicked man, this agent of a foreign power, betraying the country that had nurtured him, betraying it to the reactionary, war-mongering American imperialists, the leading enemy of our great people's democracy and of all peace-loving mankind in general*... And blah, blah, blah, blah, ad nauseam. And of course the fact that they had a real honest-to-goodness agent of a foreign power in their hot brutal hands made it all the juicier.

Interestingly enough, not a word was said at the trial about the missing files, and as far as anyone knew, they had never been found.

So Karel Novotny vanished into the prisons and labor camps of Czechoslovakia while his wife and children, who had already fled the country on the morning after the invasion, traveled the refugee route. They spent time first as guests of the Austrian government in the tobacco warehouse in Vienna, where hundreds of other refugees were housed; they surfaced next as guests of the CIA at Camp King in Frankfurt, Germany; and finally, having apparently been able to give her hosts enough inside information on conditions in Czechoslovakia, Maria Novotny was granted a visa for herself and her children and they came to the United States. Where they lived happily ever after—until now....

O'Reilly yawned, stretched, and sat up. Lighting another cigarette, he gazed out into the snow-filled street. Where is Karel Novotny now? he wondered. That's question number one, and he'd bet anyone a good hot cup of coffee that he was not in Vienna!

Question number two: Where has Paul Novotny disappeared to?

Question number three: What did lovely sister Hana see in brother Paul's bathroom?

And last but certainly not least: Where has a certain very important colonel from the USSR mission taken himself off to?

Tune in next week, folks, for the further adventures of the Novotny family!

O'Reilly let out a long sigh of frustration and watched a short, plump woman dressed in slacks, fur-topped boots, and a down parka unlock the door of a small shop called SueEllen's Collectibles that was located across the street from Hana Novotny's apartment house. On sudden impulse he climbed out of the car, locked it, and headed for the shop, keeping his head well down in his coat collar. If he didn't want to turn to stone, he had to move around a bit. He could buy his mother a birthday present even though her birthday was still two months off, but when he saw the display of dusty ceramic junk in the window, he was astonished. Did people really buy this stuff? How would his mother like a purple piggy bank, slightly chipped? he wondered.

As he pushed the door open, a bell jangled and a voice from the rear of the cramped, narrow shop called, "Be with you in a minute!"

"No hurry," O'Reilly answered. "Just looking." And suiting the action to the word, he directed his gaze across the street in time to see a man emerge from the basement apartment. He was dressed in a black parka, jeans, and rubber boots and carried a large black shovel. Following behind him came a little girl. She was dressed in a red snowsuit, red stocking hat, and red boots. She carried a small red shovel. The man's shovel cut a wide swath through the snow, the little girl's a very narrow one. After a moment the little girl paused in her work, looked at the sidewalk, then at the man's shovel. She said something to the man. He laughed, shook his head, and pointed to her shovel. The child promptly flung it down and stamped her foot.

At this point Hana Novotny appeared in the entrance doorway of the building, tall, slim, and very elegant looking. Her narrow wool slacks were tucked in the tops of her boots, the collar of her brown corduroy coat was turned up and formed a frame for the oval face. Over her shoulder swung a large pouchy handbag, and on her head a green knit stocking hat was perched, its saucy pompon bobbing up and down as she moved down the steps to the sidewalk. The winter sun struck sparks of gold in the curls that escaped from beneath the hat.

"Ah, there you are, my wild Czechoslovakian rose, my sleeping beauty!" O'Reilly murmured. "And how deeply involved are you in whatever the hell's going on, would you tell me that now?"

The child, on seeing Hana, had dashed over to her, waving angry red-mittened hands and chattering like a monkey. Hana looked across at the father with a lift of the shoulder, then bent down and spoke to the child at some length. Frowning and biting her lip, the child listened and finally, nodding her head, picked up the little red shovel and went back to work. The crisis was over. Hana waved a hand, flashed a smile at father and daughter, and walked away.

"I'm sunk," O'Reilly muttered. "God, I'm sunk!" It was the smile that did it, radiant, like a sunbeam striking the bright snow. It rocked him back. His fatigue vanished, and though it was physiologically impossible, his heart turned over in his chest. *I love you, Hana Novotny. Will you marry me?*

Bemused, O'Reilly watched Hana hop over a snowdrift into the street and hurry off toward Bleecker Street. As she passed him, he saw that she was no longer smiling. On the contrary, O'Reilly was struck by the grave, almost grim, expression on her face and by the dark circles of fatigue under her eyes. She gazed straight ahead of her and walked fast and purposefully. O'Reilly stepped to the door.

"Did you want to buy that?" A sharp voice at his shoulder stopped him.

Confused, O'Reilly glanced down at the piggy bank in his hand, then up into the accusing eyes of the plump woman. "Oh—sorry. I didn't realize—" He thrust it at her. "I'll have to think about it," he muttered, and plunged out of the shop.

You're losing your grip, O'Reilly, and that's a fact, he told himself angrily. A fine thing to be arrested for shoplifting a chipped purple piggy bank!

Pulling his cap lower on his forehead and, tucking his chin into his upturned collar, O'Reilly moved cautiously a few feet up the street. He saw Hana step into the phone booth on the corner of Perry and Bleecker streets.

Uh-huh, O'Reilly thought, phone out of order and no friendly neighbors to let you use theirs? I doubt that, I doubt that very much!

11

It was two minutes before nine when Hana stepped into the phone booth. She had checked and double-checked the accuracy of her watch in a panic at being late. In the end she had left too early, which had been lucky because she couldn't have turned her back on Emily-Jasmin, and the brief interlude had provided her with a refreshing breath of normality.

Holding the receiver pressed to her ear, she hooked the phone cradle down with one finger and leaned against the phone box to disguise what she was doing from any curious eyes. Her knees were trembling, and she wished she could sit down. For God's sake, don't be late, Paul! she prayed.

She was trying to put her scattered thoughts in order and listing the questions she wanted to be sure to ask when the phone rang. Though she had been expecting it, the shrill sound in the confined space made her jump. She jerked her finger off the hook and half shouted, "Paul!"

"Hanička..."

"Yes, yes, it's me." How stupid that sounded!

"You got my message. Good. Are you all right?" Paul's voice was pitched low as though he wanted to keep from being overheard. He kept it that way throughout the conversation.

"Of course I'm all right, but what about you? I've been worried—"

"Don't worry. Everything's under control. Now listen, I haven't much time. I'm sorry about all this hugger-mugger, but I couldn't take any chance on your phone being bugged—"

"I guessed that."

"That's my girl. I knew you would. I had to get in touch with you somehow to tell you about Father. Prepare yourself for a shock—a good shock, if there is such a thing. He's alive, Hanička. He escaped—"

"I know that, Paul."

"You *know* it? How?"

"He sent me a letter. Very brief. I received it yesterday."

"What did it say?"

Hana told him.

"That's all?"

After a split-second pause Hana said yes, that was all, and felt a sharp stab of guilt for being less than honest with her brother. They had never had any secrets from each other. Even now she didn't know why she wasn't telling him what she had discovered. It was a decision based on instinct, not reason. "It came from Vienna," she told him, as though that information would atone for her dishonesty.

"Vienna...Yes, well, that's not important. He certainly won't be there now. Have you any idea what he means, Hanička?"

Again the split second pause, then, "Except for the obvious, no."

"Well, whatever else it might mean, I think we can assume that he's coming here. For all we know, he may be here already. And the chances are he'll be contacting you. He sent you the note. He'll try to reach you because he'll need your help."

"Yes," Hana said, her heart pounding all of a sudden. "I realize that, Paul, but—"

"Hanička, listen, there are people who want to get their hands on Father. A lot of people. There's something he knows, something he has, that they want—at any price. He's not familiar with New York. He's going to need all the help you can give him—"

"Paul—"

"I haven't time to go into details now, but you must see that he is safe. Take him someplace where he will be safe. I don't know how he will get in touch with you—God help him—but

130

he will manage somehow, I'm sure, and he won't be in very good shape—not after all he's been through. Take him somewhere only we would know about and keep him there until I'm able to contact you."

"Somewhere safe..."

"There's a great deal at stake here, Hanička."

Savini had used the exact same words last night, and Hana felt very small and very helpless all of a sudden.

"One more thing," Paul went on. "I'll have to keep in touch with you at this telephone. I'm sorry. I'm sure it's inconvenient as hell, but there isn't any other way. Can you be there at the booth at nine tomorrow morning? Give me ten minutes. If I've not phoned by ten past nine, forget it for that day and come back the next. Can you do that?"

"Yes, I can, Paul, but isn't there any way I can contact you? In case of an emergency?"

"No, it has to be this way, Hanička. I'll talk to you tomorrow, then—"

"Wait, Paul!"

"There isn't time—"

"There *has* to be time. You must listen to me. I'm caught in the middle of whatever's going on, and if I'm to deal with it intelligently, I have to have some answers."

"Deal with what? What's been going on?"

As rapidly and concisely as possible, Hana described all that had happened the preceding evening, beginning with her meeting the bearded man on the sidewalk. Paul listened without interrupting until she told him of the body she had found in his bathroom. Then he let out an explosive "Goddamn the bastard!"

"Who? Who's the bastard?" Hana demanded.

"Never mind," Paul said, his voice tight with anger. "Anything else?"

Anything else! "Yes," Hana snapped. "Your friend Savini came to call—uninvited." But as she gave him the gist of the conversation, she had the impression that he wasn't really interested. When she finished there was a brief silence, then Paul said softly, "I'm sorry he gave you such a hard time, Hanička.

131

Don't worry about Savini or strange phone calls or anything else. They're not important. It's Father. He's the one you have to concentrate on. He's your responsibility. I wish I could help you on that, but I can't right now. You can handle it, though, I know you can. Keep him safe. That's all you have to be concerned with. And don't, I repeat, don't talk to anyone about this. I'll call you again tomorrow. Take care." The connection was abruptly broken.

"Don't worry about Savini or strange phone calls..."

"Damn it! Damn it!" Hana cried, slamming her hand against the phone box. It scarcely eased her frustration, but it left her palm stinging with pain. Half-blinded by angry tears, she plunged out into the snowy street and headed east on Bleecker.

12

Paul Novotny slammed the receiver into its cradle and swung around, his eyes blazing. "You bastard! You killed Krassotkin —in my apartment! What an idiot I was to give you the keys. What the hell did you think you were doing?"

"Are you angry, Pavel, because I killed him or because I did it in your apartment?" Colonel Makarov appeared in the open bathroom door. He was naked except for the large towel wrapped around his waist, his hair and beard sparkled damply, and his skin was as pink and glowing as a baby's from the hot shower. The pale blue eyes in contrast were as glacial as ever. He was rubbing a towel briskly up the back of his head with his left hand. His right hand held the umbrella.

"Both," Paul said. "Why the hell was it necessary to complicate matters?"

"I don't know why I should explain, but I'll humor you. Moscow gave the order for Krassotkin to tail me."

"How—"

"Never mind. Don't interrupt. Krassotkin wasn't very bright, but once he started a tail job, he stuck like a leech. He would have become a tiresome nuisance for me—for both of us—and too time-consuming. It was simpler to dispose of him." The Colonel's white teeth flashed briefly in the dark beard. "Nothing to worry about, Pavel. I made the appropriate phone call and it's all cleaned up now, I'm sure. That's something we've always prided ourselves—"

"The appropriate phone call? Are you telling me that you

called your own people at your UN mission—from *my* apartment—to come and clean up the mess you left there?"

"Certainly. Who else was I going to call? I only wish I could have been there to see their faces."

"Yes," Paul murmured, "so do I."

"The body will end up somewhere in the East River, probably. Perhaps under the Williamsburg Bridge, one of their favorite dumping grounds. So stop fussing. Krassotkin was expendable, a means to an end. His murder proves to your people and mine that I am a genuine defector. And that's what we want, isn't it?"

"Yes," Paul muttered, "that's what we want."

"In our business you must learn not to waste time on unimportant details. Krassotkin was an unimportant detail. Your friend Savini would no doubt agree with me."

"No doubt, but my sister went to my apartment and saw the body in the bathroom, and somebody knocked her out—"

"Yes, I figured the bathroom would be the easiest place to clean up," Makarov said as he patted his beard gently with the towel. "Pity about your sister," he added.

"Yes, a pity," Paul said, and though his eyes were still glittering with anger, his voice was cool. "I told her to forget about it."

Paul was dressed casually in faded jeans, sneakers, and a plaid sport shirt, and despite the fact that there were deep shadows under his eyes and his face was pale and drawn with fatigue, there was an air of nervous energy about him and a kind of wariness that contrasted markedly with the stolidity of the other man. A pistol was tucked into the waistband of his jeans, and the fingers of his right hand were restlessly caressing the butt.

As for the room the men occupied, it was tastefully furnished and large enough to accommodate easily two double beds with their night tables plus a desk and two upholstered chairs that were drawn up to a fair-sized round table. On the latter was a chess board with the pieces in place showing a game in progress. Two glasses and an ice bucket holding a bottle of vodka stood on the broad window ledge beside the table, and on the floor near the door leading out to the hallway was a tray holding the remains of breakfast. All the lamps in the room were lit because though there were three large windows, their drapes were tightly drawn, shutting out the winter sunlight.

Makarov tossed the towel he had been using back into the bathroom and moved over to the table, where he settled himself comfortably on one of the easy chairs. "You'll have to forgive my undress, but until my suit comes back from the cleaners..." Propping his umbrella between his legs, he waved at the other chair. "Sit down, Pavel—"

"*Paul,* goddammit!"

Makarov shrugged his heavy shoulders. "Of course. You're thoroughly Americanized, aren't you? Paul, then. But what difference does it make? You're behaving like a child, fussing over petty details. And stop fingering that gun like the sheriff in *High Noon.*" The man chuckled and bent his head over the chess board. While he studied it, he went on talking cheerfully. "I'm sure it will interest you to know, my friend, that that's always been one of my favorite films. Oh, yes! I used to recommend it to my colleagues for their enlightenment. Here you have a classic example, I would tell them, of Soviet socialist realism—good against evil—black against white—no shades of gray to confuse the issue. And the fine and final irony is that the film is the product of the most materialistic and reactionary of capitalistic countries!"

"And I would say," Paul drawled, "that here you have a classic example of the devious reasoning of Soviet socialism—taking what's just a hell of a good western movie and twisting it out of shape for propaganda purposes!"

"Ah, well... What is it you say? That's what makes horse races? Never mind. Come and sit down and tell me about your conversation with your sister—a remarkably beautiful girl, by the way."

Paul remained where he was leaning against the desk. "Among other things," he said, "she told me that Savini paid her a visit last night and she told him about finding Krassotkin's body."

"Good. Splendid! Of course he wouldn't be sure it was

Krassotkin, would he?" The man touched the scar on his right temple, adding, "Not yet, anyway. Not until he sees the body —if he ever does. But it is something for our fine Italian friend to chew on and maybe find a little indigestible. And what else?"

"She received a letter from my father."

A small bomb had exploded in the room. Makarov hissed and jerked his head up. His eyes were glittering. "What did it say?"

With a small, malicious smile, Paul told him.

"What does it mean?"

"You know what it means."

"Of course I know what the *words* mean—in Czech and in English, you fool! But what do they mean to your sister? Didn't she tell you?"

"She says she doesn't know."

"It must mean something to her. Why would Karel Novotny write her such nonsense unless it's a secret message of some kind that she would understand?"

In a flat voice Paul said, "I have no idea."

Makarov stared down again at the chess board, but without really seeing it. He was muttering to himself. "He'll be in touch with her again. He's undoubtedly on his way here. The files... It must have to do with the files." He looked up at Paul. "Do you think your sister knows anything about them?"

"No," Paul said. "I doubt it. She would have told me if she knew."

"Not if your father swore her to secrecy."

"Swore her to secrecy—Christ, Makarov, she was eight years old then!"

"True," Makarov muttered. "And yet..." He fell silent then for a long moment, gazing at Paul Novotny through narrowed eyes. "You look," he said finally, "like the cat who has eaten the mouse. Why? Are you telling me the truth?"

"Why would I lie to you, Makarov?"

Another silence. Makarov broke it, saying softly, "We made a bargain, Pavel."

Paul nodded, his face suddenly very pale. "We made a bargain."

"Are you prepared to go back on it?"

"No."

"I hope not. It would be unfortunate for a number of people. You really don't know what the message means?"

"I really don't know what it means."

"But you will think about it? You will try to figure it out, of course."

"Of course."

"Or perhaps when you speak to your sister again, she will understand it by then."

"Anything is possible," Paul said dryly.

"That's true." The white teeth flashed in the dark beard. Then Makarov reached over and plucked the iced bottle of vodka out of the bucket. "We'll have a friendly drink on that, Pavel." He twisted the cap off and filled the two glasses. "Come. Sit down. We'll drink to the success of our plan. Then we can finish our game."

Paul moved slowly to the table and picked up the drink. Except for two small spots of red burning on each cheekbone, his face was washed of all color. His eyes, expressionless, were fixed on the other man's face, whose own ice-blue gaze watched Paul with equal intensity.

Makarov raised his glass. "*Na zdorov 'e,* Pavel."

"*Na zdraví,* Colonel," Paul replied.

13

The walk in the clear, crisp air had dissipated Hana's anger, and she had managed to put behind her the troubling questions Paul's phone call had raised.

Tomorrow...I'll sort it out tomorrow. *Sufficient unto the day...!*

Now she lingered on the corner of University Place and Eleventh Street, squinting against the glare of sun on snow, trying to summon up the courage to walk across the street and enter the building on the opposite corner. It wasn't that there was anything inherently forbidding about it. It was similar to many other buildings in the area, all catering to the interior decorating trade—huge warehouselike buildings that housed a wild variety of furniture of all periods, paintings, and objets d'art. The one Hana was staring at bore the gilt-lettered legend on its plate-glass window *Novotny Antiques. Wholesale only. To the trade.* In smaller letters below this it read *Appraisals. Estates and Individual Items Purchased.* On the door, as on those of all its neighbors was a shield-shaped sticker warning everyone that the building was electronically protected against burglary.

The cold wind whipped around her ankles and sent eddies of snowflakes whirling through the air and stinging her face. Still Hana hesitated. She had wanted to tell Paul about her mother's odd phone call that morning. Odd, because neither she nor her mother made any attempt to keep in touch. There was nothing between them that mattered, no bond of any kind. There never had been. That cold, aloof woman, Maria Novotny, seemed to have had none of the ordinary emotions—at least none for her family. Her one concern had been her job at the American embassy in Prague, where she was chief translator for the military attaché. And to that she gave unstinting devotion. Or had the devotion been for her boss? That was possible, of course. If her mother had been having an affair with him, it would have accounted for all those late night hours she kept; it would have accounted for the coldness between her parents. She would like to think that that was the reason. She could handle that, but last night's dream kept intruding into her thoughts like an unwelcome guest and wouldn't go away. And when she had heard that cool voice on the phone this morning saying, "Would you be able to come over here, Hana? I want to talk to you," Hana had been too startled at first to answer.

"I want to talk to you." Just like that. No wasted words such as "How are you?" or "It will be nice to see you." Oh, hell! Hana thought. Think of it as a trip to the dentist. Something unpleasant that has to be done!

She stepped down off the curb and marched firmly across the street, though her mouth felt dry and the palms of her hands were moist inside her gloves. She pushed the heavy door of the shop open and stepped inside. It closed with a soft *chunk* behind her, setting a crystal chandelier overhead swaying and tinkling in the gloom.

The few times Hana had been in her mother's shop, it invariably reminded her of a room in a large mansion owned by someone with a great deal of money who had atrocious taste and was a very poor housekeeper. It was huge and high-ceilinged, filled with dark furniture and clumsy statuary. In one corner was a collection of large Chinese vases on little mahogany stands, in another a group of clocks, in brass, ormolu, porcelain, all shapes and sizes, their timepieces supported by nude women, wood nymphs, or coy little cupids. Too ornate and very ugly, Hana thought. The walls were covered with faded dusty tapestries and large, uninspired paintings that had the look of a third-rate Dutch school about them.

As she weaved her way through the jumbled exotic collections, Hana heard voices coming from the rear of the shop, where a partly enclosed space served her mother as an office.

Her mother's low-pitched voice: "I will, yes. You'll let me know."

A man's voice: "I'll be in touch with you tomorrow, of course." A deep voice, faintly accented and edged with impatience, vaguely familiar. Before she could give more thought to it, the man was emerging from the office, pulling on his hat as he did so. Hana stepped aside to make room for him to pass, peering up at him, trying to see his face, but his upraised arm concealed it. As he passed her, his elbow struck her hard on the shoulder, knocking her off balance. It seemed almost deliberate, for without a glance at her, without apology, he moved on toward the door, a tall, well-dressed, powerfully built man, walking with an easy lightfooted tread despite his size.

"Hana..."

Rubbing her bruised shoulder, Hana turned to face her mother. She was standing in the office entrance, straight and stiff as though at attention, her gaze fixed not on Hana but on the man's broad back. There was a curious pinched look on her pale face that surprised Hana, but there were more surprises in store for her, and as the look vanished immediately after the door closed with its soft *chunk* of sound behind the man, Hana forgot about it.

Maria Novotny drew in a deep breath, cast a quick glance at Hana, and turned back into her office. "I've made coffee," she said over her shoulder. "Come have a cup."

Too much to expect that she would greet me properly, Hana thought grimly as she followed the woman into her office. This was a small area that was crammed full with a desk, two straight-backed chairs, a file cabinet, and a tall, narrow bookcase filled with reference works on antiques. Between the bookcase and file cabinet was a door, slightly ajar, which Hana knew led to her mother's apartment on the floor above. It was curious to think that she had never been there, had no idea what kind of place her mother lived in. She squeezed between the desk and bookcase to reach one of the chairs, where she perched uneasily and watched the woman, thinking how little changed she was. Thinner, perhaps, but a handsome woman still, her skin as smooth as she remembered it from her childhood in Prague, the pewter-colored eyes as cool. She had been very young, Hana knew, when Paul was born, and she would be in her early fifties now though she looked ten years younger. Her nutmeg-brown hair had scarcely any gray in it. Curly, like Hana's, she wore it longer and pulled severely off her face, securing it in back with a barrette, exposing the fine bones of the face, which, except for lipstick, were bare of makeup. She wore a pleated tweed skirt of soft blues and grays and a slate-blue cashmere sweater. Around her neck was a string of pearls, very fine ones, Hana thought, and in her ears were delicately wrought-gold earrings studded with seed pearls.

From the coffee maker on her desk, Maria Novotny was filling two cups, lovely delicate things of bone china, white-glazed, gold-rimmed, hand-painted with pale pink roses and pale green leaves. She placed them carefully into their saucers on the desk beside a sugar bowl of delftware. Pushing one of the cups toward Hana, she said, "I have no cream or milk, I'm afraid."

"It doesn't matter," Hana said. She sipped some of the strong black liquid and remembered yesterday, the brandy-laced coffee with Conn O'Reilly in Paul's kitchen and the dead man in the bathroom. She shivered.

"Are you cold?" Sharp gray eyes fixed themselves on her face.

"Not really."

"I keep it cool in here because of the furniture, you see. A dry, cool temperature is best. Perhaps you should take your coat and hat off so you won't be cold when you go outside. I could give you a sweater."

Hana simply shook her head. She wasn't staying that long. Maria Novotny frowned and shrugged slightly before she looked down to spoon sugar into her coffee.

"It was good of you to come, Hana. I hope my call this morning didn't wake you."

"I was up," Hana said, surprised at what might almost pass for an apology.

"And how have you been?" her mother asked, stirring the coffee gently.

"Fine," Hana murmured.

"That's good. Your work is going well?"

Maria Novotny was still stirring the coffee and didn't see the startled look on Hana's face. Another surprise. Her mother had never questioned her about her work before, had never shown the slightest interest in her "nice little drawings," as she had once called them. First an apology. Now this. Small talk? Why? Her mother wasn't one to indulge in small talk. "I keep busy," she said lamely.

"That's good." Maria Novotny nodded once, replaced the cover on the delft bowl, put the spoon into the saucer, and raised the cup to her lips.

It was a little like watching a slow-motion movie, Hana thought. All her mother's movements had been so deliberate, unhurried, yet at the same time abstracted, as though her mind were only partly on what she was doing.

Hana kept her eyes on the woman's pale face, waiting for her to speak, to come to the point of her phone call, but the heavy silence continued until she couldn't bear it any longer. "I'm here," she said bluntly, "because you phoned and asked me to come, Mother. What was it you wanted? I don't have much time." She could hear Paul's urgent voice: *Keep him safe.* "There are things I must do. I don't believe you asked me here to talk about my work."

"No... or perhaps yes would be closer to the truth." The woman's voice was breathless, a little strained. "I was hoping you and Paul might have dinner with me some night next week."

"Dinner?" Hana stared at her mother, wide-eyed.

"I've phoned Paul several times in the past couple of days to arrange a date. I know how close you two are, and I thought he might be able to—to persuade you." The woman smiled faintly as though deprecating this need for intercession between mother and daughter. Hana continued to stare at her dumbly. "But I haven't been able to reach him," she went on. "And when I called his office at the UN they told me he was on

142

leave." The woman raised one perfectly arched eyebrow questioningly. "It seems a strange time to take leave."

"Not if you're going to the Bahamas," Hana said facetiously. It was all she could think to say. She was trying to come to terms with this woman who had stepped so far out of character that Hana no longer knew her.

"Perhaps when he gets back," her mother was saying, "we might arrange to have a friendly meal together at some nice restaurant. Do you know how long he'll be away?"

Hana shook her head, wary all of a sudden. The olive branch might have thorns on it. "A week or two. I don't really know."

"Have you seen him lately?"

"A week ago," Hana said truthfully. "We had dinner together."

"In that case he might be back soon."

"It's possible."

"Good." Her mother nodded and fell silent, drinking her coffee.

Impatient and ill at ease, Hana waited, her own questions hovering in her mind, but she was uncertain how to reach the point of asking them with any degree of subtlety. Her restless gaze fell on the bookcase, and she saw the clock tucked on a shelf between two large volumes. It was small and rectangular in shape, made of ormolu and bronze and with exquisite enamel paintings on its four sides. Very old, very beautiful, and no doubt very valuable. For as long as she could remember, it had been kept locked behind the glass doors of a cabinet in the living room of their apartment in Prague. No one was ever allowed to handle it except her mother.

"My treasure," her mother said softly, having followed the direction of Hana's gaze. "We each brought what was precious to us, didn't we? I would never have parted with that. And you—" She turned her head to look at Hana. "You took your music box—am I right?—the one your father gave you for your birthday that year."

"Yes," Hana said, her heartbeat quickening as she thought of the tiny rolls of film.

"And you've kept it safe, I'm sure. Does it still play?"

Her mother was smiling, her voice was light and casual, but the pewter-gray eyes fixed on Hana's face had something avid in them. The look startled and frightened her, and Hana glanced away. "I think so," she lied, "though I haven't played it for a long while."

"And is that all you brought, Hana? No other treasures? I find it hard to remember a lot of small details after so long—and so much happened on that terrible night. It's all confused in my memory."

"You must have had to make some painful choices," Savini had said, and hadn't the man's dark gaze been just as avid?

With a forced laugh Hana veered the conversation off into a safer direction. "I have to admit that it's confused in my mind, too," she said. "But I do recall very clearly how firm you were about taking one suitcase—just one—no arguments. And how Paul wanted to fill his with books and not bother about clothes at all. Surely you remember that. There was a terrific hassle!"

"Yes, I remember," the woman said in a dull voice. "It was a terrible night," she added, and fell silent.

To Hana's surprise her mother seemed to have lost all interest suddenly in the subject. She was looking down at her cup, twisting it between her fingers, her expression remote and thoughtful.

Outside a snow plow scraped and bumped its way along Eleventh Street, horns honked, sirens wailed. The city was wide awake and coping in its raucous fashion with the snowfall.

Underneath these sounds Hana heard her mother's voice speaking, so low she had to lean forward to catch the words.

"...sometimes, decisions one makes... Decisions one regrets later, but the pattern has been established and it's hard to break it. I don't know if you understand what I mean." The gray eyes lifted, gazed at Hana, unfathomable.

"I'm afraid not," Hana said. "What are you trying to say?"

The gray eyes looked down, the low voice droned on. "My job at the American embassy... It was always difficult for me; dangerous, even. I had to move very carefully. Czechs working for the Americans—or for any of the Western democracies—

144

were always suspect. Even during Dubček's time, just those eight months he was in power weren't enough to overcome that kind of—of paranoia. And of course if we had stayed after your father's arrest, life would have been impossible for me. It wasn't easy under those circumstances to function in any natural, normal way."

Puzzled, Hana said, "I don't understand."

Maria Novotny seemed not to have heard her. She went on in the same dull monotone. "The job itself was so demanding that it didn't leave me any energy for ordinary family activities. I'm trying to say—that is, so much time has passed, I hoped that now we could be friends, Hana. It isn't too late, is it? I know I was not a very good mother to you and Paul in the past, but that's all over. Things have changed. We could make a fresh start, couldn't we, the three of us?" Maria Novotny, paused for a moment. Then, with an odd smile on her lips, she lifted her gaze to Hana's face and said softly, "I'm apologizing, you see."

Hana might have believed her except for that odd, incongruous smile and a vague, indefinable something in the atmosphere, something off-key. She couldn't pin it down. Why should her mother call her on a snowy Saturday morning to ask her to come over to discuss a dinner date? Why couldn't she have done that on the telephone? And why, now, at this particular time, should this cold, self-possessed woman offer friendship, put herself in the role of a loving mother? Like the odd smile, there was something false about it. And that's what it is, she thought with a sudden flash of inspiration. It's a role she's playing, a role she's not comfortable in.

"I'll talk to Paul when he gets back. There's no reason why we can't have dinner." Hana was hardly aware of what she was saying because she had noticed her mother's hands, how the long, strong fingers were gripping the fragile porcelain cup so tightly the knuckles were white. The woman was not only uncomfortable, Hana realized with a shock, she was under extreme stress for some reason. And her recognition of this somehow worked as a kind of therapy for Hana. Her own tension eased, and she felt suddenly very sure of herself.

Pushing aside her coffee cup, Hana leaned across the desk and without preamble said, "I used to dream a lot about our escape across the border, Mother. It was a nightmare, really, and always the same. I never told you about it. I had the dream first in that warehouse in Vienna, and again when we were in the camp at Frankfurt. Even after we were here, safe and sound, it kept coming back periodically—"

"I'm not surprised. That was a very bad time for all of us, but that's—"

"Past, yes, I know, but strangely enough I dreamed it again last night. It was the same dream except"—Hana grinned crookedly—"except something new had been added. Tell me—Jan, our guide... He was killed there at the border. I'm sure you haven't forgotten that. When I asked you about it later, you became very angry, I remember, and told me he had been killed by a land mine. Then you added something very odd. You said, 'More truth than fiction in that.' What did you mean?"

Behind the woman's gray eyes Hana saw something flicker before the concealing lids dropped over them. "I don't really remember what I said, Hana. I was probably upset, not angry. Of course I was upset. And what difference does it make how the man died?"

"As far as poor Jan is concerned, none," Hana said softly.

A fleeting gleam of something through the leaves, a swaying of branches where there was no wind; two children running, running, while behind them an old man died without a sound, his face pressed into the mud.

"It's just a small piece of a large puzzle, Mother, that I'm trying to put together—that I *need* to put together once and for all for my own peace of mind, if nothing else. I hoped you might be able to help me."

"What's the point of all this, Hana? I should think if you really wanted peace of mind, you'd forget about it. It's finished, after all."

Though the woman shrugged and kept her voice casual, Hana saw the long fingers tighten their grip on the cup. Leaning closer, she said, "Jan wasn't killed by a land mine, was he? And not by any guards in a watchtower, either. I would have

146

noticed that. For some reason I don't yet understand, he was deliberately murdered by a man hidden in the forest behind him. And I think it was the man in my dream—a man *you* know—a man who was sitting with you that night at the table in our living room in Prague—a strong, heavyset man with a beard. He's another piece of the same puzzle—a big piece—and I saw him—last night—on the sidewalk in front of Paul's apartment house. And I know now that he's the man who—"

Hana broke off abruptly, halting at the brink of a precipice that she hadn't known was there until she reached it. The sheer momentum of her words had carried her there. Now she couldn't go back and she was terrified of going forward. Shocked, she could only stare at the woman whose face was just a few inches from her own. All pretense of friendliness had vanished from it. The gray eyes glittered with rage. The years tumbled away. Hana waited for the arm to raise, to strike, waited for the voice to hiss: *"How dare you pry? Get to bed and stay there!"*

Involuntarily Hana pulled back, putting distance between them. As she did so, there was a sharp cracking sound. She looked down at the woman's hands, at the broken pieces of the cup clutched in them, at the blood dripping slowly onto the desk top.

Both women stared at the desk, motionless, as though paralyzed by what had happened. Finally Maria Novotny's harsh whisper broke the silence.

"How stupid of me. How stupid!" She spread her hands wide and let the pieces fall from them.

"Let me get something," Hana said, stumbling to her feet and looking around helplessly.

Still in the same harsh whisper, the woman said, "It's nothing. Nothing. You'd better go."

"But your hands—they should be washed—they should be—"

"It doesn't matter. Do you understand? Go! Just go!"

"Yes," Hana said numbly. "All right." Like a sleepwalker, she moved to the door. There she paused and looked back at her mother for a silent moment. "I'm sorry," she said at last.

"Don't be," Maria Novotny said. The voice was hard and

flat, the face bare of any emotion, and the gray eyes as cold as Hana had ever seen them. "I've done exactly what I wanted to do."

For another second Hana lingered in the doorway, staring at her mother. She had simply meant she was sorry about the cup—or had she? But whatever she had meant, her mother had put her own interpretation on it. Feeling sick, she turned and left the office, weaving her way blindly past the dusty furniture, the ugly clocks, and the clumsy statuary. When the outer door had closed behind her with its *chunk* of sound, she stood on the sidewalk for a long time, blinking in the sunlight and drawing in deep breaths of the cold air to steady herself.

14

After the door closed behind the girl, a shadow detached itself from behind a statue in a corner of the shop. It moved swiftly and silently to the door, clicked a bolt into place, and a moment later the pleasant-faced young man appeared in the office doorway, blue eyes beaming behind the spectacles, a half smile on his lips.

Maria Novotny dropped the tissues she was pressing to the cuts on her hands and started to rise.

"Just sit down," the man said quietly. Maria Novotny obeyed. "Did you find out anything?"

The woman shook her head.

"He didn't really expect you would, but it was worth a try. Though if she knows where it is, she probably wouldn't have told you. From what I could hear, there's very little—rapport, shall we say?—between you and your daughter. There's a chance, of course, that she doesn't know anything about the film, which is all to the good. She's a smart one, though, isn't she? Makes a lot of good guesses. But she'd be a hell of a lot smarter if she'd keep her guesses to herself. Well..." The man shrugged. "None of this is any concern of yours now, is it?"

While he had been talking in a mild, chatty voice, the man had pulled a pistol from a holster under his arm, a silencer from an inside pocket of his coat, and with quick, skillful fingers had screwed the one into the other.

Maria Novotny watched him in silence, her eyes as empty of expression now as though the brain behind them were already dead.

The man stepped into the office and over to the desk until he stood close behind her. His back was to the partly open door that led to the woman's living quarters. "Just sit quietly," he said in a gentle voice. "It will be quick. No pain."

Maria Novotny made a small, helpless gesture with one hand as she whispered through bloodless lips, "I've done nothing to endanger him. Nothing. I never would."

"Of course you wouldn't, and I'm sure he knows that. But, you see, at this point in time he just can't afford to take any chances. Things are moving much too fast. I'm sorry."

The man had raised the silenced pistol and was placing it against Maria Novotny's temple when her eyes suddenly widened and her glance darted to a point beyond his shoulder. He was smiling and shaking his head, saying, "No, no, my dear, that's the oldest trick in the world, too old for a pro like—" when the knife slid into his back at just the right point below the left shoulder blade. He slumped over the desk and then fell in a slow, leisurely kind of way to the floor. The woman made a grab for the gun, but before she reached it, a hand snaked out and plucked it from the dead assassin's limp grasp.

Maria Novotny sank back in her chair and stared up at the gaunt man standing over her. Their eyes met and held for a long moment of confrontation.

The man broke the silence. "No tears of joy, Maria?" His voice was hoarse, rusty sounding, as though he hadn't used it in a long time. "No cries of welcome after all these years?" A half smile, half grimace twisted his lips. "After what I've endured because of you, haven't you even one cheerful word of greeting?"

"I knew you were free."

"And you'd been expecting me, you mean?"

"How did you get in here?"

"No mystery. You went out for pastry to the coffee shop across the street and didn't lock the door."

"I never lock the door when I do that. I'm only gone a moment."

"A moment," Novotny repeated softly, staring down at her with his feverish eyes. "A great deal can happen in a moment," he said. "You should know that, Maria. That was all it took, wasn't it, for that one betraying phone call telling me I could reach the American embassy in safety? Only a moment. God, twenty years have passed, but it's like yesterday! Oh, you didn't make the call yourself. You couldn't very well do that, but it was made at your instigation, under your instructions."

With a thin, scornful smile Maria Novotny said, "Not that it matters now, but how can you possibly know that?"

"Between beatings—" The hoarse voice faltered a little. "Between beatings Makarov took great pleasure in telling me about it. He said it would help take my mind off what was happening if I had something interesting to concentrate on. So when he wasn't asking me about the files, he was whispering: *Your wife betrayed you. Your wife betrayed you.*"

"You were lost," the woman said in a hard, flat voice, "the moment he called me and told me what to do."

"The details fit," Novotny muttered, gazing back into the past. "He must have reached a phone soon after I left him there on the floor. I heard him coming round, I remember, as I walked away." He fell silent for a moment, then added, "I should have killed him."

"It would have been better for you if you had," the woman said. "He was enraged, out of control. I'd never heard him like that." She was talking very fast, watching the man closely. The pewter-gray eyes flared with life, and as she spoke, the woman moved her left hand surreptitiously toward the gun that now dangled loosely in Karel Novotny's hand. He seemed to have forgotten that he was holding it.

"Get him there, he told me," the woman went on. "Get him to the American embassy. I'll have a reception committee waiting."

Still deep in the past, Novotny said with a shudder, "And so he did. So he did."

"I knew," Maria said, her gaze locked on his face while her hand continued its slow journey to the gun, "that if the call came from the embassy—seemed to, that is—you'd respond to it."

"Of course." Novotny nodded, and an ugly smile twisted his lips. "The thing was, Maria, you needn't have taken all that trouble. I was going to the embassy in any event. I had nowhere else to go."

"He wanted to be sure. The more confident you felt, the less cautious you'd be." The woman's hand rested now on the edge of the desk, a few inches from the gun.

"He needn't have worried," Novotny said. "When they grabbed me, I kept telling them they were making a mistake, that they had the wrong man. I kept telling them my name over and over again. They just laughed and hit me harder with their rifle butts. They were Kalmucks. I don't think they even understood what I was saying. Not that it would have mattered if they had. It was a farce. A deadly farce. I was only ten feet away from the embassy gates. Ten feet... I think I knew then—"

"*Zrádce!*" the woman cried, and in a sudden explosion of movement she sprang from her chair and lunged for the gun, scattering bits of broken porcelain to the floor. She had caught Novotny off guard. Her hand was closing around the gun when he woke to the danger. Dodging aside, he swung his left hand down in a chopping blow to her wrist. "Sit down!" he shouted.

The woman fell back with a sudden cry. At the same time Novotny, unable to suppress it, let out a groan as the pain from the knife wound in his arm shot up to his shoulder. He drew in a deep, shuddering breath and through clenched teeth said, "Don't try that again, Maria. You can't possibly change things now." He leveled the gun at her temple with a steady hand.

Maria Novotny sank back onto her chair. She was breathing hard, and her face was pale. She cradled the injured wrist in her lap and glared up at the man, repeating in a harsh whisper, "*Zrádce!*"

"No, oh, no," Novotny said, shaking his head. "You were the traitor, Maria, not I." His voice rose suddenly, strong and full of passion. "I was fighting against a system of government that even at its most benign is degrading, dehumanizing. *You* were the real traitor—you and your friends—to everything that makes life worth living anywhere in the world."

"I believed in what I was doing! I never betrayed my beliefs. You're a turncoat, a traitor to your country! What right have you to judge me?"

"How long, Maria?" Novotny scanned the woman's face with feverish, questioning eyes. "As a matter of curiosity, how long were you Makarov's agent? I have your file on the film, but there's no mention of your first contact with him."

Maria Novotny shrugged. "What does it matter? I was in college when he approached me. I didn't need a lot of persuading. I didn't need any, really. I had hated the Americans for a long time. They killed my parents in Plzeň—"

"A bomb... In wartime... They were just in the wrong place at the wrong time."

"Don't be a fool. A child doesn't take that into consideration. My parents were dead, and the Americans were responsible. It was very simple. That's all I had to know. And when Makarov offered me the opportunity to work for the cause of international communism and against the American imperialists, I didn't hesitate."

"He fed you all the slogans, all that bleak, soulless dogma, didn't he? You were Makarov's creature all along, then, even when you married me. Lead a normal life, he told you. Get married. A woman as attractive as you—it would be natural you would have suitors, would ultimately marry. And it would look better if you did. We were the 'normal' life—myself and Hana and Paul. You were not only a manipulative wife, you were a cold, uncaring mother. If only for what you withheld from Hana and Paul, you deserve to be punished. They were useful to you as cover for your treachery."

The gray eyes glared spitefully up at Novotny. "She'll be sorry to have missed you—your daughter."

"I saw her through the opening in the door. How beautiful she's become. And how brave!"

"She'll need to be brave."

"You're trying to frighten me. They won't harm her. They

153

aren't fools. Hana is safe. You know that. It's me they want—and the film."

"*He'll* find you. You don't think you've really escaped from him, do you? He's here in the city. He'll find you and you'll go right back to where you came from!"

A tremor ran through the man's frail body, beads of sweat broke out on his forehead, the hoarse voice whispered, "Perhaps you're right. Or perhaps I'll find him first, but there'll be no satisfaction in it for you, Maria, no matter what happens. As our friend here says"—with his shoe Novotny prodded the body lying at his feet—"it's no longer any concern of yours. I'm only glad I got here in time. I wouldn't have him deprive me of what is rightfully mine. The thought of this has helped keep me alive for—" Novotny broke off and cocked his head, listening.

The front door rattled, there were several loud knocks. Maria Novotny tensed and half rose from her chair, but the man waved her down with the pistol. "It's locked," he said quietly. Gesturing at the dead man, he added, "*He* locked it before he came in here to you."

There was another rattle and knock, then silence. And after a few seconds Novotny resumed speaking in a soft voice. "I used to fantasize in prison about refinements of torture for you. Why shouldn't you suffer, I thought, as I had suffered? It was an ugly kind of therapy but it helped keep me alive. Now that I'm free, I see all that as a weak indulgence. This—" He waved the pistol at her "—is just something I have to do before I get on to more important matters. I only wonder..." He gazed at her in silence for a moment, then asked, "Is there any point in asking who he is?"

The muscles of the woman's face went rigid, the eyes blank, the lips clamped into a thin line, and she turned her head away.

"A bargain, Maria?" Novotny asked. "Your life for his identity?"

The woman didn't move and made no sound.

"Is it love? Or duty? Is he really worth dying for, Maria—this *Golconda?*"

The woman swung around to face him then, eyes ablaze. "Pull the trigger, damn you!" she cried. "How could you understand? I have nothing to tell you! Nothing! Nothing! Noth—"

Before she could go any further, Karel Novotny raised the pistol to her temple and put a bullet into her brain.

15

Hana strode rapidly west along Eleventh Street, head down, hands thrust deep into pockets, oblivious to the cold, the snow, the few other pedestrians around her. Her only concern was to put distance between herself and the hard-eyed woman. Was she still sitting there in that stuffy little cubicle, gripping the broken cup in her bleeding hands? She would have liked to burn the scene from her mind, forget it ever happened. Not possible, of course, so she would file it away in the back of her mind along with everything else until she could take it out and examine it. In the meantime she had plans to make.

Eleventh Street between University Place and Fifth Avenue is a quiet residential block of well-kept apartment houses, the only commercial establishments being a small wine shop and an even smaller tailoring business. As Hana's long stride carried her toward the wine shop, a black Cadillac pulled to a stop in front of it and a man got out of the backseat. Leaving the door open, he stepped over to the shop window, where he stood gazing at the expensive display of French and California wines. Two men remained sitting in the front seat of the car, and the engine, still running, purred smoothly, sending small puffs of exhaust into the air.

If Hana had been mindful of her surroundings, she would have recognized the man standing at the shop window as the same tall, well-dressed, powerfully built man who had knocked her aside in her mother's shop. It wasn't until she was almost abreast of him that some intuitive sixth sense sounded the

156

alarm to warn her of danger, but by then it was too late. What followed took no more than four seconds.

The man stepped back, colliding with Hana with such force that she stumbled and would have fallen if he had not reached out and caught her wrist in a viselike grip. At the same time he wrapped an arm around her waist and, half lifting her, thrust her into the car. The next thing Hana knew, she was lying on the floor of the car, facedown, a hard shoe pressing painfully down on the nape of her neck, the door had slammed shut, and the car started off, gathering speed.

Panic. Blinding, paralyzing, suffocating panic.

With terrifying finality the trunk lid slammed shut. She was imprisoned in a small, dark, enclosed space, the coarse matting against her nose, dust and rug fibers suffocating her, the scream rising in her throat...

"It's all right, Hanička. Move your head over here. You'll breathe better."

"Why, Paul, what's happening?"

"We have to go away."

"Where?"

"Somewhere safe. Don't be afraid. It's all right."

"It's all right, Hana. Nothing to be afraid of." A calm, authoritative voice spoke just above her head. Then sharper, in Russian, it said, "There's no need for that, Gregor."

Immediately the shoe was removed from her neck. Hana let out a long, shuddering sigh and moved her face away from the rug, gulping in air.

"Hana will be a good girl, won't you, Hana? You'll lie there quietly." The voice spoke in very precise English, gently, as though she were a child. "You needn't be afraid. No one is going to hurt you. We only want a little talk, that's all. A few answers to a few questions."

A little talk. So many people seemed to want a little talk. The cold-eyed men at her door, Nicholas Savini and his shadow, Redstone, her mother...

But the thought of her mother brought with it a sense of betrayal so acute it pierced her body like a knife, and for a moment the pain was real and unbearable. She bit her lip to keep from crying out. Oh, God, she thought, feeling sick and shaken, at least she didn't kiss me!

It was one thing not to love... It was another...

Hana squeezed her eyes shut, swallowed hard, and told herself to concentrate on what was happening *now*.

How long had they been driving? Five minutes? Ten? Were they still in Manhattan? Brooklyn? The Bronx? No, they hadn't been traveling long enough to have left Manhattan.

A moment of black despair. What difference did it make where they were going? Afghanistan, Timbuktu, or just New Jersey—it was all the same. She was lost.

The car made a left turn, slowed, and stopped. Whatever the destination, they seemed to have arrived.

A hand reached down. It held a pair of large, dark sunglasses, wraparound style. Innocent looking, but they frightened her. The hand jerked her head back, and the sunglasses were adjusted over her eyes.

"Keep them on," a man's rough voice said.

"That's right, Hana." The voice of authority spoke. "Keep the glasses on. Don't touch them."

Someone had pasted black paper on the inside of the lenses, making a very effective blindfold. At the same time who would look twice at a woman wearing dark glasses against the glare of snow?

"Sit on the seat, Hana," the voice from the front seat directed her.

Hana obeyed, pulling herself stiffly up onto the seat.

"We're going to get out of the car now," the voice went on. "We'll guide you. Be a good girl. Do as I say and everything will be all right."

Something hard was pressed into her ribs, and as a hand gripped her upper arm, the car door opened and a blast of cold air set her shivering.

"Step down."

She was half lifted down out of the car by the strong hand, and as her feet found the sidewalk, another hand gripped her other arm. She was hurried along, the men pressing against her, concealing her, while they laughed and talked to one another. All very natural.

A voice in her ear. "Four steps."

She stumbled on the second one. The hands tightened and lifted her up the remaining steps. They moved across a threshold and through a door that was already open. Had someone been waiting for them inside the building? That meant four of them against one of her.

Unsporting odds.

Humor in adversity... Oh, Mr. O'Reilly!

She heard the door close behind her, and now she could sense walls, close, on either side, and the air was cold and damp and musty smelling. No heat in this building? Unused? Deserted?

The hands guiding Hana pulled her to a stop. A loud clang sent her cringing back. "An elevator, Hana," the soft voice of authority told her as she was led into the cage and the gate clanged shut.

All hope abandon, ye who enter here.

The elevator rose. No one spoke. The silence was a complete and stifling thing.

How many floors? She tried to guess. Three? Four? The elevator stopped. Three, she decided. The gate clanged open, and the hands led her out.

Another hallway. Again she felt the walls pressing close. And cold here, too. An empty, unheated building. No chance of help. Well, they wouldn't bring her to a building with a lot of people around, would they? she told herself with bitter irony.

Finally they pulled her to a halt, a door was opened, and she was led into a room and pushed onto a chair. A roomy chair, she couldn't feel any arms. She moved a few inches, spreading her palms along the seat. Plenty of room. A couch, probably. Covered with a rough fabric that felt like burlap.

Burlap... Oh, God, what difference did it make that she was sitting on a burlap-covered couch in a room on the third floor of an unheated, unused building somewhere in Manhattan that had four steps leading up to its entrance? It was just a game she was playing, a guessing game to keep herself from losing control, from opening her mouth and letting the screams that were coiled inside her come howling out until she was just one mindless scream.

They would want to know where Paul was. They would want to know about her father. And when she wouldn't tell them anything, couldn't tell them anything, they would kill her.

Footsteps approached her. She tensed. Then a hand ripped off the sunglasses and at the same time wrapped a dark cloth over her eyes and tied it firmly at the back of her head. During the switch she had seen nothing except the shadowy outlines of part of a large, empty room, and she was now even more effectively blindfolded than before.

Sibilant sounds came to her ear. Someone whispered on the far side of the room. Odd, Hana thought. Why should one man whisper when the others spoke in their natural voices?

The harsh-voiced man was saying, "Of course," and Hana's arms were pulled roughly behind her, her wrists securely tied.

"There, that's better." The voice of authority spoke. "Just a precaution, Hana, so you can't reach the blindfold. Not tied too tightly, are they?"

Not trusting her voice, Hana shook her head.

"You are comfortable?"

Hana nodded. *The condemned man ate a hearty breakfast.*

"Good."

Someone sat down beside her. Hana flinched away, trembling, her heart beating a tattoo against her rib cage. A hand on her knee. "There's nothing to fear," the soft voice said. "It is not my intention to harm you, Hana. Please believe me. That would gain us nothing."

The hand patted her knee, then withdrew. The voice issued a command in Russian. "Bring her a glass of water."

She heard someone sigh impatiently, then the sound of a door opening, running water, a door closing, and in a moment a glass was held to her lips. She jerked her head back.

"It's just water, Hana."

Hana took a cautious sip. If they had put anything in it, she couldn't taste it, and she was suddenly unbearably thirsty. Recklessly she gulped the water down, dribbling some on her chin. It was wiped gently away.

This is the softening-up procedure, Hana thought bleakly. The kind, friendly treatment first to throw her off balance, followed by whatever form of brutality they had in mind. It would go like that, back and forth, kind and brutal, until she broke and told them what little she knew.

Is this how they had treated her father? How brave he must have been not to tell them what they wanted to know. He couldn't have, or...

"I think you know what we want to ask you, Hana, don't you?"

It was the quiet voice of the man in charge. He was sitting beside her, and Hana turned her blinded face to him.

"There's nothing I can tell you," she said earnestly. "You've made a mistake. I think it's important that you understand that right from the start. I mean—I don't know anything you'd be interested in. I don't know who you are or what you want or why you've brought me here. This is all a mistake. You're wasting your time."

"If you don't know why we've brought you here, Hana, then how can you tell that we are wasting our time?"

Hana said nothing. She had no logical answer to such a logical statement.

"Right," the voice said, quite businesslike all of a sudden. "There are only a few things we want to know, Hana. And when you've told us, you'll be able to go home. It shouldn't take long—"

"I've explained that—"

"Just a moment. We simply want you to tell us where we can find your brother, Paul."

"I can't help you."

"A simple answer to a simple question, that's all."

"I can't help you."

"Can't or won't? Don't make it difficult for us, Hana."

"You don't understand," Hana said, trying to keep the desperation out of her voice. "I really don't know where he is."

Another voice, speaking in Russian, broke in. "This could go on and on, comrade. And we haven't time for the slow way. You can see how stubborn she is."

Hana had heard that harsh voice several times before—on the telephone demanding to speak to Paul, again in her

161

mother's shop, and in the car that had brought her here. There was suppressed violence in the voice, and Hana started to tremble. She couldn't help it, and she couldn't stop.

"I'm prepared to cope with this kind of behavior, comrade, if you'd allow me—"

"Be quiet." The man beside her answered in Russian. "When and if that is necessary, I'll let you know. In the meantime..." The voice said in English, "It is true, Hana, that we need this information quickly. Your cooperation is necessary. We must speak to your brother as soon as possible. We don't mean him any harm. I assure you of that, but we must speak to him. The matter is urgent and serious. You are very close to your brother. The two of you keep in touch with each other. I know that to be a fact. Now, where is he? Where can I reach him?"

Hana drew a deep breath, trying to ease the trembling, and shook her head. What was the use? She could tell him again and again that she didn't know where Paul was, but he wouldn't believe her any more than Savini had done or her mother.

"You're shaking your head, Hana. What does that mean?" A faint note of impatience had come into the voice.

"It means," Hana said as calmly as she could, "that I really don't know where Paul is. It means that no matter how many times you ask me that question, I will have to give you the same answer because it's the truth. It means first, last, and always that I don't know where my brother is!"

The man beside her sighed. "All right. We'll let that go for a while." A split second's pause, then, "When did you last hear from your father?"

It was too abrupt. Hana had been expecting it, but not so soon. She thought they would question her some more about Paul, threaten her, perhaps. She had been prepared for that, but for this she had no ready answer. While her mind raced off in all directions, she could only sit, stiff and silent, and when she finally started to speak, she knew she had hesitated too long. Any denial would sound phony.

"Why do you ask such ridiculous questions?" she asked, making an effort to sound indignant. "My father is in prison in

162

Czechoslovakia, has been for twenty years. You know that. You or your friends put him there!"

"A good try," the man beside her said. Hana could tell from his voice that he was smiling. "But I'm sure you know by now that he escaped, Hana. He is somewhere here in New York City. He arrived this morning at Kennedy on a TWA flight. We know that for a fact. And he must have been in touch with you—"

"Why? Why must he?"

"Why? Because he has no one else to turn to."

"No one? What about my brother? What about the people he used to work for—or my mother, for that matter?"

A chuckle. "Your mother?" Another chuckle. "No, no, not your mother. He'll come to you, Hana. I know that, and I would guess you know it, too."

Silence.

"I'm waiting, Hana."

"It's hopeless," Hana said. "What difference does it make what I tell you? You won't believe me anyway." And I've told so many lies since last night that I haven't any left over for you, she thought.

The man beside her sighed, then said in a soft voice, "I'm sure it has occurred to you, Hana, that there are other ways of getting you to tell the truth. I don't want to resort to them. Please don't force me to."

"I can't tell you," Hana said, forcing the words out through stiff lips, "what I don't know."

"You're a brave girl. I admire that."

Hana wanted to shout at him, *No, I'm not!* but what would be the use of that? Instead, in the blackness behind the blindfold, she clung to the thought of her father and brother like a drowning person clutching a lifeline and held herself rigid against whatever violence might come.

But nothing happened. There was just silence, a silence that stretched on and on, growing heavier, more menacing, itself becoming a weapon against her, adding to her fear, sending her blood racing through her body. The hammerbeat of it in her throat and temples was so loud it deafened her. Everyone in the room must have heard it.

Just when Hana thought she couldn't bear the silence any longer, that she would faint or scream, there was a scrape of footsteps on bare floorboards and the whisperer spoke. The sibilant sounds echoed through the room for several moments. When they stopped, the man beside her said, "You're right. We'll try it that way, then."

A hand gripped Hana's wrist, another hand pushed her sleeve up. She tried to pull back. *We'll try it that way, then...!* They would hurt her now, and there was nothing she could say to stop them.

"Just a little prick, Hana." His voice was soothing, like a kind doctor's. "Only a little prick and afterward you'll feel very good, I promise you. No pain, no fear, no tensions. We can have a nice long chat then."

While the man was speaking, the hand on her arm had tightened its grip, and she felt the point of a needle, thin, cold steel against her skin. Then it plunged into her flesh.

For a second she felt nothing but pure, blinding terror. Then sorrow swept over her like a tidal wave, drowning her, sorrow that it should end this way, that she would never see Paul again, or Stephen and little Sara—and what, oh, God, what would happen to her father?

She came up for air abruptly as the voice of reason took over. Don't be a fool, it told her, they aren't going to kill you. Not yet, anyway. Not until they find out what you know. They've injected you with some kind of truth drug.

Heart-pounding panic again. She clamped her lips tightly together. Don't speak, she told herself, don't open your mouth!

But she could already feel the insidious influence of the drug at work, could feel her muscles relaxing, going soft like melting butter, the blood moving slowly, warmly, through her veins. As she drifted under deeper and deeper, knowing she would soon have no control over what she said, with a final desperate effort of will, she prayed, *Dear God, don't let them ask me the right questions!*

"How do you feel, Hana?" The soft voice came from a great distance.

A sense of incredible well-being. Mindless euphoria! "Wonderful, wonderful!" she babbled words. "Drunk—no, better than that. Like floating. I've never felt like this before. It's wonderful, it's—"

"That's good." The voice cut in firmly. "But speak a little louder, please. I can't hear you very well."

Hana thought she had been shouting, but perhaps they were hard of hearing. Accommodate them, Hana, she told herself urgently and in a loud voice asked, "Is this better?"

"Much better," said the distant voice. "Now I have some questions to ask you."

"Questions? Questions... The right questions or the wrong questions? No, no, I mean—"

"The right questions, of course, Hana, and I'll expect you to give me the right answers." The distant voice sounded very stern. "Let's talk about your father first," it commanded. "Tell me about the last time you saw him. Just before he was arrested. Tell me everything you remember about that night."

And Hana talked, talked with a kind of feverish desperation, words bubbling up from her throat onto her tongue in an unquenchable flood. She talked and talked, answering simple questions with long, embellished paragraphs of answers. She talked while she floated in the air, high up and apart from her own body, and while she lay on the softest, downiest cushions.

She talked in English and in Czech, the voice of her interrogator switching easily from one language to the other. On and on, endlessly it went.

At one point through the drug haze, she was aware that someone was shouting at her. Something about her father and a mine. *Golconda?* The man was so close she felt his hot breath on her cheek. What had she said to make him so angry when she was trying so hard to please them?

Another time she heard someone singing, "Where is my home, where is my home?" and she felt the wetness of tears on her cheeks.

And throughout it all there was that distant voice, cool, implacable, inescapable, orchestrating the flow of words, stemming them, guiding them to where he wanted them to go.

Then all of a sudden with a finality that was as absolute as eternity, there were no more questions, no more answers, no more desperate need to talk, only the emptiness of total exhaustion.

In deep silence a dark cloud drifted down and enveloped her.

Hana woke, opened her eyes, and gazed vacantly up at a paint-flaking ceiling. It took her a few moments to orient herself, a few more to realize that she could see. They had removed the blindfold.

"Ah, that's my bright Hana," she muttered.

Hands? She brought her arms up from her sides. They trembled and felt heavy, but they were unbound.

So far, so good.

She moved her head sideways and looked around the room. No one. She was alone.

In slow and easy stages, not knowing how her body would react to movement, she sat up. Some dizziness, some nausea. I should be getting used to feeling like this, she thought grimly as she took in her surroundings.

She saw that she had been lying on a spring-sagging couch (where were the soft, downy cushions?) in a large, dusty room that was empty of furnishings except for the couch, a chair, and a battered desk that leaned drunkenly sideways on three legs. There were two doors in the room, both closed, and tall, dirt-grimed windows that kept more light out than they let in. Even so, she could see that the sky was gray, the sun was no longer shining.

How long had she been here? What time could it be?

She lurched to her feet and took quick inventory. She still wore her coat, thank God. On the couch lay her purse and hat. She pulled on the hat and checked the contents of the purse. Nothing missing. They had been thieves, yes, but it was her mind they had robbed when the prick of the needle had plunged her into that strange, dark euphoria.

For a moment Hana stood frozen in the big dusty room as the enormity of what had happened washed over her. A cold hand wrapped itself around her heart when she considered what the consequences might be, and her body began to tremble so hard she thought she would fall. It's a delayed reaction to shock, she insisted, trying to calm herself. It will pass.

When the trembling had eased a little, she staggered toward the door nearest her. It led into a washroom. She remembered hearing long ago the sound of running water. Nausea gripped her, and she bent over the rust-stained bowl and retched and retched. Only bile came up. She couldn't remember when she had eaten last.

After splashing cold water on her face and patting it dry with the dirty roller towel that still hung beside the washbowl, she leaned forward to adjust her hat in the streaked mirror. In astonishment she stared at the stranger who was looking back at her. Dead-white face, bloodless lips, fevered eyes. A small nerve was twitching just beneath her right eye.

"You look like Madame Dracula in need of a fix," she muttered, and turning her back on the image, she hurried out of the bathroom and headed toward the second door. This opened onto a long hallway, and a few yards down she saw the elevator they had brought her up in. The cage stood there, its gate open. Had they used it and sent it back for her? Why? A trap? What more could they possibly want from her!

The building was eerily quiet, no sounds of life at all except for her own footsteps echoing through the empty hall. Yet she had the feeling that someone was watching, waiting for her to step into the cage.

There's still some of the drug in your system, she told herself. It's making you paranoid. At any rate it had every nerve in her body twitching, each leading a separate life of its own. She couldn't stand still. She made for the stairs, running down the three flights with quick, jerky steps, pausing at each landing only long enough to peer around for an enemy who might be lying in ambush. No one. The building was empty and derelict. But on the ground floor a new fear seized her. What if the outside door was locked? What if they had left her with only an illusion of freedom, and she would have to roam through this terrible place seeking a way out? Like K in Kafka's *The Castle*. No, K had been trying to find his way *in*. More fool he!

She hesitated before trying the door, then she seized the knob and pulled with all her strength. With a protesting squeak of unoiled hinges, the door opened. In a flash she was outside, down the four steps, and standing on the sidewalk. When her eye spotted the street sign a second later, she almost laughed aloud in relief. She was standing on the corner of Spring Street and Avenue of the Americas. In fifteen minutes she could be home.

As Hana turned toward the avenue, she sensed someone behind her, and when a hand gripped her elbow, pure blind instinct took over. She shouted, "No," thrust back with her elbow, felt it jab into something soft, and she was free. Whirling around, she ran. Someone called after her, but she paid no attention. She ran wildly, without direction, plunging through snowdrifts. Down near empty streets, up crowded avenues, bumping into people, she ran without pause, without apology. Under the influence of the drug she had felt the overpowering, desperate need to talk. Now she felt the same overpowering, desperate need to run—and run—and run—until she couldn't run anymore, and she came to a halt, clinging to a lamppost to keep from falling, struggling for breath, her face and body drenched with perspiration.

Her mother stalked the rabbit with ruthless purpose, driving it back and forth, around and around, in the confined space of the vegetable garden until it couldn't run anymore and it cowered against the fence, frozen with terror. Her mother picked up the unresisting animal, holding it by the nape with its paws dangling helplessly in the air. "Here's dinner," she said, thrusting the soft, furry body into the child's arms.

A gentle hand touched her shoulder. "The race is to the swift. You win," said a familiar musical voice. "I might add that that's a powerful right elbow you've got."

Hana lifted her head, blinked, and found herself looking into the bony face of Conn O'Reilly. He was breathing hard, but the seawater eyes were clear and glowing with the same intensity she remembered from last night in her brother's apartment. "The frog prince," she croaked, and was surprised by the feeling of relief that swept over her.

"The very same," O'Reilly said, smiling, and pulling a handkerchief from his pocket, he patted her face dry. "Are you all right, Hana Novotny?"

"I'm fine, thank you."

"Of course. I should have known. It was a silly question. Can you walk?"

"I can walk."

"But don't run, please."

"No, I won't run," she whispered. "I'm not a rabbit."

The soft, furry body trembled uncontrollably in her arms. She could feel its heart against the palm of her hand pumping faster than she could count. Without a word she turned away from her mother and walked off into the woods, where she set the animal gently on the ground and watched it scuttle off into cover.

It was her father who was the rabbit now, and it was up to her to find the safe cover for him.

"Your ears aren't long enough," O'Reilly said.

"What?"

"And your teeth are prettier." O'Reilly took her arm and helped her into a taxi that seemed to have appeared by magic in front of them.

16

"Brannigan at homicide. No scar over right eye."

Herbert Redstone was tired, hung over, and depressed, and he listened with only perfunctory attention as Nicholas Savini told the others what he had learned from the police about the body they had pulled from its cold grave in the East River early that morning—perhaps from the very spot he was looking at now. The water had a dull sheen to it like dirty window glass, and he shivered a little as he perched on the window seat and sipped his drink. Behind him the men's voices murmured on in the kind of subdued tones people use when attending a funeral.

Redstone turned his back on the men and gazed with a jaundiced eye at the massive rectangular bulk of the UN Secretariat building that faced him through the murky twilight—thirty-nine stories of glass and marble devoted to keeping the world peace. What a joke! A collection of grubby politicians from grubby countries, all jockeying for power, all trying to get their hands on one another's secrets in order to give themselves ascendancy over friends and enemies alike. *"You are cynic, Herbie. You have not optimism, like me."* Eva, with the husky voice and the tip-tilted blue eyes with their sly twinkle. God, how he missed her! He shook his head and shut out her seductive image, letting his gaze move north, following the river to the Queensboro Bridge. In an eerie way the dim glow of its street lamps looked, he thought, like pale, watchful faces spying at him from out of the lowering sky.

"Krassotkin, then." That was the director's voice, hoarse

with fatigue. No country tweeds for Gilbert Halliday today, Redstone had noted. The man's big frame was dressed in a well-cut conservative business suit, and the craggy face was more lined than usual.

"Krassotkin, yes."

Savini had been right, Redstone thought, recalling last night's conversation as the two of them had walked through the city's snowy streets after leaving Hana Novotny.

"It wasn't Makarov's body she saw," the older man had said flatly, breaking his long and brooding silence.

"You don't want to believe it was."

"Have you ever seen Nikolai Krassotkin?"

"Yes, as a matter of fact, I have. He was in Prague for a while, one of the KGB's so-called liaison officers attached to STB headquarters. I was told he established a kind of record there, made so many enemies among his Czech 'brothers' so fast that he became completely ineffective and his bosses had to pull him out. There's nothing subtle about the man. He's an out-and-out bully. Everyone was surprised that someone hadn't murdered him long before he was ordered back to Moscow."

"Well, someone has now." A cab driving slowly down the unplowed street had caught Savini's attention, and he'd raised an arrogant hand, waving and snapping his fingers. The cab's off-duty sign had blinked on, and ignoring Savini's hail, it had gathered speed and headed for home.

"Can you imagine," Savini had continued, gazing after the cab with cold, black eyes, "that a man of Makarov's experience and ability would let himself be caught off guard by someone of Krassotkin's caliber? Never. In addition, Krassotkin bears a remarkable resemblance to the Colonel, black beard and all. The girl saw the Colonel once—on the sidewalk—in dim light. She drew the face with remarkable accuracy, true, but she missed the scar."

"Krassotkin must have been tailing Makarov. But we'll only be sure of who's who when and if they find the body."

Well, they had found the body and they were sure and Redstone found himself remembering all of a sudden Wesley Drumm's prescient remark the day before about corpses floating in the East River. Except, of course, they had found only one corpse, and there was still not a whisper of the whereabouts of Colonel Makarov and Paul Novotny.

"Stabbed through the heart," Savini was saying. "Very neat."

"Which means Makarov is responsible, do you think, Nick?" Halliday asked.

"Why assume it was the Colonel?" Drumm demanded. "Why couldn't it just as well have been Paul? Goddammit, we have no idea what's going on, have we? It was Paul's apartment, after all!"

"It has the mark of the Colonel's hand." Savini was quietly certain. "He carries an umbrella, you know. Started doing it shortly after he arrived in Prague in sixty-eight. Rarely goes anywhere without it now. It is an umbrella, yes, but it's also a sheath for a rapier—needle thin, razor sharp. Released by pressing a button. Melodramatic and nothing new in the way of a weapon—a variation on the swordstick—but it's the sort of thing our friend would enjoy. He's very skilled with it, I understand, and it's a sign of the man's arrogance that he's never made any secret of carrying it. People who have reason to fear him try to keep out of its range. He's been quoted as saying that old-fashioned weapons are the best, that poison pellets are chancy and cyanide gas can backfire, whereas the rapier is swift, sure, and silent. In his hands that is certainly true."

"Right. Not Paul. I'll concede Makarov is the killer, then." Drumm spoke from the bar, where he was splashing Scotch into a glass with a generous hand. As usual his clothes were as rumpled as if he had slept in them. He wore no jacket, his shirt was open at the throat, and its sleeves were rolled up to the elbows. "He's cold-blooded, he had the right weapon, and he has a key to Paul's apartment, of course. Right? There's no backup for this operation and Paul's no dummy, so he leaves a key at a safe drop for the Colonel. Then the Colonel won't be left stranded in the street in case Paul is delayed. Makarov lures Krassotkin up to the apartment and—whammo! That's the way it was played. Right, Nick?"

Savini nodded. "I think so. He was a stupid man by all accounts—this Krassotkin—but very stubborn. Once on a job he was a bulldog, wouldn't let go. Much simpler by far, Makarov would reason, to get rid of him once and for all."

"The bastard! You have to admire him," Drumm said. "If what the girl says is true, here he is, in the act of defecting, he polishes off Krassotkin, then calls his cleanup squad to come and take care of the mess. You really have to admire his nerve!" Drumm swung his glass aloft in a mock toast before downing half its contents.

"Yes, you do," Halliday said dryly. "If nothing else, it was an inspired bit of malicious mischief, wasn't it?"

"It's the sort of thing he would do," Savini said quietly.

"A bit of dust in the eyes, something to mislead...he's a master at that." From the depths of a large armchair, Deputy Director General Miles Thorsen nodded and smiled at all of them like a satisfied Buddha. "On the other hand, we have to consider the fact that Paul's apartment is now contaminated as a result of Krassotkin's murder, and the rendezvous must therefore be changed. Whereas several people knew of their intended meeting at Paul's, only two people now know where they are—Paul and the Colonel. I think we should give that some thought, gentlemen." Thorsen paused a moment, and the steel-gray eyes behind their round spectacles darted from face to face in a swift assessment of reactions. Then he added softly, "Might that not be a consummation devoutly to be wished? Something more than malicious mischief?"

There was a strange kind of artless and expectant look on Thorsen's cherub face when he finished speaking, and a faint smile lingered on his full lips. Redstone, watching from his perch at the window, was reminded of a precocious pupil in class waiting for teacher's praise for his bright remark. But the look was quite superficial, Redstone knew. Behind it there would be wheels revolving within wheels. This was not a simple man any more than any of the others in the room were. They were sophisticated, complex human beings, crafty and ruthless when they had to be, all skilled in the art of deception. And when it came to achieving their objectives, they were completely pragmatic, unhindered by any moral code. But that's the name of the game, isn't it? Some wise man had said that "morality is a private and costly luxury," and in the spy business that sure as hell was true.

"We are not, I hope," Drumm was saying with barely concealed sarcasm, "going to start playing more guessing games. We have a few facts. All the rest is conjecture. Let's for God's sake stick to the facts."

"No one's playing guessing games, Counselor." Thorsen didn't exactly lose his cool, but the smile on his lips became fixed, and the gray eyes glittered behind the spectacles. "My understanding of Colonel Makarov's temperament is based on knowledge acquired over a great many years, and I know exactly what I'm talking about."

"Well, I wish you'd let me in on the secret, then," Drumm rasped. "What the hell *are* we talking about? And what are we doing here? I have more than enough to keep me busy in Washington, but Nick calls us, tells us to come, we come. All right, here we are. Now what?" He swung around on Savini. "Now what, Nick?"

The dark eyes in the thin, austere face gazed up at the big, burly man standing over him. "We wait, Wes," he said. "That's all I can tell you. No miracles. We wait."

Redstone turned his back on the others and stared out the window. His thoughts went back to the night before.

He and Savini had spent the night here in the AIC building on Tudor City Plaza, occupying one of the apartments always kept ready for any agency people who might find themselves stranded in New York.

They had had food sent in, had chatted briefly with the night staff at the top of the building, and then had returned here to this room in the fourth-floor apartment, where a cheerful fire burned and heavy drapes effectively shut out the cold winter night—helped considerably by the bar's stock of fine brandy. Brandy for him, that is, the inevitable Perrier water for Savini.

And it was from here that Savini had summoned the others with his own special brand of arrogance. "Novotny's in the city, I'm sure," he told them. "The girl knows it or suspects it and is waiting for him to get in touch with her. He'll have some kind of plan to smoke out the enemy. It would be wise if we were here at the scene of the action, ready to move."

After hanging up the phone, Savini studied Redstone for a silent moment. Then with his thin smile he said, "You're telling yourself that Savini is a fool for trying to predict how Novotny might act now. Isn't that right?"

"As you've just read my mind, I guess *I'd* be the fool for thinking you couldn't read Novotny's. But you're right. I was thinking that a man who has survived first Makarov's treatment and then twenty years in places devoid of humanity does not—"

"Does not follow the normal rules of behavior? I agree. But I knew Karel Novotny very well. I'm not exaggerating when I say I knew him better than anyone else did. One's agents are like one's children. You can understand that, I'm sure, Herb. One teaches them, nurtures them, watches them grow, worries about them, and at crucial times one even gets inside their skins."

It was true, Redstone had to acknowledge. A very spooky feeling. And yet...

"I've seen a good many men released from police state prisons after long terms there," Savini went on, "in those places, as you say, devoid of humanity. And what impressed me most about them was their own lack of humanity. They had taken on, at least for the time being, the coloration of their jailers. They had lost the ability to care. They had turned inward, concerned only with themselves, with their sufferings. And most of them were bent on revenge. They wanted to get back at the people they considered responsible for what they'd been through. So it's simple logic. Karel Novotny is here in New York City because his family is here, because Makarov is here, and though he doesn't know we're in the city, our headquarters are only a short distance away. As soon as I heard that he had avoided all our stations in Europe, I knew he had us on his list of enemies."

"Or *one* of us."

"Or one of us."

"I can understand how he might think that we had let him down, but you said 'revenge' and in the next breath mentioned his family."

"It was a fake, of course."

"A fake? What...?"

"Their escape across the border. You're tired, Herb, you're not thinking clearly. Didn't it strike you that there was something *off*, something not right about the girl's story?"

"I'd swear she was telling the truth."

"Of course she was—as far as she knew it. And that's exactly what they had in mind. The escape had to look real for the children's sake. It had to seem hard and dangerous and frightening so if they were questioned about it in the future, they would describe it exactly as Hana did tonight. But you must have found it odd that except for two guards who stood near them and chatted for a while, the girl made no mention of the usual amenities of the closely guarded border—watchtowers, dogs, barbed wire? Their guide tells them to follow their mother carefully. The mother has been briefed where to run to avoid the mines. The path may have been outlined with stones. It's been done before. And, of course, there must be no witnesses left to talk about the phony escape, so the guide must die. But not by a land mine, or Hana would have remembered a different kind of scene altogether. More likely he was shot by someone concealed in the woods behind him—perhaps the person who arranged the escape. It could have been Makarov. Certainly it was someone with the power to arrange for guards to look the other way, to have barbed wire conveniently pulled aside at a certain spot, to see to it that the dogs were kept quietly in their kennels for the requisite time."

"All planned to protect the mother."

"Yes. Payment for past services—and future ones, no doubt."

"She was checked out by us, wasn't she? Debriefed? How did she manage to slip through?"

"We were had. She made fools of us." A cold, hard note crept into Savini's voice. "She was so completely cooperative, so pathetically grateful to all our people at Camp King, answering their questions with wide-eyed candor. You must understand, too, that she was a very attractive woman, and she knew how to use her attractions to the best advantage. Yes, she was good, very good. Came out with high marks all around."

"Who was responsible for her debriefing? Who was the one who was really had?"

Savini slanted a dark, enigmatic glance at him. "Gil Halliday was in charge at the time."

"Oh, yes, that's right. Yes." Why he should feel surprised, even a little shocked, Redstone didn't understand. He had known Halliday was at Camp King. What he hadn't known, of course, was that Halliday had been responsible for Maria Novotny's debriefing.

"Don't forget," Savini went on, his voice as unemotional as if he were talking about the weather, "that Czech refugees were pouring into the camp then—a lot more than our staff could adequately handle. There were bound to be slipups. Another thing one must remember—it was Karel Novotny who was the focus of everyone's attention at the time. He was the traitor, so-called, the Czech intelligence agent we had doubled. I don't suppose anyone thought of Maria Novotny in any context but that of his wife. And as such she was only of peripheral interest."

"Understandable, but—"

"Not really forgivable, do you think?"

"I like to think I would have probed deeper."

"In light of what you know now, of course you would."

"No, in light of all the rules I've learned. In light of what you yourself have taught me."

"I'm flattered," Savini said with a slight smile.

"Surely you would have done the same."

"Who knows? Hindsight is easy. Gil had a lot on his mind then, and when her boss at our embassy in Prague gave her a clean bill of health..."

"She worked for our military attaché—isn't that right—as translator-secretary."

"Actually her immediate superior was Miles Thorsen, the attaché's aide."

He just slipped that in under my guard, the bastard! Redstone thought angrily. He closed his eyes for a moment while he absorbed the shock, muttering angrily to himself, "I should have known that."

"All of this is in the computer," Savini said blandly.

Still angry, Redstone snapped, "I haven't had a chance to get at it yet."

"I understand," Savini said soothingly. "I'm not expecting miracles."

Like hell! Redstone thought. Aloud he said, "At any rate, we sponsored Maria Novotny. We arranged for visas for herself and the children."

"That's right."

"All things considered, do you think that Makarov himself was her case officer?"

"Perhaps he'll tell us," Savini said dryly, "after he's accepted our hospitality. That may be one of the tidbits he'll offer." He fell silent for a moment, then added in an undertone, "Nothing like closing the barn door and all that, but we'll put someone on her in the morning."

"And the next logical step in our thinking," Redstone said, going to the bar to pour himself another large brandy, "is that the wife betrayed the husband in 1968 at the instigation of the Colonel, and the husband has since found out about it—which may be one of the reasons he's come to New York."

The sleek dark head nodded a few times but in an absent way, as though that were a foregone conclusion and Savini had already passed on to something else of more immediate importance. When he spoke it was as though he were continuing some inner dialogue.

"He may be coming in for just one purpose," Savini said. "To protect his agent."

"Makarov." Redstone made it a statement as he adjusted to Savini's switch of subject matter.

"Or he may have more complicated motives," Savini went on. "We'll have no way of knowing until he's in our custody and is being debriefed. And even then we may never know. At any rate whatever he gives us will have to be checked and rechecked against all our sources, every word he utters examined microscopically. We must be very much on our guard—" Savini broke off, seeing the look of perplexity on the younger man's face. "Oh, you mustn't imagine," he said, "that I *want* this man to be anything but the real thing, Herb. Don't imagine that for one second. Just think of what he can tell us."

All kinds of goodies, Redstone thought. My God, names and locations of agents, not only in the United States but in the Western world; descriptions of operations being run against them now, perhaps something of future KGB plans, because Colonel Makarov was a man who helped *make* the plans, who *placed* the agents.

"There's nothing I'd like more than to sit down with Sergei Sergeivitch," Savini said, "and have a long, long chat. And yet..."

His voice trailed off into silence, and Redstone, watching him, was surprised at the odd expression on the man's face and the strange light that glittered in the dark eyes as he added in a soft undertone, "You see, in a way the successful conclusion of this affair might at the same time be a disastrous failure for all of us." He nodded his head a couple of times in Redstone's direction and said, "Think about that, Herb." Then he set his glass down on the table carefully and rose from the chair with the grace and elegance that marked all his movements, and wishing the younger man a cool "Goodnight," he went off to bed. After another large brandy Redstone did the same.

To bed, but not to sleep. Savini's cryptic remark had him tossing and twisting from side to side.

"... *a disastrous failure for all of us.*"

Suppose there was a "mole" in the agency, and Makarov, as a bona fide defector, exposed him. How could you measure the size of such a disaster! The knowledge that for years there had been a deceiver among you, a man who has been feeding your secrets to the enemy, a man whom you might have called a friend, whose company you enjoyed, with whom you ate and drank and talked agency business...

And if it leaked out to the public... Redstone shuddered as he visualized the screaming newspaper headlines. They'd be back to doing business in a storefront window, as Savini had put it, *if* they were able to do business at all.

The impact on any intelligence service when a "mole" is discovered within its ranks is shattering, its consequences wide-spread and long lasting. From Philby in England, to Felfe in Germany, to Paques and Roussilhe in France... These men had not only laid bare the secrets of their countries to their KGB masters for years, but the discovery of their treachery finally had destroyed the morale of their own services and had undermined the trust of their allies—a trust that even now had not been fully restored. This destruction of morale and trust was a "mole's" crippling side effect and one that was fully appreciated and exploited by the Russians. "See how powerful and clever we are," they could gloat. "And how weak and vulnerable you are!" It added to their aura of superspy, false though it was.

And if there was a "mole" at Langley, what then? Quietly dismiss him and go about the disheartening business of trying to repair the damage he had done? Not bloody likely, as his British cousins would say.

Redstone rolled over on his back and stretched his tense muscles, staring with hard eyes up at the ceiling. No, he thought, not bloody likely if he had anything to say about it. No flying off to peaceful retirement in a little dacha outside of Moscow for a man like that, nor even to another kind of retirement—to a cell in a federal penitentiary. Both would be too good for him. A fine and fatal "accident" for the traitorous bastard should be his retirement! Yet even then questions would remain, wouldn't they? Insidious, poisonous questions. Who else is there? If there's one, might there not be two? Or three? How deep does the rot go? Wouldn't they all be contaminated somehow?

All right, Redstone thought, that's all very well, but what about the other side of the coin? The phony defector and the damage he could do. Redstone punched his pillow and tossed restlessly onto his side. If Makarov was coming in to protect his man, not expose him, he could point the finger at any number of loyal men, identify them as KGB agents, and who could prove he was lying? Certainly not the poor bastard who was accused. Hadn't people been saying for years that there must be a "mole" within the agency, for how was it possible that the KGB had not been able to breach the security and infiltrate the ranks of its greatest enemy? How could they have failed to do that?

'My God, the kind of discord and suspicion a false defector could spread through the agency would for all practical purposes make it impotent for years!

As for the film Novotny was supposed to have secreted somewhere twenty years ago... He hadn't forgotten about it, no, it was just that he found it hard to believe in. Too much like a deus ex machina, something magical that would solve all their problems.

Redstone rolled over onto his other side, twitching the blanket up around his shoulders and thinking that if the film did exist and if the girl had it, would it incriminate one of their people? And if so, which one?

What reasons, for example, could a man like Halliday possibly have for selling out his country, for sacrificing his family, his friends, a whole way of life? Here was a real establishment man, an essential product of the capitalist system. Halliday's father, an investment banker, had made a fortune, and son, Gilbert, had gone the privileged route of prep school, Princeton, graduate school, from there to the State Department, and a few years later into the CIA, having been recruited by Halliday's predecessor, the former director. Gilbert Halliday was said to be a devoted family man, married for more than thirty-five years to the same woman (a record in this day!) and happily so, by all accounts (though who could really know?). He had three children and four grandchildren.

Redstone found it difficult, if not impossible, to believe that a man like Halliday could be leading a dangerous double life that might end finally in some drab dacha in Russia.

Stranger things had happened, though, hadn't they, and some men were arrogant enough to believe they would never be caught.

And Halliday had been in Frankfurt in August 1968...

And he had debriefed Maria Novotny and had given her a clean bill of health...

There was that.

Still, all things considered, Redstone found it easier to believe that Wesley Drumm might be the deceiver, Drumm of the raspy voice and the quick temper, whose clothes never seemed to fit and who appeared to have very little regard for material things, but whose crude outward manner concealed a brilliant legal mind and whose position as general counsel for the agency placed him in a very powerful position. Drumm had gone through three marriages and was now two years into the fourth with a woman some fifteen years younger than himself, and rumor had it that the icing was off that cake and the marriage was foundering. He had four children whose pictures in every stage of growth covered all available space in his office. He talked of them often and seemed devoted to them. If the crunch came, would he be able to leave them? And what about his close friend, Halliday, who had brought him into the agency? Could he sell him out?

That, too, had been known to happen.

And he had been in Prague in August 1968 . . .

Of course, he might betray the service, Redstone thought sardonically, just to spite Thorsen!

Which brings me to the agency's deputy director, Brigadier General Miles Thorsen, a vain and pompous man, whose record at West Point, so Redstone had heard, had been quite unspectacular, but who had found his true calling with army intelligence first, then with the CIA. Though Redstone disliked the man, he sensed that they had something in common—the enjoyment of the arcane practices of the spy business for their own sake. His marriage to a beautiful and wealthy woman had ended in tragedy. Husband and wife had been on a holiday in Slovakia's Tatra Mountains, skiing, and the wife had taken a spill. Somehow her ski pole had pierced her skull—three inches of pointed steel. This happened in February 1968, and though Thorsen stayed on at the embassy in Prague, he was apparently so devastated by his wife's death that he was of little use in his job, and finally in September of that year, he had been shipped home on extended sick leave.

But . . .

He had been in Prague at the key time of Karel Novotny's arrest. And his character reference of Maria Novotny must have influenced Halliday's judgment.

All very well, Redstone thought, twisting restlessly over to his other side, but what would motivate a man like Thorsen to jeopardize his way of life? He had a grown son on the West Coast and a mistress, so rumor had it, tucked away somewhere in Watergate. He had a fortune, he could retire any time he liked, live in luxury, satisfy any whim. Why should he take a chance of losing all that? Thorsen struck him as something of a sybarite, someone who would not enjoy an ascetic life.

And thinking of the ascetic life brought him last but not least to Nicholas Savini, the Monk, the mystery man. No one knew much about his private life—or if he really had one. Maybe when he left his office at Langley he simply ceased to exist, faded away like the Cheshire cat in *Alice's Adventures in Wonderland,* leaving behind only that thin, sardonic smile floating over his desk—on guard, so to speak.

The image amused Redstone for a moment, but the amusement faded as he considered the possibility of his boss as the "mole." By calling attention to his suspicions of a traitor in the agency, Savini, of course, was diverting suspicion from himself. By continually casting doubts on the validity of Makarov's defection, he was preparing the way for discrediting anything Makarov might tell them during debriefing. And if the Colonel should point the accusing finger at Savini, who would believe him if Savini had convinced them that the Colonel was a plant?

He would hate to discover that he had placed his faith in someone whose apparent singleminded devotion to the agency concealed his treachery.

But...

Under the cover of head of the U.S. Information Service in Prague, Savini had been the CIA's chief of station in 1968, and as Karel Novotny's case officer he had been in a position to command Novotny's complete trust. If Savini had directed him to the embassy that night (and into the arms of the Russians), Novotny wouldn't have hesitated to go.

Redstone wished he were clairvoyant or had some magic formula that would enable him to look into the hearts of these men and discover if there was a traitor among them. He could put an end then to the abnormal insanity of "find the mole" so they could all return to the normal insanity of the spy business;

so he could go back to where he belonged—to his base in the embassy in Prague on that street with the unpronounceable name, Tržiště, to his comfortable apartment in the lovely baroque building on Loretanská, and most of all to those evenings when he could relax at the ancient tavern, U Fleků, with a stein of the rich, amber Pilsner Urquell on the old carved table in front of him and across from him Eva of the golden hair and the wicked blue eyes and the lush, sensuous body...

Goddamn him to hell! Whoever he is... If he is...

Behind his closed lids Redstone tried to hold on to the pleasurable image of Eva, but the more recent one of Hana Novotny kept intruding. He saw again her dead-white face and blazing eyes, heard again the pain in her voice as she shouted at Savini. And when at last he had fallen into a troubled sleep, he carried her image with him.

"And what's that damned Irishman doing, sniffing around?"

"Were they sure?"

"Absolutely!"

Redstone came back to the present with a start. He had been far away, so lost in his thoughts of the night before that he must have missed something here. Drumm, he noticed, was at the bar again. Or hadn't he left it? The man seemed to have an endless capacity for Scotch. "We're going to *have* to liaise with Polson now, Gil," he was saying. "There's just no way of getting out of it."

"Not yet," Halliday said sharply.

"There'll be hell to pay if we don't, I'm warning you. They'll raise a stink from here to Nome, Alaska—and they'll be within their rights, I might add."

"O'Reilly may be off on a tangent of his own," Thorsen put in gently. "He's done that before—and been called on the carpet for it."

"We hope," Drumm rasped. "But I don't think we should take the chance. Besides, our friends in the Bureau have resources here in the city that we don't have, avenues of inquiry that are closed to us. They could prove useful. I can call Polson and explain—"

Halliday cut him off, his voice knife sharp with impatience. "I said not yet, Wes. We'll bring them in on the debriefing at some point, but in the meantime I repeat what I said last night —this matter remains strictly between us. I'm prepared to handle whatever flak there may be in the future. Our out is very simple—we had no choice. Makarov said he would come to us and only to us. We didn't want to take the chance of losing him."

"Only to Paul," Thorsen reminded Halliday.

"It's the same thing."

But was it? Redstone wondered. If it was the same thing, then why wasn't Colonel Sergei Sergeivitch by now securely ensconced behind the high stone walls of that very luxurious safe house "somewhere" in Virginia?

"And that's not all," Drumm went on, taking a kind of gloomy pleasure, it seemed to Redstone, in listing what could go wrong. "We'll soon have coldly courteous gentlemen from the Soviet embassy knocking on our door. Have we heard from the Colonel by any chance? they'll want to know. Have we seen him at all lately? We just wondered, they'll say, if he might have dropped in for a cup of tea. *Nyet?* Well, we'll just toddle over then to your State Department and check up there. There'll be a hell of a stink from that quarter when they find out that we *have* heard from his nibs!"

Waving a weary hand in the air, Halliday said, "All right, Wes, don't belabor it. They'd have no way of finding out when the Colonel contacted us, and we'll cross that bridge when we come to it. We're all pretty tired. I think we should save our energy for concentrating on the essentials—"

The discreet buzz of the phone on the desk interrupted Halliday. Thorsen, being closest, picked it up and after identifying himself listened in silence for some time. From where he sat, Redstone could only hear squawking sounds from the other end of the line, but as he watched the General's round, bespectacled face, he saw his eyebrows go up in surprise. Then he pulled a yellow pad from the drawer and began to make notes, his lips drawn into a tight, disapproving line. At one point he asked sharply, "And a man as well, you say? Any ID? . . . What did he look like?... I see." Another long period of listening followed, a few more notes, then a curt "Very well. As soon as possible."

Thorsen cradled the receiver and turned to face the others, pausing just a moment before dropping his bomb.

"Speaking of essentials, Gil, that was Storm and Wallman reporting in. Maria Novotny, Karel's wife, has been killed. She was found in her shop this morning by a customer. A young man's body was found with hers. No ID. Maria Novotny was shot. The young man was stabbed. The gun is missing, but the knife was still in the man's body. His back, to be precise."

There was just a split second's silence. Then Halliday turned to Savini and in a quiet, dispassionate voice said, "I assume this is what you meant, Nick, about being at the scene of the action? Did you expect this?"

With equal dispassion Savini said, "Let's just say there is logic in what happened."

"Logic!" Drumm stabbed the air with his cigarette and paced back and forth in front of the bar. "Novotny's here in the city, then, as you thought he might be, Nick, is that right? He's responsible for this? That's what you're saying? If what you told us is true, he's killed his wife in retribution. And the young man? What about him?" For some reason Drumm directed these last questions to Thorsen. "Was he just an innocent bystander, someone who got in the way? Or someone—"

"I'm sure the police will sort that out, Wes," Thorsen said, his voice acid-coated. "But there's more, if you can settle down long enough to listen."

"More?" rasped Drumm, swinging around to the bar. "Hallelujah! This is our lucky day, isn't it, Miles? Well, let's have it. I'm fortified." He splashed a large dollop of whiskey into his glass and turned to face Thorsen, grinning wolfishly at him.

"Storm and Wallman will be here soon to give us detailed reports," Thorsen said, turning his back on Drumm and directing his remarks to Halliday. "But they thought we would like to know soonest—their word—that in their search of the girl's apartment, they found two things of interest. One was a small pistol. I think you'll agree with me that that is irrelevant to our problem, though it isn't the sort of thing you regularly find in a girl's apartment, and though it's beside the point, I would suspect that Paul gave it to her. At any rate, Storm said they left it where they found it—which was one of their smarter moves."

"Hard to get reliable help these days," Drumm murmured into his drink.

Thorsen cast a look at Drumm that would have cut into steel before he went on. "What is interesting and much more to the point is the second thing they found—a music box. It was in her bedroom, and it's the kind where you lift the lid to set the music playing. This one has a tiny figure of a ballerina that dances to the music. Storm said the figure's head was snapped off, and though its body cavity was empty, the size was right to conceal a roll or two of microfilm."

"That's pretty slim evidence, Miles," Halliday said. "The film might have been hidden in the figure of the ballerina because its head was broken off? Doesn't prove anything, does it? And how do they know where the music box came from? She could have picked it up here in New York—or anywhere, for that matter."

"They're on firmer ground there. Storm described a snapshot that stood beside the music box—a family group showing her as a child, holding it. The background was unmistakably Prague. And the music it played," Thorsen added with a wry smile, "was the Czech national anthem, of all things."

"The treasure an eight-year-old child carried with her across the border," Savini interjected softly. "The one thing she wouldn't part with. And of course Karel knew that very well. He probably gave it to her."

"I see," Halliday said. "Well, it still isn't absolutely conclusive, is it?"

Halliday uncertain, clutching at straws? Redstone wondered. He tried to shake off the heavy sense of foreboding that was taking hold of him. He wasn't all that imaginative a man, but he felt that they were heading for a bloody confrontation. He even felt he could hear the faint ticking of a bomb somewhere in the background. If the girl had the film and if the father was here in the city, they would certainly get together. There

187

couldn't be any doubt about that. And when they did, the bomb would be armed.

Which one?

You pays your money and you takes your choice, Redstone thought grimly. Deception was a way of life for them, after all. They were all masters of the art. His gaze moved swiftly from one man to the other. To Halliday, whose craggy face had an unhealthy gray tinge to it and looked as though it had been carved from granite; to Thorsen, leaning against the desk, arms folded across the gaudy expanse of the brocade waistcoat, his steel-hard eyes behind the horn-rimmed spectacles busy on their own assessing journey around the room; to Drumm at the bar, pouring himself yet another drink, cigarette dangling from his lips, eyes narrowed and frowning against the smoke; finally to Nicholas Savini, seemingly the most relaxed of them all, lying back in the armchair, his thin face impassive as he gazed past Redstone's shoulder out of the window. Only the dark eyes were coldly alive, glittering beneath their heavy lids.

Which one might the bomb destroy?

Redstone picked up his glass and joined Drumm at the bar. He needed another drink, a large one.

17

"Not fancy but nourishing," O'Reilly said as he put two mugs of hot coffee, two bowls of steaming soup, and a plate of ham-and-cheese sandwiches on the small table by the window in Hana's kitchen. "This domestic side of my nature," he added, flashing her a smile, "is one of my more endearing attributes, don't you think?"

The man had refused to leave Hana at the entrance to her building, had followed her up the three flights of stairs and insisted on coming in "for a few minutes only, sleeping beauty, just to check that everything's all right."

Hana didn't argue. She was too tired, disoriented, and still strung out from the drug. Actually, if she had thought about it, she would have admitted that she found his presence comforting. The wide smile on the bony, clever face and the warmth and concern in those seawater eyes were soothing to her jangled nerves.

Immediately upon entering and without bothering to ask her permission, O'Reilly loped off on a tour of the apartment, nodding his head from time to time and remarking, "Nice, yes, *very* nice," as though he were thinking of moving in or of taking over the lease. It was quickly done, but Hana noticed that he didn't miss dark corners and even pulled open her closet door and rummaged through her clothes.

She watched it all with an objective kind of interest as though she weren't directly involved, neither protesting nor commenting. Only later did she connect the quick skill of his search with his prompt reaction the night before in dealing with her drunken messenger and wonder about the professionalism of such behavior.

In the kitchen he waved her to a seat with a flourish, saying, "No need to show me where things are. When it comes to food, my instincts are infallible. Rest. Take it easy. You look beat."

"No, Mr. O'Reilly, I'm not beat. I've just begun to fight."

The words had come out before she knew what she was going to say. Hana bit her lip and looked down, avoiding O'Reilly's startled gaze. She told herself angrily to be careful. Some of the drug was still in her system, putting words into her mouth, or it could simply be the carelessness of fatigue.

Strangely enough, O'Reilly didn't ask her what she meant. He seemed to have his own ideas about that, for with an odd look on his face, he said softly, "I don't know whether to be glad or sorry to hear that." Then he turned away and poked through a drawer until he found the spoons he was looking for. "We'll eat first," he said, sitting down opposite her. "Then you can tell me about your friends in the big black Cadillac."

Hana spooned soup into her mouth voraciously, but kept her gaze fixed on the man. She chewed, swallowed, and said, "Déjà vu. We played this scene yesterday in my brother's apartment. And they weren't friends of mine, Mr. O'Reilly— not by a long shot—though I don't need to tell you that, do I?" She went back to her soup without waiting for an answer, eating swiftly, neatly, and with single-minded concentration. By the time she had finished, a little color had returned to her face and some of the tension had eased around the eyes and across the cheekbones.

"That's better," Hana said with a sigh. "I was hungry." She dropped the spoon into the soup bowl and reached for a sandwich, adding with a note of surprise, "I was very hungry."

"It was all that exercise," O'Reilly told her. "For someone who's not a rabbit, you can sure run like one."

"You're not eating your soup," Hana said coolly. "It will get cold. And I would like some more coffee, please." She pushed her cup across the table. "And while you're up, you could get me a glass of water as well."

190

"How do you expect me to eat my soup," O'Reilly demanded in a pained tone of voice as he got up, "if you continue to make these unreasonable, insatiable demands on me?"

"How is it," Hana asked, ignoring his clowning, "that you always turn up at these times of crisis in my life, Mr. O'Reilly? Could you tell me that?"

"Just luck, I guess. Do you want ice in your water?"

"No, thank you, and no, I wouldn't call it luck. It's more than that, I'm sure. It must have a part in the overall scheme of things, though I don't know what that is yet—neither the part nor the scheme, that is. You were following me, weren't you? Why were you doing that?"

O'Reilly, standing on the other side of the table, stared down at her for a moment, and if Hana hadn't known it was impossible, she would have thought he was embarrassed. There was a slight flush on his cheeks, and his eyes were wary. He started to say something, changed his mind, and turned away. "I'll get your water," he murmured, and became very busy looking for a glass, opening and closing cupboard doors with a lot of banging until he found one. He filled it with a gush of water from the tap and set it down in front of her. As he did so, Hana, who had been watching him with a thoughtful frown, nodded once sharply and rose from her chair.

"Thank you for the water," she said, "and excuse me."

She headed for the living room, and after a quick consultation with the phone directory, she picked up the telephone and dialed a number. On the second ring a voice answered, "Federal Bureau of Investigation. Can I help you?" Hana told the voice she would like to speak to Conn O'Reilly, and when the voice matter-of-factly told her that Special Agent O'Reilly wasn't there right now and could someone else help her, Hana said, "No, I'm afraid he's the only one I can speak to on this matter. Thank you." She hung up and returned to the kitchen, where she found O'Reilly sitting at the table with two cups of steaming coffee in front of him and a rueful expression on his face.

Arms folded, honey-brown eyes glowing with anger, Hana faced him across the table. "What, may I ask, is so special about you, Special Agent O'Reilly?"

191

O'Reilly held his hands out, palms up. "I'm sorry. What else can I tell you?"

"Plenty! You might start by telling me why you lied to me."

"It wasn't that I lied, exactly. It's just that I didn't tell you the truth."

"That's sophistry."

"Be reasonable. In the beginning am I going to say to a semi-conscious woman, I'm with the FBI, ma'am, and I'm investigating... well, something or other. I'm not sure what it is, exactly, but there is something around here that smells mighty fishy, and I wonder if you could tell me what it is."

"You're evading the issue. What about later?"

"Later..." O'Reilly paused, then added, his voice dropping low, "Later it began to get complicated."

"Like your thinking maybe I might be involved in some kind of hanky-panky?"

"Something like that." Seawater eyes gleaming, O'Reilly grinned up at her. "Impossible, isn't it?"

Hana ignored the grin. "And what about Paul? Was that a lie about your being his friend?"

"No," O'Reilly said firmly. "It was not. I've known your brother for a couple of years now, mostly in a professional capacity, it's true, but we're on friendly terms. Ask him—when you see him, that is."

"I will," Hana said coolly, ignoring the implication in his statement.

"Don't stand there looking like a hanging judge, Hana me darlin'. Sit down, please, and say you forgive me. I'm on your side. You know that, don't you? You can trust me."

After a moment's hesitation Hana sat down, surprised to feel that her anger had almost completely dissipated. She felt that she was letting herself down somehow, that she should stay angry longer over the man's deception, but the fact was that she was just too tired to dredge up the energy to remain angry. And there was an element of relief, too, in the disclosure. O'Reilly's manner toward her had never been the least bit threatening. On the contrary... She broke off there, not wanting to pursue that thought any further. At any rate, she decided, trust him or not, she must guard what she said for her father's sake.

"If you're one of the good guys," Hana said, accepting with a nod of thanks the cup of coffee O'Reilly pushed over to her, "perhaps you'll tell me why you didn't rush to the aid of the maiden in distress when you saw my friends, as you called them, pick me up and literally carry me off in their Cadillac?"

"I didn't fancy the odds—three against one."

"A likely story. Only it was four."

"Four? I saw three escort you into the building."

"There was another man waiting inside. That is, I'm assuming it was a man. I call him the whisperer."

"Oh?"

"He never spoke aloud. He only whispered."

"Because you might recognize his voice. Someone you know already, or someone you might meet later."

Hana smiled slightly. "Or he could just have had a severe case of laryngitis."

"That's my girl. Up to her old tricks again." He beamed at her across the table. "Tell me, what would happen when this man whispered? Did he seem to be giving orders?"

"It was more like he was making suggestions. He was not subordinate but equal, I'd say, to the one I called the boss, the one who was asking the questions. *He* wasn't taking orders from anyone. He was very much in charge. But he listened to the others and followed advice where he agreed with it. At least that was my impression. You understand first of all I was blindfolded all the time, and second, I didn't feel—that is, I wasn't—" Hana broke off, swallowing hard.

"You weren't altogether calm and in control." The light, musical voice was gentle and reassuring. "I know that. You were frightened—"

"I was terrified. I had no idea what they might do."

"They wouldn't have hurt you," O'Reilly said, and his voice was not gentle anymore but hard and cold. "That's for sure."

"How do you know that?"

"They would have nothing to gain by it. I have a good idea of how their devious minds work. Now that my life is an open book and my hideous secret is out...I'm on the Soviet desk of the FBI's Counterintelligence Section here in New York. These men who picked you up were Russians, of course, KGB officers from their UN mission here. I recognized one of them, probably the one you call the boss."

Hana, who had been crumbling a piece of bread crust between her fingers while listening, nodded and murmured, "All members in good standing of the leather coat brigade. I did have my suspicions of them." She then swept her crumbs into a neat pile, picked up her empty soup bowl, and holding it below table level carefully brushed the crumbs into it.

Frowning, O'Reilly watched her. When she finished he said, "Now that everything's tidy, would you tell me, please, what these men wanted to know? What questions did they ask?"

"Where is your father, Hana?"

"Kde domov můj."

"No nonsense, Hana. Let's have the truth. He's here in New York. We know that. He must have been in touch with you by now. Tell us where he is. Where have you arranged to meet him?"

"Praha."

"Stop playing games, you bitch!" A new voice, hard and vicious. Very close. A spray of saliva on her face. "Tell us the truth, goddammit, or I'll make you sorry you didn't! Where is your father? Where is he?"

"Hana..."

Hana blinked and brought her eyes up to meet O'Reilly's.

"Where were you off to, girl? Are you all right?"

"Just something I remembered. I'm fine."

"Holy Mother of God, will you listen to the girl? She's fine. Sure it's superwoman herself I'm talking to, right enough!"

The rolling eyes, the thick brogue, the prayerful hands flung into the air, broke through Hana's defenses and brought a quick, involuntary smile to her face. It came and went in a second, but for that second bright sunshine filled the kitchen for O'Reilly, giving him the same kind of jolt it had given him earlier when he had been watching her through the shop window. His breath caught in his throat, and his heart turned around in his chest. He looked away for a moment, muttering something under his breath.

"Beg pardon?" Hana said.

"I said—" O'Reilly cleared his throat. "What questions did they ask you?"

"I don't remember all that well. They gave me something—"

"They gave you something? You mean they injected you with a drug?"

Hana nodded and said dryly, "To make the question-and-answer period go more smoothly, I suppose."

"The bastards! I didn't think they'd go that far. I'm sorry, Hana. The bastards!" O'Reilly was so upset by what she had told him that he spilled his coffee and had to spend several moments wiping it up. He cursed all the while under his breath. When he finished, he tossed the dishrag into the sink, refilled their cups, and sat down.

"Now that everything is neat and tidy..." Hana said with a lifted eyebrow.

"I have only myself to blame for that, haven't I?" O'Reilly sipped some coffee, then said, "All right, panic time is over. Do you know what they gave you?"

"I don't think that's a very realistic question. My only experience with drugs is taking a couple of aspirin when I have a headache, which hasn't been very often—up to now."

"No need to get huffy, girl. I wasn't implying that you were a hopeless drug addict. I withdraw the question. How did you feel when it took effect?"

"Incredible," Hana said after a moment. "Dreamy, euphoric, on cloud nine. All of that and more. There aren't any comparisons I can make because it's way out of range of anything I've experienced. It was wonderful and terrible at the same time."

"Terrible?"

"Not to be in control. Without a mind of one's own. Not only willing but eager to do whatever they wanted." A shudder ran through her body, and for a while Hana's voice wasn't steady. "It seemed to go on and on. I suppose one's sense of time is distorted. Whatever they asked, I answered. At least... At least I think I did. It's all rather foggy."

195

"And what did they ask you, Hana?"

Before she realized it, Hana had answered on a note of indignation. "What everyone's been asking. Where is Paul? Where is your father? Over and over and over—" Hana checked herself abruptly. How stupid of her! How thoughtless! The question of Paul's whereabouts had come up yesterday and had been dealt with in a way. Her father, though, was a new and dangerous subject. The trouble was that O'Reilly's presence here, FBI notwithstanding, the warmth of his sympathy, and the security of her own kitchen after the cold and terror of that derelict building and the casual ruthlessness of her captors had easily beguiled her.

"Hana..." O'Reilly's voice, soft and casual, broke into her thoughts. "You haven't mentioned your father before," he said. "Why should anyone be interested in him? Where does he fit into this 'overall scheme of things,' as you put it?"

Hana gave the man a long, measuring look before she said slowly, "My father was a prisoner in Czechoslovakia. A political prisoner." She paused.

"A political prisoner. Yes, I've got that."

"And he escaped somehow—a week or so ago."

"How do you know he escaped?"

"He sent me a note."

"Saying what?"

"Just that he was all right. That he was safe."

"You must have been very happy to hear that. Where did the note come from?"

Hana shook her head. "I didn't notice. I was too excited. It had been such a long time since I had had any word from him at all."

"You could check the postmark on the envelope."

"No, I couldn't. I destroyed it along with the note. I wouldn't want anyone to find them."

"No, of course you wouldn't," O'Reilly said. He stubbed out his cigarette in his soup bowl, stared for a moment at the mess he had made in doing so, then in a casual voice asked, "Do you think he's here—in New York, Hana? He would get in touch with you again somehow, wouldn't he? Or with Paul?

196

Do you think that's where Paul might be—with your father? If he's on the run from these friends of yours in the black Cadillac, he would need some help, surely."

Hana said nothing, and though her gaze didn't shift from his face, her eyes suddenly went out of focus, and O'Reilly knew she was no longer seeing him. The glow from the ceiling light turned the cinnamon-colored cap of curls into a bright halo and washed the face beneath it of all color. It brought the bones of the skull under the taut flesh into sharp prominence and laid dark shadows below cheekbones and honey-colored eyes. As O'Reilly stared at her, some atavistic gene, some ancient Celtic superstition, seized hold of him. My God, he thought wildly, she looks fey! And for that fleeting, frightening moment he felt he could really see an aura of doom surrounding her, could sense the foreboding of death that lay behind the shadowed eyes. Involuntarily he reached out a hand to touch her, to establish physical contact and bring her back from wherever she had gone, but the movement itself in the still kitchen broke the illusion. It vanished altogether as Hana began to speak.

"When we were children, Paul and I," she said, her voice low and a little husky, "my father used to read to us whenever he could. One of our regular favorites was *The Good Soldier: Schweik* by Hašek, a Czech writer. It's a famous antiwar book —you probably know it—about a lowly Czech soldier in the Austro-Hungarian army during World War One. It's about his adventures—misadventures, really—as he tries to rejoin his regiment up at the front. At least he *seems* to be trying. Is he simple-minded? Or a scoundrel? I was never sure. No matter how explicit his orders are, he always manages to march off resolutely—in the wrong direction. He's thrown into prison for desertion, into a lunatic asylum for being an imbecile, he's vilified and cursed, but throughout it all he never loses his sunny good humor. With a bland gaze and innocent smile he accepts everything that happens as perfectly reasonable under the circumstances. There's something good in everything, Schweik insists, and he is always willing to point it out. Take that battlefield over there, he says at one point. A lot of soldiers died there, and after the war it's going to make very good farmland. All that fertilizer..."

Hana paused and sipped her coffee. Then she smiled slightly and said, "And toward the end, true to form, Schweik is taken prisoner of war by his own side as he's trying on a Russian soldier's uniform to see how he looks in it!"

"I suspect this all has a point," O'Reilly said after a brief silence. "And that you'll get to it in time."

"Oh, yes, in time," Hana said, casting a quick glance at the clock on the wall above the refrigerator. "I thought you'd find it interesting. It's claimed by some experts that Schweik embodies the characteristics—or some of them—of the Czech people, traits they developed in their own defense during the hundreds of years of subjugation by the Hapsburg empire—that ability to *appear* to go along with, to accept, whatever the masters are dishing out. Like my grandmother during the Nazi occupation in World War Two. She was forced to work for the Germans in a factory in Prague. Her job was copying blueprints. Copy them exactly in every detail, the German foreman told her. And she did. If a speck of dust or a hair happened to fall on the print, or a flake of plaster from the ceiling, it went into the copy. It was surprising how many loose hairs and flakes of plaster there were floating around. The foreman would storm and shout that she was an idiot, an imbecile, or worse. But like Schweik, she was all wide-eyed, sweetly smiling innocence. What had she done wrong? Hadn't he told her to copy it exactly as it was? There was no way he could prove it was sabotage. It was an effective way for the weak to deal with the powerful and still stay alive."

"Sure it's a long and tragic history, so it is," O'Reilly said as Hana paused and drank some coffee. "And my grandparents and their grandparents and all before them back in County Mayo would know exactly what you mean by powerlessness. And God forgive me for asking the question, but what relevance does all this have?"

Hana's wide-eyed gaze mocked him as she set her coffee cup down, and though she was smiling slightly there was a red spot burning on each cheek like a warning flag. In conscious imita-

198

tion of his brogue she said in a silky-smooth voice, "Why sure, Mr. O'Reilly, it's just that I find it wonderful, really wonderful, that so many people are taking such a kind interest in the welfare of Paul and my father, how truly concerned they all seem to be, includin' yourself, Special Agent O'Reilly."

"Hold it, me darlin', hold it. I haven't read the book, but I've seen the movie. Save your Schweikian reactions for someone else. I'm on your side, remember? I've told you that and it's true. I want to help. Trust me." O'Reilly leaned forward and placed a large hand over hers. "You need a friend you can trust. You're in the eye of the storm. I don't want to see you hurt."

Hana pulled her hand away. "If I'm hurt, is it any business of yours?"

"If I love you, is it any business of yours?"

Hana blinked and stared at O'Reilly for a long, startled moment of silence.

"Goethe," O'Reilly said matter-of-factly. "You know your Schweik, but I see you don't know your Goethe."

Hana said coldly, "You're a very extravagant man, Mr. O'Reilly. I don't find you amusing."

The man's bony face flushed slightly. "Hana," he said softly, "I wasn't trying to be amusing. I'm sorry if I gave you that impression. I tend to treat serious things lightly and vice versa. That's something you should know about me, though we can discuss that in depth some other time. I repeat, I think you need a friend. You can't go it alone—" He held up a hand as Hana started to speak. "And don't go asking me what I mean by the 'go it alone' bit. Now, you've given me some past history and the synopsis of a novel, all of which I found very interesting. In exchange, I'll give you some history of a more immediate nature. Stop me when I come to the parts that you know. Yesterday a man disappeared from the USSR Mission to the United Nations. He walked out of their headquarters on Sixty-seventh Street and no one has seen him since. Makarov—Colonel Sergei Sergeivitch Makarov—is his name and espionage is his game. Are you with me so far?"

The soft, distant voice: "Do you know the name Makarov,

199

Hana? He was—a friend of your brother. Did your brother ever talk to you about a man named Makarov?"

"I'm off to slay the dragon."

"The bitch is talking nonsense again!"

"Do you think so? I wonder. Tell me about the dragon, Hana."

"Yes," O'Reilly said softly. "I can see you're with me."

"My friends," Hana said, fighting to control the trembling that had seized her, "the ones in the big black Cadillac—they mentioned him."

"Yes, I'm sure they would. They can add two and two. So can I. Not to beat around the bush...Makarov, number-one KGB man here on the East Coast, stationed in New York, disappears; your brother, Paul, CIA agent also stationed in New York, disappears; your father, former agent for the CIA and until a few days ago a prisoner in Czechoslovakia, escapes from his jailers and is either here in the city or soon will be. But to all intents and purposes, he too has disappeared. Now you could draw some very neat conclusions from all of that."

After O'Reilly finished speaking, Hana sat in silence for a moment, staring at him, her eyes bright and wary. Finally she shrugged and said, "It's a free country. You can draw any conclusions you want to, Mr. O'Reilly."

"I wouldn't want you to kid yourself, Hana. You're up against tough, ruthless, resourceful people. You should know that after this afternoon. If they think your father is in touch with you, they'll not stand idly by, not if they want to get their hands on him. You can't hope to handle this by yourself. You'll need help."

Hana said softly, "Maybe so." She glanced up at the wall clock above the refrigerator, then stood up, her face very pale and drawn. "Maybe so," she repeated, "but what I need right now is a rest. It's been a long, hard day and I'm very tired."

"Yes, I can see you are."

"And I'd like you to leave."

"I can tell easily enough when I'm not wanted. No need to get aggressive. No, no, don't apologize!" O'Reilly rose, took his sheepskin jacket from the back of the chair where he had hung it, and pulled it on. "Tell me," he said, "as a matter of curiosity, if your call to the FBI had been a bust, what then?"

Hana smiled. "I had a little list. Nicholas Savini, at a number he gave me. The New York Police Department..."

"And you wouldn't have gone wrong with any of them. I'm well known in certain quarters. Just one more word."

"Only one?"

O'Reilly shook his head. "It's a sharp tongue you have, lass, and that's a fact. But listen, please—" Resting his palms on the table, he leaned across, face close to Hana's, and said, "I'll be around—frog prince with friendly sorcerer—available and at your command whenever you want me. Don't forget that. And you know my number."

O'Reilly's face was grave, there was only the faintest touch of banter in his voice, and the silver highlights in the seawater eyes were dazzling. Hana turned hastily away from their piercing gaze and moved toward the foyer, feeling a little out of breath. She was glad to close the door behind him. Her feelings toward the man were getting rather complicated, and she couldn't have that. At this time she had to keep her life as simple as possible, her mind free of all distracting influences.

She could hear his footsteps, noisy, on the stairs. Too noisy? Was he making sure she heard him go? Or *seem* to go? Hadn't he left a little too easily?

He was singing in a light, clear tenor. Hana pressed her ear to the door. "He never will be missed. I've got him on the list..." Gilbert and Sullivan. *The Mikado.* Hana shook her head, smiling, while she slid the chain into place and shot the bolts home. Then she turned and went into the living room, where she made a quick phone call.

In her bedroom Hana dressed slowly, paying careful attention to every article she put on because each one had its purpose. The tailored black wool pants suit and the white silk blouse with the lace frills around the throat and wrists. Sufficiently dressy, but giving her freedom of movement at the same time. No heels. She would wear her flat-heeled, ankle-high boots. They were comfortable, and she could move fast in them if she had to. Good, thick socks. They wouldn't show anyway, and she wanted their thickness and elasticity. From her closet she took her lined raincoat and dropped it on the bed. It had a hood, but she would not be wearing that. She would have to wear the same green stocking hat with its floppy pompon. Not fancy, but she could tuck it into her coat pocket when she went inside.

At her dressing table she applied lipstick, a touch of rouge to conceal the pallor, and brushed her hair till it gleamed. As she replaced the brush in the tray, her eye fell on the music box. She frowned. Hadn't she put the lid down and tucked it behind the photograph where she usually kept it? It stood alongside the photograph now, and the lid was raised, the broken head lying, forlorn, beside the tiny figure of the ballerina. Thoughtfully she closed the lid and set the box back in its accustomed place. Then she pulled open the top dresser drawer, the middle one, the bottom one. None of her things were quite the way she had left them. For some reason the two cold-eyed men who had waylaid her at her door came to mind, and she imagined their careless, alien hands pawing through her clothes. The image sent anger flashing through her, but it was mixed with fear as she realized just how easily these men moved in and out of her life, doing what they wanted to do without concern for her. Wasn't there even something a little too careless about this search, as though they didn't care if she discovered it? Perhaps even wanted her to?

"But you didn't find what you were looking for, did you?" she muttered grimly. "And what's more, you're not going to!"

She slammed the drawers shut, still trembling with anger and telling herself to calm down. It was worse than useless to waste precious energy like this. In order to cope with tonight she needed a cool head and a clear mind.

Hana did not deceive herself that there was no danger in the coming hours, but she knew that if she thought about what she was up against, *really* thought about it, she would become immobilized with fear. Tough, ruthless, resourceful people, O'Reilly had said, and he certainly ought to know. She could not take for granted that her "friends in the big black Cadillac"

202

had not found out what they wanted to know, and Savini, she felt, had chosen to disbelieve most of what she had told him.

There had been no more phone calls, and though she was thankful for small favors, it didn't mean they were finished with her. They were out there, watching, waiting for her to make a move. And when she did, they would make *their* move. The danger time was when she would rendezvous with her father.

She would be followed. She must be prepared for that. She must be prepared too for the possibility that they had found and read her father's note. It had been in her coat pocket all along. O'Reilly could easily have read it while she lay unconscious on Paul's bed. The Russians could have done so while she was drugged, and Redstone could have searched her pockets when he went to the kitchen last night to make coffee. She could only hope and pray that they had missed the significance of a word and a date.

The word: Praha. Not the city at all, but a Czech restaurant here in Manhattan in the East Seventies, owned by her father's old friend, Josef Slavik.

The date: 20–2–88. That taken-for-granted notation in the upper right-hand corner of the letter. Her father had written it the European way, putting the day first instead of the month, so it read the twentieth of February, 1988. That was not the date he had sent the note. It was today's date, and an important part of the message which she had recognized so belatedly when she'd stared at it early that morning in the kitchen.

The message was clear, the mystery solved, once she had noticed the date. *Meet me at the Praha Restaurant on Saturday, February 20.* As for the time…The year 1988 could mean eight o'clock, perhaps. Or it might mean nothing at all. The time was the least important factor. She wasn't worried about that. If he was there at the restaurant, he was safe until she came. Safe with Josef Slavik, the chef-owner, an old friend of her father, whose family had fled the country and come to the States in 1948 at the time of the first Russian-engineered coup in Czechoslovakia. Somehow, despite the separation of time and an ocean, their friendship had remained firm. On the infrequent occasions when she had eaten at the Praha, usually with Paul, Slavik always joined them at their table, and over bottles of Plzeň Urquell he talked of the good times he and their father had had together as students at Charles University. He never seemed to run out of stories, nor the need to tell them to his friend's children. He was always smiling, but the kind blue eyes behind the rimless spectacles were damp and melancholy. The whole routine had become too painful for Hana, and she had stopped going to the restaurant. And it occurred to her only now that her father, after he escaped from prison, must have been in communication with his old friend, else how would her father have known where to send the note? Thanks to Josef, kind, reliable Josef.

It all made sense, and she would have tumbled to the meaning of her father's message sooner, but the *Kde Domov Můj* had thrown her off. Which is why he had written it in the first place—to confuse the unwanted reader.

Yes, her father was at the restaurant now. Hadn't the softspoken Russian told her they knew he had arrived in New York? Somehow he had given his followers the slip and had made it to temporary safety. And he was there, waiting for her.

Despite her good intentions to keep a cool head, Hana's heart started to pound, sending the blood flowing fast and hot through her veins. She felt dizzy, but before panic could take complete control, she ran from the bedroom into the living room, dodged around the screen into her "studio," and knelt down in front of the filing cabinet. Pulling the bottom drawer all the way out, she reached behind the files and brought out a shoebox. Inside, wrapped in an oiled rag, was a pistol. It was small—only a little over four inches long and weighing less than a pound—but it was deadly enough. Paul had given it to her, had taught her how to load it, shoot it, keep it clean. "I'll never use the thing," she had told him. "Put it away somewhere," he had said. "It's just in case." This was the "in case."

In addition, as Paul never did anything by halves, there was an ankle holster for it. She strapped that onto her right leg, tucked the gun into it, and pulled the heavy sock over both. When she rose and the leg of her slacks fell back down around her ankle, she couldn't see any bulge. No one would know the gun was there. On the other hand there was no way she could get at it with any speed if she had to. "I'll never be known as Quickdraw McGraw," she muttered. But she felt less vulnerable just knowing it was there.

With a feeling of shock she remembered how blithely she had jumped off the bus yesterday, looking forward to a pleasant social evening with Steve and with a lovely contract in her pocket for the illustrations of two children's books—not one, but two! Now, some twenty-four hours later, she thought, I have a gun strapped to my ankle and am worrying about reaching it fast enough if I have to!

It was useless, she knew, to wish that her father could visit her in her apartment like any normal father could visit his daughter—without fear. Without fear...

At that moment O'Reilly would have recognized the "fey" look on Hana's face as she gazed off into space, her eyes shifting out of focus and the skin stretching taut across the cheekbones.

"Golconda," *the soft-voiced Russian said. "Did your brother ever mention* Golconda *to you, Hana?"*

"A mine?"

"That's right. What else, Hana?"

"I don't know. I'm not—I—I don't—know—"

"No, Hana, you can't sleep yet. We're talking about Golconda. *How did your father describe* Golconda *to you?"*

The whisperer: "Do you think this is wise? Don't you—"

"Be quiet, please. Hana? Hana! Tell me about your father and Golconda."

"A mine—in India—very rich..."

Sternly: "You know that's not what I mean, Hana."

"Oh, God!" With a long, shuddering sigh, Hana swung around and headed for the kitchen. There she poured herself a glass of white wine, which she drank down fast. She poured another and carried that to the living room. Sipping it, she stood at the window watching the delicate flakes of snow drift lazily down from the slate-colored sky and tried to plan how to reach her father at the restaurant without being followed. Or was that by now only an academic problem? It was if the Russians had found and read the note or if she had betrayed it during the interrogation. Bits and pieces of their questions and her answers came back to her at odd times, but would she ever know the whole of it? Or know it before it was too late?

She leaned her hot forehead against the cool windowpane and decided that she would *have* to assume that the meeting place was still secret, that her father was safe with Josef Slavik, and act accordingly. There was nothing else she could do.

Her attention was caught at that moment by movement on the sidewalk below. The lone figure of Andy Johnson, building superintendent and father of Emily-Jasmin, was striding rapidly along toward the door of his basement apartment. He was wearing a brown corduroy jacket, black jeans, and a jaunty red stocking hat that bobbed up and down with each step. He carried two large sacks of groceries. Long after he had disappeared from view, Hana continued staring down at the sidewalk, frowning, lost in thought. Finally she turned and moved slowly back to the bedroom.

When Hana left the apartment a few moments later, she was wearing the familiar brown corduroy coat and the green stocking hat. The lined raincoat remained behind, having been carefully hung back in its place in the bedroom closet.

Just before she stepped out into the hall, she reached out and touched her charcoal drawing of Paul with gentle fingertips. "For luck," she whispered.

18

Hana's long strides carried her rapidly along Perry Street. She wasn't conscious of anyone around her. Enclosed in her own world now, she was aware only of herself, her own body, the swing of her legs and arms, the striking of her booted feet on the hard-soft surface of the snow-covered pavement. But most of all she was aware of the heavy, knotted feeling in the pit of her stomach and the tingling sensation in her fingertips—fear and excitement over what the future held.

She had kept O'Reilly with her as long as possible with talk of Schweik (she smiled a little to herself) so she wouldn't have time to think, only time to act, to move, to get to the restaurant, to meet her father and take him off to the secret, safe place. If anyone was following her now, it didn't matter. They were welcome to do so. It was when she picked up Steve's car that she would have to worry about that.

"You're ill," he had said when she phoned him. "You're supposed to be in bed!" He was both indignant and concerned. What did she want the car for? he wanted to know. Where did she have to go on a night like this, and if she *had* to go out, he would take her. Sara was feeling better. He would get a babysitter and drive her to wherever she wanted to go. She hated the idea of another lie, and she had fudged it by saying she would explain when she got there. You pay for your sins as you go, she thought with a wry smile.

Rounding the corner onto Greenwich Avenue, she saw a cab dropping off a couple in front of the Chili Bowl, a restaurant

207

that served so-called Texas-style food. She had eaten there once, a concoction called a chiliburger—dubious chili poured over dried-up hamburger. She ran for the cab. Someone else ran for it, but she won the race and climbed in without so much as a backward glance of apology. After giving the driver Steve's address, she sank back, closing her eyes, and tried to relax.

Stephen Karr lived in the Seventies on West End Avenue in one of the fine old pre–World War I buildings that was just converting to condominiums. The doorman knew her, smiled at her, and held the door open. When she emerged from the elevator onto the tenth floor, she figured the doorman must have called up because Steve was waiting for her in the open doorway. He put an arm around her shoulders and drew her into the foyer, a large, spacious room that could hold about six of her own little foyers.

"Your phone call left a lot to my imagination," he said after he kissed her. "Are you going to tell me what's going on?"

"I don't want to lie to you, Steve, but I can't tell you the truth. It isn't mine to tell."

"I could call Vicki," Steve persisted with a quick glance toward a bedroom door. "Sara's asleep now, and Vicki only lives a block away. If she's free, she can be here in a few minutes to baby-sit. I can drive you then. It's such a lousy night, Hana."

"I have to do this alone, Steve," Hana said firmly. "If you don't want me to use the car, all you have to do is say so—"

"Hana, for God's sake! I don't give a damn about the car. It's you I'm worried about."

"Don't be. I'll be all right."

It took several more minutes before Steve admitted defeat and let her go.

"But I'm making a condition," he said. "You can't have the car unless you promise to call me later tonight to tell me that you're all right, that you've landed safely wherever it is you have to land." His kind, round face was all knotted into one big frown of worry. "You promise?"

"I promise, Steve, cross my heart." Hana smiled and stretched up to kiss him on the cheek. "Give my love to Sara," she said, trying to make it all sound normal. Then she turned quickly and hurried away.

The building had an underground garage with its exit on Seventy-ninth Street. When Hana drove Steve's Buick out of it and turned right to head crosstown, over her own coat she was wearing Steve's old olive-drab trench coat buttoned straight up to the neck and on her head was his Irish tweed hat, which concealed her hair and shadowed her face. "I wish," Steve had said, helping her into the coat, "that I could believe you were dressing up for some kind of costume party."

Hana felt very tense now, and when she hit the red light on Central Park West and Eighty-first Street, she peered into the rearview mirror at a taxi behind her. It had been following her now for several blocks, hadn't it? It was dark, and through the thin veil of snow she couldn't make out any definition of the figure in the backseat. If they (who?) had picked up her trail despite her precautions, what would she do? Park the car some distance from the restaurant, walk and try to lose them? And if she couldn't lose them, what then? It was the "what then" that made her feel desperate. If she couldn't contact her father, what then?

He needs you, Josef Slavik had told her when she phoned the restaurant. She had called him from Steve's apartment, not daring to use her own phone in case it was tapped. He is resting now, so just come, Hana. He is not well. You can understand, of course. How could he be well—after everything.... But he knew you would come.

Where there's a will...? Hana set her jaw and, when the light changed, swung right into the park, keeping an eye on the taxi. With a roar of its engine it zoomed north, and Hana let out her breath on a long sigh. So far, so good.

The second coating of snow on the roads might conceal icy patches, and Hana drove very slowly and cautiously through Central Park and across town. The restaurant was located on Seventy-third Street between First and Second avenues, and by the time she reached it she was perspiring freely.

Directly across the street from the Praha was a fine, cleared parking space, and it was only after she had backed in that

Hana realized she was blocking a fire hydrant. She rationalized that she wouldn't be gone long enough for the car to be towed away, and she didn't care if she got a ticket. Fire hydrant or no, she was parking facing west, the direction from which she had come and where she would be returning.

She took off Steve's trench coat and tweed hat and laid them on the backseat. She ran her hand through her hair, combing it with her fingers, checked that the green knit stocking hat was in the left pocket of her corduroy coat, took the keys out of the ignition and put them into the right pocket. Then she placed her trembling hands on the steering wheel, gripped it tightly, and bowed her head over it, waiting for the panic to subside. The past twenty-four hours had been leading up to this moment, and she couldn't come apart now. Too much depended on her. Abruptly she raised her head, took in a deep breath, flung open the car door, and climbed out. A quick glance up and down the street satisfied her that none of the few people nearby looked suspicious. And you would know, wouldn't you? she told herself wryly.

Hana hesitated beside the car for a moment. Should she lock it or leave it unlocked? She finally opted for locking. Though it would slow her down when she came out of the restaurant with her father, she couldn't take the chance of leaving it open to a thief—or worse.

She entered the restaurant behind an elderly couple who started to discuss the weather in Czech with Josef Slavik, who had greeted them at the door with smiles and bows and *dobrý večer*s. When he saw Hana standing just over the threshold, his smile froze on his face. He dipped his head at her in a nervous little nod and said, "I'll be with you in a moment, miss—uh ... as soon as I have seated this lady and gentleman. Perhaps—" Another dip of the head, toward the bar this time. "Perhaps you would care to order something to drink while you wait?"

Hana took the hint and sat down at the long, mahogany bar. After ordering a bottle of Pilsner Urquell, she let her gaze roam casually over the tables. She didn't expect to see her father. He wouldn't come out of wherever Slavik was hiding him until her arrival.

The restaurant had three rooms, each opening through wide archways into the other. There was the barroom, which you entered from the street; to the right of that was the main dining room; and beyond that was a smaller, more intimate room that was sometimes used for private parties. A few tables lined the inside wall of the barroom, the last one being in the undesirable position next to the kitchen door.

Only a scattering of tables was occupied, and as Slavik led her to that undesirable table, he murmured in her ear, "Everybody stays home on a night like this," adding as he seated her, "Forgive me, Hanička, it is not a good table. I'm sorry. But it is—you understand—safer."

Hana murmured, "I understand."

When Slavik placed her beer and a menu in front of her, Hana noticed that the man's face had a greenish, pasty hue and beads of sweat lined his forehead. Poor Josef, she thought, he's not a very brave man, and wished that he wouldn't make them both conspicuous by whispering like a conspirator in her ear. She would have felt more comfortable, too, if the restaurant had been as busy as it usually was on a Saturday night. The noisy, crowded bar, the tables filled with chattering customers, the waiters rushing to and fro—all would have provided good cover for her father. She ran a nervous hand through her hair, which was damp from the snow. She unbuttoned her coat but did not remove it.

Slavik had seated her with her back to the kitchen wall, facing out toward the bar. The occupant of the chair across from her would have his back to the customers.

The occupant... Her father... Panic gripped her again, twisted her stomach. She turned her face to the wall quickly and closed her eyes, fighting nausea.

With a faint swish of sound the kitchen door swung open, then with a soft thump it closed. As a blind man would sense something solid in front of him, so Hana sensed someone standing beside her. In another second she heard the scrape of a chair leg. Someone had sat down. She took a deep breath and raised her eyes to meet the eyes of her father.

You must be prepared for a change in him, Josef Slavik had

told her on the phone. And she thought she had been, but nothing could have prepared her for the shock she felt at the sight of the man sitting across from her. His face bore only a shadow of resemblance to the one she had carried lovingly in memory for twenty years. Long and thin and ravaged, with sunken cheeks and sharp cheekbones—a suffering El Greco face without the color. Beneath the gray hair, cropped and sparse, the pale skull was plainly visible, each bump and ridge clearly defined. His cheap jacket simply hung on the skeletal frame, having no flesh to cling to. Certainly no one could ever have described to her the haunted, fevered eyes that peered out of their dark caverns at her. Their expression, a kind of fearful joy, pierced her like an arrow. Unbearable... Pity followed shock, tears sprang to her eyes.

"Hanička..." Karel Novotny's voice was no more than a rusty whisper, and there were tears in his eyes as well. "My dear, dear Hanička." His hand reached across the table to take hers. It was thin and veined, almost transparent, but its grip surprised Hana with its strength. For a long moment neither spoke. They simply stared at one another, coming to terms with what they saw.

"I was afraid," Karel Novotny said at last, "that you might not understand my note."

"I almost didn't. It was only this morning that I realized—" Hana broke off, shaking her head. "I don't believe it," she went on in a low, tense voice. "Even now—sitting here— looking at you—I don't believe it."

"I'm here, all of a piece, my dear Hanička, and intend to remain so. I have things to do." The whispering voice was harsh with bitterness. "But we'll have time to talk later, won't we? You have some place for us to go? Josef is—" Karel Novotny broke off as Josef Slavik appeared beside them, holding a tray with three small glasses of slivovitz on it. "Concerned about our safety, aren't you, Josef," he finished, looking up at the man with an odd smile on his face.

Carefully, Slavik placed a glass in front of each of them. His fingers were trembling, and some of the colorless liquid spilled onto the tablecloth. "You know I would have no way of protecting you, Karel," he said. "If they came here and found you, it would be hopeless." He turned to Hana, his eyes damp with sorrow. "You understand that, don't you, Hanička? They would simply kill both of us. There's no question in my mind. What could I do? They will be looking for him now, going to his friends..."

"We're leaving right now, Josef, don't worry," Hana assured him. "I have a safe place to go—"

"You mustn't tell me where it is," Slavik said quickly. "I don't want to know." He raised his glass. "Here's to your safety and good health. *Na zdraví.*"

"*Na zdraví.*"

"*Na zdraví.*"

They all drank the burning liquid quickly, then it was time to go. Karel Novotny rose and put on the shabby hat and coat that he had been holding in his lap. Hana noticed that he winced as he slipped his left arm into the sleeve.

Josef Slavik, clutching a sheaf of menus under his arm and with a fixed smile on his lips, escorted them to the door, hurrying a little more than was necessary.

"You've been a good friend, Josef," Novotny said, holding out his hand. "I'm grateful for everything you've done."

"Nothing, it was nothing," Slavik muttered. "I hope all goes well with you, Karel, and you, Hanička."

"Thank you, Josef. Good night. We'll be in touch." Hana pulled her coat collar up around her throat and stepped out into the dark street.

The wind had risen, and just a few scattered flakes of snow were falling now. Hana headed for the car, pulling the keys out of her pocket as she did so. There were no pedestrians around, and the street was empty except for a lone car at the far end of the block. Its engine was idling, sending little puffs of exhaust smoke into the air.

Novotny, who had lingered behind in the restaurant doorway to say something to Slavik, was stepping off the curb into the street when Hana, who had been watching the car for no reason except that it was there, suddenly heard a voice in her mind scream, *Danger!* She swung around to shout a warning to her father, but it was Josef Slavik's cry, *"Pozor, Karel, pozor!"* that saved Novotny's life. Flinging his arms over his face instinctively, he was already falling when the car drew abreast of him. It slowed, the long, thin muzzle of a revolver slid through the open window, two *phut-phut* sounds were followed by a spat against the restaurant wall and a cry from Karel Novotny. Then the big black car was gathering speed, and without waiting for the light to change, it had slewed around the corner, vanishing in a cloud of snow. And Hana was running toward the prone figure in the gutter, crying, "Not now, dear God, not now!"

Josef was on his knees beside Novotny when Hana reached them, and she heard him babbling about doctors and hospitals and her father whispering, "No doctors, no hospitals, Josef. Help me up. Tell Hana—there you are. All right. Just help me get into the car, that's all. Just help me up and into the car." There was something in Novotny's voice that cut off further argument, and between them Hana and Josef half carried him across the street and settled him gently in the backseat. Hana climbed quickly into the driver's seat and switched on the engine.

"Go back, Josef," Novotny whispered. "Go back to your restaurant. They might return."

Josef hesitated, shifting from foot to foot and peering anxiously into the car window. He seemed to be in an agony of indecision.

"Josef..." Hana said sharply.

"Please call me, Hanička," Josef said. "I will want to know. Please." Then he turned quickly and trotted back across the street and into the restaurant, a small round, anxious figure. Somehow through it all, Hana noted with surprise, he had managed to hang on to the sheaf of menus. They were tucked firmly beneath his arm.

The light was red at Seventy-third Street and Second Avenue, and Hana skidded to a halt. She would have to watch her driving. If she had an accident now, it would be fatal. A glance in the rearview mirror told her that so far the street behind her was empty. They would be back, though, she was sure of that, to see if they had accomplished their purpose. Her "friends in the big black Cadillac" hadn't followed her here. They had been lying in wait until she appeared with her father. She had betrayed the rendezvous under drugs, or they had decoded her father's note. Only one good thing—they couldn't know about the safe place because she hadn't decided on that until a short time ago.

Hana twisted around for a quick look at the man in the backseat. His face was the color of ashes, and his right hand was clamped to the upper part of his left arm, the sleeve of which was stained a damp, dark red. He was sitting bolt upright, his gaze directed out of the window.

"This is a one-way street," Hana said softly, reading his thoughts. "They would come from behind us."

Her father nodded and whispered, "We must go—now."

"Yes, but I have to know before I can drive—safely, that is—that you'll be all right, that you're not so badly hurt that—"

"It's my arm, Hanička. Painful but not fatal. I'm not ready to die yet."

The forced smile, the attempt at humor, the look in the fevered eyes shook her, sent the tears stinging her eyelids. She swung around. "All right," she said, looking in the rearview mirror. "The sooner we get there, the sooner it can be taken care of. I may have to go fast, make some sharp turns. If they follow us, I'll have to lose them. I don't want to hurt you."

"Do whatever you have to do, Hanička," Karel Novotny whispered. "Don't worry about me." His head fell back weakly against the seat. He closed his eyes.

Don't worry! For a split second Hana was shaky with panic again. Do we run because we're afraid, or are we afraid because we run? After the past twenty-four hours, she thought, I should know the answer to that.

Two cars swept around the corner from First Avenue onto Seventy-third Street, their headlights outlining briefly the exteriors of the buildings and picking out the delicate drift of snowflakes. Two cars...the lead car, medium-sized, nondescript; the second car, the black Cadillac.

Hana accelerated across the avenue, keeping an eye on the

rearview mirror. The big car was almost nudging the bumper of the smaller car and honking angrily. The smaller car continued to move at a snail's pace in the dead center of the road, until about midblock it seemed to hit a patch of ice and despite its slow speed went into a skid, slewing right, then left, and coming to a stop finally straight across the road, completely blocking the Cadillac. The angry horn blared, but Hana didn't wait to see the outcome. It was a lucky break, and she took advantage of it. Swinging north on Third Avenue, then west on Seventy-ninth Street, she was soon winding her way through Central Park again. At Columbus Avenue she picked up Seventy-ninth Street and continued driving steadily west.

In the backseat her father rested quietly, head back, eyes closed, breathing evenly. At one point he somehow became aware of her scrutiny and without opening his eyes whispered, "I'm fine, Hanička, I'm fine," and Hana could hear O'Reilly's light, musical voice in her ear: *Like father, like daughter, and that's a fact.*

She was able to smile a little, feeling calmer, more in control. The physical activity of driving the car safely on the snowy roads, the concentration it demanded, had pushed the panic away. We *are* fine, O'Reilly, or soon will be. The Cadillac was nowhere in sight. Who knows, perhaps it was still blocked behind the other car on Seventy-third Street. The only car behind her now was a taxi that had been picking up a fare at Seventy-ninth and Third as she had been driving by, and she wasn't worried about that.

The cabdriver swung left onto Riverside Drive and immediately pulled over to the curb. His passenger jumped out and trotted into the Seventy-ninth Street Riverside Park entrance, passing under the West Side Highway overpass and coming to a halt at the parapet. Some fifty feet below lay the boat basin. Dozens of boats of all sizes and descriptions were moored along the piers that reached out into the Hudson River. Many of them were used as permanent residences by their owners, and light beamed through their portholes, smoke curled up from the chimneys.

In a few moments the passenger of the cab saw Hana and her father emerge from the underground garage that served the boat owners. They were walking slowly. The man was limping and held his left arm bent and close to his body, while the girl kept a supporting hand under his other arm. By the light of the street lamp the girl's pale face, upturned to her father, looked tense with concern. For a moment the man was stirred by compassion for Hana Novotny, who was caught in this tricky, dangerous situation through no fault of hers at all. She just happens to be a member of the wrong family, he thought wryly. He watched her unlock a gate leading into the basin. She held it open for her father and, after entering herself, clicked it firmly shut behind her.

The gate through which the two had emerged was one of several set at intervals into the chain-link fencing that enclosed the boat basin. They were always kept locked, and only the boat owners had keys. For additional security rolls of barbed wire topped the fencing. Rather crude but effective against intruders, thought the watcher. He remained leaning against the parapet, shivering in the cold wind, until father and daughter reached their destination—a houseboat moored at the very end of the northernmost pier. They disappeared inside, lights sprang on, drapes were drawn. The man turned and jogged back to the taxi.

"He doesn't look all that well. He's limping, and something seems to be wrong with his left arm. She's taken him to one of the houseboats moored there in the basin," the man told the driver.

"Smart girl," the driver said. "Okay. Better check in with headquarters. There's a phone booth across the street. I'll keep an eye out here, though I'm sure they won't be going anywhere tonight."

19

Hana leaned against the deck railing and gazed down into the black water of the Hudson River, brooding over what tomorrow might bring. The argument, if you could call it that, hadn't lasted long. Even while she was objecting to what her father wanted her to do, she knew that in the end she would give in.

"I can't do it. How can you ask me to?" she had said.

"It has to be this way. I've planned it. It has to be this way."

"Have you thought of what's involved? Have you really thought of that? If what you believe is true, it would be like signing your own death warrant—no, like *my* signing your death warrant, and how can I—"

"Hanička..." The thin hand reached for hers and clung to it.

"No. No, give them the film, Father, please, or let me do it. Savini—he's a friend of yours. You can give it to him. He'll know how to handle it." Hana gripped her father's hand tightly in both of hers. "Don't throw it all away now. You're safe here. We could go somewhere, anywhere in the country. They won't be able to find you. We'll change our name. I don't have to be in New York City now for my work. I have an agent, I have a reputation..."

But none of her arguments, none of her pleas, would make him change his mind. Finally he shook his head in silence and a shuttered look came over his face, a look she remembered as a child that meant the discussion was closed and she had to give in.

218

"All right," she said with a sigh. "I'll do it if we can manage to make it as safe for you as possible."

Hana had been afraid she would feel shy and awkward once she was alone in the houseboat with this stranger who was her father. She needn't have worried. There was too much to do. The walk from the garage to the boat had used up whatever reserves of strength her father had. Blood soaked the sleeve of his overcoat, and he was breathing hard. Hana switched on the lights and helped him to an armchair. Then she locked the door and drew the drapes. The room was comfortably warm because Rosie's neighbor had come in earlier to switch on the space heaters.

This was the "safe place" Hana had chosen, this houseboat belonging to her friend, Rosie. It was less boat than house, a very modern little house set on a raft. Though it had a wheel-house on the top deck, Hana didn't know if it was seaworthy or not because Rosie never took it anywhere. Like most of the others in the basin, Rosie lived on her boat. It was her home, her castle, her studio, and it was permanently moored here in the Seventy-ninth Street Boat Basin.

The one large room, or cabin, though Rosie never bothered with boat terms, was comfortably furnished with easy chairs, bookcases, and two wide bunk beds built in on either side of the room beneath the thermal-pane picture windows. There was a telephone, television, and in the small kitchen a micro-wave oven and a large, well-stocked refrigerator-freezer.

Extending a third of the way out over the living room was a balcony reached by a narrow iron staircase. This was Rosie's studio. Rosie was a painter with something of an international reputation, and she was in Paris at this time arranging for a spring show of her large and slightly mad abstract paintings. "There's plenty of everything," Rosie had said when she gave the keys to Hana. "Use and enjoy."

The "plenty of everything" included a well-stocked medicine cabinet, and Hana blessed Rosie for being the mild hypochondriac that she was. When she carried what she thought she would need to where her father sat, she saw that he had removed his coat and jacket and shirt and was lying back with his eyes closed. His face looked more ashen than ever, if that was possible.

The bullet wound itself didn't look so bad to Hana, a clean wound in the fleshy underpart of the upper arm, but when she had removed the bloodstained piece of shirt that was wrapped around his lower arm and saw the torn flesh from the knife, red and swollen and suppurating, she could only stare at it, shocked and speechless for a moment.

"Oh, God, how...?"

"Just do what you can," Novotny whispered.

"It looks bad. I think it's infected. A doctor..." Hana felt suddenly helpless to cope with this. "You have to see a doctor, Father. I don't think—"

"Not now," Novotny broke in. "Do the best you can, Hanička. Please." His voice sank to that rusty whisper, and the "please" sounded desperate.

So Hana did the best she could, gritting her teeth and holding back the questions that wanted answers. Where did it happen? And when? And who did it to you? And why? Perhaps there would be time for them later.

She cleaned both wounds with warm water first and then sponged them with a solution of hydrogen peroxide, hoping all the while that she was doing the right thing. She patted the skin dry very gently, then bound the wounds with gauze.

"Well, I've done a pretty good job—for an amateur," Hana said, fashioning a sling out of one of Rosie's dish towels, "but you need an antibiotic of some kind. That's obvious. And for that you'll have to see a doctor. I won't let you put it off too long."

Karel Novotny nodded his head and agreed absently to see a doctor, but Hana could tell it was a kind of reflex action and that his mind was elsewhere. He ate one of the sandwiches she had prepared and drank some coffee with the same absent air. He refused aspirin but asked for whiskey, and when she brought it to him, he took it with a hand that shook, swallowed it greedily, and asked for another. He sipped this slowly while he rested against the pillows on the bunk bed, a blanket around his shoulders. "It's healing already," he said with an attempt at a smile. "Thanks to you, my dear Hanička. And what's more important," he added, "is that I feel that I'm on my way at last to rejoining the human race. It's been a long time."

Looking at the gaunt, gray face, at the feverish eyes and the trembling fingers, Hana felt a lump rise in her throat, she wanted to weep. "You can rest now, can't you?" she asked softly. "We'll talk later. There'll be plenty of time to talk now." Now that you're here, now that you're safe, was what she meant, but that was before he had told her what he wanted her to do, what his plan was.

"Not yet, not yet. There is something..." An urgent note came into his voice, and he struggled to sit up. "Your music box, Hanička. I put something—"

"In the little ballerina. Yes, I found it. Wait." She had forgotten for a while about the film, and no wonder. Her coat lay on a chair by the door where she had dropped it. From its pocket she pulled out the green knitted hat and brought it to her father. Turning it inside out, she pointed to a circular piece of green wool material sewed at the top of the hat beneath the pompon. "It's here," she said, guiding his fingers so they could feel the two small lumps under the concealing cloth.

"How clever you are, my darling Hanička. How clever." For a moment Karel Novotny became quite animated, nodding and smiling at his daughter while his emaciated fingers probed at the hidden film.

"That was the safest place I could think of," Hana explained, perching on the coffee table in front of her father. "Something I would naturally have with me. I didn't want to leave it behind in the apartment. I didn't want to leave it in the music box. I figured if I could find it, someone else might. My apartment was searched, you see. I don't know, but it's possible it was done by Savini. He had been—"

"Savini?" Novotny's voice was sharp.

Hana nodded and said gently, "Oh, yes, a great deal has been happening over the past twenty-four hours."

"Tell me," Novotny said.

Her father put his head back and closed his eyes while Hana

told him about Savini's visit, about the questions he asked, the answers she gave. She even included the description of the escape across the border as she had told it to Savini, realizing that her father wouldn't know about that. The haggard face against the pillow remained impassive except when she described Jan's death at the border. Then a muscle in his cheek twitched, and he rolled his head from side to side as though to rid himself of the picture in his mind. But he raised his head and opened his eyes to stare at her when Hana, near the end of her story, told him how Savini had reacted to the drawing she had made of the bearded man on the sidewalk.

Hana said carefully, "Savini called him Makarov."

"Makarov!" Novotny spat the name out like a curse, shocking Hana with the expression on his face, a combination of fear and virulent hatred.

"But he is dead," Hana went on. "I saw his body—"

"Never. It's not possible. I don't believe it. Did you see a scar?" He placed a finger on his right temple. "Just here?"

Hana admitted she hadn't noticed anything like that. "The first time I saw him, I was too startled and his hat was pulled low. The second time...well, I didn't get close enough to examine it."

"It must have been a frightening experience for you, but one man's bearded face looks very much like another man's bearded face," Novotny persisted stubbornly. "I don't believe that the dead man was my friend Makarov—Major Makarov, when I gave him that scar." He paused a moment, then added, "He's alive. He must be alive." His voice was low and harsh and so filled with hatred that Hana, looking into those burning eyes, sensed for the first time the obsession that possessed her father, an obsession so strong she knew it must have been at least partly responsible for keeping him alive through the long ordeal of his imprisonment.

As though he had read her mind, Novotny said, "Where *he* is concerned, I am not rational, as you can see." He tried to smile. It was just a grimace of twisted lips. "I hated him, not only for what he did to me personally, but for everything he stood for—the joyless, barren, dead-end kind of life his people

222

forced our people to live. Makarov was just one of their instruments of repression, just one of those who stifled any spirit, any independent thought." The man's voice rasped in his throat, and he was shaking with some strong emotion.

"Don't," Hana said, leaning forward to take his hand in hers. It was hot and dry. "Don't make yourself suffer like this."

"I want you to understand, Hanička. I'm trying to explain why I became a spy. No," he said as Hana started to say something. "There's no point in dressing it up in fancy language. I was a spy. Nominally I worked for the STB, our secret police. Or to put it more realistically, *their* secret police. It's been an arm of the KGB since 1948. In reality, of course, I was working for the CIA under Nicholas Savini."

"Yes, I know that now. The odd thing is, when I understood what you had been doing, I never thought of questioning it. I simply accepted it. That's the way it was."

"I'm glad it didn't distress you. I never had a chance to talk to you about it, to explain. At any rate, when I was arrested and charged with all those terrible crimes, they were only telling the truth—discounting their more hysterical exaggerations, that is. I *was* subversive. I was giving information to a foreign power. The fundamental purpose of any country's secret service is to preserve the status quo. My job as a double agent was to subvert it."

Novotny broke off to finish what was left of the whiskey in his glass. Then he held the glass out to Hana, who took it to the kitchen and refilled it. When she returned she found him leaning back against the pillow with his eyes closed, breathing heavily. Throughout the hours they spent talking together, periodically he would withdraw like this and remain quiet as a way of replenishing his small supply of energy. So Hana simply waited until her father opened his eyes. With a sigh he resumed speaking as though there had been no break.

"I paid for it—my hatred—a heavy price. The others who were arrested with me were quickly tried, quickly executed. I was kept alive. Makarov's orders. I know that now. He wanted this." He held up Hana's hat. "He wanted it very badly."

Makarov had visited him in Pankrac, Novotny went on, first

on a daily basis, then weekly, then monthly. "I never knew when he would come, of course, which was part of the whole sadistic process."

Her father was perspiring freely now, and Hana got up and paced around the room, unable to sit still and watch his face as he recalled the pain.

"His visits finally stopped altogether, but I didn't know that until a long time had gone by. And in the meantime I had the guards to cope with. As a traitor, I was fair game for whatever nasty little tricks they could think of. You'll never know how hard I tried to be a 'good' prisoner, to follow all the rules and regulations very, very carefully. The only problem was the rules changed at the whim of the guards." Novotny paused, took a long swallow of his drink, then set the glass down and added in an almost inaudible whisper, "It was unbearable—but I had to bear it."

"But it's over now. Finished. There's no need to go through it all again!"

"Hanička, my dear, I'm hurting you. I'm sorry. I shouldn't have—"

"That doesn't matter. I can take it. It's you I'm worried about." She knelt down in front of him, gripping his hand in hers. "Why must you go through with this? Why? I have such a bad feeling about it. What can I say? Please don't, *Tatá*, please don't!"

Tatá... How many years since she had called him that?

Even while he acknowledged the childish title with a faint smile, Novotny was shaking his head. "I can't give it up, Hanička, I can't—"

"What good will it do? What difference does it make to you? To me? I couldn't bear it if anything happened to you now, after—after everything."

"All that suffering has to have a reason, don't you see?" Novotny's voice dropped to the harsh, rusty whisper. "In destroying him—*Golconda*—I'll be destroying Makarov—his work. His most important work. That's the reason. And, forgive me, but whether you help me or not, I intend to do this. I don't want to argue with you, Hanička. I love you, I love

224

Pavel. You are the only two people in the world I care about. You are the only ones I thought about over the last twenty years with love. For all the rest, it was hate."

"That's the first time you've mentioned Paul. I didn't understand. I didn't know what to say."

It was only some days later, when it was all over, that Hana realized that during the time they were together, neither she nor her father ever mentioned Maria Novotny.

"Someone told me—I'm not sure who—a guard, another prisoner—and taking pleasure in it, I remember that"— a shadow passed over the haggard face —"that Pavel is working for the CIA."

"That's true, but surely you don't think—"

"I couldn't afford to take any chances. You can understand, can't you? How could I be sure—"

"Paul would die before he would betray you!"

"That's not what I mean. It isn't what he would have done consciously. But only one careless word to the wrong person..." Novotny fell abruptly silent, closing his eyes and resting for a moment. "But it doesn't matter now," he whispered finally. "It's close to the end. Tomorrow, ask him to come. I would like Pavel to be here."

It was after one in the morning. The snow had stopped a couple of hours before. The sky was a clear ice blue, and the air was crisp and cold. Overhead a plane broke the silence as it roared north up the Hudson, fading gradually in the distance. The boat rose and fell very gently on the ebbing tide. In a few boats around her Hana noted that lights still burned, smoke drifted out of their metal chimneys. To the north the George Washington Bridge was outlined like a Christmas tree with its festoons of lights.

The boat basin had always reminded Hana of a carnival, particularly in the summertime, a charming river carnival without the hoopla and honky-tonk of a real one. Normally the scene charmed her and soothed her, but not tonight. The lights on the Jersey shore, even the lights on the bridge, seemed too bright for some reason, glaring and watchful. She felt cold and

225

alone and exhausted. She turned away from the threatening lights and went inside, locking the door behind her.

It was then she remembered she hadn't called Steve, and guilt drove her to the telephone. The fact that he picked it up on the first ring told her he'd been waiting for her call. Watching some god-awful horror movie, he told her. Are you all right, Hana? Tired, but fine, she lied. I'll talk to you tomorrow, my dear. Sleep well. Sleep well...

After she hung up, Hana put the heaters' thermostats on low and covered her father gently with a quilt. For a moment she remained there, gazing down at his face, at the lead-gray skin, the sunken cheeks, at the lavender eyelids closed in uneasy sleep. *Tatá*... Her heart ached for the *Tatá* she had known, the gentle, handsome man of twenty years ago. But that man had died in the prisons and labor camps, and this one had taken his place. A sick man, emotionally as well as physically. Had his obsessive hatred, perhaps, destroyed his healthy emotions, like cancerous cells destroy the healthy cells? Could she have found any way to refuse to do what he had asked her? At least she would take what precautions she could to safeguard him.

I want you to call them—these men. I want them to come here tomorrow. We have things to talk about.

If tomorrow just wouldn't come. If she could go to sleep and wake up on Monday...

Hana climbed into the other bunk bed fully clothed except for removing her hat and coat and dropping her boots on the floor. The little gun in its ankle holster she tucked under her pillow. It didn't make her feel less afraid. Everything in her life that was familiar and safe and comforting seemed very far away.

226

20

At a quarter to nine Sunday morning Hana stepped into the phone booth at the corner of Perry and Bleecker streets to set in motion the final act of what was later to be titled "The Novotny Affair" in the files of the CIA.

She had left Steve's car behind in the boat basin's underground garage, subways and taxis being more efficient for the day's errands. The little gun in its holster, however, was again strapped to her ankle for no reason she could think of except that she felt more comfortable with it there. And though she was once more wearing Steve's old trenchcoat and Irish tweed hat, that was more a concession to her father's fears for her safety than from the belief that *they* would not be able to penetrate this thin and, as she thought of it now, silly disguise. If the ubiquitous *they* found her, she didn't think they would harm her—not as things stood now. But if they managed to kidnap her again, gun or no gun, and question her under drugs, then her father would be lost.

Consequently she had stayed close to people, not allowing herself to become isolated and in a position where they could pick her up easily. Leaving the boat basin, she had attached herself to a family group whose conversation told her they were churchbound. On Broadway she had parted from them to flag down a cruising taxi, which had deposited her here at the phone booth, where she seemed to be surrounded by people— coming and going, in and out of shops open on Sunday despite the snowstorm, or perhaps because of it. There was a kind of celebratory air about them all, and Hana thought, not for the first time, that New Yorkers were a gallant, intrepid lot. A little snow wasn't going to keep them from their appointed rounds.

One deep breath, one quick prayer, and Hana pushed a quarter into the slot and dialed the AIC number. It rang just once, then a courteous male voice said, "AIC. Can I help you?"

"I would like to speak to Nicholas Savini, please. This is Hana Novotny."

"Yes, Miss Novotny. Hang on a moment." The man sounded as though he had been patiently waiting beside the phone, knowing she would call.

God, Hana thought, it isn't that they are omnipotent. It's just that they *believe* they are!

A brief silence on the other end of the line was followed by a series of electronic bleeps, then Savini's smooth voice was saying, "Yes, Hana, I'm glad you called. You have something to tell me?"

"I'm calling for my father—"

"He is with you?"

"Yes—that is, no—"

"I must see him as soon as possible. You understand how important it is for me to see him, don't you?"

"You've made that very clear. Now I've arranged for him to be in a safe place, but he—"

"And where is that?"

Hana exploded. "I will not be bullied, Mr. Savini. Do you understand? I will not be bullied! My father insisted that I make this call, but I'm doing it against my better judgment. If you want to listen to what I have to say, fine. Otherwise I'll just hang up and walk away."

After a brief silence Savini said very gently, "I beg your pardon, Hana. I'm so anxious to see your father I'm forgetting my manners."

"And he, unfortunately," Hana said, her anger still carrying her along, "wants to see you."

"Good," was all Savini said.

"He would like you to come to see him this afternoon along with these other people—Mr. Halliday, Colonel Thorsen, and

Mr. Drumm. He said you would understand why he's inviting these men."

"I do, Hana, and tell him it's General Thorsen now." Savini's tone was light. He was trying, perhaps, to dissipate the anger he could still hear in Hana's voice.

"Will they be able to come?"

"I can guarantee it. And where are we to come?"

"We are staying on a houseboat belonging to a friend of mine. It's moored in the Seventy-ninth Street Boat Basin in the Hudson River. Not difficult to find."

"I know where it is. What time do you want us to be there?"

"Would you be able to make it by five o'clock? If not, I must know what time you can make it because I'll have to come to the gate and let you in."

"We are in the city, Hana, all of us. We'll be able to make it easily."

"There's more than one gate, Mr. Savini, so if you'll come to the northernmost one, I'll be there."

"The northernmost gate, yes."

"One more thing. My father wants to know—that is—do you have any information about this man, Makarov? I told him the man was dead, that I saw his body in Paul's bathroom, but he doesn't believe that it was Makarov I saw any more than you did, if I'm not mistaken."

"No, you're not mistaken, Hana. Tell your father I'll be glad to talk to him about Colonel Makarov when I see him this afternoon."

"All right." Hana fell silent for a moment.

"Was there anything else you wanted to tell me, Hana?" Savini asked softly.

"Only that . . . I want to repeat that I'm only making this call because my father insisted on it and I couldn't find any way of making him change his mind. But he isn't well. He's changed a great deal, as you can imagine, and I'm concerned about his health. I'm concerned about his safety. I don't want him hurt. You said you were his friend. I'm sure you don't want to see him hurt, either. If I thought he might be, I would call this meeting off and take him where none of you could find him.

After all that he's been through, he deserves to be allowed to live in peace and safety. Do I make myself clear, Mr. Savini?"

After a split-second pause, Savini said, "Perfectly clear, and I assure you there's absolutely no reason why I should want to hurt your father. On the contrary, I'm as deeply committed to his safety as you are."

"Yes. All right. I'll expect to see you later, then."

Hana hung up and leaned her head against the cold glass of the phone booth. "All right, that's done," she murmured. She was shaking, and the perspiration was dripping down her temples from beneath the Irish tweed hat. She pulled a tissue from a packet in her purse and wiped her face dry.

It was a couple of minutes to nine now. She had timed it right. Stepping out of the phone booth for a moment, she drew some cold air into her lungs and cast one swift glance down the street to her apartment house. No obvious watchers, but they would be there, she felt sure, well hidden somewhere, waiting.

The phone rang.

"A houseboat on the Hudson River. What a clever girl your sister is. Clever *and* beautiful. Remarkable."

"You heard, obviously."

"She has a clear voice, excellent enunciation, and I have had no problem understanding the English language for a good many years. You surely weren't planning to keep the rendez-vous a secret from me, were you, Pavel?" For a split second malice flashed in the pale blue gaze that was fixed on Paul's face.

"Why should you think I'd do a thing like that, Makarov? We're on the same side in this, aren't we?"

"That was my understanding, yes. Tell me this. What did your sister mean when she told you to come as soon as you can? We need you, she said. Why is that? An emergency? What has happened to make an emergency?"

"I don't think there's any emergency. Not in the sense you mean. I suspect from what she said that she's concerned about my father. He can't be very well after... But why do I have to tell you that, Makarov? You'd know more about his state of health than I would."

230

"I've been a bit out of touch lately, I'm afraid. But whatever your father suffered in the past, he brought on himself with his foolish obstinacy."

"You mean he could have lived the good life, every whim satisfied, if he had handed the film over to you?"

"You are being sarcastic, of course, because neither you nor your father would be simple enough to believe that."

"He would have been a dead man."

"Of course. Don't be stupid. That goes without saying. But wouldn't that have been preferable to the living death he endured for twenty years? On the other hand," Makarov went on, his tone changing, very jocular now, "if your father had given me the film then, Pavel, fate might have traced very different paths for us altogether. Right? We might have been denied this opportunity to meet, to spend this time together, to enjoy our games of chess, the vodka, here in these—uh... luxurious surroundings." There was a flash of white teeth in the dark beard as the man swept an arm out to encompass the room, which had acquired a rather dusty and uncared-for appearance with its unmade beds and litter of empty bottles, dirty dishes, and clothes.

Like the room, Paul, too, was unkempt. He still wore the sport shirt and jeans, both of which looked wilted and slept in. His thick curly brown hair was uncombed, and yesterday's stubble of beard shadowed his chin. There were dark circles of sleeplessness under his eyes. The gun remained still tucked in the waistband of his jeans, and for most of the time he rested a hand on it.

In contrast with Paul's appearance, the Colonel looked fit, jaunty, and as well groomed as the chairman of the board of General Motors. He was dressed in a perfectly tailored three-piece, navy-blue, pin-striped suit, fresh from the cleaners, a white shirt with gold cufflinks, and a silk paisley tie. The pale blue eyes were clear and alert, and his beard seemed more luxurious and glossier than ever. With the umbrella swinging from his arm, he moved around the room with an energetic stride.

"I will confess something to you, Pavel," Makarov said. "Your father was one of my few failures. Yes, now that the affair is drawing to an end, I can tell you this. It was a very important failure, considering what was involved. I never thought, you see, that he would be able to withstand my—persuasions. Who would have thought he could? There were times when it was difficult even for me—"

"I'd rather you skip the details, Makarov." Paul's voice was harsh, his face very pale.

"You are squeamish. Very well. I simply wanted you to know that I am human after all, propaganda being to the contrary." Again the flash of white illuminated the dark beard.

Paul remained silent, simply watching the other man with wary eyes.

"I have never forgiven your father though, for holding out against me. What, you say, not even after twenty years? No, never. And I suspect"—a thick, blunt finger stabbed the air in Paul's direction—"that he feels the same about me. In our business, as you will learn, we have long and ruthless memories. Your father was rarely out of my thoughts in all that time, and in the prisons and the mines I always had someone with him. A kind of baby-sitter, you might say. Someone to watch him, talk to him, listen to him, awake or asleep. All observations were reported to me. Your father was not allowed to receive letters or to send them. His only means of communication, his only outlet, was to talk to his 'fellow prisoner.' And what did he talk about, when he talked at all? About the weather or about a book he was reading. We took his books away. Even then—" Makarov broke off. Sudden anger glinted in his eyes, set the pulse in his temple throbbing.

"My father would have known you'd put a man on him, Makarov. I'm surprised you were unrealistic enough to think otherwise."

"Unrealistic? What was unrealistic was for him to think he could get away with what he did."

"He was a clever man—my father. If he had acted on his own initiative, he wouldn't have been caught, I'm sure of it."

"Your father was lucky, not clever. If I had arrived at STB headquarters a few minutes earlier, he would never have escaped with the files. Never!" Again the anger glowed in the man's eyes and throbbed in his temple as he paced rapidly

232

around the room, flicking his umbrella wrathfully at the un-made beds. He came to a halt finally at the window, where a fresh bottle of vodka cooled in the ice bucket on the ledge. For some reason the man's mood changed abruptly. He plucked the bottle out of its nest of ice and, holding it up, dripping, turned to face Paul. He was smiling, his voice was relaxed and genial.

"You'll join me, Pavel," he said, breaking the seal on the bottle and unscrewing the cap. "No reason why we shouldn't enjoy a final drink to celebrate the success of our plan, is there?"

Paul said, "I'll have the drink, though I'd say the celebration is a little premature." He pushed himself away from his post at the desk and moved around the beds to where Makarov stood between the window and the table that held the chess set.

"Nonsense," Makarov said cheerfully, "not premature at all. You Novotnys have given me a great deal of trouble in the past. All of you. But then you would say the same of me, am I right? That Colonel Makarov has given the Novotnys a great deal of trouble. But that's coming to an end now, isn't it, Pavel? For both of us. Soon our problems will be solved." Makarov poured the liquor carefully into the two small glasses, filling them to the top with a steady hand. Giving one to Paul, he raised his own glass and with a kind of mock bow said, "*Na zdorov'e*, Pavel."

Paul raised his glass. "*Na zdraví*, Colonel."

Makarov tossed the vodka down his throat, pressed the button on the umbrella that released the long, slender blade from its shaft, and stabbed Paul in the chest—all at the same time. If anyone had been watching the two men and had blinked his eyes, he would have missed the action, so swiftly had Makarov accomplished his purpose.

Paul's eyes widened with shock. The glass slipped from his fingers as he crumpled to his knees. He pressed one hand to his chest, where the blood swiftly dyed it red, with the other he scrabbled at his waist for his gun. Makarov bent down and grabbed it from his nerveless fingers, swung it in an arc, and brought it slamming against Paul's cheek, sending him sprawling to the floor.

"That," Makarov hissed, "is for your father." His face was flushed with passion. "You don't think," he went on, "that I ever really trusted you to keep our agreement, do you? Like father, like son—traitors all!"

"The pot—calling the kettle..."

"I'll leave you with this fact for your consideration during the time you have left, Pavel." Makarov dropped Paul's gun on the bed and retracted the blade into the shaft of the umbrella after wiping it on the rug with two swift strokes while he went on talking. "I've been running an agent against you since 1968. Against your impregnable agency. You understand? Something no one else I know of has ever succeeded in doing. And he was safe—my man—while your father was in prison. Nobody had any idea where the film was—or *if* it was. For all anyone knew, it might have been at the bottom of the Vltava or the Atlantic Ocean. That's all changed now."

Makarov flung open the door of the closet and peeled his coat off the hanger. In one of its pockets was the cashmere scarf, in the other the astrakhan hat and the fur-lined gloves. He dressed carefully but quickly, without wasted motion, casting a dispassionate glance from time to time at the man at his feet.

"Poor Pavel," Makarov said at last, his voice heavy with mock sympathy. "Are you trying to guess who this man is—my 'mole,' *Golconda*? He holds a very important position in your organization, I assure you, and has been extremely useful to me over the years. Are you going over certain names in your mind now? Are you thinking could it possibly be your director himself, Gilbert Halliday? What a coup that would be! A man who embodies all that capitalism stands for. And what splendid cover for a 'mole'! Or are you asking yourself is it his deputy, General Miles Thorsen? There's a shrewd, cunning man. He weighs every pro and con before he makes a move. I would like to have him on my side. A very useful ally. Or I would be pleased to work with your man Drumm. A clever man who conceals his brilliance under the guise of a loudmouthed bumbler. A little too obvious sometimes, perhaps..."

Makarov fell silent for a moment as he pulled on his gloves

and smoothed each finger. When he spoke again, his voice was very soft, his eyes very cold. "We mustn't forget, of course, the most likely candidate of all. Nicholas Savini, that devious Italian. The 'Monk,' as you call him. A subtle and ruthless man. Is he the one, Pavel? Is he the one?" The man bent over suddenly and whispered something in Paul's ear. When he straightened up, the white teeth gleamed through the black beard in a broad smile. Paul could only stare up at him helplessly, his eyes filled with anger and despair.

Still smiling, but paying no further attention to Paul, Makarov picked up his umbrella, tucked Paul's gun into his pocket, and left the room, taking the key with him and locking the door from the outside.

Paul, gray-faced now, closed his eyes and tried to regulate his breathing to slow, shallow breaths while he listened to the retreating footsteps. When he could no longer hear them, he began his long, painful crawl to the telephone.

21

By four o'clock in the afternoon the sky had become heavily overcast again and like an inverted bowl had lowered itself over the river, shutting out the light as the gray winter day faded rapidly into a dark winter night.

Inside Rosie's houseboat the drapes were drawn, the wall lights gleamed cheerfully from their recessed niches, and the space heaters hummed gently. But to Hana the warmth and comfort of the room meant nothing. Carrying her mug of coffee, perhaps her tenth of the day, and sipping from it from time to time, she moved in restless circles around the room, using the physical activity to keep herself from pushing the panic button. Paul hadn't come. She wanted him here. She wanted him badly. She had been counting on his help in the approaching confrontation. On the phone he had sounded relaxed and at ease and had assured her he would be at the boat soon. That had been hours ago. She was afraid to ask herself why he hadn't arrived by now.

Exactly where the time had gone since she'd returned to the boat after making the phone calls, she had no idea. Hours drag when you're looking forward to something, she thought, but how fast they go when you're dreading it.

The first order of business, of course, had been to change the bandages on her father's arm. She repeated the hydrogen peroxide cleansing and thought that the knife wound looked a little less inflamed. Or was that wishful thinking?

Rummaging through Rosie's bureau drawers, Hana found

an old sweater, paint-daubed but thick and warm and baggy enough to fit her father's gaunt frame. His own jacket and shirt were hopelessly torn and bloodstained, and the shabby suitcase he had carried from Europe to New York held nothing of any use at all. He had discarded it without regret at Josef Slavik's.

Over a breakfast of scrambled eggs and toast, which neither of them ate, Hana told her father what little there was to tell about the phone calls. He listened in silence, responding only once with any animation when she mentioned Makarov's name.

"And Savini said nothing else? Nothing else at all?"

"No. To use his words, he said he will be glad to talk to you about Colonel Makarov this afternoon when he sees you."

"Colonel..." Something flickered in the depths of those hollow eyes, and the hand that held the glass of whiskey trembled. Novotny whispered, "I see," then lapsed into silence.

Hana didn't like the fact that her father had been drinking whiskey almost steadily since morning, though she had to admit that he sipped it slowly and it seemed to have no effect on him as far as she could see. So she continued to pour it for him because if it gave him the strength and courage he needed, she couldn't refuse him. She watched him now as he brought the drink to his lips. In the quiet room the tinkling of the ice against the glass was the only sound. As the time of the rendezvous drew nearer, Karel Novotny's silences grew longer. He withdrew deeper and deeper into himself, shutting Hana out. When she tried to talk to him, he would reply in monosyllables, if he replied at all. Hana felt more and more alone.

In preparation for the meeting they had placed a chair beside the door leading out to the deck. With the door slightly ajar, Karel Novotny would be able to see a fairly broad section of the deck and the pier, but no one would be able to see him.

"When they come, you'll stay here in the chair, won't you, *Tatá?* Out of sight?"

"Yes, certainly," Novotny said.

"You must promise me you will," Hana insisted. "Promise."

He had promised like an obedient child, an obedient, absent-minded child.

Now he sat there at his post beside the door, silent and withdrawn. At his elbow was a small table, and on it lay a large, ugly revolver, which he had removed from his overcoat pocket that morning. It hadn't surprised Hana that he had a gun. It would have surprised her more, she realized, if he had not had one. She didn't know, of course, and never would know, that this was the gun he had snatched from a dead man's hand, the gun her father had used to kill her mother. Her own small one she had transferred now from her ankle to her coat pocket, where it was easily accessible. She planned to stand guard on deck when the men arrived, though she had no intention of telling her father this. She would simply remain outside after she had led the men to the boat. What good she could do—an amateur among professionals—she didn't know. She only knew she had to do it.

She glanced at her father. He had set the now empty whiskey glass down beside the gun and was resting, head back, eyes closed. How vulnerable he looked. His face, Hana thought, seemed thinner than it had last night, if that was possible. Beneath the skin the bones were scraped clean of all flesh.

Pehaps he felt her watching him because his eyes opened suddenly and looked directly into hers. She saw in them for one unguarded moment the raw fear that lived inside him. In two swift strides she was beside him. Kneeling down, she caught his hand in hers, saying, "Change your mind, *Tatá*, please. Change your mind. There's still a half hour. We can be well away before then. I have a friend who lives close by. We can stay with him until I can arrange a safe place for us to go."

But they didn't have a half hour. Before Karel Novotny had a chance to reply, there was the sound of footsteps on the deck, a sharp rap on the door. They both froze. Another rap, arrogant, followed by a voice familiar now to Hana.

Savini said, "I would like to talk to you, Karel. May we come in a moment?"

Novotny's gaze went from Hana's face to the door and back to Hana's face. At the same time he was fumbling the sling off his arm and reaching for his gun. "We?" he called hoarsely. "Who is that?"

"Nicholas Savini, Karel."

Novotny's eyes went questioningly to his daughter's face. Hana nodded. "I know the voice," she said reassuringly.

"You said *we*," Novotny called.

"Herbert Redstone is with me. You don't know him. He's filling my old spot in Prague. We neither of us intend you any harm. Ask your daughter. She will corroborate what I say."

Again Novotny's gaze rested on Hana's face and again she nodded. "I've met this man Redstone," she said. "He seems all right."

Exhausted suddenly, Novotny whispered, "Ask them if they are armed."

Hana spoke through the door. "My father would like to know—are you armed?" It seemed a naive question. If they were armed, they wouldn't be likely to say so, would they?

"Of course not, Hana," Savini said impatiently. "We're as concerned for his safety as you are. I repeat, Karel, we only want to talk with you."

"I would like to know first," Hana said, "how you got into the boat basin?"

"That was the only flaw in your plan. I happen to have a friend who moors his boat here."

"I should have known," Hana muttered bitterly.

"Otherwise it was a smart move to bring your father here. I do congratulate you. Now let us in, please."

Hana turned to her father. "Do you want to hear what he has to say, *Tatá?*" she asked gently. "Should I let him in?"

Novotny was silent for a long moment, staring at nothing, withdrawing into himself to take counsel while Hana waited on one side of the door, the two men on the other side. When he finally raised his head and looked at Hana, she saw the raw fear again in his eyes, but something else was there as well—a look of such dogged determination that it sent a stab of pain through her and she cried out, "You don't have to, *Tatá*, you don't have to!"

"Let them in, Hanička." Her father's voice was low and

quite firm. And as she hesitated with her hand on the bolt, he repeated, "Let them in."

Hana slid back the bolt and opened the door. At the same time the morbid, melodramatic thought flashed through her mind: I'm letting death in. And when Savini appeared in the doorway with his narrow, olive-skinned face and dark, hooded eyes, dressed in his blacks and grays, he might have been Death—or Death's emissary.

Holding his arms away from his body, gloved hands open and palms out, Savini moved slowly into the room. You see? he was saying. No weapon. You have nothing to fear from me.

Redstone entered silently behind him, closed the door, and leaned back against it. Both men sent one swift glance to the gun in Novotny's lap, noting it, noting the trembling hand that held it. Then for the rest of the time they seemed to ignore it.

Savini had come to a halt in the center of the room and turned slowly to face Novotny. Fixing his dark gaze on the other man's face, he studied it with a strange intensity as though, Hana thought, he were trying to find a message in its grooves and hollows. Whether he succeeded or not, she couldn't tell. The man's face might have been made of stone for all the expression it had.

"It's good to see you, Karel," Savini said at last. "It's been a long time."

"A lifetime, Savini," Novotny said in his rusty whisper. "A lifetime. But let's not waste any time on the social amenities. They are meaningless here. It's perfectly clear to any objective observer that you are in very good health and that I am not. And despite your assurances to my daughter that you are concerned with my welfare, we both know that that is not your primary interest here, so come to the point."

Savini smiled his thin smile and said, "You weren't as blunt as this in the past, Karel. You used more subtlety in your approach to things. You've changed, of course."

"Yes, I've changed—in ways you can't see. Being in prison is a—a very refining process. But before we go on, I would like your man here to move away from the door, please." Novotny gestured in Redstone's direction with his gun. "If he stands behind you, or sits, if he prefers, then I can see you both easily."

"Karel..."

The gun gestured again, and Savini, lifting one elegant shoulder in a shrug, nodded at Redstone, who moved immediately to a spot behind him. Hana watched as Redstone lowered himself to a perch on the arm of the easy chair beside the coffee table, resting a hand on the table for support. Less than an inch from his fingers, where her father had left it last night, lay the green knit stocking hat.

Hana's heart started to pound, and she could feel the blood draining from her face. What if the man picked it up? Just because it was there? Toyed with it as her father had done last night? Even as the thought occurred to her, the man's fingers had reached out and were fondling the soft wool of the hat brim. In another moment...

Before she realized it, Hana had moved swiftly over to Redstone and had pushed rudely between him and the coffee table, compelling him to lean back to let her through. In doing so, he dropped the hat on the table. Hana scooped it up along with her empty coffee mug and gave her father, whose eyes, too, had been glued on the hat, a quick, almost imperceptible nod. Then she turned with a smile to Redstone and Savini. "Would you like some coffee?" she asked. "It will only take a moment."

"No, thank you," Redstone said, staring at her with a puzzled frown, and Hana knew that her bright hostess smile looked as forced and phony to him as it felt to her. Savini said nothing, simply watched her with cold black eyes as she headed for the kitchen.

There she had to lean against the stove until the trembling eased and the strength returned to her legs and she was able to fill her mug with black, lukewarm coffee without spilling it. She put the hat on the shelf of a small utility closet, shut the door firmly, and returned to her post beside her father.

Redstone, Hana saw, had moved from the arm of the easy chair and was now perched on the bare coffee table, and Savini with his elbow propped on its back was leaning gracefully against the easy chair. He looked so relaxed and at ease that even though he was still wearing his overcoat, he fit the part of host much better than either her father or herself. He directed his dark gaze at Hana and asked, "Is everything all right now?"

"All right? I don't know what you mean," Hana said sharply.

"Well, you've cleaned the debris off the table like a good housewife, you've offered your guests refreshment like a good hostess. Now if you're finished with these chores, perhaps we can proceed."

Hana, flushing with both anger and relief, snapped, "I apologize. Please, by all means, carry on."

With exaggerated courtesy, Savini said, "Thank you," then turned his attention to Novotny.

"We will forgo the amenities as you suggested, Karel, and get to the point. You know why I'm here, no doubt."

Novotny nodded.

"You made a microfilm of the files you stole that night at STB headquarters, didn't you?"

Novotny nodded again.

"And you hid the film in your daughter's music box—the safest place you could think of at the time."

A faint smile touched Karel Novotny's lips as he cast a glance up at his daughter's face. "That's right," he said. "And if you know where the film was hidden, then you must know that it isn't there anymore."

"Of course I know. I also know there must be some information of extraordinary value in it for you to have suffered so much to protect it." Savini paused, watching Novotny closely, waiting for him to speak. When he didn't, Savini sighed and went on.

"I have an idea of what your film might reveal—something as dangerous, as volatile, as nitroglycerin, something that would cause terrible damage to the agency. I'm here to ask you to give me the film."

"Do you think after going through a dozen different kinds of hell for it that I'll hand it meekly over to you?"

"Why not? You were going to give it to me in the first place,

242

weren't you, that night in Prague? You intended it for me, for the agency."

"I suppose... I don't really remember, but I suppose I must have had something like that in mind. But—things have changed. I've changed. I'm not about to give the film to you so you can hide it away in a vault somewhere or destroy it altogether."

"I wouldn't destroy it, Karel, and I wouldn't hide it away. I would act on it. Whatever needed to be done, I would do." Savini paused a moment. When he went on, his voice was very soft. "You don't trust certain others in the agency, is that it? All right, then we'll work together on this, you and I. It will be like old times. We used to work well together, didn't we, Karel? We respected each other's abilities?" Savini started to move toward Novotny, who immediately raised the gun and waved it rather wildly at the other man. Savini came to a halt, but he didn't step back. Smiling slightly, he raised his hands, palms out. "You don't need the gun, Karel." He spoke slowly and carefully as though speaking to a frightened child. "You have nothing to fear from me. You can trust me. I'm your friend. Surely you know that."

"I have no friends. I trust no one—except my daughter and myself."

"I understand, of course, but—"

"No, Savini," Novotny said hoarsely, "you can't possibly understand."

"Believe me, I do. You feel you've been betrayed by the people you most trusted. Someone you worked with, perhaps. Or someone—someone even closer to home."

Like raindrops on leaves, soft and persistent, the hiss of the whispering voices drew her to the door. Three heads, close together, silhouetted against the fiery glow of the window...

Something was there—in the dark part of her mind—drawing her closer and closer to the danger.

Hana's heart was pounding, she couldn't catch her breath. She swayed, put a hand on the chair for support.

"Are you all right, Miss Novotny? Are you all right?"

Hana opened her eyes. Redstone had risen and was standing

243

beside Savini, staring at her, his eyes anxious and kind. He obviously wanted to come to her but was being held at bay by her father's gun.

"Tired, that's all," she said, running a hand through her hair and trying to smile. She noticed that she had set her cup down on the table so hard that coffee had splashed out and run off onto the floor. It should be cleaned up, she supposed, but it didn't really seem important enough to worry about.

"What is it, Hanička?" Her father's voice was low and tense, and he didn't remove his gaze from the two men. "Is something wrong?"

"No. Tired, that's all," she repeated. Fatigue and fear, fear and fatigue. She'd been coping with them now for almost forty-eight hours, and it had left her with few reserves of energy. "But there's no need to worry," she told her father, putting a reassuring hand on his shoulder. She could feel the sharp bones even through the thick sweater. "It's getting late, though." She turned to Savini. "And—"

"And we are only here on sufferance so get on with it," Savini said dryly. "Yes, I know, Hana, I know."

All of a sudden and with a passion that shocked her, Hana hated the man—hated his arrogance, his cool self-assurance, his elegant clothes. Most of all she hated that aura of well-being and invulnerability that seemed to emanate from him. She glanced down at the skeletal figure of her father in his shabby trousers and the paint-stained sweater. Exhaustion and pain had cut even deeper furrows in the gray, unhealthy face. Only the fevered brown eyes showed any life. How could he stand a chance in this ill-matched confrontation!

Hana's face must have given her away, or Savini was able to read her mind. "We are all of us at risk sometimes, Hana," he said. "It is unrealistic to think otherwise." His eyes were dark and brooding, and he had a strange smile on his face. "Your father knows that. He knows he is at risk now." He directed that brooding gaze at Novotny. "Don't you, Karel? But I am not your enemy—no matter what you think. I really have only your best interests at heart. All you have to do is give me the film and your job is done. You can relax." Savini paused a moment. When he went on, his voice was very low, very seductive. "You will be able to live the way you want to live, where you want to live. You have money coming to you. I will see that you get it. Our finance department will arrange for your pension. You'll have no worries in that regard. As for your staying here in the States, I'll personally see to it that nothing hinders you getting U.S. citizenship when the time comes."

Say *yes*. Give him the film, Hana found herself praying. Even if all the rest doesn't follow.

But Novotny was saying, "You're trying to bribe me, Savini."

"I'm only offering what's yours by right. You've had a bad time. I want to try to make up for that. I want to give you the means of living in peace and security."

"And if I don't hand over the film, I'll find myself without rights. You'll withdraw the offer."

"If you won't think of yourself, then think of your daughter." Savini's voice hardened. "This is a dangerous game you're playing, not only for yourself but for Hana as well."

"Now you're threatening me, Savini, but it won't work. It's me they want, as you know very well. No one is going to hurt Hana." Novotny's voice trembled a little.

"If she gets in the way, they will."

Savini's flat statement was followed by a brief, heavy silence broken only by the creaking of the mooring lines against the pilings outside as the boat rose and fell on the swelling tide and a voice in the distance calling a cheery good night across the water.

Hana was angry. It had been deliberately cruel on Savini's part to bring up the idea of danger to herself. She had avoided any mention to her father of her being kidnapped by the Russians and questioned under drugs. Nothing would have been gained by telling him. It would only have upset him.

"They..." Hana heard her father whisper, and because she still had her hand on his shoulder, she felt the long shudder that ran through his body. "My daughter said you would be glad to talk to me about Colonel Makarov, Savini. I would like to know where he is. Can you tell me that?"

"He's here in New York."

"Here..."

"And he should be in our hands right now."

"In your hands? What are you saying?"

"I am saying he is defecting to us."

"Defecting?" Novotny closed his eyes for a moment. His face was bloodless. "Never," he whispered, "never."

"It was all arranged," Savini said. "He made only one firm condition." The man paused a moment. Hana had the feeling the pause was for dramatic effect. "One condition—that your son, Paul, bring him in."

"Pavel?" Novotny whispered.

"Paul?" Hana cried. "You know where he is—"

"Wait, Hanička." Her father reached up to touch her hand but kept his gaze fixed intently on Savini. "*Should*, you said. *Should* be in your hands."

"We are waiting to hear from them," Savini said.

"He knows I'm here," Novotny whispered. "That's why. He knows I'm here." An ugly smile appeared on his face. "He'll give you fairy tales, Savini, fairy tales. He only wants what you all want."

"We'll see," Savini said coldly. "When the time comes, we'll see."

"The debriefing, you mean? You don't think he'll give you anything worthwhile, do you? It won't be *in*formation you get, Savini. It will be *dis*information. Or is that what you want him to give? Is that what's behind his defection?"

Savini's face flushed a deep red, and his eyes narrowed as he took a quick step toward Novotny. He stopped as the gun came up to point directly at his chest. Novotny's hand was steady. The gun didn't waver.

"*Tatá*..." Hana bent down and placed a hand on his wrist. "Don't!"

At the same time Redstone rose and moved quickly to Savini's side. For a long moment the four of them remained motionless, forming a deadly kind of tableau. Then Novotny dropped the gun into his lap and said, "Get out. Wait on the pier until the others come. And it's time for you, Hanička, to go to the gate."

Hana stepped around her father to the door, unbolted it, and pulled it open. Savini, keeping his black-gloved hands at shoulder height in sardonic surrender, walked toward her. When he reached the chair where Novotny sat, he paused and looked down at him. His face was expressionless, his eyes hooded. There was no way of knowing what he was thinking.

"I doubt that we'll have another chance to discuss this matter, Karel," Savini said, "and I regret that very much. I'm sorry we couldn't reach an agreement. After tonight, I'm afraid, it will be too late to do anything about it."

"It was too late," Novotny said in a barely audible whisper, "a long time ago, Savini."

The man shrugged and stepped gracefully across the sill onto the cold deck, followed by the silent Redstone.

Hana shut the door and bolted it, then turned to her father. "I'll put my coat on," she said. Her father nodded and held out his empty glass to her. Hana took it from him quickly because his hand was shaking so hard, she was afraid he would drop it. She brought him the fresh drink and then went to the closet to fetch her corduroy coat and to the kitchen for the green knit hat. The time for Steve's old trench coat and Irish tweed hat was long past. It was the end of the line for deception. This was truth time. What happens after...

She wouldn't think about that.

She put on the coat, then the hat, pulling it securely down so it hugged her ears and forehead. "It's better if I wear it, isn't it." It was a statement, not a question, and her father, who had been watching her through half-closed eyes, nodded very slightly. Otherwise he didn't move. He had reached, Hana could see, a point of almost total exhaustion. His face was livid, and he was breathing hard through his mouth as though he were having trouble getting enough oxygen.

"Will you be all right, *Tatá?*"

"Yes, Hanička, don't worry," he whispered.

Don't worry.

She leaned down and pressed her cheek against his wasted one. "I wish—"

"No, no," he whispered before she could finish. "That's

pointless. This course was set a long time ago. There's no altering it."

Tears blinded Hana as she straightened up. She wiped them angrily away with the back of her gloved hand and fumbled the door open. Stepping out onto the deck, she waited until she heard the bolt snick back into place before she jumped down to the pier and headed toward the gate. Redstone smiled at her as she passed him, then resumed his pacing. But Savini, standing motionless as a statue, seeming impervious to the cold, watched her in silence with hard black eyes.

It was cold and bitterly damp. She couldn't stop shivering as she walked with leaden steps along the slanting pier, past the brooms and shovels leaning against the railing, past the tarpaulin-draped bicycles with the little mounds of snow covering them. A gust of wind blew some into her face. She scarcely felt it. Like a sleepwalker she moved past the brightly lit boats, not hearing the laughter and music, the clink of glasses. She wasn't aware of any of it. She had withdrawn into her father's nightmare world.

Hana's fingers curled around the gun in her pocket as she drew near the gate. She could see the dark figures of three men moving restlessly on the other side. Just three dark shadows in the dim light, bundled up against the cold, scarves, hats, upturned collars all helping to conceal faces.

One of the men detached himself from the others and stepped forward, a tall, broad-shouldered man, his face half-hidden by the brim of his hat. "Miss Novotny," he said. "I'm Gilbert Halliday."

"I wonder if—that is—could I—"

Halliday had anticipated her stumbling request and was pushing a card through the fence. Hana read his name and beneath it the fact that he was chairman of the board of AIC.

"Thank you," she said, pushing the card back to him.

"You're welcome," Halliday said gravely. "Mr. Savini, I believe, has already arrived."

"Yes," Hana said, opening the gate. "He's waiting on the pier."

"And your father, Miss Novotny. Is he...?" There was a delicate pause.

"He's fine," Hana answered with a touch of belligerence. "And he's waiting as well. I'll lead the way." She swung around and headed back toward Rosie's boat, hearing the self-locking gate click belatedly shut behind her. As it did she felt a sudden change in the atmosphere, something that set every nerve in her body quivering. The winter air was filled with menace all at once. It wasn't her imagination. She could feel it. Something violent and hate-filled was directed at her back. Fear, cold as ice, circled her heart. The urge to run almost overwhelmed her. She forced herself to walk.

"You all know who I am and where I come from, so I won't bore you or waste your time by telling you what you already know. Let me state my case very simply: One of you is a traitor, gentlemen. Your code name is *Golconda*. In Prague twenty years ago Major Sergei Sergeivitch Makarov—now Colonel, I understand—turned you, made you his man. I don't know what pressure he used to do it or even if he needed to use pressure, but you have been working for him ever since under his exclusive control. Makarov and only Makarov has had the running of you."

Like the voice of a long-distance caller with a bad connection, Karel Novotny's voice, coming through the partly open door, would sometimes waver, fading to a whisper, then it would grow strong suddenly, increasing in volume.

Hana, standing on the deck with her back to the railing, listened to her father with mixed emotions that she didn't try to sort out. She was still shaky from the fear that had seized her at the gate, and she was now trying to watch both the door and the men on the pier at the same time. Though they were all standing quite still, listening intently, she sensed a kind of menacing impatience in the group, a restless energy that could explode in her father's direction or hers at any moment. She accepted this possibility fatalistically. There wasn't anything else she could do, and though she was no match for these men, she kept her hand on the gun in her pocket.

"Because you are so important to Makarov," Karel Novotny went on, "because not the faintest hint of who you are must ever leak out, your identity was known to only three other people—the chairman of the KGB himself, the head of the First Chief Directorate, who was Makarov's superior, and—and a third person, who is—who is no longer important." Novotny's voice had fallen to a whisper. Now he paused, and Hana could hear him drawing in deep, shuddering breaths. When he spoke again, his voice was stronger. "I stumbled on your file, *Golconda,* while I was researching something else. The file was thin and marked only with your code name, *Golconda.* I don't know who was responsible for putting it in the records or who even knew enough to do it. I tried to find out who the agent was but never succeeded. At any rate, there it was—"

"Cut out the chatter and come to the point, Novotny!" a voice rasped from the pier. "You said you wouldn't bore us. If you know who this man is, or *think* you know, out with it. What the hell's all the grandstanding for, anyway?"

Silence followed the interruption, but Hana heard faint movement behind the door and thought she could make out her father's white face peering through the opening, trying to see who had spoken.

"I've come a long way for this. A long way."

Hana tensed when she heard her father's hoarse whisper. He *had* moved. He must be standing now at the doorway.

"And whoever you are, if you want to hear what I have to say, then listen to me." Novotny was speaking rapidly and angrily, running the words together. There was some slurring, too. All that whiskey, Hana thought, is finally catching up with him. That and his anger could push him beyond rational action into something dangerous. Tensely she waited and listened.

"I assume you want to hear what I have to tell you or you wouldn't be here. So, if you please... What set me finally on the path that led me to *Golconda*... It might have been a coincidence. Maybe it was, though I don't believe in coincidences like that. You'll remember—all of you—the electronic tracking station we had—the CIA had—in the mountains in northeastern Iran, a few miles east of Mashhad. Nicely located on the borders of Russia and Afghanistan. And you'll remember, I know, that early in August 1968, when Russia and her allies

250

were on war maneuvers, that same station suffered a mysterious and timely mechanical failure. As a result we lost track of an entire Russian tank division. Two weeks later we found it again on the streets of Prague on the night of August twentieth."

"I don't get this!" The raspy voice again. "What coincidence? What the hell are you talking about? You sound drunk to me, Novotny. We all know when the Russians invaded Czecho and caught us all with our pants down. Right. Ancient history. What's it got to do with now? What's it got to do with this file you're supposed to have, and what the hell are we doing here, anyway, on a whim of yours when we could all be home snug in front of a fire with a drink in hand. Will you tell me that, Novotny?"

Was the man being deliberately provocative? Hana wondered. If so, why? What was he trying to do?

"Yes, I'll be glad to tell you, whoever you are," her father was saying, his voice tight with anger and slurring badly now. "One of you—the traitor among you—was in Iran at the key time when the tracking station suffered its breakdown. You have only to study the files, and—"

"Novotny..." A voice interrupted, calling the name softly. A dark figure detached itself from the shadows several yards away up the pier. "Novotny," the voice said again.

Hana, who had been facing the cabin door intent on forestalling any rash move her father might make, swung around toward the pier. She watched the broad, heavyset man move with slow, deliberate steps to a spot on the pier just below the boat deck where the light from the overhead street lamp fell on his face. It caught the gleam of teeth in the dark, luxuriant beard. It gave false warmth to the ice-blue eyes.

The dragon was not dead.

As it had when Hana first saw the man two days ago, the alarm bell in her mind jangled its loud, insistent warning: *Danger!* She straightened up, looking from the cabin door to the pier. There was movement among the men; Halliday said something she didn't catch; the bearded man said rudely, "Not now, my friend, not now." Then he planted himself facing the

251

boat, feet wide apart, arms spread out, umbrella dangling from his wrist.

"Here I am, tovarich," the bearded man called, his voice carrying clearly in the crisp winter air. "We are a long way from Prague, but we have unfinished business from there, haven't we?"

"Who is that? Who is that?" Novotny flung the door wide open with a bang and stood swaying on the threshold, eyes burning in his dead-white face, hands pressed against the jambs on either side for support. Hana saw a glint of light along the blue-steeled barrel of the revolver he held in his hand.

"Go back!" Hana cried. "You promised. Go back!"

If her plea was heard, it was ignored. Makarov was saying in a voice filled with vicious contempt, "The film you claimed to have taken of those files you claim to have burned . . . you were lying to me, weren't you. There is no film, there never was."

"Makarov? Makarov! Is that you?"

"I'm here, Novotny, yes."

"I see. I see. That's good. No film? You'd like that, wouldn't you?" On Novotny's haggard face as he stared across the deck at the bearded man a look of triumph struggled with fear which struggled with hate. His features were so distorted by the warring emotions that for Hana it became a stranger's face.

"You've lost, Makarov," Novotny went on. "This is Judgment Day." A long, thin arm whipped out in Hana's direction, a long, thin finger pointed at her head. "There—in the hat— the film—my clever daughter... It's finished for your *Golconda*. It's finished for you. It's finished, Makarov, you devil!"

Then Novotny leaped. With a terrible cry he launched himself at the bearded man.

"*Tatá!*" Hana screamed. "No!" She had the gun out of her pocket when the first bullet ripped through the pompon of the green knit hat. It lifted it from her head and carried it out into the river. The second bullet followed immediately, striking her with a force that knocked her back against the railing; from there she slumped to her knees. As she toppled slowly to the deck, she saw...

A gun in a black-gloved hand pointing in her direction...

Two dark figures struggling on the pier, locked in a dreadful embrace...

A round, cherubic face under the dim light glaring at her through horn-rimmed glasses...

The gray eyes glared; the arm rose; the voice hissed, "How dare you pry? Get to bed and stay there!" The blow fell. Through her tears she saw the head turn, saw the round, cherubic face, eyes behind horn-rimmed spectacles gazing at her. Briefly. Then the door slammed shut. She stumbled to her room.

After her mother struck her. Not before. For a split second only.

To have the last piece of the puzzle now when it was too late—a fitting end for a nightmare. Though somehow it didn't seem important, one way or the other, anymore.

Hana closed her eyes. The sounds on the pier and the scramble of activity there faded away. She wasn't in pain. She was surprised at that. As a matter of fact she felt nothing at all. Except for being tired she had no feeling of any kind.

Just tired. Very, very tired.

In the distance she heard the wail of police sirens. Drawing nearer. Coming here? she wondered vaguely. How would they get through the locked gates? On the pier someone saying harshly, "God, what a mess. We'll have to call the police." Someone answering quickly, "I already have, Mr. Drumm. They're on their way." Voices calling out anxiously. Footsteps sounding on the pier. An authoritative voice saying, "Clear the pier. Let's keep the spectators away."

A light step on the deck near her. "Hana..." A soft, musical voice, not quite steady.

A hand on her forehead, warm and soothing, something soft under her head, a warmth over her body. "Hana..."

Her eyelids seemed to be made of lead, but by concentrating very hard, by sheer force of will, Hana managed to lift them and found herself looking into a pair of eyes a few inches from her own, blue-green eyes like seawater with gleaming silver highlights, heavily fringed with dark lashes.

"The frog prince," Hana croaked.

253

"At your service."

"You're late."

"I am, God help me. Things moved faster than I thought they would. Hang on, girl. The ambulance is on its way."

"That's nice. I think I'll sleep now."

"In a minute—"

"We've played this—this scene—before—haven't we?" Hana whispered painfully.

"Not the same, no, not the same at all. How do you feel, macushla?"

"I'm fine."

"Yes, of course. You're fine. I'll never learn, will I? How is it I keep asking these stupid questions?"

"How is it"—Hana's whisper grew fainter and fainter—"you keep—turning up at these—times of crisis in my life—Mr. O'Reilly?"

"Conn." The seawater eyes were wet, the silver highlights were blazing at her.

Hana gave him her sunshine smile—and fainted.

22

A week later Redstone boarded a plane for Prague.

"Wind down any operations you're running and do it fast," Savini had instructed him. "The word so far is that you have not been blown, and we'll assume you'll be safe for a few days. We've no way of knowing yet what kind of a trail Thorsen and Makarov laid down for others to follow. It would be safer all around, of course, if you didn't go at all, but—"

"I can't leave my people high and dry—"

"As I was about to say...no, you can't do that."

"That happened once before in Prague, you'll remember, and the stench of it is still there. There has to be a—a rearrangement of priorities. I don't want to leave any of them open to more risk than is necessary when I pull out."

"I expect nothing less of you, Redstone," Savini said with his thin, humorless smile. "But no one is indispensable. Someone will take over after you've gone. And your people knew they weren't joining a Boy Scout troop when they signed on."

"Of course they knew it. Still..."

He spent half the trip sleeping and dreaming of Eva, which was very pleasant, and the other half reviewing the events of that night on the pier at the Seventy-ninth Street Boat Basin, which was very unpleasant.

To himself he referred to it as the shootout at the O.K. Corral. Everyone had suddenly seemed to have a gun in hand, even the girl. When the medics were lifting her onto the stretcher, a small gun had clattered to the deck.

The actual sequence of events was still difficult to establish. Makarov's unexpected appearance had triggered Novotny's violent reaction, which in turn had set off a chain reaction of violence. Redstone closed his eyes for a moment trying to block out the image of that wild-eyed, skeletal figure hurtling to the pier and impaling itself on the Russian's upthrust sword. Poor, doomed man. Redstone could still see those thin fingers wrapping themselves around the other man's throat in a death grip that Makarov couldn't break. Locked together, the two men had plunged into the cold river, and before anyone could make a move to save them, they had been swept away on the tide. Were they still joined together—hands clutching throat, sword skewering body—somewhere at the bottom of the river?

"The bodies have not been recovered yet," Savini had told him, adding with cold objectivity, "And let's hope they never are. Let's hope they're a long way out to sea."

Something else that was probably a long way out to sea was the green knit hat. What a shock that had been! To see it lifted from the girl's head and carried off into the river. He had watched, horrified, as a wave caught it, tossed it, drew it under.

How ironic that two tiny rolls of film responsible for Karel Novotny's long years of suffering and all that mayhem on the pier should lie buried in the mud somewhere on the bottom of the Hudson River, lost forever. And to add to the irony, except for the *Golconda* file, practically all of the information contained in the films would have been mainly of historical value now. After twenty years agents would have moved to other posts, taken new cover, would have retired or died. Operations would have been successfully or unsuccessfully concluded.

Except, of course, for *Golconda*...

Neither Makarov nor Novotny could have been quite sane at the end. Novotny, under the accumulated weight of his years of hatred for Makarov, seeing him there suddenly on the pier, had simply exploded with a kind of mad, vengeful rage.

And Makarov, with his cold-blooded, overwhelming arrogance, had refused to accept the possibility that *his* "mole," *his* creature, could be exposed. Never! So the day after he'd learned of Novotny's escape, he had sent a message to Paul to set up a secret meeting. There he had made a kind of "your money or your life" proposition to Karel Novotny's son.

"The film your father has or his life," he had said. "If your father is willing to give me the film, I will let him die in his own good time. Otherwise there's no place in the world where he will be safe from me."

And Paul, who had long been nursing the hope that he might someday rescue his father from prison, had agreed. So Makarov had "defected," and the two men had holed up in a hotel and waited for Karel Novotny to get in touch with Hana. When that happened, they would make their moves. Neither man intended to keep the arrangement. In the end the Colonel had just been faster and more ruthless than Paul.

Savini had received the news of the "agreement" with narrowed eyes and rigid face. Not so much a Medici monk as a Torquemada then. It would be some weeks before Paul would be well enough to be questioned, but when he was he would have a hell of a lot to answer for.

It was odd that Makarov hadn't waited to see that his victim was really dying. He must have been sure of it, however, because in a moment of bravado, sadism, or whatever, he had whispered the name of his "mole."

General Miles Thorsen, deputy director of the CIA, second in authority to Director Gilbert Halliday.

In the end, of course, it hadn't mattered that Makarov had told Paul. They not only had Hana Novotny's testimony, but Thorsen gave himself away. He had come to the boat basin with revolver fully loaded and ready to hand in his pocket. He had fired four shots in quick succession, the first two at Hana Novotny, the third at Karel Novotny, and the fourth at Makarov. A last desperate attempt to prevent his exposure as *Golconda*?

Redstone was convinced that Thorsen had come to the boat basin to kill the Novotnys, but the man couldn't have known that Makarov would show up as well. He couldn't have known, either, that the Colonel's defection was a fraud, planned to protect *him*. Their line of communication had broken down when the Russian had gone into hiding with Paul, the former having to assume that Thorsen would understand why he was "defecting." Either the General hadn't understood, or he had just grown tired of playing the double game and was putting an end to it.

What had led the man into the role of betrayer in the first place? Money is the only suitable reward for a spy, Napoleon had said, and Thorsen would have agreed with that.

Describing his last conversation with the dying man in the hospital, Savini had told Halliday, "His treachery began in Prague. A simple matter of greed."

When Thorsen's wife had discovered that he was having a passionate affair with his secretary, Maria Novotny, she'd demanded a divorce. Thorsen wouldn't have that. His wife was very wealthy. He wanted her money. He also wanted Maria Novotny. So on the slopes of the Tatra Mountains a skiing accident had been arranged. It left Eleanor Thorsen dead. It left Miles Thorsen a very rich man. It also left him in bondage to the KGB for the rest of his life.

Who, Redstone wondered with a shudder, had actually plunged that ski pole into the woman's brain? Maria Novotny? Miles Thorsen? Both were dead, and they would probably never know the answer to that question.

As to other questions Thorsen could answer...

The fifth bullet fired from the pier that night had come from Savini's gun. "I knew who the bastard was when he sent that first bullet at Hana Novotny. I aimed at his stomach because I didn't want him dead—for the time being. I wanted to have a talk with him first." Hard and cold, those black eyes. Redstone was glad the coldness wasn't for him.

Thorsen had died four hours later in the hospital with only Savini at his side. "He didn't survive his wound," Savini had reported to Halliday. And a long, steady look had passed between the director and his deputy director for operations. "I didn't think he would," Savini had added blandly.

"They're very nasty—stomach wounds," Halliday had said simply.

In the same hospital they had paid a visit to Hana Novotny,

where, suave and bullying by turns, Savini had questioned her memory of a face from the past.

"Yes," Hana had insisted, "he was there that night in our apartment. He was the third person at the table."

"And why, after all this time, should you suddenly recognize him? In all the confusion there on the pier, you could have caught only a glimpse of him. What makes you so sure he was the same man?"

"Perhaps..." Hana looked down at the blanket, pleating it with her fingers. "Perhaps because the circumstances were—seemed to be—similar. The dark... The atmosphere of tension..." Her voice was low. It trembled a little. "I don't know, but he *was* there that night in Prague."

She had seen Thorsen briefly but clearly, had recognized him, and Savini couldn't shake her. Redstone noticed that Hana's refusal to give way and admit she might have been mistaken made Savini angry. As though punishing her, he had told her bluntly, without compassion, how her father had died. Hana had closed her eyes and listened, white-faced and silent. When Savini finished, she had whispered, "But Paul...?" And a faint smile had touched her lips when Savini told her he was alive.

"You were lucky, Hana," Savini had said as he was preparing to leave. "That bullet was meant for your heart."

"Yes, I know." Hana put a hand over the bandage just below her left shoulder.

"Yes, very lucky," Savini had continued, adding after a brief pause, "I do hope that you're not going to 'remember' anything else about all this in the future, are you?"

In a weak but belligerent voice, Hana had asked, "What did you have in mind?"

"It's just that your brother—works for us, you see. He's in a very tight spot at the moment. We wouldn't want to place him in any danger, would we?"

The honey-brown eyes that stared at Savini for a long moment were empty of expression. Finally Hana had said, "No, Mr. Savini, we wouldn't." And she'd smiled a cold, thin-lipped smile that Redstone had found to his astonishment was remarkably like Savini's.

"Good!" Savini had said cheerfully. "I wish you all the best, Hana."

It was then, after leaving Hana Novotny, that Savini had gone alone to see Thorsen.

The whole affair had been very neatly hushed up, and Thorsen's death was referred to simply as a tragic accident. Nothing that happened at the boat basin that night had found its way into print. Only a few outside the charmed circle of Halliday, Drumm, Savini, and himself knew the facts, and they never talked about them. When the police arrived on the pier, Halliday and Drumm vanished. For the next several hours they were closeted with New York City's police commissioner, and as a result no charges were made and nothing appeared in print or on police files.

Another meeting, acrimonious and heated, where old animosities flared, took place the following day. Because of that "damned Irishman," Special Agent Conn O'Reilly, mixing in, there had been an unholy row with the FBI. It started at Federal Plaza in Manhattan and ended in the Oval Room in the White House, where everyone shook hands under the avuncular eye of the president, smiled icily at each other, and agreed to abide by the rules in the future and behave like gentlemen.

Redstone sighed at the memory. That was the least of their problems—behaving like gentlemen. He flagged down the stewardess and ordered a double Scotch. When she brought it, he drank it in one long swallow, then put his head back and closed his eyes.

At any rate, he thought, though it would take time to repair the damage Thorsen had done, at least they could all get back now to normal, everyday spy business. The game of "Find the Mole" was finished. The man who had deceived the deceivers was dead, wasn't he? But just before he dozed off, Redstone remembered something that he had overlooked in the turmoil on the pier and the rush of events that followed—Thorsen, after he had been shot, writhing in agony, muttering, *"Et tu, Brute,"* just before he lost consciousness.

Shakespeare, not La Fontaine. But just as cryptic under the circumstances.

260

And what the hell had the son of a bitch meant by that?

Had he been looking at Savini when he said it?

Sowing discord right up to the end?

Anyway, one thing was certain: Those bastards in Moscow wouldn't give up. They'd never give up. Their "mole" was dead. Long live their "mole"! And *glasnost* be damned. They were probably making plans right now for another assault on the agency!

23

As for Hana...

Steve brought her home after she was released from the hospital. When he visited her there, Hana told him just the bare facts of what had happened on that fateful weekend. And as they stood at her door, though Steve had many questions to ask, he knew from the shuttered look on the pale face that she couldn't or wouldn't answer them. He sensed as well that she needed to be by herself for a time in order to heal, to find a way to reconcile herself to what happened, to lose that vacant look in her eyes. So he said, "You have work to do, don't you? A contract? A deadline to meet? That's probably what you need right now—work." He smiled. "Dr. Karr's prescription: hard, absorbing work. But if you want me for anything, call me, Hana, please."

Hana nodded, thanked him, touched his cheek with her lips, and went inside her apartment. There she locked herself in, shut herself off from everyone and everything. Though her left arm was in a sling and she was often in pain, she worked and worked feverishly, resting only when her fingers could no longer hold the pen or watercolor brush. She left the apartment just twice to buy food and art supplies, the art supplies being far more important than the food. She ate little, slept less, grew thin and pale. The apartment showed uncharacteristic signs of neglect. Dust collected on tabletops, dirty dishes filled the sink, clothes lay strewn carelessly through the rooms.

Except for brief talks with Paul on the telephone at the "safe" house where he was recuperating, Hana had no contact with anyone. She let the answering machine take the calls, slipping in fresh tapes when needed, letting the used ones pile up beside the phone, unheard.

During the day she worked, at night she mourned. The pain of the gunshot wound was sometimes bad, and Hana took pills for it. The pain of the wounds to her spirit was worse, but she had no pills for that—only work.

There on the boat that night the one real thing for her in the end had been the shock of the bullet's impact, then the blackness. What went before had taken on the quality of a bad dream. But Savini's visit to her in the hospital—the questions he'd asked, what he had told her—had brought her harshly back to reality. Her father had been dead to her for twenty years, then he had been alive for a few days, now he was dead again. And she came to terms with it in slow stages, with the guilt she felt for having contributed to his death by agreeing to the confrontation on the pier, with the bitterness she couldn't help but feel when she faced the fact that his hatred for his enemies was stronger than his love for her, until at last she was able to accept that her father had accomplished what he'd set out so obsessively to do. Makarov and *Golconda,* the traitor, were dead. The circle was closed.

On the last day of March Hana finished the illustrations, packaged them carefully for mailing, and then spent the rest of the day cleaning the apartment, dusting, vacuuming, polishing, scrubbing, with a kind of ferocious energy, ignoring the pain of the wound, until the place had been returned to apple-pie order. After a dinner that included a large dish of pasta, salad, and a half bottle of wine, she showered, went to bed, and slept for twelve hours.

The next morning she rose early, ate a large breakfast, and, dressed in plaid slacks, the Irish fisherman's sweater, and a navy-blue blazer, left the apartment with the package tucked under her arm.

As she stepped outside she heard running footsteps and a small voice calling, "Hana!" Emily Johnson, dressed in jeans and a red jersey with bits of egg yolk stuck to its front, came bounding up the steps of the basement apartment. She was puffing and frowning fiercely. "I've been waiting and waiting to ask you. Daddy said I shouldn't bother you 'cause you were prob'ly working, but I wanted to tell you it's Milly. My name, I mean. Least I think so. Milly's a nickname for Emily, see, and I won't have to change my name really. My Daddy likes it and my teacher does too and my friends said they'd call me that if I remind them. Do you think Milly is as nice as Jasmin?"

The child waited, tensely, expectantly. Hana thought she had stopped breathing.

"Milly...hmmm..." Hana gazed off into space for a moment, then with a judicious nod of her head, she said, "Yes, I like it. I like it very much. It's better than Jasmin. Milly...it suits you. You've made a very good choice." She smiled down at the child, who smiled broadly back. Then with a flap of her hand in farewell, Emily-Milly turned and raced down the steps to her apartment, shouting, "So long. Be seeing you!"

"So long, Milly," Hana said softly. "Be seeing you."

The sun was bright and warm, the sky was blue, and the little ginkgo tree in front of the apartment house was in bud. Spring came when I wasn't looking, Hana thought with a smile. And after mailing her package, she walked—and walked—and walked—until she was exhausted and couldn't walk any more. Looking around, she found herself on the corner of Fifth Avenue and Seventieth Street facing the elegant facade of the Frick Museum.

She paid the admission fee and went into the Garden Court. There she sat down on the stone bench under the vaulted skylight and gazed at the marble fountain with a dreamy look on her face. When someone sat down beside her, she didn't for a moment turn her head. She addressed the fountain.

"You're late," she said. "What took you so long?"

"I had to finish reading *The Good Soldier: Schweik.*"

She turned to him then, and O'Reilly saw how thin she had grown. The light from overhead cast highlights on the cheekbones, hollowed the cheeks. He could only stare silently at the gaunt, beautiful face until she smiled at him and said, "I'm glad to see you, O'Reilly—and that's a fact." Then he took her hand in his, saying, "O'Reilly, is it? All right, me darlin', I'll settle for that for the time being."